Sunset at Dawn

In a novel that is at the same time a satire,
a love story and a story of war, Chukwuemeka Ike has drawn movingly and con-
vincingly on his own experiences of the
Biafran tragedy.

On 30th May 1967, Eastern Nigeria
broke away and the new state of Biafra
was born. Then economic blockade, bitter
fighting, a mammoth refugee problem and
above all, sheer starvation drove the new
state into surrender.

Throughout the crisis Chukwuemeka Ike
was there and the characters in his novel
were there, drawn from a cross-section of
those he met under the exigencies of wartime. The armchair soldiers; the self-
important 'brass-hats' sending others into
action; the callow youngsters exposed to
the horrors of the front line – they all come
alive and are made utterly believable,
described with Ike's individual brand of
warmth, sympathy, and sheer humanity.

GW00640736

Available in Fontana by the same author

Toads for Supper
The Naked Gods
The Potter's Wheel

Sunset at Dawn

a novel about Biafra

Chukwuemeka Ike

Fontana/Collins

First published in 1976 by William Collins Sons and Co Ltd
First issued in Fontana Books 1976

© 1976 V. Chukwuemeka Ike

Made and printed in Great Britain by
William Collins Sons & Co Ltd Glasgow

CONDITIONS OF SALE
This book is sold subject to the condition
that it shall not, by way of trade or otherwise, be lent, re-sold, hired out or otherwise
circulated without the publisher's prior
consent in any form of binding or cover
other than that in which it is published and
without a similar condition including this
condition being imposed on the subsequent
purchaser

For my Father-in-Law
AARON OGUNNAIKE ABIMBOLU
who died on 28 June, 1968
during the Nigeria-Biafra War

And my Mother-in-Law
EMILY EFUNYEMI ABIMBOLU
who died on 6 June, 1960

AUTHOR'S NOTE

From 6 July 1967 to 14 January 1970, a fierce, widely publicized war raged between the Federal Republic of Nigeria and the short-lived Republic of Biafra – born 30 May 1967, ceased to exist 14 January 1970. (Prior to 30 May 1967 Biafra was known as Eastern Nigeria. It has now been split into four states within the Federal Republic of Nigeria: Anambra State, Cross River State, Imo State, and Rivers State.)

The Nigeria-Biafra War provides the setting for this novel, and reference is made to some actual battles and a few other historical events, including some peace conferences and diplomatic recognitions of Biafra. The book is, however, a work of fiction. The plot as well as all the characters are imaginary, and any resemblance to actual experiences during the war or to persons living or dead is accidental.

An explanation of the Igbo and other uncommon expressions used in the text is given at the end of the book.

PRINCIPAL CHARACTERS

Dr Amilo Kanu	Director for Mobilization
Fatima	his wife, a Nigerian radiographer
Ami and Emeka	their small sons
Love	Dr Kanu's mistress
Mazi Kanu Onwubiko	Dr Kanu's father
Egwuonwu	Dr Kanu's brother-in-law
Geoffrey	Dr Kanu's orderly
Luke	Dr Kanu's chauffeur
Professor Emeka Ezenwa	Professor of History
Chike Ifeji	barrister
Duke Bassey, 'Indigenous'	owner of a chain of supermarkets
Nma	his wife
Ndubuisi Akwaelumo, 'Akwa'	a civil servant
Rose	his wife
Ikem Onukaegbe	a civil servant
Uko	Director-General of War Services
H.E.	His Excellency the Commander-in-Chief
Ofo	Chief of Obodo
Madukegbu Ukadike, 'Ezeahurukwe'	self-styled Chief of Obodo
Prophet James	a wandering preacher
Justus Chikwendu	a fifth columnist
Halima Uche	a Hausa refugee with one surviving child
John Nwosu	Secretary of the Obodo War Council
Dr Azinna Obinani	doctor at Umuahia
Ndiyo	village fisherman, friend of Bassey

BIAFRA AT THE OUTBREAK OF THE WAR: JULY 1967

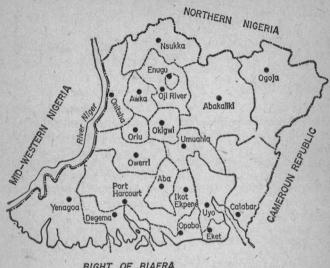

International boundary
Provincial boundary
Provincial Capital

1

We are Biafrans
Fighting for our freedom;
In the name of Jesus
We shall conquer.

'Lep! Ai! Lep! Ai! . . .' shouted a young Second Lieutenant, trim and smart in his well-starched green khaki uniform, shiningly ironed in a manner that displayed three horizontal lines across his back. The brand-new Biafra Sun emblem, a yellow half sun on a black background, symbol of the four-month old nation, Biafra, distinguished him from his trainees: he was a soldier, an officer, albeit commissioned only the week before; his trainees were young volunteers who had poured into Enugu like soldier ants from all over the young republic, to save their capital from the Nigerian 'vandals', as every Biafran called their former compatriots now turned enemies.

We are Biafrans
Marching to the war;
In the name of Jesus
We shall conquer.

'Lep! Ai! Lep! Ai! . . .'
The trainees hardly heard the shouting young officer. They sang their war song with great emotion, and its rhythm was all they needed to keep the beat. It was a mixed group, comprising boisterous-looking teenagers and young adults, male and female, primary school leavers, secondary school students, school teachers, traders, civil servants, shop girls, roadside mechanics, all dressed in the brown khaki trousers, yellow round-necked vests and brown khaki caps of the Port Harcourt Civil Defence Corps. The vests carried the picture of Biafra's Head of State, below which was boldly inscribed the popular slogan: ON ABURI WE STAND. Each volunteer carried his dummy gun, carved out of any available piece of wood – some amateurishly, some very expertly done – as if he was clutching the one weapon that could eliminate the entire Nigerian army.

As the Port Harcourt contingent disappeared into the all-

9

engulfing examination hall of the Enugu campus of the University of Biafra, the Aba contingent followed close behind, in their white VIGILANCE vests, each vest carrying the symbol of vigilance – an eye as large as a cola nut pod. Their dummy guns looked so identical that they must have been carved by the same craftsman. They rendered their marching song with gusto to the tune of 'John Brown's Body':

Our great Biafra stands for Truth and Justice, nothing more;
We shall never be enslaved or bow to Nigeria;
Whatever the result we shall still defend Biafra,
Our republic shall vanquish.

So-lidarity for ever,
So-lidarity for ever,
So-lidarity for ever,
Our republic shall survive.

All over the extensive grounds of the University campus, including even the private lawns behind the aristocratic-looking senior staff houses, the ten thousand young men (and a sprinkling of girls) who had been 'contributed' by the twenty provinces of Biafra received hurried doses of physical fitness exercises in their provincial groups before being marched into the hall for briefing on their crucial assignment. In normal times this would have been an occasion for ovation and shouting of praise names. Large crowds of idlers, relations and friends of the trainees would have formed a thick hedge on each side of the drive through which the volunteers marched into the hall, cheering, teasing, shouting praise names. But late September 1967 was not a normal time throughout Biafra, particularly in Enugu. An attempt that same month by some highly-placed army officers and civilians to subvert the Government and take Biafra back to Nigeria had been thwarted, but the mere fact that the attempt had been made at all by such highly-placed and popular personalities had shaken most Biafrans. They remembered the fate of so many Eastern Nigerians in one of the incidents that had prompted the breakaway of Biafra from Nigeria some months earlier – the 1966 pogrom. If the sabos (as the saboteurs were called) had succeeded there would have been a repetition of those nauseous scenes of gouged eyes, ripped wombs and headless bodies.

The abortive coup dealt its most devastating blow to the army, grinding to stockfish powder the unparalleled rapport which had existed between soldiers and civilians. The public now saw in a new and painful perspective all Biafra's previous tactical withdrawals which had led to the loss of Ogoja and Nsukka and progressively brought the enemy within shelling distance of Enugu. The ten thousand youths parading on the grounds of the university campus symbolized the spontaneous reaction of the people to the mid-ocean desertion by the men trained and equipped to defend the republic. The war must be fought to the finish, even if it meant using bare fists!

'Enugu kwenu!'
'Ha!'
'Port Harcourt kwenu!'
'Ha!'
'Aba kwenu!'
'Ha!'
'Biafra kwezuenu!'
'Ha-a-a!'
'Onitsha! Give us a song! Ready? Go!'
'We shall not . . .' began one of the boys from the Onitsha contingent. Everyone in the hall knew the song by heart and immediately joined in; it was one of those war songs, otherwise known as songs of the revolution, which had the effect of marijuana on the singers.

> . . . We shall not be moved,
> We shall not, we shall not be moved;
> Just like a tree that's planted by the wa-ter,
> We shall not be moved.

Dr Amilo Kanu, recently appointed Director for Mobilization, beamed his broad infectious smile as he took over the leadership of the song. He was just short of six foot, athletically built except for the rather broad hips. He was remarkably handsome, with a smooth face and chin which, at the age of thirty, gave him the appearance of a teenager. He sang the first part of each line in a beautiful tenor voice while the audience joined him in the second half as well as the chorus:

> The workers are behind us, we shall not be moved;
> The students are behind us, we shall not be moved;
> Just like a tree . . .
> Africa is behind us, we shall not be moved;
> The world is behind us, we shall not be moved;
> Just like a tree . . .

God is behind us, we shall not be moved . . .

A shrill sound from the powerful roof-high loudspeaker planted in front of the hall suddenly interrupted the singing. The shrill sound was followed by a piece of highlife music which was so gritty that it set your teeth on edge. It was the air raid alarm.

'*Ewo!*' shouted a driver outside the hall. 'It's a plane!'

Everyone in the hall reacted as if he had a split second to escape from the vicinity of the examination hall before Kill-We (the Biafran Superman) smashed the building, roof, wall and all. Chairs and volunteers were jostled and trampled upon in the stampede to take cover outside. One volunteer made for one of the glass panels on the folding door with the speed of a ram and the blindness of a millipede. He did not notice that he had any cuts until he was a safe distance from the building, squatting inside a cassava farm whose leaves offered him the protection he badly needed from the enemy plane.

'Remove that white shirt!' shouted a frightened girl taking cover in the cassava farm clutching her high-heeled shoes in one hand and her rosary in the other. It was while removing the shirt that the volunteer observed the blood stains.

The Second Lieutenant's batman had lost sight of his master in the stampede. Unable to locate him anywhere outside, he climbed the bonnet of an empty passenger lorry standing outside and opened fire at the plane with his 'she-beret' S.M.G. His attack triggered off a reassuring barrage of anti-aircraft fire. Policemen and civilians living in a nearby student hostel took the cue and fired in the direction of the plane with double-barrelled shotguns and No. 4 rifles. Similar outbursts came from other parts of the town. The enemy plane was clearly visible in the cloudless sky, flying apparently slowly as if defiantly oblivious of the bullets far below. Those who had the courage to follow its path with their eyes say it dropped a number of bombs, though there was no consensus as to the actual number, a detail that had little significance since the bombs fell into a yam farm and the only one among them which exploded did so harmlessly in mid-air.

'How's that!' shouted Dr Kanu light-heartedly, as he brushed dust off his elbows, knees and backside. 'How many of you are taking cover for the first time?' he enquired as the volunteers reassembled. Several hands went up into the air.

'Congratulations on your baptism! To celebrate the occasion, let's have another song: '*Ojukwu bu eze Biafra . . .*'

The volunteers joined in thunderously:

Ojukwu bu eze Biạfra,
Edere ya na Aburi;
Awolowo, Yakubu Gowon,
Ha enwegh ike imeri Biạfra!
Biafra win the war:
Armour'd-u car,
Shelling machine,
Heavy artillery,
Ha enwegh ike imeri Biạfra!

Biafra win the war:
Armour'd-u car,
Shelling machine,
Fighter and bomber – kpom!
Ha enwegh ike imeri Biạfra!

'If the Anglo-Soviet armoured cars, shelling machines and heavy artillery can't overcome us, will Nigeria's Egyptian-piloted borrowed war planes do so?' shouted Dr Kanu, back on form.

'No!' thundered his audience. The song had restored order in the hall and so pepped up the volunteers that many had already forgotten the scare caused by the war plane.

'Again!' shouted Dr Kanu.

'No!'

Kanu was visibly pleased with the response of the volunteers. 'Know who taught me how to take cover? My mother's chickens ...'

An outburst of laughter interrupted the revelation.

'I mean it. One bright afternoon, a hawk flew past. The chickens – old and young – reacted with incredible presence of mind. Absolute silence as each chicken instantly dived under anything that shielded it from that hungry hawk overhead, and stayed there as if paralysed. The foolish hawk flew past, and life returned to normal thereafter for the chickens. Do like the chickens and Nigeria's war planes will never get you. Sarge!'

A Sergeant whose moustache stood six inches in front of him gave the fly-catching salute popularized by Biafra's Head of State before handing over a file to Dr Kanu who flung it open as he made for the blackboard.

'Now to business. This is Enugu, our capital city ...' He marked an X on the blackboard to indicate the location of Enugu. 'That's where we are now. The Nigerian vandals are around Okpatu. There!'

He indicated the spot with another X.

'Those vandals want to enter Enugu. We do not want their jigger-infested feet anywhere in our capital. The army which should have stopped them has done – well, you know what some of them have done. While the army is being reorganized to remove any further traces of sabotage, Biafra relies on you to stop the enemy from entering Enugu.'

'With matchets?' The question came simultaneously from at least a dozen volunteers.

'Of course, with matchets!' Dr Kanu shouted as if he was enraged that a Biafran could ask such a stupid question. 'Do you want to go in your armoured car? OK, take it along with you! Biafra has given you what it has, and if you knew how we obtained these ten thousand matchets at short notice, you would thank God for small mercies. Biafra win the war!' The audience took over the chorus:

> *Armour'd-u car,*
> *Shelling machine,*
> *Heavy artillery,*
> *Ha enwegh ike imeri Biafra!*

'Yes,' ridiculed Dr Kanu, 'let those Nigerian *sho-sho* come with their armoured cars, shelling machines, and heavy artillery. With these matchets, and with God on our side . . .'

'We shall vanquish!' echoed the volunteers, including the many who had only a minute earlier entertained fears as to the wisdom of matching machine gun with matchet.

'We shall divide you into groups, and each group will be taken to its location tonight,' Kanu continued. 'We all go into operation tonight, and our objective is to catch those vandals in their sleep. Then! I shudder to think of it! We'll teach them that the best head hunters in former Nigeria came from these parts! And if you catch your group unawares, their guns and shelling machines become useless! Regrettably they can't be up to ten battalions strong, so I can't promise each of you a head. Don't you wish they were thirty thousand so that each of you could bring back three heads and avenge the pogrom overnight?'

'Yeah!' The thought of avenging the atrocities perpetrated on Biafrans by the Nigerians, particularly in Northern Nigeria, was enough to unsex damsels and turn them into Abam head hunters. Hardly any family in Biafra escaped donning the black cloth of mourning in 1966 as a result of the massacres. Living

Biafrans regarded it as their duty to the spirits of the departed to avenge their death, and this was the opportunity.

The smiles of enthusiasm instantly evaporated as a noise louder than the cannon fired at the funerals of the great resounded in the distance. As glances were being exchanged it went off again, this time from another direction. The siren had not sounded any alarm, and no aeroplane could be heard. What sounds were they? Another boom. And yet another. Only Dr Kanu's presence of mind quelled the restlessness spreading among the volunteers.

'Don't be afraid,' he shouted. 'Those sounds come from explosives manufactured by our scientists. They are being tested before being turned on the vandals.'

Dr Kanu wiped the sweat off his brow, uncertain of the plausibility of his explanation. He told himself he must be right, even though his sixth sense feared that the sands were fast running out and that the sounds came from Nigerian soldiers. He hoped there would be no further scares before the volunteers went into action. The officer in charge of catering announced the arrangements for feeding the ten thousand volunteers. Dr Kanu, still inwardly perturbed by the sounds of shelling (which had died away), decided to assure himself that he was not rushing any young people to untimely death; so in his final announcement he asked any volunteer who no longer wished to join in the defence of Enugu to stay back in the hall when the others marched off to the different feeding and embarkation points.

The Sergeant with the six-inch-long moustache received the folder from Dr Kanu and gave the fly-catching salute. The Second Lieutenant in the shiningly starched military uniform with three horizontal creases at the back of his khaki shirt flung his officer's stick under his armpit and shouted the volunteers to attention. An awkward moment followed as the volunteers wondered how to combine their matchets with their dummy guns, but it did not last long. A resourceful volunteer demonstrated that the matchet could conveniently lie flat on the gun and both be securely held by the left hand. A clear sonorous tenor voice raised a song:

> Oh my father, don't you worry;
> Oh my mother, don't you worry;
> If I happen to die in the battle field
> Never mind, we shall meet in heaven . . .

'Lep! Ai! Lep! Ai! Akaekpe Akanli ka oyibo n'akpo Left!

Right! Lep! Ai!' shouted the young officer, introducing a bit that he had picked up from a teacher in his elementary school years ago.

All ten thousand volunteers joined in the march. Not one remained in the examination hall.

2

The Rising Sun, beacon of hope for all Biafrans, had been born four months earlier on 30 May 1967, the day the Republic of Biafra was proclaimed. The Green Eagle – Nigeria's emblem – had failed to protect the lives and property of Eastern Nigerians, the people from the Land of the Rising Sun. Rather it had behaved like the vicious hen which eats its own offspring. The campaign against the Eastern Nigerians, and in particular the pogrom of 1966, had driven the Biafrans to reject the Green Eagle on 30 May, and declare their loyalty instead to the Biafra Sun.

The Biafra Sun shone brightly from 30 May until the outbreak of war on 6 July. Its presence as an emblem on a soldier's uniform instilled in him a sense of national identity and pride. Civilians clamoured for the emblem as a keepsake, or to sew on to military uniforms made for their little boys. The Sun's dazzling rays dispelled the clouds of insecurity and hopelessness which had eclipsed the lives of Eastern Nigerians, particularly the Igbo, for over a year. They infused a new determination and hope in the 'returnees' – an estimated two million Biafrans who had returned home after being hounded from other parts of Nigeria, most of them with nothing more than they had brought to the earth at birth, some with an arm or a leg or an eye less.

The university dons who had fled for their lives from the universities of Ibadan, Lagos, Ahmadu Bello and Ife; the businessmen and industrialists who had been compelled to abandon their concerns in Lagos, and in Northern and Western Nigeria; the students who now had to find new schools, colleges and university places for themselves in Biafra; the civil servants who had given up exalted positions in the Nigerian Federal Public Service, including the highly sought-after diplomatic service; the employed and the unemployed, farmers, traders and others who had lived in Eastern Nigeria all along and who were now required to carry the burden of providing for several thousands of their dispossessed kinsmen – all looked to the Biafra Sun for security and for a brighter future.

Declarations of support and loyalty had come from all over Biafra. Students' associations, trade unions, women's associations, village progressive unions, university staff, market associations, every identifiable group had rushed in declarations of support and loyalty. Never in remembered history had any government received the pledges of support and loyalty which besieged the Government of the Republic of Biafra in its first month.

The road ahead was strewn with thorns. No one had any illusions about that. The economic blockade imposed by Nigeria was already hurting. The decision by Lagos to carve Nigeria into twelve states with effect from 27 May had been a clever move to undermine and then destroy the solidarity of the people who now constituted Biafra. It threw a most enticing bait to the non-Igbo among the Biafrans, by offering them two states of their own. The extended family system which had always enabled the 'have-nots' to share in the bounty acquired by the 'haves' had well-nigh been stretched to its elastic limit: it was not designed to absorb two million people overnight.

Yes. Everyone knew that the road ahead was bound to be rough. But they thought it was better to walk on thorns with dignity and self-respect than to accept the role of tenth-class citizen in Nigeria, hiding in roofs or in toilets to escape torture and death at the hands of their fellow countrymen. The Biafra Sun held out the only rays of hope. Biafran ingenuity, industry and determination were proverbial. Granted security, the initial hardships and starvation would soon be things of the past, topics for reflection and conversation. Moreover Biafra had rich oil fields: Biafra's future economic viability was no major problem. What mattered most was whether Nigeria would allow Biafra to exist as a nation.

Would the Nigerians go to war to compel Biafra to remain in Nigeria? Many Biafrans dismissed the possibility. Who were the Nigerians anyway, they asked. The Northerners had no moral justification, argued many Biafrans, to want Biafrans back in Nigeria, unless their aim was to kill off those who had escaped the 1966 massacres. The Westerners had always seen the Eastern Nigerians as their greatest rivals for the plums of the Federal Public Service, the Federal Corporations and the Federal Universities. They should therefore be only too glad to see their rivals throw in the towel and vacate the arena.

The Nigerians did decide to go to war, and when the fighting began on 6 July 1967 the hollowness of Biafra's confident proclamations of its readiness to crush any Nigerian invasion – be it by land, sea, or air – became obvious. The first week of the war had hardly ended before the tragic fact was established that Biafra had neither the trained military men nor the military hardware to repel any serious invasion. The pattern was consistent in each of the three initial sectors of the war – on the Nsukka, Ogoja and Bonny sectors. The hastily assembled and ill-equipped Biafran forces could not dig in anywhere. Biafran territory shrank like a cheap fabric after its first wash. The yellow-on-black Biafra Sun lost its dazzle and much of its authenticity.

Then came August.

The August break began with geography book regularity, sweeping the rain clouds off the horizon and rescuing the sun from obscurity. The week before, the sun had been driven into hiding, abdicating its exalted throne for ominous clouds which had enveloped the earth in daylight darkness and unleashed torrential downpours on a saturated earth. The August break enabled the sun to assert its supremacy once again over the powers of darkness, and the sun responded by showering down its rays lavishly.

The Biafra Sun burst free from near ignominy and shone radiantly from its position of supremacy, triumphant as a cockerel descending heroically from the back of a hen it has conquered. Even the BBC carried the news, so it could not be dismissed as mere Biafran propaganda. While Nigerian troops were gaining ground slowly in Biafra, Biafran forces sprang a surprise on them by taking the war onto Nigerian soil. The success of the lightning operation stunned even the Biafrans, most of whom had no inkling that any such invasion was contemplated. It was one of the few secrets which remained secret inside Biafra. An unbelieving world woke up one morning to hear that gallant Biafran forces had captured Mid-Western Nigeria. The commander of the invading force proclaimed Mid-Western Nigeria an independent state under the new name of the Republic of Benin. A BBC reporter announced that the advancing Biafran forces had already reached Ore, some seventy miles beyond Benin on the way to Lagos.

The war had suddenly taken a new turn. Nigerian success in the Nsukka, Ogoja and Bonny sectors became meaningless as Biafran forces marched confidently on Lagos. Biafran traders lost no time in moving into Benin City, thereby smashing Nigeria's economic blockade of Biafra overnight.

The Nigerian Federal Military Government, which had hitherto described its military offensive in Biafra as 'police action', reacted to the Biafran capture of the Mid-West by declaring full-scale war on Biafra.

Songs of the revolution rent the air as jubilant Biafrans celebrated the capture of the Mid-West. When Professor Emeka Ezenwa and Barrister Chike Ifeji arrived at the Progress Hotel, Enugu, to celebrate the big event, they saw a group of young children, all boys, parading in front of the hotel singing their own composition:

> *Gowon, itiwe, tiwe, tite nwa agu n'ura,*
> *Gowon, itiwe, tiwe, tite nwa agu n'ura,*
> *Gowon, itiwe, tiwe, tite nwa agu n'ura,*
> *Mgbe nwa agu tetere, ebenebe egbuela!*

'How appropriate,' observed Barrister Ifeji, throwing a shilling to the boys. 'The vandals have roused the lion from its sleep, and so should take all the trouncing that comes their way!'

The Progress Hotel, Enugu, had been nicknamed the House of Assembly. Since the early months of 1967 when the Nigerian military leaders held the abortive meeting at Aburi in Ghana to attempt to save Nigeria from disintegration, the hotel had become the focal point for social contact. From midday until closing time at 10 p.m., senior civil servants, university staff, businessmen, 'returnees', undergraduates, came and went. Some came for lunch – it was one place where you could get a good meal of pounded yam at a very reasonable price. Some came for the delicious pepper soup, with chunks of oxtail, washed down with draught beer or lager. Many came to pick up the latest news or speculations on the prosecution of the war. Some came in an attempt to escape from their sorrows. Generally, the Progress Hotel had taken over the essential function of the House of Assembly (or Parliament), disbanded with the army take-over in January 1966 – it had become the venue for letting off steam!

'I haven't been able to conceptualize how we pulled off such a brilliant victory,' Professor Ezenwa said as if he were thinking aloud. 'The whole of the Mid-West falling like a young banana stem at the stroke of a matchet . . . To capture the entire eighty-eight miles from Asaba to Benin, and to push seventy odd miles further west into Ore! All in the twinkling of an eye, as it were.

And to think that for so many weeks we had been contesting as to who controlled Nsukka and Ogoja . . . Difficult to conceptualize!'

Emeka Ezenwa, a 35-year-old Professor of History at the University of Biafra, had become sceptical about Biafran military capability since the loss of Nsukka, the university town, to the enemy. As soon as he heard that the Nigeria-Biafra war had broken out and that a fierce battle raged at the border with Northern Nigeria, which was uncomfortably close to Nsukka, he decided to take his family to his home town, Onitsha, for a long week-end. He had hoped that the whole thing would blow over and that they could return to their peaceful life on the campus early the following week. For that reason, they had taken only a change of clothing for each member of the family. His television set, hi-fi equipment, most of their clothes, his wife's electric sewing machine, his grand piano, their silverware and china, his books – his entire library and his unpublished research papers – he had left behind, assured that the Biafran Army would guard the campus. Even if the vandals were to set foot on the campus – which God forbid – they would be looking for Biafran soldiers, not for abandoned property. If they strayed into one or two houses to ensure that no Biafran soldiers were hiding inside, they might pick up a souvenir or two – a camera, a work of art, the kind of thing they could tuck away into their knapsack. Television sets, libraries, trunks or suitcases would be of no interest to soldiers on the march. He had reasoned it all out beautifully.

The week-end had lengthened into weeks. The Biafran Army, quartered next door to the campus, had pulled back to Opi, nine miles away, leaving Nsukka without any defence. Members of the university staff who were still sticking around, led by the few who had had some weeks' drill in the Militia, mounted guard at night round the campus, armed with double-barrelled shotguns, revolvers made by Awka blacksmiths, and cudgels, looking more like night watchmen than a defence line. Even they had had to withdraw, following orders from Enugu that everyone should get out of Nsukka by a given deadline within the first week of the war, to enable the Biafran Army to use 'something' on the enemy.

The week-end over but not the war, Ezenwa had moved to Enugu, where he stayed with Chike Ifeji, a lawyer with a flourishing legal practice there. He and Chike had been classmates at the Dennis Memorial Grammar School, Onitsha, where people mistook them for twin brothers. Their years of separation after leaving school appeared to have reduced their resemblance. Ezenwa had developed a fat belly and his hair had become unusually white for his age. Ifeji remained thin, but his years of study in Belfast had made him respectably bald in front. Professor Ezenwa, unable to put up much longer with his wife's tongue, had thought it best to leave her and her tongue at Onitsha when he moved to Enugu. He was not the adventurous type, and the way his wife moaned over the precious things she left behind at Nsukka – her precious Singer electric sewing machine, her irreplaceable wedding album, her box of trinkets valued in four figures, her expensive silverware, her precious wedding presents, her boxes of clothes, her precious this and irreplaceable that – he knew that if he remained at Onitsha he would either die of hypertension or give in to her pressure to take a lorry to Nsukka and evacuate their personal effects. God forbid that he should risk his life for material possessions, when all they needed was a little patience. The storm would blow over, the vandals would be driven back and the displaced peace-loving people of Biafra would return to their homes and property. When his wife named two of his colleagues who had driven to Nsukka and evacuated their personal effects, he told her he would move to Enugu where he could assess the military situation more reliably and from there move to Nsukka at an opportune moment.

Professor Ezenwa had had one other reason for moving to Enugu. He was anxious to identify himself with the war effort. Every human being in Biafra, no matter what his station in life, had a part to play in the war. While at Nsukka, before fighting began, he had served on the Civil Defence Committee. To remain longer in Onitsha could be misconstrued as a withdrawal from his responsibilities to the nation. Enugu offered many opportunities for non-combatant duties.

'. . . Difficult to conceptualize!'

'The trouble with you professors is that you talk too much grammar and philosophy.' Mr Duke Bassey, better known as Indigenous, had materialized from nowhere. 'The matter is simple. The Nigerians said they were engaged in "police action" against us, so we left our women and our grass to deal with them in the Nsukka and Ogoja sectors, freeing our boys to take some pepper down to them in Lagos!'

Mr Bassey instinctively pulled together the folds of a nonexistent *agbada* as he slumped into one of the two lounge chairs he had dragged towards Ezenwa and Ifeji to make a foursome. He had discarded western suits since Nigeria attained political sovereignty in October 1960, replacing them with *agbada*. Within a couple of years he had established a reputation at Enugu for

21

his lovely, beautifully tailored, expensive and well-kept *agbada* which sat most becomingly on his neat frame. With the birth of Biafra, the *agbada* had become one of the symbols of Nigerianism which must be cast overboard. Any Biafran found wearing it in public at Enugu learnt his lesson the hard way: his voluminous robes were stripped off him and set ablaze. The *agbada* had become so much a part of Mr Bassey that for months after discarding it he still gathered the non-existent folds of a non-existent *agbada* whenever he was about to sit down.

'All that talk about police action was balderdash,' Barrister Ifeji said in reply, stroking the gold chain on his waistcoat. In what he often claimed was the highest legal tradition, he was wearing his usual three-piece-suit of dark, striped, woollen material, complete with gold chain across his waistcoat and black bowler hat. 'The vandals have been waging outright war against us from the word go when they fired the first offending bullet.'

'Now that their mouthpiece in Lagos has come out into the open and admitted that they have launched full-scale military operations,' Mr Bassey said, 'let's see them produce mosquitoes from their arses!'

'Have you heard of the message which our boys intercepted?' asked Mr Ikem Onukaegbe, a Senior Assistant Secretary in the Civil Service, as he occupied the chair Mr Bassey had reserved for him. The blank look on the faces of his three friends gave him his answer, so he went on, 'It's the usual transmission line, Oturkpo to Makurdi. Oturkpo was asking Makurdi to confirm the story that the big men in Lagos were escaping in large numbers to Dahomey. It appears that the news of the capture of Ore by gallant Biafran forces had hardly filtered into Lagos when the big shots began to flee to neighbouring Dahomey! Our Air Force boys who sprayed a few bombs over them with the B26 confirmed the story. They talked about the terrific commotion in Lagos. I don't now remember who told the story about the people of Ondo in the West. They are already composing new tunes on their talking drums, for welcoming our gallant boys into Ondo town. Trust the Yorubas!'

'That's great!' cried Mr Bassey. 'I'll stand you a pint for the news.'

'I think I want to start with pepper soup,' Onukaegbe replied, tugging at his shirt to save it from splitting. It was amazing that a man so chubby should make such tight-fitting shirts and trousers for himself.

'I've already ordered four bowls,' announced Barrister Ifeji. 'If only the steward would bring the orders quickly; my mouth has been watering all the time we've been talking . . . Oh, here he comes at last!'

'I'll stand everyone a drink,' announced Bassey, 'if Chike is taking care of the pepper soup.'

'Let's split it,' offered Onukaegbe. 'After all, I am still intact. It's the Professor who is a refugee!'

'God forbid that I should be a refugee anywhere,' Professor Ezenwa said quickly. 'Certainly not in my own country. Don't our wise men say that the onus to quit lies on the visitor, not the host? The way things are going, it shouldn't take more than a week or so to clear the vandals from Nsukka. If we can overrun the Mid-West and penetrate deep into the West, why can't we push the fellows at Nsukka back to where they belong?'

'If I may cut in,' said Bassey, 'did I hear that some of those professors who suddenly disappeared from the country when the going was tough – ostensibly to attend learned conferences or on medical grounds – are now sneaking back following our conquest of the Mid-West?'

Professor Ezenwa knew the swipe was intended for him and countered immediately. 'You always generalize when you talk about university professors. How many university dons have left Biafra since the beginning of the crisis? Only one. And if you ask my opinion, I don't care a hoot where that idiot goes. A black man, black even in his gum, and yet he calls himself an Englishman! Such a man has no place in Biafra as far as I'm concerned.'

'I am sorry, O,' Bassey apologized. He always took the slightest opportunity to embarrass academics, even though he went out of his way to court their friendship. Unconsciously he bore a grudge against academics for the fact that he was not a graduate. He had had a brilliant secondary school career, and had nursed an ambition to go to the United Kingdom for higher education. His father had the funds, being a successful produce-buying agent in Ikot Ekpene, his home town. Unfortunately he failed to obtain a pass in English Language, and this resulted in his failure to obtain the School Certificate, notwithstanding his brilliant performance in the subjects directly relevant to his proposed studies. Contrary to all appeals by his family and his teachers, he refused to repeat the year or the examination. He would go into business, and prove that one could succeed in life without seeing the four walls of a university. He would own a car before any of his classmates who went on to the university.

He did achieve his ambition. In no time he had established a chain of supermarkets – in Enugu, Onitsha, Port Harcourt, and Ikot Ekpene – each bearing the name INDIGENOUS SUPERMARKET, and all combining to give him his popular name 'Indigenous'. He built himself a lovely country house on the outskirts of Ikot Ekpene, breaking the monotony of statues of dead parents guarded by cement leopards which provide the commonest landmarks on the Ikot Ekpene-Umudike road. It was a three-storey mansion with twenty bedrooms, four lounges, two dining-rooms, and a kitchen. His feeling was that his home town deserved the largest and best designed house he could afford to build, even if he made use of it less than half a dozen times a year. A powerful generator supplied electricity whenever he was at home; whenever the road connecting his mansion to the major road was lit up at night, you knew that Mr Bassey, alias Indigenous, was at home.

He ploughed his profits back into the business, into real estate (with houses for lease in Enugu, Port Harcourt and Aba), and into motor cars. He drove a Mercedes Benz 220SE coupé automatic, one of the most expensive cars in pre-war Eastern Nigeria, his wife a Ford Mustang, and each of his supermarkets had a Peugeot 404 station wagon.

Not only did he make money and acquire property, he lived well too. A handsome young man in his early thirties, he was always impeccably groomed, and anything he wore – from *agbada* to his underwear – was of the highest quality. Only one thing bothered him: his lack of higher education. He did not want to admit that it bothered him, but you could see evidence of it in practically all he did. He cultivated the friendship of university professors, lawyers, medical doctors, top civil servants, and wanted to be seen in their company rather than among his fellow businessmen, even though he lost no opportunity of letting his learned companions know that all their learning was of no consequence without money. It was evident, too, in his obsession with white girls. Only the threat from his mother to commit suicide stopped him from marrying a white girl who had moved into his house at Enugu. He finally married a girl from a village close to his own, the first person from that area to obtain a university teaching appointment. It made him feel great, the thought that he had a university don as his wife!

'Prof.,' Mr Onukaegbe belched as he spoke, emitting a smell of beer. 'I wouldn't be too optimistic about recovering what you left behind at Nsukka.'

'What do you mean?' asked Ezenwa anxiously.

'One Nsukka man who had been cut off by the enemy managed

to escape alive. He told the D.H.Q. that the vandals are looting even toilet floats and cement blocks, let alone suitcases and television sets.'

'But how can they?' Ezenwa asked.

'From what he said their fighting men are followed at a safe distance by a looting squad. The squad is equipped with trailers and lorries, and their looting is systematic and thorough.'

'God forbid!' cried Bassey. 'Is that the kind of war we are fighting?'

'I pray your information will prove inaccurate,' Professor Ezenwa said. 'It would be tragic to lose all one has taken a lifetime to acquire, just like that. And my research papers as well?'

'They'll probably burn those,' Bassey replied, smiling.

'They'd better not!' shouted Professor Ezenwa in protest, as if the Nigerians were within earshot.

For a while no one spoke. Pints of beer went round a second time.

'Any *suya*?' enquired Bassey, turning to the waiter. 'No, sir,' he replied. 'They're finished.'

'A second round of pepper soup?' Bassey asked, looking from one face to another.

'One is enough for me,' Professor Ezenwa replied.

'What's the matter?' Bassey asked the Professor. 'We're here to celebrate, and you're looking sad.'

'May our boys capture Lagos as rapidly as they captured Benin,' proposed Onukaegbe raising his mug.

'Yes!' The glasses clinked against one another, and a mouthful of beer raced down each throat.

'This Lagos adventure puzzles me, though,' muttered Professor Ezenwa.

'Why?' asked Barrister Ifeji. He knew why. Ezenwa had raised the matter before they left the house, and he had been unable to provide any satisfactory answer. He asked now in the hope that Bassey or more probably Civil Servant Onukaegbe might supply the missing link.

'I can understand the capture of the Mid-West,' Ezenwa continued. 'The Republic of Benin would give Nigeria two countries to fight instead of one. Morever it would serve as a buffer between us and Lagos. But the purpose of the march to Lagos is not quite so clear to me.'

'The Prof. has come out with his philosophy again,' remonstrated Bassey. 'It seems straightforward to me. If you capture Lagos then there will be no further opposition to Biafra's existence as a sovereign state. Doesn't that make sense?'

'I can see your point,' Professor Ezenwa admitted, taking a mouthful of beer. 'But did you listen to the broadcast made by the commander of our forces in the Mid-West when he proclaimed the Republic of Benin?'

'What did he say?' asked Bassey, perching on the edge of his chair.

'He appealed to "fellow Nigerians" to remain calm.'

'What!' cried Bassey.

'I heard it myself,' Onukaegbe said.

'I didn't hear the broadcast,' commented Ifeji, 'but Emeka told me about it and we haven't quite been able to figure out what the commander was talking about. A Biafran talking about "fellow Nigerians"!'

'Well,' Onukaegbe spoke in a whisper. 'The information I picked up just this morning is that that statement is causing concern at D.H.Q. I understand the commander has been summoned back to Enugu.'

'You see what I mean, Indigenous?' Professor Ezenwa was pleased to observe that his fears were well-founded.

'I hope there's no monkey business going on!' Bassey replied heatedly.

'Please keep what I've told you secret,' continued Onukaegbe. 'Technically, the commander was correct in addressing Nigerians as fellow Nigerians, being himself a Nigerian fighting on the side of Biafra. But there's probably more to it than meets the eye.'

'Come on, Ikem,' Bassey prodded; 'na we-we here. Tell us what is happening.'

'Quite frankly there's nothing more to tell you now,' replied Onukaegbe. 'The D.H.Q. is still studying the whole matter.'

3

September 1967.

The fine weather had come to an end. Heavy rains again took over, driving the sun from the sky, even at noon. The Biafra Sun found itself similarly chased off the sky. August had been its month of glory. Its place in the galaxy appeared to have been firmly established and recognized, on earth as well as among the heavenly bodies. Biafra had made it. There was no question about that: expatriates were beginning to return as news of Biafran victories in the Mid-West reached them. It was over the future of Nigeria that the giant question mark now hung. What were the implications of the establishment of the Republic of Benin, the second sovereign state to be carved out of Nigeria? What if Biafran soldiers marched on to Lagos? Would the West declare the Republic of Oduduwa, as they once threatened to do? What would the Biafrans do if they captured Lagos?

On 23 September, the commander of the triumphant Biafran forces who had proclaimed the Republic of Benin was condemned to death in Biafra. He and three other well-known Biafrans, two of them high-ranking army officers, were publicly executed by a firing squad for attempting a coup d'état.

Biafran occupation of Mid-Western Nigeria ended as dramatically as it began. To prevent any further expensive escapades by the Biafran Army, the Nigerian forces pulled out all the stops in their bid to crush Biafra. The Organization of African Unity, meeting in Kinshasa, resolved to send a consultative mission comprising the Heads of State of Cameroun, Congo Kinshasa, Ethiopia, Ghana, Liberia and Niger to assure the Head of the Nigerian Federal Military Government of the organization's support for Nigeria's territorial integrity, unity and peace.

The sound which Dr Amilo Kanu and the matchet-carrying young men heard as they prepared for the defence of Enugu did not come from Biafran explosives. It came from the first Nigerian mortars to be lobbed into Enugu. Dr Kanu's wife, Fatima, and their elder son, five-year-old Amilo Junior, were standing outside their Progress Hotel Chalet, waiting for Emeka, the three-year-old son, who had gone to the toilet. Something suddenly landed with a crash on the ring road in front of their chalet. Almost simultaneously, Fatima heard a whistling sound followed a split second later by a cry of agony from Ami Junior, standing beside her. He was a bloody heap before she could wake up from the nightmare.

Fatima broke down completely as her husband rushed into the chalet which had been their home since December 1966.

'Here he comes,' she cried. 'Gallant Biafran! Hero of Biafra! See whether you can recognize your firstborn son wrapped up there! If you could have spared just a little time for your son if not for me, if you could have listened to the words of your nagging wife, we would have been out of this mess a long time ago and

27

Ami Junior would not be lying there dead!'

She slipped down from the pouffe on which she sat and sprawled on the floor weeping her soul out as if this was one moment when she did not care one *anini* about inhibitions.

Dr Kanu stood stunned. Then he walked unsteadily to the bed where a nursing sister was tucking away the white sheet used to wrap the body in a small coffin, after a doctor from the General Hospital had pronounced death by misadventure. He bent low over the body, and then began to unwrap the little bundle that now represented the vivacious young rascal he had kissed goodbye earlier in the day.

'Sure you can stand it?' cautioned the nursing sister.

'Don't forget . . .' He wanted to tell the sister not to forget that he was a medical doctor but the words stuck in his throat. His gesticulation, however, transmitted the message.

'Oh no!' he shrieked as the outline of a smashed skull showed through the blood-soaked sheet. He shut his eyes tight but that could not hold back the tears. Yes, his worst fears had come true. Those awful sounds which had revived his stomach ulcer did not come from Biafran explosives as he had told the volunteers. They came from the enemy, and the first to land had selected his innocent little son and instantly smashed him to death.

He sat beside the coffin and bit his lips hard to save himself from sobbing in the presence of the nursing sister. The rhythmic heaving of his chest and the frequency with which he blew his running nose showed what a success he made of it.

'Come on, doc. If you do that, who will comfort your wife?' Mr Akwaelumo's voice took him unawares. Although he had not known Akwaelumo before his arrival at Enugu nine months earlier, both of them had grown to be palm kernel and fried breadfruit in their attachment to each other.

At thirty – Dr Kanu's age – Mr Ndubuisi Akwaelumo (popularly abbreviated to 'Akwa') was the youngest Permanent Secretary in the Civil Service, with the additional wartime duty of Director for Procurement. He always looked relaxed, even in a storm, and had such a pleasant, gentle disposition that you had difficulty in reconciling such a refined man of culture with the Neanderthal gorilla style afforestation all over his body. He grew hair even on the ridge of his nose. His beard was thicker than His Excellency's.

Dr Kanu blew his nose hard and tried to dry the tears all over his face before turning towards his friend.

'I know how difficult it is to bear, but what has happened has happened. Our one consolation is that the pitcher is not broken;

it's only the water that has spilt.'

Dr Kanu was surprised to hear his own voice reply 'thank you' without faltering. It was as if the deluge of tears had rolled aside the heavy rock which had pressed down on his chest only a moment before.

'It isn't safe to be here much longer,' Akwa helped Kanu to his feet as he spoke. 'We're probably the only souls still lingering around the hotel premises. Sympathizers had been discouraged from coming here – that's if they needed our discouragement. One can't be sure what the Nigerian vandals will try next. Let's hurry over to the cemetery and come back later in the evening to move your things to my house, at least for tonight.'

'I feel ashamed to ask what burial arrangements have been made for my son,' said Kanu apologetically.

'Why be ashamed?' Fatima broke out in a voice hoarse with excessive weeping. 'Director for Mobilization, mobilizing the youth to defend their new-found land. That's much more important than the burial arrangements of a little rat, isn't it?' And without waiting for an answer she shouted 'Non-sense!'

Akwa smiled at her pacifyingly, 'It's OK Fatima.' He then went on to summarize the hasty arrangements he had made for the burial, thanks to the telephone and to the decision taken a week earlier to dig several graves in the military cemetery every day in anticipation of war casualties. No church service; the pastor in charge of Kanu's church feared it was within range of enemy shells, although it was believed his fear was more of air raids. Everything would be done at the graveside. The pastor reckoned all would be over in thirty minutes at the outside.

'It's now 3.30,' observed Dr Kanu, taking a prolonged look at his watch. 'I think I can make it, even if it goes on till 4.30. After that, I'll have to rely on you, Akwa, to take care of Fatima and the packing. I don't know why the two events should coincide today, but in spite of my grief I have to carry out an assignment for His Excellency tonight. I'll tell . . .'

'You hear him?' Fatima shouted hoarsely, turning towards Akwa and bursting into another spell of weeping. 'You hear what a husband is saying? An assignment from H.E.! An assignment from H.E. is more important than his dead son! An assignment from H.E. is more important than his dead son! An assignment from H.E. is more important than the safety of his wife and his remaining son! An assignment from . . .'

Doom – Dooom! Doom – Dooom!

Husband and wife, Akwaelumo and nursing sister all instinctively dived for cover under the double bed which held the remains of Ami Junior.

Doom – Dooom! Doom – Dooom!

Hardly anyone breathed under the bed. Fatima's running nose stopped running. The thought that you were within range of the Nigerian shelling monster was enough to chill your blood.

'If they have advanced since their first shelling, this place ought to be safe.' Dr Kanu broke the silence after it appeared the shelling had stopped. 'If anything, the shells should pass well over our heads.'

'We'd better get out of here quick, old boy, safe or unsafe.' Akwa emerged from under the bed as he spoke. He looked himself over and brushed the cobwebs and dust off his trousers.

'Who knows where these ones landed,' Kanu wondered aloud.

'We'll soon discover when we get out of here,' replied Akwa. 'The Reverend Aghamelu must be at the cemetery now, if he hasn't been frightened out of his collar by this latest shelling. Off we go.'

'I see no alternative,' Dr Kanu argued with himself as the Reverend Aghamelu sped through the burial rites for young children, reading the prayers faster than a stage-frightened elementary school pupil who finds himself reciting a passage in front of an unfamiliar audience. 'I have to forget that Ami Junior died today . . . My duty to the state, in a national emergency such as this, must take precedence over any personal considerations . . . I must go ahead and lead my group of volunteers tonight as planned . . . Yes, I must . . . I'll explain to Fatima later . . .'

Dr Kanu concluded that he had no choice but to participate in this precarious venture even before the coffin bearing his first son had been lowered into the bowels of the earth. In the eyes of some Biafrans, he was still security risk number one. Before the war, he had been an outspoken advocate of a united Nigeria, and had had occasion to cross swords with many of his more parochial colleagues while working in Western Nigeria, as Senior Registrar at the University College Hospital, Ibadan. Some of these colleagues, who had then dismissed him as misguided, were known to have peddled vicious propaganda against him on their return to Eastern Nigeria. The fact that he and his family stayed on at Ibadan after the assassination of the Supreme Commander, an Igbo, on 29 July and after the massacre of thousands of Eastern Nigerians in Northern Nigeria on 29 September, 1966 had lent credence to the rumours. He was alleged to have dissuaded fellow Eastern Nigerians from returning to the East, and his more malicious colleagues even alleged that it was he who supplied the Nigerian vampires with the list of Eastern Nigerians in Ibadan and Lagos to be exterminated. Only a man in the good books of the Northern and Western Nigerians could consider himself safe in a city from which his kinsmen had fled for their lives.

The rumours had become so strong that his parents and next-of-kin began to find them rather suffocating. The climax had come the day his father stood up to address a meeting of his age-grade at Obodo, his home town. 'Obodo kwenu!' he had shouted in the traditional manner of 'buying' the floor. Not one word was uttered in reply. The exuberant expression on his face vanished as he looked round and found that every eye avoided him. This was one of the occasions on which silence spoke more forcefully than words. The wise man understands when a proverb is used on him; Kanu's father was wise enough to understand the unuttered proverb, and he had sat down to snuff his tobacco while another member was granted the floor and the age-grade meeting continued.

Pressure thicker than sandbags on an army officer's bunker had piled upon Kanu's parents and next-of-kin to drag him back to the East, not only by his father's age-grade meeting but by persons and organizations inside and outside Obodo. Letters from his parents requesting him to come home had been of no avail. Faced with the threat of ostracism, his father had allowed a telegram announcing his own death to be sent to his son as a last resort.

Dr Kanu had stayed on at Ibadan for a number of reasons. He feared that the mass exodus of Eastern Nigerians would lead to a breakdown of a federation he felt committed to uphold. 'Disintegration or regionalization or secession,' he had argued on one occasion, 'is the short cut adopted by people who are not men enough to face up to the challenge of group living.' He had regarded it as a short-cut that would ultimately lead to the creation of one state for one person, if carried to its logical conclusion. He firmly believed the federation of Nigeria could stay together if only every Nigerian would be man enough to face up to the challenge.

His marriage to Fatima, a Northern Nigerian girl studying radiography at the hospital in England where he had pursued his clinical studies, had been one of his own attempts to face up to this challenge. The prospect of a break-up of the federation now posed serious problems for him. How would his wife fit into this? Would it be fair to drag her with him to the East? Would she be welcome to the East with those tell-tale marks of her tribe on her face? Would he himself not be held suspect by the mere fact that he lived with a wife from a part of Nigeria which held anything but pleasant memories for every Eastern Nigerian? To make matters worse, Fatima came from a wealthy and well-known family in Northern Nigeria. One of her uncles, who had held a federal ministerial appointment in the ousted political régime, was known to have spearheaded the carnage on Eastern Nigerians in his Emirate.

Yet another headache delayed Dr Kanu at Ibadan. He had been assured of appointment as Lecturer in the Faculty of Medicine at the University of Ibadan in January 1967, an appointment that would have launched him into a life career to which he very much looked forward. To go with the tide would have meant losing this golden opportunity for which he could not visualize any adequate compensation. The East had no Faculty of Medicine and he had not forgotten the insult a colleague received from the Eastern Nigeria Ministry of Health not long before. His colleague had offered to serve under the Ministry and was requested to travel third class by rail to an interview at Enugu, even though he had pointed out to the Ministry that he drove his own car.

His father's fake telegram had brought him home in December 1966, months after most of his colleagues had left him at Ibadan. He had gone alone, hoping to rejoin his wife and two sons within a week. He did not leave the East thereafter. Having set foot in the Land of the Rising Sun he began to see the situation through new eyes. He was affected by the feeling of inevitability which pervaded the region. If the federation was bound to break up in spite of him, it was crucial that he should be found on the proper side of the River Niger when the moment of separation came. And since no one could say when the sands would run out, was it wise for him to go back to Ibadan at all?

He saw the dangers to which his parents and relations were exposed by his continued stay outside Eastern Nigeria. He saw how his name had already begun to stink because he refused to go with the tide. He sought interviews at the highest levels and received assurances of safety for Fatima everywhere in the region, her tribal marks notwithstanding. These discussions revealed that there were still men and women of consequence in the East who believed in a united Nigeria and sought acceptable ways of surmounting the obstacles in the way. It had been in the course of these discussions that someone had put it to him that he and his wife could serve the cause of a united Nigeria better if they moved to Enugu. Their contacts in Ibadan, Lagos and Northern Nigeria, and their influence with some of the more powerful forces in Lagos and the North would make them very useful for negotiations which seemed likely to follow. It was this possibility that encouraged Fatima to join him at Enugu later that month. They were given free accommodation and subsidized meals at the Progress Hotel, Enugu, and he was designated Officer on Special Duties and placed on the salary he was to have earned as a Lecturer in Medicine.

It took him no more than a month to redeem his reputation in Eastern Nigeria, and he soon found himself acting on committees, preparing briefs for the Government, and serving on official delegations during the months of negotiation with Nigeria. His charismatic qualities made him a popular crowd puller and favourite of the innumerable mass rallies.

Hardly a day passed without Dr Kanu doing or saying something of news value to the radio, television or newspapers. His was one of the photogenic faces which the television cameramen always succeeded in shooting at every rally or party. He became one of the regular guests at any state or society party, and he himself threw parties frequently. Some of his former colleagues resented this meteoric rise to prominence which, they argued, as did the more responsible brother of the prodigal son, was a slap in the face to the diligent and loyal. They lay low, waiting for an opportunity to strike.

The chicken overturned the offerings for the sacrifice when the final act of separation took place and Biafra became an independent nation. Dr Kanu was absent from the public ceremony to mark the occasion, and his sudden undisclosed illness thereafter provided additional ammunition for his detractors. To the chagrin of those who thought he was out for the final count, he emerged even stronger than before. At the outbreak of the war he was given a crucial appointment as Director for Mobilization.

It was the abortive coup that brought him closest to public renunciation. Two of the four leaders of the coup were associates of his who were often seen drinking with him at the Progress Hotel bar. Although his name did not come up in the official trials, public reaction to him wherever he went left him in no doubt that his name was being freely associated with the coup, albeit unofficially. It was as part of his effort to blot out this dangerous suspicion that he identified himself with what he recognized was clearly a crazy idea – sending matchet-carrying young men to destroy the Nigerian Army on the march to Enugu. He even offered to lead one of the groups himself. The matchet parade idea had not originated with him; he had merely seen in it an opportunity for demonstrating his loyalty to Biafra. By the time the matchet boys were about to set off, the idea had become identified with him as if he had invented it.

He knew Fatima would die of heart failure if he admitted her into the secret, so the matchet campaign did not come into their conversation at any time. If he could not tell her about it when Amilo Junior was alive, it would be double death to mention it after the boy's death. Yes, Ami Junior's death. That was a greater sacrifice than anybody else had made in the cause of Biafra. Now that he had sacrificed his first son, was it in his own best interests to endanger his own life as well by leading the matchet operation? What if he died? What could Fatima do in Biafra without him? Was it fair to bring her all that way only to abandon her before she had put down roots in her new environment?

He dismissed the thought. He was committed to the matchet operation, however crazy and precarious it might sound. Even if he paid the supreme sacrifice . . .

'Sand to sand, earth to earth, dust to dust . . .' The Reverend Aghamelu's voice and the sound of the red earth on the diminutive coffin reminded Kanu that he was at the burial of his son. He looked around him guiltily. Fatima was holding on to his arm and biting her lips hard as the tears flowed down her now swollen face. He offered her his handkerchief.

4

'Here's my find, gentlemen,' smiled Barrister Chike Ifeji as he and his three friends stepped into the bar of the Hotel Rising Sun, Enugu, one of the innumerable public houses which had assumed a new name to reflect the emergence of Biafra as a nation and the severance of all links with Nigeria.

'Service!' he called.

A waitress who had been struggling to stop her blue mini-skirt from exposing too much of her fair-skinned, beautifully rounded thighs as she mopped up a table, dropped her cloth and approached the three men to take their orders.

'We want four chairs round that table,' Ifeji instructed, pointing towards a far corner.

'Not too bad,' declared Ikem Onukaegbe as he balanced on his all-metal chair. 'Doesn't compare with the good old House of Assembly in comfort, but no shell will land around here in the near future, and that's more important to me than air-conditioning or Dunlopillo cushions!' He tugged at his Biafran-style tunic: as usual he had made it so tight-fitting that he could hardly raise his foot twelve inches from the ground or bend down without causing a split. 'Morever, you don't have to open your boot and disclose your identity X times to innumerable Civil Defenders each time you want to have a booze.'

'The Rising Sun has another advantage, especially for university dons who seem to have inexhaustible energy.' Ifeji laughed as if his lean frame would break in two. He was noted for enjoying his jokes more enthusiastically than his audiences, quite often going into hysteria at the mere thought of the joke he was yet to crack. As always, he was impeccably dressed in his three-piece, striped suit, complete with gold chain.

'Wetin masters want?' asked the waitress.

'The usual thing?' enquired Professor Emeka Ezenwa who had insisted on paying the bills this time, arguing that although he had been unable to recover his belongings yet, he still received his professorial salary.

'Draught for everybody,' he ordered.

'Yes, sir.' The waitress disappeared, and returned with a draughts board which she deposited loudly on the table to await the order for drinks.

The tears flowed freely down Ifeji's cheeks as he laughed his ribs sore. 'Don't confuse the poor girl, Prof.,' he rattled out. 'There's no draught beer here.'

'Beg your pardon! You got G.G.?'

'Yes, sir.'

'OK. Three bottles.'

As the waitress turned away to collect the three bottles of Golden Guinea lager, Onukaegbe added: 'And one plate of Congo meat!'

'Why do you bring us here, Chike, if the *bozos* have no draught?' queried the Professor, wearing a frown on a face that was becoming overgrown with hair. Having forgotten to include his shaving set among the few belongings he took out of Nsukka, he had decided to join the band wagon and sport a beard. It made you look like a revolutionary, Cuban style. It identified you with His Excellency.

'You wouldn't let me get to the end of my list of attractions

35

here,' replied the lanky lawyer. 'What the Rising Sun lacks in draught it compensates for in skirts! They satisfy all tastes. Moreover, if you hi-jack a dame from somewhere else and have no place to "shell" her, you can get a bunker here for as many hours as you like. Now tell me, Prof., whether that doesn't give this place the edge over our good old House of Assembly!'

'What do you know!' The Professor wrung his hands excitedly as though he was squeezing the bitterness out of the bitterleaf. 'And only yesterday I gave a lift to one of the Port Harcourt Civil Defence girls who was actually prepared to move in to my house right away. I was at my wit's end where to sample her, not wanting to embarrass you by bringing her to your house.'

'Thank God you didn't take her anywhere.' Onukaegbe took a bite of fried snail as he spoke. 'I avoid those Civil Defenders, especially the groups from Port Harcourt. They leave a trail of Bonny disease wherever they go, and our doctors are too busy with shell shock and battered bones to find time to tackle that killer effectively.'

'What difference does it make whether you are killed by a bomb or by Bonny disease?' asked the Professor. 'Death is bound to catch up with you sooner or later, if the war continues at this rate.'

The fate of Enugu had become a major concern. Most people were already wondering how much longer the Biafran forces could hold out. The first sound of enemy mortar had been widely believed to have come from Biafran forces trying out new equipment. It was inconceivable that the enemy could be that close to Biafra's capital. When the ominous sounds persisted, a more plausible explanation had to be found: they came from enemy collaborators among the Biafrans.

Most of the Enugu population remained because clear instructions had been issued that no male should be allowed to leave the city. You could sense in the atmosphere a general feeling of insecurity and uncertainty. The Government residential area (including the popular Progress Hotel) had been deserted: the early mortars had landed there. The senior civil servants who wanted to demonstrate their courage put in an appearance at their houses once or twice during daylight hours but spent their nights in parts of Enugu considered outside shelling range and therefore safer.

Hardly any Biafran civilian, however, expected Enugu to capitulate to the enemy. It was inconceivable. Enugu was the nation's capital. Hardly any other Biafran town could boast of such natural defences. The enemy could shell Enugu from the surrounding hills, but let them attempt to pour in troops from Okpatu down the Iva Valley or the steep, meandering Milliken Hill and they would never return home to tell the tale. If Biafran military might and expertise could not save Enugu, what hope for Biafra's survival as a nation?

The cold facts were beginning to stare everyone in the face. The presence of thousands of young men in Enugu and the story that they were to defend Enugu with matchets dramatized Biafra's predicament. For the first time Biafrans were doubtful whether or not to accept the assurances, blared out to them from a Ministry of Information public address van, that Enugu would be defended to the last man. Who would remain behind to be the last man?

Professor Ezenwa had gradually reconciled himself to the cruel fact that he could not get back to his house until the war was over. He and three other colleagues had been requested to stand by, to be escorted to Nsukka by the army whenever it was considered sufficiently safe to do so. On one occasion they had gone as far as Abor, but had had to abandon the trip following instructions from Tactical Headquarters. It was during this time that he moved out of Ifeji's house into the Enugu Campus of the University, where rooms had been made available at the students' hostels for Nsukka campus staff engaged in war duties at Enugu. The Directorate of Manpower Utilization had also employed him in the Research Division of the Directorate of Propaganda. The pervading atmosphere of uncertainty and hopelessness, the fact that the Research Division had not yet quite got off the ground, which meant that he was not fully occupied, and the absence of his family, all conspired to make him spend more time than usual drinking and bird hunting (as he and his friends nicknamed going after girls).

'Wait a minute . . .' Professor Ezenwa peered at a man in a blue shirt and khaki shorts who stood at the entrance as if he were making up his mind whether to take a seat or to turn back. 'That's Dr Osita.' He rose and walked towards Dr Osita for a handshake.

'Hi, Prof.!' Dr Osita shouted, pleasantly surprised to see a familiar face in the strange environment. 'Haven't seen you since we ran from Nsukka.'

'You're the last person I expect to find here,' Professor Ezenwa said. Dr Osita was one of Biafra's best-known physicists. Even

37

before his appointment as a Senior Lecturer at Ibadan, he had been internationally acclaimed for his outstanding contributions to learned journals. His curriculum vitae had been sent to the Inter-University Council for Higher Education Overseas (in London) for external assessment shortly before he fled from Ibadan in August 1966. There was no doubt that the assessors would declare him eminently suitable for a professorial appointment. He was the kind of man most African women would like to have as a husband. He had no passion for wine, women (other than his wife), or song. If he was not at home any evening, you were sure to find him in his laboratory.

'I had been dying to see you, and someone told me that this was the place to find you!'

'Whoever could have told you that? This is my first visit here.'

'I'm joking,' Dr Osita said, smiling. 'Seriously, I've just achieved a major breakthrough and I thought I should indulge myself a little. So I just popped in to the first pub I found for a bottle of beer.'

'Well, be our guest! We're here to commiserate with one another after our disaster in the Mid-West and the abortive coup . . .'

'What's this about the breakthrough?' Professor Ezenwa asked after Dr Osita had settled down to a glass of Golden Guinea lager.

'Gentlemen,' Dr Osita began in reply. 'Rise with me and drink to Biafra's first rocket!'

Dr Osita was even more excited than his audience as he told the story. He had taught rockets for years. He had read every available publication on rockets and followed with keen interest the various blast-offs at Cape Kennedy. But the thought had never crossed his mind that *he* could launch a rocket successfully. When Major Ejimofor of the D.H.Q. first enquired at a meeting with the Science Group about the possibility of producing Biafran rockets, he had dismissed the project as one of Major Ejimofor's wild ideas.

Major Ejimofor had persisted: 'Those countries which manufacture the rockets we buy, do they have scientists with two heads? Did their scientists study in special universities?'

'We don't have the equipment,' Dr Osita had contended.

'What equipment?' Major Ejimofor asked.

'We don't have the technicians,' continued Dr Osita.

'We have them!' shouted the Major. 'We have them. A few in the university, but many more in places where you probably never thought of – in market places, by the roadside, anywhere you see any sign board advertising a mechanic or fitter, or "doctor" of electronic and other equipment . . .'

Major Ejimofor had set Dr Osita thinking. 'I could hardly sleep that night,' Dr Osita told them. 'I was so anxious to get out and begin assembling what we would need to make a start. What the Major said made sense. There was no reason why rockets could not be made and launched in Biafra! It has taken us two weeks, knocking bits and pieces together. And, man, if anybody tells you Biafra lacks technicians don't believe him! This afternoon we went to an isolated spot beyond Okunano, and I could hardly believe my eyes when I saw that rocket go off!'

'D'you mean we now have Biafran rockets?' Professor Ezenwa asked, starry-eyed.

'There's still a lot of refinements to be made. The rocket we launched today only rose ten yards. If we are to shoot down planes with them or lob them into enemy locations, we must aim at a much longer range. But these are refinements. The important thing to me is that we *can* make rockets!'

'Great!' shouted Barrister Ifeji, shaking his fist in the air.

'Biafra win the war . . .' began Onukaegbe, rising and clapping his hands to keep the beat. The others joined in:

> Armour'd-u car,
> Shelling machine
> Heavy artillery –
> Ha enwegh ike imeri Biafra!

'Service! Three more bottles of G.G.,' ordered Ifeji.

'I can't take more than this glass,' Dr Osita announced. 'But I'll pay for the bottles.'

'No such thing,' protested Ifeji. 'You are the hero today. You have produced something vital to our survival.'

'I don't know that I qualify as a hero for sending a rocket ten yards into the air,' replied Osita modestly. 'Not when our engineers have produced an armoured car.'

'So the story is true?' asked Ifeji.

'Oh, sure,' replied Osita. 'Some foreign journalists visiting Biafra had the surprise of their lives two days ago. The D.H.Q. took them over to one of our workshops to show them some of the things our scientists had produced. They admired the different types of grenades and the locally-made guns. Then an armoured car drove towards them, stopped opposite them, and out jumped a Biafran girl smartly dressed in army uniform and gave the salute to the officer accompanying the journalists. They could not believe it when they were told the armoured car was made in Biafra.'

'Stories like that make me proud to be a Biafran,' Barrister Ifeji announced.

'I see the dawn of a major scientific and technological revolution in Biafra . . .' began Professor Ezenwa.

'Here comes the historian,' cut in Onukaegbe.

'The Prof. is correct,' said Dr Osita. 'If only we can survive as a nation, I see a great future ahead for Biafra.'

'You've hit the nail on the head,' concurred Professor Ezenwa. 'If only we can survive as a nation. The way things are going at the moment, the prospects are not that bright.'

'We in the Science Group were particularly frustrated to learn that a large number of the grenades we had manufactured had been used by one of the saboteurs against our own boys!'

'I see you are celebrating without waiting for me!' shouted Duke Bassey as he rushed into the bar. 'Service! Get me one bottle of champagne! And one roast chicken! We must celebrate.'

'Celebrate what?' cried the lawyer, the civil servant and the professor all at once. Dr Osita introduced himself to Mr Bassey.

Bassey was amazed. 'You mean you haven't heard?'

'What?' enquired his three friends, rising as if buoyed up with hope. The bartender and the waitresses drifted towards the group, their ears tuned to catch the sound of a feather landing on the floor.

'You mean you haven't heard that the Yorubas have toppled the Hausas in Lagos? And that the Yorubas have announced over Radio Nigeria that they will let us go our way in peace, if that is what we want?'

'D'you mean it?' Dr Osita asked.

'You know some of the Yorubas had always wanted to go it with us,' continued Bassey, happy to monopolize the floor. 'The realistic ones among them know that with the Biafrans out of the way, the Northerners will turn on them next and crush them. They must have been afraid of the consequences, so they backed out when we decided to break away. They've finally realized that it's now or never. So they have seized power in Lagos. Who knows? They may soon proclaim the Republic of Oduduwa!'

'You don't say!' shouted Ifeji.

'I'm surprised you haven't heard. The news is all over the town. The boys in the barracks have been throwing their guns up and catching them. There's no space to stand at the House of Assembly; so many people want to celebrate that they've forgotten about mortar bombs. Service! Where's my champagne and chicken?'

Bassey sat down in the chair which had been reserved for him, and pulled out a freshly laundered white handkerchief which he used to mop up the sweat on his face, neck, chest and arms.

'You don' hear now?' the waitress said to the bartender. 'You go pay me my one pound today. Next time when I tell you something, you . . .'

'Service! Where's my champagne and chicken?'

The waitress scuttled off to the kitchen to fetch water for washing hands before eating the chicken.

'Long live the Yorubas!' toasted Bassey as the glasses went up. The bartender and the two waitresses in the bar also raised their hands, without glasses.

'Long live Biafra!' added Barrister Ifeji.

'I hope that means I don't have to move from Enugu,' Onukaegbe observed, 'and that the Professor can return to his books at Nsukka, leaving the good things of Enugu for us!'

'I'd pay anything to get into my house at Nsukka, to see if I can still find my unpublished research papers, my lecture notes, my crockery, my cutlery, my travel souvenirs, my . . .'

'Depends on how soon orders from Lagos reach the vandals at the fronts,' suggested Onukaegbe. 'I hope they travel fast. I don't want to die of a heart attack!'

'The orders have already reached some of the vandal troops,' replied a man in a blue shirt with bell-shaped sleeves, sitting on a bar stool waiting for his bottle of G.G. The shirt had a light blue inner lining, which made you wonder whether the man had erroneously picked his wife's blouse from the wardrobe. 'One of our soldiers who came from the front said that the Nigerian soldiers are packing up and have sent emissaries to our boys proposing an immediate ceasefire.'

'Strangely enough' – Ifeji looked philosophical as he spoke – 'I'm not sure that I want the war to end that way . . .'

'Wetin dat man dey shit for mout',' asked one eavesdropper.

'You dey min' am? Na dem dey chop when man pikin dey die for trench,' opined another.

'What I mean,' continued Ifeji, pretending to ignore them and yet taking the hint that it was suicidal to do or say anything which could be construed as detrimental to the war effort, 'what I mean is that I do not want those vandals to think or say that they have *allowed* us to leave Nigeria. I want them to be made to realize that they cannot stop us from going. You see what I mean?' He canvassed for support from one face to another, receiving no more than a bland 'Well' from Onukaegbe.

'Why hasn't our radio announced such a major development?' asked Professor Ezenwa, looking puzzled.

'The dog stung by a bee flees at the sight of a house fly,' Bassey replied. 'Didn't the Director for Propaganda tell us last week how he put pepper into the anus of each of those radio boys for rushing to the microphone after the discovery of the abortive coup without first clearing the details at the appropriate quarters? None of them will commit a similar blunder so soon again.'

> *Ole ebe unu no, Bi-afra!*
> *Ole ebe unu no, Bi-afra!*
> *Agaghm arapu Bi-afra ga Nigeria ga biri.*
> *Agaghm arapu Bi-afra ga Nigeria ga biri.*
> *Biafra gadi ndu!*
> *Umu Biafra ibe mu,*
> *Jikerebenu, na heme – heme!*

A group of jubilant boys and girls, chanting one of the popular war songs, stopped at the entrance to the Hotel Rising Sun as if to ensure that everyone inside the bar was celebrating the good news.

The man in the blouse with the bell-shaped sleeves promptly joined in the singing and dancing, carrying his glass of beer in one hand and the half-empty bottle in the other, as if to make sure that it did not disappear while he danced.

'Biafra win – ' he shouted.

'War!' replied the singers.

'Biafra win – '

'War!'

'Service!' he shouted 'Give them two big bottles of G.G. on my account!'

'And two on mine!' shouted Bassey.

> *Umu Biafra ibe mu,*
> *Jikerebenu na heme-heme . . .*

The jubilant group danced away, carrying their prize and giving the solidarity sign with their fists. They picked up more dancers as they proceeded, like a magnet collecting metal filings.

'It's all over the town,' said Bassey. 'Let's finish up the chicken. I must find champagne quickly – there's none here. Beer is not the thing for such an occasion. Will you come with me?' he asked his three friends. 'We can all go in my car and, if we find the champagne, we'll come back here to drink it. Come with us, Dr Osita.'

Onukaegbe and Ifeji nodded assent; the dog has good reason for hanging around a gourmand.

'I want to be sure of what I'm celebrating first,' was the Professor's reply.

'Of course you university people don't accept what non-academics tell you . . .'

'It isn't that. Experience has taught me to check on the origin of any major news items such as this, to see whether or not it's the Voice of Rumour – the 'Radio without Battery'. Moreover, even if it's true, we ought to study the matter carefully to make sure there's no catch in it. The Yorubas are too slippery for my liking, and this sudden outburst of love for Biafra beats me. They couldn't have forgiven us overnight for letting the N.C.N.C. team up with the N.P.C. in 1962 to crush the Action Group in the West.'

'OK. Look for us here when you're through with your research! What about you, Doc?'

'I'll have to go back right away to the workshop, I'm afraid,' Dr Osita replied.

'Professor Ezenwa of the University of Biafra, employed at the Directorate of Propaganda. Here's my pass!' The Professor generally recited these words at every checkpoint, to save himself the often irritating cross-examination of half-literate Civil Defenders and policemen who manned them. It generally worked like magic. He was allowed to drive through without touching the ground with his feet, and often in addition received the military salute for V.I.P.s.

'Pleased to know you, sir. Good evening, sir, please clear your car here, sir.'

'Look, I'm in a desperate hurry. I must catch the Inspector-General of Police within five minutes and I can't afford to waste any time. I pass this checkpoint several . . .' The irritated Professor discovered that he was talking to himself. The police constable had moved on to the car which had pulled up immediately behind him.

'Driver, you don' pay?' enquired a man carrying a tin of something looking like coal tar, and banging on his car bonnet.

'Will you stop banging on my car?' raged the Professor.

'Onyenwem, make you no vex, O,' apologized the painter. 'I dey aks weder you don' pay two shilling for paint your headlamp.'

'I don't want anybody to mess around with my headlights. I don't drive at night.'

'Please sir, we get order not to allow even Hetch-Ee to pass without painting 'im light. Make you co-operate wit' us. You see how you dey make traffic jam . . .'

'OK. Take the money. Paint the whole car if you like.' The Professor flung two shillings at a second police constable who had come to find out the reason for the delay. The constable picked them up patiently and ordered the painter to work. The cross-bar went up barely thirty seconds later; the painting job was as brisk as that. The Professor's Opel Admiral shot forward angrily, dripping black tears from both eyes. He had hoped he could save his car from the coal tar by designing a more dignified hood for each headlight to tone down the effect of the light in the event of night raids by enemy planes. He had now paid for his procrastination. He drove into a nearby petrol station to see how much havoc had been done.

'How many gallons?' enquired a female petrol attendant, wearing khaki trousers with patch pockets everywhere and a soldier's khaki cap.

'Fill the tank,' Professor Ezenwa replied mechanically as he inspected the headlights which had been blackened unevenly. After hearing how some of his colleagues had to abandon their cars at Nsukka at the approach of the enemy, simply because their tanks were dry, he had decided to keep his tank full all the time. That way he could dash off at the first sign of the enemy. He had also decided always to carry in the car his suitcase and the briefcase containing the only uncompleted research paper he had taken out of Nsukka. They now constituted his only possessions and he was determined not to leave them behind for the vandals.

'You no like am?' the attendant asked him as she found him still inspecting the painted lights after she had filled his tank.

'It's messed up the whole car!' Professor Ezenwa replied angrily.

'We fit remove am for you, sir.'

'Sure?' A ray of hope lit up the Professor's face.

'Yessir. Jus' now.'

'OK. Go ahead.' The Professor could hardly wait to see the work begin.

'Only you go pay us five shillings, O.' The attendant looked coquettishly at him.

'Never mind about that. You get that black stuff off first.'

We are Biafrans,
Fighting for our nation;
In the name of Jesus
We shall conquer!

Twenty little boys, aged about five to eight years, marched into the petrol station, chanting their war song with great feeling. Each of them wore a camouflage headgear, some made out of banana leaves, some out of green climbing plants. Their rifles were fashioned from the raffia bamboo. Their leader, hardly into his teens, also wore camouflage headgear but carried an officer's baton instead of a rifle. He announced that his boys would divide into two groups and demonstrate a typical battle between gallant Biafran troops and the vandal army.

'Take cover!' he shouted to the Biafran contingent after the 'Nigerians' had gone into their trenches. All the boys fell flat on the ground, their legs spread out behind them at the proper angle.

'Advance!'

The Biafran soldiers crawled stealthily forward on all fours.

'Halt!'

The boys went flat again, each pair of legs forming an acute angle behind.

'Steady.'

One of the boys crawled on his belly towards the 'Nigerian' trench, stopped, gave a sharp pull at something and hurled a hand grenade right into the trench.

'Fire!' shouted the Biafran commander as the grenade exploded and wrought disaster on the Nigerian soldiers. The Biafran boys closed in on their disorganized enemies, mowing them down systematically.

'Flush out the trench!' ordered the C.O. to the applause of his spectators.

'I don' finish 'am sir,' the petrol attendant announced proudly to Professor Ezenwa who had temporarily forgotten all about his blackened headlights, completely captivated by the mock battle being staged by the little boys who fought as if they were actually defending their mothers' soup pots.

'You like am?' she asked, knowing quite well that he would. No trace of the black paint remained.

He paid her for the job. The expression on her face showed that she had expected something more. 'I'm afraid that's all I have left after paying for the petrol. Unless you'll follow me to the house ...'

She smiled coquettishly again, as if to ask 'why not?' Professor Ezenwa seized an opportunity when it presented itself. She gave him the time she would close for the day and he agreed to pick her up at an arranged spot.

The Professor felt much lighter at heart as he drove off from the petrol station. The irritating tar on his headlights had gone. The impressive and moving exhibition by the little boys had fired his zeal to defend Biafra at all costs. And to crown it all, Pep (that was the petrol attendant's name) had dropped from the clouds right into his lap. He did not know whether Pep stood for Pepper or for the famous tomato sauce, Tomapep. The full version of the name was irrelevant; Pep had the hips to give pep to a nonagenarian! Her khaki trousers made them obvious. Professor Ezenwa had not imagined that he would require the 'other facilities' at the Hotel Rising Sun that soon.

He made for the G.R.A.* with characteristic speed, slamming on the brakes here and swinging sharply away from a stubborn cyclist there. Since the shells landed at the Progress Hotel premises and killed Dr Amilo Kanu's son, many civil servants had fled from the G.R.A. He hoped the Inspector-General of Police would have the guts to stay behind.

As he approached the last checkpoint before entering the G.R.A. he saw three parked cars and instinctively slowed down to find out what was going on. He saw a man holding a small tin of coal tar and a brush. He rushed back into his car, negotiated a U-turn at break-neck speed and gave up his quest for the Inspector-General. He drove straight back to the petrol station, lied to Pep that he had decided to leave his car under her care to remind her of their date, and walked to the Hotel Rising Sun to see if his friends had returned. They had.

'Where's my champagne?' he enquired.

'Don't rub it in, Prof.,' Ifeji replied.

'I don't mind,' said Bassey, smiling. 'I did some boxing at school so I know how to receive hard knocks. It was my fault. Next time I'll do research like the Professor before accepting anything anybody tells me about this war!'

'You mean the story about the Yorubas is not true?'

'Haven't you done your research?' Onukaegbe asked in reply.

'I've been doing other things instead – I'll tell you about them later. What happened?'

'No coup in Lagos, that's all,' Ifeji replied.

'Another instance of monitoring from the Voice of Rumour?'

* Government Residential Area for senior civil servants.

the Professor said, laughing.

'The Director for Propaganda says it's nothing short of sabotage deliberately thrown in to give us a false sense of security and make us relax our vigilance, thereby giving the vandals easy entry into Enugu. He says Government is trying to smoke out the peddlers of the false rumour.'

'How I wish it had been true,' Onukaegbe yawned. 'I'm getting tired of this whole thing.'

'Come on, man,' reprimanded Bassey. 'You talk as if the war had been going on for a year!'

5

'*Eti-hei! Eti-hei!*' sneezed Mazi Kanu Onwubiko, Dr Kanu's father, as he supervised the repair of the roof of his house at Obodo, a village tucked away in Orumba Division.

'Don't let them!' His son-in-law, Egwuonwu, gave him the customary good wish offered to any one who sneezes. It is as if a sneeze symbolized a conscious effort by the person sneezing to thwart the efforts of the evil spirits who were trying to whisk him away.

'My life and yours,' Mazi Kanu acknowledged. It was the kind of sneeze that did three things to you at once: it released tears through wide open eyes, it sprayed saliva from your mouth, and it set your nose running.

'Who knows if it is my brother-in-law, Doctor, calling you?' suggested Egwuonwu.

'Doctor calling whom?' Mazi Kanu used the back of his hand to wipe his nostrils. 'My present concern is to stop the rain from pouring on my head inside my own house. Andrew' he addressed one of the men Egwuonwu had brought with him to mend his father-in-law's thatched house, 'push that mat right in. If you don't, the next rain will pour in from there. *Eti-hei! Eti-hei!*'

'Don't let them!' said Andrew.

'Oh!' Mazi replied. 'Whoever thinks he can take me will retire earlier than his chickens! I know I haven't stolen yams from anybody's barn.'

It was unusual for Mazi Kanu to sneeze like a boy having his first experience of snuff. He did not feel his normal self, but he could not pin down the cause of it. The previous night he had slept on his right side, on his left side, and flat on his chest, but no side had offered him any comfort. He had had a strong urge to try sleeping on his back as well, in his restlessness; his pathological fear of witches had, however, outweighed his discomfort. Things did not improve with daybreak. The cassava *foofoo* he ate for breakfast had refused to settle down since morning, and yet the usual symptoms which preceded an attack of 'go-slow' were not there. It was the kind of day he normally spent at Olie Post, sharing palm wine and snuff with members of his age-grade and picking up items of war news from those who owned or had access to radio sets. He could not do so today because his son-in-law, Egwuonwu, had sent a message that he would bring four men to help him mend his leaking roof.

The late rains had been very heavy in Obodo. The torrential downpour two days before had been preceded by a storm strong enough to tear an only child from the back of a possessive mother. By the time the storm had expended its fury, several mats had been ripped from Mazi Kanu's roof and flung over the mud walls demarcating his compound. When the rain itself began to pour down, hardly any patch in the mud house remained dry.

'In-law,' Egwuonwu began, removing an *omu* from his lips and tucking it away behind his right ear until he needed it for tying a mat. 'What is this we hear about Enugu?'

'Did you hear anything?' Mazi Kanu asked, stroking his hair which closely resembled a lawyer's wig, without the exotic curls. It was appropriately white for a man in his early seventies, but there was no sign of baldness.

'If you didn't hear it then it can't be true.'

'What did you hear?'

'I had better put back the *omu* into my mouth before a soldier arrests me for starting a bush fire with my mouth! If the Hausas have taken Enugu, Doctor should have run home with his wife and children.'

'May God forbid that we run from Enugu,' Mazi Kanu prayed. 'We have run from Nsukka. We have run from Ogoja. We have run from Abakaliki. If we also run from Enugu, to which place shall we all run? Please don't talk about any such thing happening, lest the gods act on our words!'

'*Kpulum!*' exclaimed Egwuonwu. 'Let my words return to me! If anybody reports that I ever said such a thing, I shall deny it outright.'

'Let nobody say that I said it, either,' Andrew put in, 'but I heard Eleazer Nwankwo say that his brother Peter, who works in the Public Works Department at Enugu, ran home last night. He said that Peter said that nobody is left at Enugu.'

'I won't judge with Peter, though,' observed Egwuonwu. 'He fears more than *iyiya*. Remember the story he told the first time he ran from Enugu over a month ago. That was even before the Hausas came near to Okpatu. He talked of rockets falling inside his neighbour's bedroom and of enemy shelling machines and ferrets* combining to warn every civilian to leave town as they shouted *kwapu kwapu unu d-uum!*'

'Was it from his mouth that my grandson Obiora picked up those words?' asked Mazi Kanu.

'Yes,' Egwuonwu replied. 'Peter can tell such convincing lies!'

'I am not saying that Enugu has run, O,' one of the workmen said cautiously, 'but I overheard – who was it now? – say that somebody who came from Awgu yesterday saw many cars moving out of Enugu towards Okigwi. The cars were overloaded with beds and mattresses and their drivers said the Hausas had entered Enugu.'

'Let's talk about something else.' Mazi Kanu found that the discussion aggravated his feeling of discomfort. 'If Hausa people are not satisfied with driving us from Ugwu Hausa and think they can also drive us from the land of our fathers, God and our dead fathers will bend their necks.'

'*Ise!*' Egwuonwu responded.

'Those whose powers are greater than ours will teach them that it is the stranger who has to take leave of the owner of the land, not the other way round.'

'*Ise!*' The other workmen joined Egwuonwu in the response.

'In-law,' Mazi Kanu addressed Egwuonwu, 'remember to tell me when you want breakfast to be served so I can tell Enyidie to bring it out to you.'

'Not until we can point at what we have accomplished,' replied Egwuonwu. 'We had some early morning palm oil before setting out from my house, but if you can pass your snuff-box round we would be thankful.'

As Mazi Kanu produced his rectangular snuff-box from the folds of his heavy woven wrapper where he usually concealed it, a Peugeot 404 station wagon pulled up in front of his compound.

'Push that mat right in,' Mazi Kanu instructed one of the workmen in an attempt to steady his nerves as a Sergeant stepped out of the car. His moustache gave him a forbidding appearance. The

* Armoured cars fitted with guns.

arrival of the car had stirred the hookworms in Mazi Kanu's inside, and he hoped the Sergeant would soon discover that he had stopped at the wrong house.

'Who de hell dey here?' shouted the Sergeant as he stepped into the compound. The way he carried himself, you would have sworn he was the General Officer Commanding the Biafran Army rather than a Director's orderly. No one knew what to reply so no one replied.

'Which is the road to Dr Amilo Kanu's house?' he asked in the vernacular when it became clear to him that no person in the compound spoke English.

Mazi Kanu and his son-in-law, Egwuonwu, spoke to each other with the eyes. Egwuonwu understood that he was to be the spokesman. 'Officer, we are Agbenu workmen,' he replied, 'and know nothing about people living here. The doctor you named, does he work in this village so that we can ask from one of the villagers?'

'I have no time to waste,' stormed the Sergeant. 'If you are strangers here, take me to the villagers so that I can ask them myself.'

'The people have gone "combing", and I don't think the officer will want to trek to the bush where they have gone. I can send one of my men there to check if you can tell us where the doctor works and who wants him.'

The Sergeant saw there was no alternative but to allow himself to be interrogated by an idle civilian. 'Dr Kanu works at Enugu.'

'Why doesn't the officer look for him at Enugu?' Egwuonwu asked, plucking up courage. He very nearly went on to ask whether it was true that the Hausas had entered Enugu but he knew the dangers of toying with a lion's tail.

'I am not looking for Doctor,' the Sergeant replied, showing that he was getting irritated. 'Doctor gave me a message for his father who lives in this village.'

'So it is Doctor's father you want?'

'Yes.'

'Hm.' Egwuonwu saw the Sergeant's eyes staring ... ...ke a cat about to pounce on its prey. That ruled out the possibility of consulting his father-in-law with the eyes. Mazi Kanu came to his rescue.

'This is Doctor's father's house,' he informed the Sergeant.

'Who de hell you tink you fit dribble like football, you bloody fucking idiot?' the Sergeant roared at Egwuonwu in pidgin.

'Officer, don't be angry,' pleaded Egwuonwu, who saw the

Sergeant's anger without understanding his pidgin. 'You people asked us to be vigilant, especially nowadays when we don't know who is with us . . .'

'Sharrap there, or I put you for bunker for fourteen days! Me I look like sabo?'

'Please, my son, don't be angry,' pleaded Mazi Kanu. 'Were we not warned by you people who control the Government not to open our mouths too wide in the presence of strangers, until we find out who the strangers are?'

The Sergeant felt elated at being grouped among the rulers of the young nation. He made a show of forgiving Egwuonwu and turned to Mazi Kanu.

'Do you say this is Doctor's house?' he asked incredulously. What he saw would not have qualified as the servants' quarters in the kind of home he had imagined Dr Kanu living in.

'Doctor has no house here,' replied Mazi Kanu. 'This is my own house.'

'Are you related to Doctor?' the Sergeant asked.

'I am Doctor's father.'

It was as if the Sergeant suddenly discovered that a man he had insulted was his commanding officer. He promptly stiffened and gave the fly-catching salute. The driver who was stretching himself outside the compound also instantly stiffened and puffed out his chest when he saw the Sergeant salute.

'Pardon me, sir!' the Sergeant apologized. 'I didn't know, sir!' Egwuonwu bit his lips so as to suppress a giggle.

Mazi Kanu took the Sergeant to his wife's house within the compound, to receive the message from his son, a son who could not keep the rain off his old father's bamboo bed.

'Has anything gone wrong?' Egwuonwu enquired of his father-in-law who had remained in his wife's hut after the Sergeant had driven off.

'I did not know I could ever sit in my own house with goats eating palm fronds off my head.'

'What is it, in-law?' pressed Egwuonwu. 'Did anything happen to Doctor?'

'No. It is my little Amilo. Doctor's first son. Five years and three months old. It is him that the Hausas killed yesterday. Just tell me what evil I have ever done to any Hausa man or woman, that they should pursue me to my house and kill a child who does not know his right hand from his left . . .'

Mazi Kanu gave as much detail of the child's death as he had picked up from the Sergeant. 'I warned that the marriage to a Hausa girl would bring no good to us. But Doctor attaches no weight to my words. Now my words have come true. In the whole of Enugu, the Hausa people saw nobody else to kill with their shelling machin' except my little grandson Amilo . . .'

'In-law, you are not the person to be taught how to take any blow. Ndo.' Egwuonwu allowed a decent interval before asking the question uppermost in his mind: 'Does it mean that the Hausas have entered Enugu?'

'I am not one of those who can see the moon from under a shade so I cannot stay at Obodo and talk about what happened at Enugu. But the soldier said Doctor sent him to warn me that his wife and the remaining child will be coming to Obodo by the time the sun begins to set. He said that after the death of his son Amilo, the Government decided that all women and children should be removed from Enugu. That is all I was told.'

'So that thing is true!' Egwuonwu cried.

'What is true?' enquired Prophet James in his white ankle-length robe and his white headgear shaped somewhere between a royal crown and a chef's hat. He held a small bell in his right hand which he stopped from ringing as he walked by holding it upside-down by its ball-shaped pendulum. In his left hand he held his second permanent companion on his rounds – a small wooden cross which he usually held in front of him as he talked to any one as if to halt any evil spirits which might attempt to jump from his hearers to him.

'The Hausas have entered Enugu,' Egwuonwu replied.

'Eh!' the prophet shouted. 'I saw it clearly in my vision four weeks ago! Yes, the Holy One of Israel showed it to me very vividly. When I cried about my vision, when I called the nation to observe dry fasting for seven whole days, those possessed of the evil one said it was Prophet James carrying on again . . .' He began to ring his bell and to shout ecstatically.

'Please Prophet James, not here,' Egwuonwu shouted, pleading.

'Don't ask me to shut up. When the Holy One of Israel speaks through me no earthly mortal can silence Him!'

'Please, my in-law has just been told that Amilo, Doctor's son, was killed yesterday . . .'

'Eh?' Prophet James could hardly wait for Egwuonwu to finish before shouting and ringing his bell. 'Killed yesterday? That completes the picture. That explains that other vision. Yes. I said it. The Holy One of Israel – may His name be praised – Alleluia! The Holy One of Israel showed me a gold coffin, the sign that an important person would die unless we prayed and fasted for our sins. You see, the doctor has lost his son. It wasn't a poor man's son, but the son of a big man. Now the Hausas have entered Enugu. More big men will die, and small men too – unless the world listens to Prophet James. Seven days' dry fast. No food, no water, not even the chewing stick; nothing but prayer and dedication. No man should go in to his wife. No dancing, no drinking, no merriment, not even farm work. A big disaster hangs over all of us, worse than what befell Sodom and Gomorrah. A disaster that will make all ears which hear about it tingle . . .'

Prophet James rattled on as he jingled his bell, held high his cross and took to the road without excusing himself.

'It's amazing that that man's voice never fails him,' one of the workmen broke the silence which followed the prophet's departure, 'even though he shouts from morning till night every day.'

'If the hen loses its *kwom*, with what will it feed its brood?' observed another workman. 'It is his voice that fetches him his food, so how can he allow it to fail him?'

'I had never taken James' words seriously,' said Andrew. 'But what I have just heard has set me thinking.'

'Divination is no more than sheer common sense,' Mazi Kanu remarked, his first utterance since Egwuonwu gave the spark to the highly inflammable Prophet James. 'No eyes see the gods. I did not need any prophet to see for myself that Doctor's marriage to a Hausa girl would bring trouble with it.'

'In-law, did you say Doctor's wife will be coming to live here?' Egwuonwu asked, conscious that he was fanning the flames.

'That's what the soja said.'

'We had better hurry then to complete the work before she arrives. Andrew, Joshua, Moses, quick quick!'

'She is not coming to this house,' Mazi Kanu announced, vibrating his legs and looking pensively ahead of him.

'Where else could she go?'

'Are you asking me? I told the soja to tell Doctor that his wife is not entering my house. My house has none of the things which I hear they were enjoying so much in Ibadan and Lagos that they forgot they had an old man at Obodo. Even if it had everything desirable, she would still not enter my house. So I told the soja to tell Doctor that he will have to find another house at Obodo for his family if they decide now to live in the bush.'

'But, in-law, how will it sound in other people's ears, to hear that your son's wife is living in another person's house instead of your own?'

'What is there the ear has not heard before?' asked Mazi Kanu in reply.

'Nothing, in-law. But do you think Doctor will be happy that you refused entry to his wife?'

Mazi Kanu laughed without mirth. 'A man who was drenched to the skin entered the house of a man in Umuawulu and asked to be allowed to warm himself by the fire. The Umuawulu man asked at what point on his journey the rain descended on him. The man could not tell. So the Umuawulu man threw him out of his house and back into the rain, arguing that the man who took no note of the point where the rain began to soak him will also fail to take note of the house in which he warmed himself dry. That is all I have to say . . . What am I hearing?'

All five men strained their ears.

'Is that not the sound of the *ikoro*?' Egwuonwu said.

Mazi Kanu nodded assent. It was certainly the *ikoro*. The sound was unmistakable, even though he had not heard it for several years. Something grave, very grave must have happened. It could not be that the Odo of Obodo, Chief Ofo, was dead? He and Mazi Kanu had exchanged snuff-boxes only the night before. What else could call for the sounding of the *ikoro*? Could it be that Prophet James actually sees the gods? *Ko – ko – kom . . .*

Mazi Kanu picked up his walking stick and the brown plastic helmet Egwuonwu had presented to him the previous year. Every Obodo male who had tied cloth round his waist was required to proceed to the chief's compound immediately he heard the sound of the *ikoro*, without waiting to complete the work on hand or to be summoned personally.

'In-law, I'm going to find out what those above say it will be today. Thank heavens, you and your workmen are not Obodo people so the *ikoro* is not meant for you. Please hurry up with the work before something happens which may prevent you from completing it today. Nothing is more ignoble than that an old man like me should be drenched by rain in his own house.'

Mazi Kanu took a pinch of snuff to steady his nerves in preparation for whatever shock lay ahead, and made for Chief Ofo's compound. He found that his thoughts focused on the death of his grandson rather than on the message of the *ikoro*. Nothing from the *ikoro* could be more depressing to him than the shocking death of the little boy. He had seen the boy only once. Shortly after Dr Kanu's wife and children had joined Dr Kanu at Enugu he had brought them home one Sunday morning. It had been a flying visit. They hardly even sat down. Amilo Junior had stuck to Mazi Kanu during that short period, not minding the rags he wore, as if the two of them were of a kindred spirit. Mazi Kanu had seen in the little boy signs of someone who would show greater interest in and respect for his village and his kinsmen than his father had. That was the child the Hausas had decided to kill. Harmless, innocent child. It was an abominable act. Its perpetrators were not worthy to be allowed to set foot in any society which had a sense of values.

Doctor's wife and second child to come and stay with him? His in-law Egwuonwu was correct. Absolutely correct. He could not reject them. It would be abominable. Fatima was his son's wife, and therefore his wife . . . But was she? No, she was not. He could reject her. To bear a child for a man does not in itself transform the woman into the man's wife. A concubine can bear children for her lover; that does not in itself change her status from a concubine to a wife. Marriage means more than cohabitation and procreation. It is a binding together of two families, not only the man and the woman, into something almost as tight as blood relationship. It has its rituals, without which there may be cohabitation and procreation, but no marriage. He knew nobody in Fatima's family. There had been no marriage rituals. There had been no marriage. He could reject Fatima . . .

Could he, really? Doctor had sent him a photograph of their wedding in England. Obodo did not recognize such ceremonies as constituting marriage but it could well be that Fatima's people did. And since Fatima was not a daughter of Obodo, one has to reckon with the traditions of her people rather than the tradition of Obodo.

What about Doctor's surviving son? If anything happened to Doctor that boy would be the only hope of perpetuating his name. He could not reject the boy, could he?

The noise from Chief Ofo's compound reminded Mazi Kanu about the *ikoro*.

6

'Is there anybody who has not yet come?' enquired Chief Ofo as he scanned the sea of masculine faces from his outsize chair elevated on a platform from which he could see and be seen by all present.

The meeting was in his *ogbaburuburu* – as the name suggests, a circular hut, which he had inherited from his father. Unlike the custom at the *ogbuti* which once served both as a court and as a hall for receiving large groups, the mud benches in the *ogbaburuburu* were arranged in a horseshoe formation and in four tiers. The skins of leopards, sheep, deer, and other domestic and wild animals slaughtered during the reigns of Chief Ofo and his forbears lined the circular wall, available to any person who wanted to sit on them rather than on the naked mud benches. The benches were usua ly rubbed hard with special pebbles by the wives of the compound, leaving a glossy finish which generally protected clothes from the red laterite while the gloss lasted.

Chief Ofo, in his late seventies, looked a centenarian that morning. His characteristic humour seemed to have dried up *kpamkpam*. Even his once hairy head had lost some of its gloss as if the harmattan had already set in. There was no doubt that somebody – Prophet James or someone else – had pumped fear into him; so much so that his small figure looked still more diminutive as he sat on his chair to address the men of Obodo.

'Our people, greetings. I salute you for answering the summons of *ikoro*. Some of you here were not born the time *ikoro* last sounded in Obodo. That was when our father died thirty years ago. Nobody sounds the *ikoro* for fun, so we have not gathered here for fun. Our people say that something has gone wrong when a thing which did not exist in the private part of a she-goat is found in the private part of the she-goat's offspring. Something has happened in Obodo which has not happened since my mother bore me, nor did it happen in the days of our fathers and the fathers of our fathers. No food can be so sweet that a sensible man will for its sake bite off and swallow his tongue. Never has an Obodo man betrayed his kinsman for the sake of reward, much less that thing called money, paper money. I cannot remember any Obodo man who, because of love of meat, has ever eaten a deer stricken with hernia. All this has happened today. *Ikoro* has summoned all of you here so that everybody will wash his eyes in water and get at the root of this matter. I salute you all.'

'Offspring of Akajiofo, *kwenu*!'

'Ha!'

'Men renowned for wiping out any rival town before dawn, *kwenu*!'

'Ha!'

'Pillars of Obodo, *kwenu*!'

'Ha!'

'*Kwezuenu!*'

'Ha! ! !'

'We cannot stay as full-blooded men and stink like putrefying corpses. It is true that the *ikoro* announces the death of a great man, but it is not only the death of a great man that the *ikoro* announces. In the days when men were men, the *ikoro* summoned men to war. The *ikoro* we have just heard summons us to war . . .'

That was Chief Madukegbu Ukadike, the Chairman of Obodo Civil Defence Committee (C.D.C.), and somebody every Obodo man had to reckon with. Any decisions taken in his absence which went contrary to his wishes had to be reversed as soon as he appeared in person. Nobody conferred any chieftaincy title on him. As Chairman of the Obodo Local Council, he had made no bones of the fact that he was the effective head of the town, describing Chief Ofo as a mere figurehead and an anachronism. His appointment as Chairman of the local Civil Defence Committee brought him yet more powers, and he decided the time had come to acquire the cap of chieftaincy to take his many feathers. So he killed a cow, called in the people and in the midst of the feasting announced that he had renounced his English name, Christian, because of the atrocities the British were perpetrating on his fellow Biafrans, and wished to be known thenceforth as Chief Madukegbu Ukadike. He also announced that he had taken the title, Ezeahurukwe – the chief you acknowledged at sight. That title stung Chief Ofo more than anything else; it focused attention on the contrast between the diminutive, inconsequential size of the anointed chief and the domineering, impressive personality of the pretender.

Chief Ukadike did not care one grain of *garri* about Chief Ofo's feelings. He did not care about anyone else's feelings either. Before he took the title of Ezeahurukwe, he was popularly known as Idere – the flood that can flow uphill! He had been a braggart all his fifty years or so, and his two years of service in the West African Frontier Force during World War II gave him the opportunity to lay claim to limitless achievements. As the saying goes at Obodo, the traveller has the licence to tell countless lies about the places he has visited; no one in his audience has shared his experience so no one can challenge him. Name any battleground – in Burma, in India, in North Africa – and Ukadike would claim to have fought the battle of his life there. The Arakan Yoma jungle was for years after his return to Obodo a regular feature of his conversation. He claimed to have earned four of the six medals he usually lined across his left breast in one fierce operation within that jungle. If you asked him why, in spite of such a meritorious career, he did not rise beyond the rank of private, he would show you the scar on his right hand. It was his penalty for beating up a British Officer and stuffing his mouth with sand for attempting to take one of his innumerable Indian mistresses to bed and adding insult to injury by referring to him as a monkey. The army command did not take kindly to a black private trouncing a white officer in public. A decision was therefore taken that he must pay dearly for his temerity – by remaining a private for the duration of the war, and by losing the source of part at least of his strength. The latter was accomplished by pulling off the power-packed sinews from his right hand, hence the scar. Everybody at Obodo had dreaded him ever since.

'My Civil Defence Committee decided to summon this gathering here in Chief Ofo's *ogbaburuburu* to show you that the Nigerians have already entered Obodo without most of you knowing it. You will soon see that Radio Kaduna knew what it was talking about when it announced last week that Obodo had been "liberated". When you have heard what we have to tell you, we can then decide the best way to fight the enemy . . .'

Ukadike felt buoyant like the fully-inflated advertisement for Michelin X tyres as he described the intelligence network he had cast over the enemy agent, Justus Chikwendu, and the record catch it had netted. Information had reached him about Justus which had roused his suspicion. With his Arakan Yoma jungle experience, which, thank God, he had not forgotten, he planned a careful investigation, details of which he had been advised by the General Officer Commanding not to disclose. As a result of the investigation, the army swooped down on Justus early that morning. He listed the items discovered in Justus' compound, some hidden underground in boxes, some hidden in the ceiling: brand-new army uniforms, including boots, dozens of grenades, hundreds of rounds of ammunition, several Madsens.

The reaction of the men of Obodo was a spontaneous outburst of disgust. The gathering had been summoned soon after the discovery; the news had not therefore had the time to filter through the length and breadth of Obodo, with the result that most men at the gathering were hearing about the treachery for the first time.

Ukadike informed the gathering that Justus was one of many agents planted in many parts of Biafra by the men who planned the abortive coup. When the agreed time came, soldiers loyal to the organizers of the plot, disguised in plain clothes, would be sent to the agents who would fit them out in military uniforms and supply them with arms and ammunition. Thus armed, these specially trained soldiers would cause confusion by firing a few shots, leading to the desertion of the village and the easy entry of Nigerian soldiers. Ukadike emphasized that the uncovering of Justus' treachery could not have been more timely. As soon as Justus was informed that some soldiers wanted him he immediately shouted the password 'One Nigeria!' as he had been instructed to do in order to identify himself; apparently he had been told to expect his own group of soldiers later that day and thought they had decided, for one reason or another, to arrive some hours earlier.

'Enough of that abominable account,' shouted someone in the audience in utter disgust. 'What we want to know is what you did with that Justus!'

'I would have done to him what I did to thousands of Germans in Arakan Yoma jungle,' Ukadike replied, his medals rattling as he struck his chest. 'But the soldiers begged me to leave him for them.'

'What can the soldiers do to him?' one man asked. 'Don't people say he claims no bullet can penetrate his body?'

'If only the soldiers had left him for me,' replied Ukadike, 'I would have taught him how the flood flows uphill.'

'Idere!' shouted some of his admirers.

'What about the man's compound?' asked the man who had asked earlier about Justus himself.

'That's one of the questions we have called you here to answer,' Ukadike replied.

The gathering disposed of Justus' treachery to his fatherland speedily and without any controversy. Fifty young men were despatched to the compound which had harboured such a white sheep and such lethal weapons, to ensure that no wall was left standing. Fortunately the ancestors had foreseen the fate which awaited Justus and denied him any children. His wife was ordered back to her home town, but not before her hair was shaved off and she had been clothed in mourning. No matter what the soldiers did with Justus, he was proclaimed a dead man in Obodo, his home town, and his wife was free to return to her parents or to marry another man. Because of the unprecedented crime he had committed against his kinsmen, he was to be deprived of the traditional funeral rites, thereby condemning his soul to perpetual restlessness.

Having dealt with Justus, the gathering turned its attention to a much more problematic assignment – to ensure that the 'jigger-infested vermin' (as Radio Biafra described the Nigerian soldiers) did not get too close to Obodo, let alone actually take the town. Enugu was much nearer to Obodo than the official distance of 50 miles along the trunk road would suggest. Every man in Obodo knew that Enugu was barely a day's walk by the bush path taken by pedestrians carrying palm produce and palm wine to a famous pottery market midway between Obodo and Enugu; the distance was probably less than 20 miles. If the enemy discovered that route, Obodo would be in trouble. Since the route was not defended by Biafran troops, the enemy could cover the distance and storm Obodo while everybody was still snoring in bed.

'How much soup must stick to the bottom of the soup pot before a sensible man takes the trouble to get at it?' one man had asked during the discussion of the matter. 'What is there in Obodo, what has Government ever established for us here, that the Hausas will want to waste their time and bullets coming here?'

'What did Ibagwa have which Obodo does not have?' another man asked in reply. 'Did the Hausas not go there and refuse to get out?'

'Don't mind Okeke,' retorted another man. 'Ask him what Obodo had when Radio Kaduna announced that the Nigerians had captured it. Ask him what Obodo had when the saboteurs made their plans with Justus. I appeal to everybody: any person who does not know what to say should shut his mouth – *kpilikom*!'

Everyone agreed that Okeke was wrong. The pattern had been established that the Nigerians usually 'captured' a town first by radio, followed days, weeks or months later by a concerted effort to capture the town militarily. Since Radio Kaduna was alleged to have announced the capture of the town of Obodo, a push by the Nigerian troops towards Obodo must be expected. The gathering accordingly empowered Ukadike, as Chairman of the C.D.C., to lead a delegation to the Brigade Commander drawing his attention to the significance of the Enugu-Obodo route and requesting immediate deployment of troops to guard the bush path. The villagers would feed the soldiers for the duration of their assignment, and offer every other assistance they might require, including the building of obstacles and the digging of trenches.

How best could Obodo guard against the emergence of other Justuses? *Igba ndu* won unanimous support as the answer. The next *Nkwo* market day was chosen for the solemn ceremony. Every Christian would swear by the Holy Bible, and every non-Christian by the *Ofo* that he would never assist any enemy to attack or enter

Obodo nor sell his town or fellow townsman in any other way; if he did, the Bible or the *Ofo* should kill him outright.

'Mazi, Mazi. I salute you all. My words are few . . .' The speaker deliberately spoke in low tones.

'You are addressing yourself, O!' protested one man who could not hear the speaker from where he sat. There were nods from many others.

'My words are not the kind that require the *ogene*,' the speaker explained. 'Therefore don't ask me to shout.'

Everywhere was silent as the speaker cleared his throat and spoke as aud'bly as he could in low tones: '*Igba ndu* is good. Every other thing we have today agreed to do is good. But we have left out the most important problem, the problem which will determine whether we shall run from Obodo or we shall not. We have said nothing about the foreigners in our midst. I mean the refugees [pronounced 'riverju']. These people are not happy that they cannot return to their home towns. They covet our farms, our barns, the fact that we are still living in our own homes, forgetting that if they had stood behind our army the enemy would not have set foot in their towns. Many of them will do anything possible to show the enemy the way to Obodo so that we too will become refugees. If my wishes were to prevail, I would say we bundle all of them out of Obodo today and tomorrow. No town which receives them will remain standing long after. My words are spent.'

The speaker received several handshakes as he resumed his seat. Mazi Kanu adjusted his wrapper as he rose to speak.

'Our people, I salute you all. Our people say that the time a dead man's funeral arrangements are being discussed is also the best time to discuss who is to inherit the dead man's widow. So while you consider what to do with foreigners, I want you to know that Doctor, my son, sent me word just now that he will send his Hausa wife to Obodo today. As if I sniffed my fingers and knew what we would discuss today, I told his message bearer to tell him not to send her here, but you all know how much my words mean to Doctor! That is why I decided to let all of you know it before she arrives. I salute you all.'

Mazi Kanu had stuffed each nostril with snuff before he remembered that the unwritten standing orders governing meetings at Obodo required any person wishing to snuff or to smoke while the meeting was in progress to do so outside the place of meeting. He was boiling over with rage at the thought that the son who should have been a source of pride and sustenance to him

61

in his old age should be the person to whitewash his face and expose him to public condemnation at each turn of the road. On the other hand an inner voice reminded him of the inward debate he had had on his way to the chief's compound. Is Fatima not his wife? Could she be his wife and be a foreigner? What about their son? Should he not get up again and withdraw or modify his words? Or should he wait and see the reaction of the group first? The provost who had come to demand the customary penny fine from him for breach of the standing order on snuffing, read his feelings and walked away without demanding the fine.

For a while, the meeting broke into whispering groups. As the collective thoughts of the different groups began to crystallize, the noise gradually subsided. When finally the man who introduced the discussion about foreigners raised his hand and took the floor, the nods of approval from all sides showed that he spoke the consensus:

'Our people, I salute you all again. Please let nobody accuse me of "buying" this matter. It is as a result of the strength of my feeling that I am speaking again on it. Mazi Kanu, we salute you for your words. We know that if you had your way, Doctor would not have married a Hausa woman. We know that you do not want the woman inside your house. We shall heap sand round your waist to give you reinforced support. Tell your son, Doctor, that the group owns the individual, the individual does not own the group. Any decision taken by the group is therefore binding on every individual member of that group. After all, did not Mazi Nwankwo Ijoma name his first-born son Okwuasoeze – truth is no respecter of royalty? Our people, I have nothing further to say.'

Having agreed that any decision on foreigners should apply to Dr Kanu's wife, the gathering proceeded to discuss what should be done to non-indigenes of Obodo seeking refuge at Obodo. The initial consensus was to chase every non-indigene out of the town post-haste. The arguments in favour of this line of action were overwhelming. Just as it was impossible to say which lizard was male and which was female by merely watching them run around the house, so it was impossible to tell which foreigner was a true Biafran and which a Nigerian in Biafran clothing. By admitting foreigners into the town, the people of Obodo might be admitting some of those enemy collaborators who carry small talking machines for telling the Hausas where to drop their bombs. More-over to admit foreigners would mean swelling the population of Obodo and heightening the military significance of the town, thereby turning it into a military target. Another argument advanced was that any sizeable influx of refugees invariably ushered in a sharp rise in the cost of living.

Chief Ukadike needed all the bragging, jingling of his six medals and bloated accounts of conversations he had had with the Provincial Secretary, the Provincial Administrator, unidentified top Army officers, etcetera, to tip the scales. Chairmen of C.D.C.s and members of the Provincial Leaders of Thought Assembly had been warned not to encourage acts which could be construed as discriminatory to Biafrans of any other ethnic group, town, or province, as this would puncture the slogan 'Every Biafran is his brother's keeper' a slogan upon which the success of the war effort largely depended. Ukadike employed every workable technique to brush aside any dissenting views, not because he was an altruist, but because he knew that any unfavourable decision would be made applicable to Dr Kanu's wife and, although he was not fond of Dr Kanu, he saw in him a ladder reaching to greater heights. He was sweating profusely by the time it was finally agreed that foreigners should be received into the town, subject to adequate security measures to be developed and enforced by the C.D.C.

Before the gathering rose, it decided on a weekly 'combing' of every bush in Obodo, including even the dreaded evil bush which, years past, received the corpses of men and women who died in ignominy. Any male who failed to join in each combing exercise would be fined one goat. The C.D.C. was empowered to mount checkpoints at strategic points on all roads and footpaths throughout the town. Wherever possible, a veteran of the world wars was to be placed in charge of each checkpoint. An all-night curfew was to be imposed as soon as the C.D.C. could organize night watches for all villages making up the town.

Ukadike gave the closing charge: 'We are fighting what people who speak the English language call a war of survi-'

'-val!' echoed the gathering.

'War of survi-'

'-val!'

'Our sons who studied history assure us that no nation fighting a war of survival as we are now fighting has ever been defeated. As the Big Man says, by the grace of God we shall van-'

'-quish!' echoed the audience.

'We shall van-'

'-quish!'

'Our people say that no degree of misadventure can uproot a man from his home. God forbid that the Nigerians will uproot us from

63

our home. If they venture in this direction, we shall teach them how water can flow uphill. After all, some of us did not commandeer these medals as some of them commandeered their military ranks!'

'I am not trying to speak after the Chairman of the C.D.C. has gathered our words together,' apologized a lanky man as he rose to his feet. 'I only want to touch on the last point he raised. As all of you know, I am one of those who invested all their money in Northern Nigeria. I put up four buildings. I owned a petrol station. I had a transport business. Where are all those things today? The Hausas have taken all of them. But for our Reverend Father, they would have taken my life too. Our people, the Hausas now want to follow me even to my father's compound. Did I mount the wife of any of them? Did I steal any yams from their barn? Now, forget me. What about you? What has any of you done to any Hausa man? Has he squandered all that we left for him in the North that he should come here to take your homes and farms from you? If you will leave them to enter Obodo, I will not! I will take at least one head before I lose mine!'

There was complete unanimity as the meeting rose. The enemy must not be allowed to step inside Obodo.

7

'Director for Procurement. Can I help you?' Mr Ndubuisi Akwaelumo answered the telephone in his usual authoritative yet courteous telephone voice. You at the other end of the telephone could never tell from the way he announced himself whether he was harassed or happy, fresh or fatigued. No matter what his mood or temper, no matter how busy and harassed, whenever his secretary buzzed him to take a call he did so in the same calm, collected, slightly affected but clear voice as if he was momentarily oblivious of everything around him except the telephone call. It was a habit he had picked up from his boss when he was a fresh recruit in the Administrative Service. His boss had maintained that it was unfair to greet a telephone caller unknown to you with any hostility or frustration for which he was not responsible.

'Yes, Rose. I didn't recognize your voice. Any problems?'

His wife's voice contrasted sharply with his as it bruised its way through the receiver. The personal secretary heard the shrill sound, read the anxiety in his face and vacated her room for him. He was taking the call in her office.

'Yes, Rose, but I'm at a meeting now,' Akwaelumo replied, hoping that his wife would take the hint and keep her voice down.

'Mee – what?' she yelled into the speaker. Akwaelumo quietly moved the receiver some distance from his ear. The harsh sound set his teeth on edge as if he had bitten into an unripe pineapple. 'You're at a mee – what!'

She was mad with him for reporting so calmly that he was at a meeting of heads of the various War Directorates known as the War Services Council.

It was always work, work, duty, duty for him. No time for his wife, no time for his two children. No time to consider their welfare. It was only a husband like him who, for the sake of his work, would abandon his family to the bloodthirsty sex maniacs fighting for Nigeria when every other considerate husband had evacuated his family and property from Enugu. She could not accept any pleas to keep calm. If he didn't send her the car immediately, she would set off on foot with the kids! To hell with his meetings!

Mr Akwaelumo walked over to the window. It looked out onto a parking lot for the Government Secretariat. In normal times that parking lot bustled with activity – girls selling oranges, peeled and unpeeled, news vendors displaying their newspapers, Chinese magazines, Onitsha market love literature, and pornographic magazines on vacant lots or on the bonnets of parked cars. A large mango tree at the near end gave the hawkers and vendors shelter from the blazing sun. A hawker popularly known as 'Manpower' had carved out for himself a vantage position between the tarmac and the mango tree, where he did brisk business selling roast groundnuts and puffed up popcorn, a combination he had nicknamed 'generator' because of its high rating as an aphrodisiac! The parking lot was virtually deserted as Akwaelumo stared vacantly through the window collecting his thoughts. The young men had become Civil Defenders. 'Manpower' had travelled to his village, to evacuate his belongings to the mansion he was alleged to have built from his huge profits from the sale of his 'generator'. Little drops of water certainly made a mighty ocean for him.

Mr Akwaelumo's glance swung from the parking lot to the old Parliament Building, a uniquely designed complex which was at one time the most outstanding parliament building in Nigeria.

A much more imposing parliament building had now been erected on the commanding heights of Independence Layout; it had been deliberately designed to symbolize the transformation of the Eastern Region of Nigeria from the poor relation it used to be to the oil-rich region.

'We're waiting for you, Akwa.'

Mr Akwaelumo turned round and followed the voice into the conference room.

'You were so long away that we wondered whether you had evacuated yourself!' Mr Uko, Director-General (War Services), who usually presided over the War Services Council, laughed convulsively in his characteristic manner. Anybody unfamiliar with him would think he was epileptic, the way he roared and coughed with laughter.

'It was Rose . . .'

'Which Rose?' the Director-General interrupted.

'The only Rose, of course! My wife.'

'Is she still here?' asked the Director-General in wild disbelief.

'Yes, why not?' Akwa replied. 'It's in accordance with H.E.'s directive that no evacuation should be permitted to avoid causing panic.'

Mr Uko burst out laughing. This time the laughter was short-lived as nobody seemed anxious to keep him company. He took a bite from a cola nut, his usual habit, and turned to Akwaelumo. 'Go and arrange the evacuation of your family. I'm sure all your colleagues here have done so. H.E. can't expect you to concentrate on your work with your wife and children hanging round your neck like millstones. Ask your deputy to join us so that he can brief you on our discussions about contingency evacuation plans when you return.'

It was clear that Biafra did not have the military capacity to keep the Nigerians out of Enugu. It had therefore been decided to move the War Directorates, Government Ministries, Banks, University of Biafra, University Teaching Hospital and other important establishments in Enugu to different locations. The war must continue, no matter what became of Enugu.

The meeting chose Umuahia, Aba and Owerri as the main locations to which the War Directorates and Government Ministries would be transferred. The University of Biafra and the University Teaching Hospital were also to find new homes in any of the three towns. The Directorate of Accommodation was requested to send scouts out immediately to take stock of all available office and residential accommodation in the three towns, to enable the Directorate to allocate space to the various approved establishments as a matter of extreme urgency.

Radio Biafra was to transfer to Aba without delay, to ensure the continuation of its broadcasts whether or not Enugu fell to the enemy. It was, however, to continue to broadcast as 'Radio Biafra, Enugu'. Similarly, all establishments transferring from Enugu to new locations were to retain their Enugu address for correspondence. The Post Office would be advised of their new locations, to ensure that their correspondence got to them. All approved establishments would also receive in confidence the list of the new addresses of all important public establishments.

The contingency evacuation plans included the evacuation of all government files, typewriters, duplicating machines and other essential equipment; all important Government documents, including the records in the Government archives, the public library and the University of Biafra Library at Enugu Campus. Hospitals were instructed to move their patients, beds, drugs and equipment.

Clear instructions were, however, issued that all adult males must remain behind for the last-ditch defence of Enugu. Women and children could now be evacuated, but any adult male seen leaving Enugu must be turned back. Men were requested to arm themselves with guns, matchets, anything available, and to be prepared for street fighting with the enemy. If the order to leave Enugu was finally given, all food and water left behind must be poisoned.

'Hello, Prof.! What brings you to my house?' Mr Duke Bassey, alias Indigenous, warm as ever, gave Professor Emeka Ezenwa a pat on the back.

'My car, naturally,' Ezenwa replied, attempting to be humorous.

'Oh, of course. I thought you were one of the people afraid to drive their cars in daylight – for fear of air raids!'

'I have been toying with the idea of camouflaging my car, but not just yet. If what the Nigerians have so far displayed is all they know about air raids, I wouldn't have sleepless nights over them. That's why I didn't want anyone to mess up my headlights.'

'Did you hear of the enemy plane shot down with a dane gun?' Bassey asked laughing.

'No.'

'Well, sit down, let me nack you tory!'

Each man sank into an enormous lounge chair, imported from

Holland. 'You know the tactics adopted by the timid pilots: fly high over Enugu to avoid our rockets, then make for a cassava farm where they harmlessly off-load their bombs. take photographs of any of the bombs which happen to explode, complete with any dust raised by the explosion, and then fly back safely to report to Lagos that they set ablaze an ammunition dump or a fuel depot. Unfortunately for this one, a vigilant Biafran hunter was near the cassava farm it selected. The hunter took a cool aim with his dane gun and *gbuaaam*! He scored a bull's eye. That's why we haven't had an air raid for the past two day . The vandals have rushed to Britain and Russia to beg for a replacement! Have something to drink. Whisky or brandy?'

'I'm not sure I'm in the mood to drink,' Professor Ezenwa replied, shifting uneasily.

'Come on Prof.,' urged Bassey as he handed a glass and the bottle of White Horse whisky to Professor Ezenwa, 'it's one way of forgetting everything. You don't look particularly bright today. Hope you don't allow thoughts of the belongings you left at Nsukka to weigh you down unnecessarily.'

'I would be a hypocrite if I said I wasn't upset about leaving all I have acquired in my life for those vandals. But right now, that's not my problem. It's you I'm concerned about.'

'What is it?' whispered Bassey, retrieving the glass that was already half-way to his mouth.

'It was either Ikem or Chike who told me that you had not evacuated any of your property, apart from the few things Nma took when she went home with the kids. If you don't want to lose everything as I have done, you should begin to pack right away and evacuate at least one lorry-load before midnight. Tonight.'

'What!' Bassey jumped to his feet. 'Has it come to that?'

Bassey took a quick look at his property within the lounge alone. The value ran into thousands of pounds. He had furnished his Enugu house extravagantly – deliberately. Enugu had become his second home. That was where he had his friends having lived most of his adult life there and held key positions in the Enugu Municipal Council. If there was a place where creating a favourable impression paid off for him, it was Enugu. The furniture, the fittings, the wall-to-wall lounge carpet, practically everything in the house had been imported from Holland.

'I couldn't be happy losing these things,' Bassey said. It had never occurred to him that such a thing was possible. 'But what would be the reaction of the public if I began moving my property out of Enugu? Would the Government not consider it an act of sabotage?'

'What Government?' Professor Ezenwa interrupted. 'Give me the name of one single permanent secretary or director who has not evacuated his family and his property from Enugu.'

'You don't mean it.'

'Go and check, if you doubt me,' Ezenwa continued. 'Most of those who talked rubbish about university dons fleeing from Nsukka did not even wait for the war to begin. As soon as H.E. gave the zero hour broadcast on 30 June, they evacuated their property to their respective villages. Some of them even went to the extent of evacuating window blinds, carpets and cushion covers. The wife of one of them was turned back by angry Civil Defenders at a checkpoint near Aba as she tried to evacuate the drinks in their refrigerator.'

'You don't mean it,' repeated Bassey, for want of any more appropriate remark.

'I mean every word of it, and my advice to you is to do as they have done. I have no more property to lose. My one and only suitcase and my briefcase are constantly in the boot of my car. If the alarm goes any time, I'll jump into the car and off I go.'

'Thank you for the tip, although I can't tell you that I know what to do with all these things here . . . and in my supermarket . . . What do I take, and what do I leave? . . . And what if my neighbours cause a stir?'

'If you want to worry about your neighbours, go ahead.' The Professor sounded impatient.

'The Civil Defenders too,' Bassey added. 'They often turn back vehicles carrying household goods . . . And you know how doubly difficult they become when they discover that you speak a different language.'

'My friend, I know you wouldn't have achieved so much success in business if you didn't know how to cope with this sort of thing. You speak fluent Igbo, and I'm sure you know that you can hire a uniformed and armed soldier or policeman to act as escort for the vehicle carrying your property. Moreover I shouldn't be surprised if the Government authorizes what they may call "quiet evacuation" of women and children today or tomorrow.'

'Are things as bad as that?' an anxious Indigenous asked.

'We shall vanquish!' chuckled Professor Ezenwa, draining his whisky and taking his leave.

'That's at least one load off my mind,' sighed Mr Ndubuisi

Akwaelumo as he walked to the wash basin to wash his hands, soon after his wife and two children had left in his car bearing the special VIG (for Vigilance) number plates introduced by the Biafran Government and sold at £20 a pair to raise additional revenue. He had chosen VIG 200 for his white Mercedes Benz 200 car, and VIG 1100 for his wife's Austin 1100 car. A five-ton lorry accompanied by armed military escort preceded the car, loaded with their personal effects as well as items of furniture belonging to the Government.

'I know what you mean,' Dr Amilo Kanu replied, taking his turn at the wash basin. 'I'm sure I would have cracked in no time if I hadn't got Fatima out when I did.'

As the steward was sweeping and tidying up the near empty house, the two friends moved into the garden, each carrying a dining chair. They settled by the entrance to an uncompleted bunker at the back of the house.

'It's only one load, though,' Akwaelumo picked up the thread. 'The much bigger load on my mind is the fate of Enugu, of Biafra, and of all of us. I have been terribly upset since we saw the latest sitrep* at the meeting this morning. Try to piece together the various pieces of the jig-saw puzzle – the sabotage in the Mid-West, resulting in the loss of the lives of several of our best fighting men, the attempted coup within our army leadership, our unprepared-ness and lack of military hardware, our consistent loss of ground to the enemy, the fact that many officers do not want to fight, and that most of the few who wish to do so are already killed – I could go on and on. Piece the various parts together and what do you get?'

'The thought has given me sleepless nights, too' Dr Kanu replied. 'We knew all along that we didn't have the guns and ammunition to challenge Nigeria, even when we boasted that no power in Black Africa could beat us. I am not sure I'll ever recover from the nightmares I had before H.E. ordered the termination of that matchet parade to the war front . . .'

'Excuse my interrupting you, but in the past week we have been able to get in thousands of rifles and rounds of ammunition.'

'Agreed. But rifles and ammunition in themselves alone cannot win battles. You need dedicated and committed soldiers to use them. The rank and file were extremely enthusiastic. The civilians were more than prepared to play their part. Our scientists have been performing wonders. It's the army leadership which appears to be letting Biafra down. They are the people proclaiming the

* Situation report.

70

Republic of Benin and talking about marching down to Lagos to redeem their fellow Nigerians (whatever they meant by that). They are the people betraying the enthusiastic and dedicated officers among them, thereby exposing them to untimely deaths . . .'

For some time neither man spoke. Akwaelumo stared at the zig-zag entrance to the uncompleted bunker. Part of one side had already caved in. To prevent the other side from doing likewise, the sides had been lined with wooden pegs driven into the earth. At the far end of the bunker lay long palm tree trunks to be used for the roof.

'It would be a shame to be forced back into Nigeria,' Akwaelumo remarked. 'Apart from the utter humiliation, we must be prepared for even more outrageous pogroms, if anything can be more outrageous than the 1966 massacres.'

'I don't think it has come to that.' Dr Kanu spoke slowly. 'Biafra does not belong to army officers alone. Even H.E. cannot claim that it is his personal property. Biafra belongs to all of us. We cannot therefore leave its fate entirely to any one group of people.'

'What do we do?' enquired Akwaelumo. 'Take over the guns?'

'Why not? Do soldiers have two heads?'

'They don't, but they are soldiers, you are a lecturer in medicine and I am a permanent secretary.'

'Akwa. I agree with you.' Dr Kanu spoke deliberately slowly as if the words came in drips. 'We are not soldiers. But there's an idea that I have been chewing over for some time. I nearly mentioned it to the Director-General the other day when we called on him to discuss the Mid-West fiasco, but I wanted to sound you out first . . .'

Dr Kanu proceeded to unravel his plan. As Director for Mobilization, he had been struck by the tremendous enthusiasm on the part of young Biafrans to join the Biafran Army. Young men turned down at one provincial recruitment centre offered themselves for recruitment at another centre, hoping for better luck. Bribes were even offered to enhance the chances of recruitment. So high was the enthusiasm that Dr Kanu found the Director's job not one of appealing to reluctant young men to apply for recruitment but, on the contrary, one of devising methods of *rejecting* large numbers of enthusiasts who satisfied all the prescribed requirements. With such high motivation, all that seemed to be required was the right kind of training for the boys and effective leadership.

Dr Kanu had devoured all available literature on military

71

strategy. He read all he could find on Che Guevara, Fidel Castro, Adolf Hitler, Mao Tse-Tung and Ho Chi Minh. He picked the brains of field commanders. He also probed soldiers returning from the war fronts, including the stragglers, some of whom told stories of commanding officers who were the first to flee at the sign of danger, leaving the boys under their command to save their necks as best they could.

One boy convalescing in a hospital ward after losing an arm, had been asked by a curious nurse what the enemy Hausa soldiers looked like. His reply, in the Awka dialect of Igbo, had become a popular joke: 'The Hausas? Who sets eyes on them? All you do is to obey orders. When you are ordered to spray bullets, you spray them. When you are ordered to stop, you stop. Nobody sees the enemy.' Yes, you emptied your magazine into the air; with luck one or two bullets might hit the unseen enemy!

The imminent collapse of Enugu presented a tremendous challenge to every Biafran, particularly to the prominent Biafrans who had stuck their necks out in the attacks on Nigeria and the declaration of secession. Dr Kanu knew this, and was certain that he numbered among the Biafrans to be eliminated by the Nigerians at the earliest opportunity. There was also the matter of pride. Surrender by Biafra was tantamount to a subjugation of the Easterner to a position of inferiority in Nigerian politics for a long time to come. The Hausas and the Yorubas would see to it that the Easterner, particularly the Igbo, constituted no further threat to them in the Nigerian scene.

'When you talked me out of a commission in the army . . .'

'You mean when we were both talked out of seeking commissions in the army,' Akwa corrected Kanu. 'You remember you wanted to avenge your son's death, while I wanted to avenge the brutal murder of my elder brother, Uchendu, in the North . . .'

'I took the point that no sensible nation sends its intellectuals to the front line to serve as cannon fodder,' Dr Kanu continued. 'I don't remember now who made the point, the Director-General or someone else. However, subsequent events have confirmed my conclusion that Biafra cannot succeed militarily unless its brain power is made to permeate every facet of military planning from now on. An illustration of my point is already evident in the establishment of the Science Group. The special officer-training camp which I propose to establish will be another channel for such interaction.'

Dr Kanu had every detail at his fingertips. A secondary school would be an ideal site for the camp. The trainees would be young officers commissioned since the birth of Biafra; it would be risky to take in any of the old guard, not only because an old dog does not readily acquire new tricks but also because you could not be certain of the loyalties of the pre-Biafra officers. The ideal trainees would be undergraduates and young secondary school leavers, bubbling over with idealism and faith in Biafra. The training would include physical fitness, karate or kung fu (the ancient Chinese art of self-defence), guerilla tactics, political orientation (aimed at ensuring absolute loyalty to and love for Biafra on the one hand and mortal hatred for Nigeria and everything Nigerian on the other). The instructors would include eminent Biafrans, H.E., clergymen, trusted army officers, women leaders, psychologists, and war scientists. The officers would be trained to *lead* their men into battle, not to remain at the rear. Systematic training of groups of officers that way would provide the Biafran Army with enough company commanders to rout the rag-tag Nigerian Army.

'Sounds fascinating,' observed Akwa. 'The first problem would be to gain access to H.E. The second would be how to present the idea in a way that would convince him that it is not another method to subvert the Government. You have to sell it first to the Director-General . . .'

'If we can get him in the right mood!' cut in Dr Kanu.

'You can leave that to me,' Akwaelumo replied. 'Most Permanent Secretaries know how to turn him on!'

October 4, 1967.

Down came the curtain. The melodrama had ended. Enugu changed hands.

The matchet offensive had earlier been scrapped, minutes before its midnight take-off deadline, allegedly by H.E. himself. Its architects had borrowed the idea from China, where they claimed it had always worked. You fought the enemy with human bodies rather than with ammunition. The enemy mows down the unending line of human beings until they run out of ammunition. Then begins the matchet offensive. The matchet becomes the superior weapon when your enemy has nothing but his fists and the butt of his rifle. The Nigerians at the Enugu sector would run out of ammunition before they killed 10,000 Biafrans. The Biafran survivors would then move into their trenches and not only save Enugu with their matchets but also bring back many more heads than Biafrans had lost in Northern Nigeria in 1966! It would have been as simple as that, if only H.E. had allowed the offensive to take off. But he did not.

There had been no street fighting, either, nor any last-ditch defence. The loudspeaker pronouncements along every major street and back street of Enugu in the dying days of September, threatening fire and brimstone on any vandal who set foot on Enugu and commanding every male Biafran to stay on his toes in readiness for the gruelling battle ahead, must have been intended to scare the enemy believed to have been in hiding in the surrounding hills from where they lobbed shells into the city. When the long-awaited moment came, there were no battle orders; no officers; no men.

No attempt had been made to capitalize on those natural defences of Enugu which soldier and civilian had talked about with so much confidence. Even the famous herbalist brought all the way from Anambra had not been given the opportunity to save Enugu. Everyone had talked about the efficacy of his mysterious medicine pot. Take it to the war front, and place it in position in front of the forward trenches. Every enemy bullet would whistle past its target, mowing down the surrounding vegetation instead of Biafran soldiers. The medicine pot had not performed its wonders on this occasion because there had been no war front and no forward trench.

Enugu changed hands with hardly a shot fired in its defence. Biafra moved to Umuahia. H.E. was the last to move. He lingered on in the outskirts of Enugu, in the tradition of the captain of a sinking ship reluctantly drifting away on a raft after everyone has been evacuated, his eyes full of sorrow at his inability to save his ship.

'Is that the Mompo stuff from the Ministry of Home Affairs?' Dr Kanu asked as he accepted the glass of red wine extended to him by Mr Akwaelumo.

'Hmm . . .' Akwaelumo gulped down a mouthful as he nodded assent. 'Until we can find the foreign exchange to import what the two breweries say they require to operate, Mompo table wine takes the place of beer!'

'Not bad at all,' was Dr Kanu's verdict. 'I saw a four-gallon jar in my house yesterday, but I haven't opened it.'

'It was found by our boys during one of their treasure hunts in Port Harcourt. Several cases of White Horse whisky as well. Off-loaded by a cargo boat before the blockade; destined for Chad or the Niger Republic.'

'That's the kind of operation in which our boys win their laurels,' observed Dr Kanu cynically. 'What's become of the whisky though?'

'I gather some clot in Home Affairs decided to send the whole lot to H.E. to take what he wanted and pass the rest to the top army officers.'

'Army officers, my boots!' exploded Dr Kanu. 'H.E. apart, I don't see any army officer who deserves a cup of even the cheapest palm wine.'

'I wouldn't condemn all of them . . .'

'Yes, I know there are exceptions,' interrupted Dr Kanu. 'The architects of the January 1966 coup. They have an ideology, a sense of mission. You can see it in the way they fight. Any nation would be proud of them. I would say the same for the officers who master-minded the capture of the Mid-West. But how many are they? Only a handful. And where are they? Killed in action, betrayed by their fellow officers who prefer stiffly starched uniforms, shining shoes, goat meat and other comforts of city life to the war fronts. I'm disgusted with them!'

'It doesn't pay to be disgusted,' Akwaelumo remarked. 'The war took all of us by surprise. Or perhaps I should say that it has turned out to be something much more serious than any of us, including the top army officers, ever anticipated.'

Akwaelumo's words had little conviction. He felt exactly the way Kanu felt: terribly let down by the very army boys who had encouraged the civilians to believe that Biafra could defend her territorial integrity should Nigeria decide on a military confrontation. Every Biafran felt the same way on learning that Enugu had fallen to the enemy. For Kanu, Akwaelumo, and others who knew the details, the effect of the loss of Enugu was even more shattering and frustrating. No other event in the history of the young republic had had such a demoralizing effect on the people, not even the abortive coup and the loss of the Mid-West.

The loss of the Mid-West had been disappointing, but it was in fact the loss of territory that was never Biafra's, and it did not change Biafra's territorial boundaries. Ogoja had fallen to the enemy, and so had Nsukka, the university town, and Bonny in Port Harcourt Province. These were border towns; their fall in the first month of the war could be explained away: Biafra needed some time to organize its hastily assembled army and to set up the supply lines.

The fall of Enugu was something entirely different. Enugu was several miles away from the nearest border. It was Biafra's capital city, the seat of Government and of the Biafran Army. It was the nerve-centre of all Biafra's military operations. The Milliken Hill and the Iva Valley jointly provided it with a unique natural defence. If there was any town which every Biafran expected to hold out against the enemy, it was Enugu. Yet no such thing had happened. The mobilization of thousands of matchet-carrying young men was the only visible effort made to defend the city. Biafra had simply abandoned Enugu to the Nigerians.

'It irritates me to think that the Nigerians are drinking champagne in Lagos and bragging how the "gallant" Federal troops "liberated Enugu according to plan"!' Dr Kanu nearly choked as he swallowed the Mompo.

'It doesn't matter how it happened. What matters is that they have taken Enugu from us.'

'I guess you are right,' Kanu conceded. 'I hope they'll go on drinking champagne until H.E.'s plans materialize. Then they'll realize that being down for a count does not mean being knocked out.'

Akwaelumo broke the silence by asking how Fatima was settling down at Obodo.

'She doesn't like it one bit,' Dr Kanu replied, 'and I'm having to use all sorts of tactics to tie her down there. Thank goodness we can still get all the building materials we require for the house. As soon as the contractor completes the bungalow, she should have little to complain about. She is normally a most reasonable wife; the shocking death of Ami Junior was too much for her.'

'It would be for any woman. Rose might have cracked up completely.'

'Fatima has never been in love with village life,' continued Dr Kanu, 'neither have I – I hadn't built even a one-room hut at home. I'm sure she will begin to insist on joining me here, as soon as she feels I'm comfortably settled. I couldn't complain about lack of good accommodation, what with these luxurious bungalows allocated to us by the Directorate of Accommodation. I would, in fact, have preferred to have her close to me here. That way I wouldn't worry about what was happening to them at Obodo. It's only that I don't know whether the tensions of war will drive her into making the kind of remarks she did before I sent her away from Enugu. I don't delude myself into thinking that I have no enemies in Biafra, or that I enjoy going into detention or, worse still, facing mob justice!'

Mr Akwaelumo switched on his transistor. It was nearly seven o'clock, time for the evening news. The 'drum' signal was on. It was the sound of the Igbo xylophone, played at the fast tempo characteristic of the shoulder-vibrating dance common in the old Owerri Province. The drumming was followed by a fanfare of trumpets. Then: 'Eternal vigilance is the price of liberty! This is Radio Biafra Enugu. Here is the news, read by . . .'

The news broadcast actually came from the town of Aba, nearly 200 miles from Enugu, where Radio Biafra had already installed a mobile transmitter. The contingency plans had been faithfully executed. The War Directorates, Government Ministries, etcetera, had moved as planned – to Umuahia, Owerri, and Aba primarily. The town of Umuahia, equidistant between Owerri and Aba, and about the most central in Biafra, took over from Enugu as the seat of Government, receiving a large number of Directorates and Ministries. The Enugu commercial banks dispersed like the seeds of the oil bean tree. Some found new homes in villages which seemed safe from enemy incursions, some followed concentrations of their clients to the big towns of Aba, Owerri and Umuahia. Each Directorate, Ministry, Bank, etcetera, retained its Enugu address in its new location. The Post & Telegraphs Department was settling down to its own assignment, matching Enugu addresses with current addresses.

The news broadcast ended with another fanfare of trumpets, and a pre-recorded declaration: 'To save Biafra for the free world is a task that must be done.' There had been no reference to the war in the news bulletin. The daily 'War Report', a programme always anxiously awaited by every Biafran every day, had been off the air since the beginning of the evacuation of Enugu. The pattern had become discernible: it was better to be silent in moments of serious military reverses than to broadcast lies. No news had become bad news. On such occasions, the Voice of Rumour immediately took over from the Voice of Biafra.

'Well,' Akwaelumo sighed, *'na'im dat,* as the Creoles would say in Freetown!'

'Meaning what?' Dr Kanu enquired.

'That's that. I take it we've lost Enugu.'

'Were you expecting the radio to tell you that we had recaptured the town when you know that the enemy have even advanced beyond Enugu on the Awgu road?'

'Well. Somehow one has a lingering hope that a miracle will happen,' replied Akwaelumo, rising. 'Should we move into the lounge or take a walk down the road?'

'I probably ought to be going,' Dr Kanu replied, also rising.

'What's the hurry? You are not keeping Fatima or anyone else waiting. Have dinner with me.'

'If you'll come over and share mine with me.'

'That's fine by me, if that's the way you want it.'

'Then we could go over together to see the Director for Accommodation about my house. I haven't gone to see him because I gather he can be difficult, especially with university dons.'

'But you are a fellow Director,' Akwaelumo said. 'How could he be difficult with you?'

'I'm sure he thinks of me first as a university don rather than as a fellow Director. Otherwise why did he not allocate a house to me in this part of Umudike where all my fellow Directors are?'

'You forget that yours is one of the most modern buildings in Umudike. Built by the American Government for Americans. Ours are old fashioned colonial-type senior service houses designed and built by our P.W.D.!'

'Yes,' said Dr Kanu. 'But think how thickly wooded your compounds are compared with mine, which is a wilderness. You can see my house from miles away, standing on a hill with nothing but grass and flowers as cover. Easy target for the most inexperienced air force pilot.'

'Never mind; we'll see the Director. I bet he'll offer you a house at the G.R.A. in the township.'

'G.R.A.? Count me out of that one!' Dr Kanu stretched himself, yawning in the process. 'We're lucky the vandals haven't bombed Umuahia yet, but now that it has become our capital they're bound to do so, and when they do, to live in the G.R.A. would be no better than living at the war front.'

'You remember his report at our meeting yesterday? Every possible accommodation in Umuahia and Umudike has been allocated, including even boys' quarters attached to the houses. Yet there are still several people sleeping in their cars or in classrooms. It's simply chaotic. I don't envy the Director for Accommodation his job, trying to accommodate not only those engaged in war duties but also chiefs and other V.I.P.s whose homes are disturbed and have nowhere to live. And you would think some of those chiefs would take whatever is given to them and be thankful. No. They may have lost their chiefdoms, but not their dignity!'

'We'll see the Director, and if he has nothing better to offer I'll stay put here,' Dr Kanu replied. 'After all, how many daylight hours do I spend in the house? And who knows how much longer the war will last at this rate?'

'You can't be sure. As they say, anything can happen in war. And with God on our side . . .'

'Don't kid yourself, man. God is on the side of the big battalions, and thank heavens most people in Biafra are beginning to recognize it. I'm especially pleased with H.E.'s decision to establish the "S" Brigade. A Commander-in-Chief without even one company of his own to command and upon which he can always rely is unfortunate. How I wish he had thought of it earlier. With one crack battalion, reasonably well-equipped, Enugu would have been firmly in our hands today. But the day is young yet. If my proposals for a special training school had found favour, I could have ensured that only the best young officers were sent to H.E.'s Brigade. All the same, I have already asked the Director-General to assure H.E. that I will send our best recruits to him.'

'You know some army chaps are not happy with the idea?' remarked Akwaelumo. 'They regard the decision as a calculated attempt to divide the army.'

'What are they ever happy with? The mistake many military men often make is to think that because they can easily plan a coup and overthrow an elected government at gunpoint, they have the answers to every problem.'

'Our chaps are piping down now. They know that the public is fast becoming disenchanted . . .'

'And that the public has also seen from the performances of our civilian war heroes that a committed civilian can pick up all the basic military training he requires in a matter of days and proceed to acquit himself more creditably at the front than some of our veteran officers! I am not against the military. We couldn't do without our army men, not at this time. What I keep saying at every opportunity is that the soldiers should recognize that we too have brains, and that the army cannot do without the civilians. If they recognize that, Nigeria would be no match for us. But I see I'm beginning to preach again!'

9

Go-gom! Go-gom!
Go-gom! Go-gom!
Men and women of Obodo-O!
Hear the words of the War Council!
Every taxable male, one big yam – O!
Every taxable male, one big yam – O!
Every woman, five cassava tubers or one cup of *garri* – O!
Every woman, five cassava tubers or one cup of *garri* – O!
Every village, one tin of palm oil – O!
Every village, one tin of palm oil – O!
First thing tomorrow morning – O!
First thing tomorrow morning – O!
All for our soldiers – O!
Whoever hears should spread the word – O!
Go-gom! Go-gom!

'What council did he talk about?' Mazi Kanu enquired as the towncrier's *ogene* grew silent and Aniche, the towncrier, moved towards the next village on his itinerary. Kanu wore a warm, brown jumper over his woven wrapper. Fatima, his daughter-in-law, had insisted that he should always wear something over his wrapper, and had ordered some new jumpers for him.

'War Council,' replied Chief Madukegbu Ukadike, who was paying Mazi Kanu a visit. Both men sat under a cola nut tree enjoying the cool evening breeze.

'Is this a new council?'

'No. I prefer the name War Council to Local Civil Defence Committee. So I've changed our name to Obodo War Council. Stops people confusing us with the Committee, that is the Church Committee. Also it sounds better.'

Mazi Kanu replied with an anecdote: 'One *itibolibo* like me who never as much as heard the school bells ringing was eating food one day in the company of those men whose heads have been split in two by too much learning. The learned men kept speaking *istafablushbulfa* . . . and so on in English. As their conversation in English dragged on and on, the *itibolibo* like me told them in

Igbo: you may speak whatever language you like; the pieces of meat in the soup are four and we are four, one piece of meat for each of us! Likewise, call it committee or council, every day the demands will be the same – every male, one big yam, every woman, one cup of *garri* or five cassava tubers. Tell me, those of you who know what is happening, will this thing ever come to an end?'

'Is there any story that has no end?' asked Ukadike stroking his beard. 'You should thank your *chi* that you have the yams to give. What of those people who have been driven out of their homes? I am sure they would be happy beyond words if they were given back their homes and asked to donate one stick of yams or one bag of *garri* every day.'

'*Bo*, that one has no comparison.' Mazi Kanu used his finger to eject a bee which floated on the top of his cup of wine after drinking itself to death. 'Each time I see a "riverju" the tears begin to form in my eyes. How can a man with a wife and children live in a school hall day in day out, with no compound of his own, waiting for gov'ment or the mission to bring food for his family. Who was it saying in jest the other day that these riverjus have become gov'ment workers in their old age, being sent on transfer from their homes to riverju camps or from one riverju camp to another. I told him to stop laughing; it is not good to laugh at evil. You know death is preferable to this kind of life. God forbid that I should ever be a riverju!'

'Thank your *chi* that the Nigerians changed their mind after Enugu, and went to Calabar and Onitsha instead of heading for Obodo as we had feared. Who knows in which refugee camp each one of us would have been today?'

'Our ancestors cannot let such abomination come to pass with their eyes wide open. Whoever says yes, his *chi* will say yes; whoever says no, his *chi* will say no. God forbid that a person who has eaten out of a plate all his life will suddenly find himself eating out of earthen pots.'

'I hope every man at Obodo will view the situation as seriously as you do, Mazi,' Ukadike said. 'Perhaps it is a good thing that we have a chance of seeing the suffering of refugees . . .'

'Evil cannot be a good thing,' Mazi Kanu interrupted.

'I know what I'm saying,' continued Ukadike. 'Sometimes when the few of us who have fought in world wars tell our people what to do, they react as if somebody oiled their ears into deafness. It's only when they see a refugee and his family running out without even a mat on which to sleep, let alone a wrapper with which to cover up, that what you tell them about gathering their important things together for any eventuality means something.'

'Don't blame anybody, Idere. I know you people have said it. Doctor's wife still cries about some of the things she left behind at Enugu, and has asked me to pack some of my things together to avoid the mistake they made. But, tell me, what will a man like me pack? My yam barn? My palm trees? My lands? My household property? Our goats? Our chickens? Tell me, what am I to pack? After packing, will I carry them on my head when the time to run comes?'

'Why am I arguing my voice hoarse,' Ukadike asked, 'when I know that Doctor will arrange your evacuation? What I should request is that you squeeze me on the tailboard when the time comes, God forbid!'

'It is better to wish that such a time never comes. As for Doctor, you think he remembers that his old parents and relatives still exist on this side of the earth? Maybe, now that his wife is living here, I may join the well-to-do in drinking hot soup!'

'Thank you for mentioning Doctor's wife; I nearly forgot that I came to see her. There's a bone sticking stubbornly in my throat which I'm sure Doctor can help me to remove. That's why I want to see his wife to find out when Doctor is expected at Obodo or how I could contact him where he is now.'

'I knew it wasn't me you came to see,' Mazi Kanu protested. 'My mistake is that I gave you my evening "special"; I should have left you to drink proper whisky with Doctor's wife!'

'If I come to see Doctor's wife, I have also come to see you,' Ukadike wriggled out grinning. 'After all, Doctor's wife is your wife.'

'A child owns a goat only in name.'

'You cannot liken a son's wife to the child's ownership of a goat,' Ukadike disagreed.

'All right. I agree. Doctor's wife is in.'

Ukadike lowered his tone: 'You know I have fought in the white man's land and know them inside out. So when I come across our own people who behave like white people . . .'

'Not now,' Mazi Kanu interrupted. 'This evil war is dragging every person's arse through the ash. Blowing the firewood in the kitchen has not given anybody the chance to behave like the white man.'

Chief Madukegbu Ukadike straightened himself on his chair and fingered his six medals as he awaited the emergence of Fatima, wife of Dr Amilo Kanu. The presence of the medals usually reassured him, especially when he was scheduled to appear before persons he wanted to impress favourably but could not take for granted. The medals invariably gave him a good start: only a man who had excelled himself in one sphere or another of human endeavour received medals of honour. On this occasion, the medals hung from a thick high-necked grey sweater which he had saved from World War II. The sweater had leather patches at the elbows. He rose as Fatima walked towards him.

'Good evening, Madam.' Ukadike beamed a warm smile of familiarity as he bowed low and offered both hands for a hand-shake.

'Good evening.' Fatima's tone was not very inviting, and it certainly did not give any indication that she knew her caller from Adam.

'It seems Madam has forgotten me. I am Chief Madukegbu Ukadike, Chairman of the Local Council and Chairman of the Obodo War Council.' Ukadike fidgeted with his medals before continuing. 'You remember I was the person who ordered our Civil Defenders to return that machine they seized from your car at the Afo checkpoint.'

'Pardon me,' Fatima apologized. 'Of course I remember you. Oh yes. Only I didn't notice your medals.'

Ukadike took a quick glance at his famous medals, and fidgeted with them before thrusting his hands behind him.

'I'm ashamed that I failed to recognize the man who returned my projector to me,' continued Fatima. 'There was nothing I didn't do to explain to those men that the projector was nothing to fuss about, but they were certain it was a transmitter for com-municating with Lagos.'

'But, Madam, do you blame them? Which of them has seen the po . . . – I mean, something like that before?' Ukadike knew that even he had not. He could not even repeat the name of the machine without prompting.

'I wouldn't have felt so annoyed if they had admitted their ignorance,' Fatima replied. 'One of them, who claimed he had spent twenty years in Lagos, irritated me so much when he went on to demonstrate how my projector was used as a transmitter! And the others were gullible enough to swallow the rubbish.'

'Won't you sit down, Madam?' Ukadike offered his chair, at the same time moving towards the chair Mazi Kanu had vacated as soon as the couple began to speak in a language which meant nothing to him.

'I shouldn't really stay,' replied Fatima, sitting down on the chair she was offered. 'I'm stinking after a spell of firewood cooking, and I ought to have a wash now that my son has slept. I ran out of kerosene for my cooker, and the only way to get my food cooked is to blow the firewood. We're moving backwards!'

'Madam, as Chairman of the Obodo War Council, I've come to find out whether you still receive any molestation of any kind from anybody in Obodo because of the marks on your face – I mean, because you are not a native.'

'I don't know whether I should call it molestation,' replied Fatima rubbing her cheeks with both hands as if to stroke the horizontal tribal marks on each cheek which immediately marked her out as a stranger wherever she went, 'but there's hardly a day I go out when I don't run into one incident or another. I thought my marks would make it clear that I'm not Igbo. Yet people will insist on speaking to me in Igbo. They are angry when I can't reply in Igbo, as if there was a law that only speakers of the Igbo language can use the roads in Biafra!'

'Many of our people cannot understand English.'

'You should remove such people from the checkpoints. They merely irritate road users.'

'I'll see what I can do about that, Madam, if I can find enough people who can speak English to replace them.'

'Why do you need so many checkpoints anyway?' enquired Fatima.

'Ah! The price of liberty is eternal vigilance!' cried Ukadike proudly, smacking his be-medalled chest joyfully at remembering the slogan popularized by Radio Biafra.

'Stuff and nonsense!'

'Don't say that O, Madam. Did you not hear of the white reverend father carrying the coffin of a child in his car? When vigilant Civil Defenders at Ndikelionwu checkpoint opened the coffin, they found that it contained explosives which were to be used in blowing up the Hotel Presidential. But for the vigilance of the men at the checkpoint . . .'

Fatima interrupted him: 'We heard that story before we left Enugu. My husband checked on it and found that no such thing ever happened!'

'But this newspaper reported it,' protested Ukadike. 'This newspaper – I've forgotten the name of the newspaper. Anyway, what of the woman who was caught carrying a bomb inside her brassière?'

'And you believe that?'

'In this war, there's nothing I can't believe.'

'Stuff and nonsense! That's why one sheepish-looking man at a checkpoint was scared to touch my toilet bag, even after I had told him what it was. He actually retreated one or two steps as I pulled the zip open to show him the contents of the bag; he probably feared I was connecting the fuse to activate an explosive! I'm sure state security will be none the worse and motorists will be relieved if most of the road blocks and checkpoints are dropped.'

'Prevention is better than cure,' observed Ukadike rather weakly. He was an advocate of checkpoints and was not pleased to see someone try to demolish them.

'Admitted,' replied Fatima. 'But what do checkpoints prevent? Did I not hear that you discovered several dangerous weapons in a man's house in this town? How did those weapons pass through your innumerable checkpoints? Checkpoints are useless and irritating to motorists unless you have trained and intelligent people to man them.'

'I agree with you there.' Ukadike was glad that Doctor's wife did not condemn checkpoints completely. 'Perhaps Madam can help me to train our men for their work.'

'Me?' asked Fatima. Without waiting for the reply, she went on: 'I'm afraid not! Your people don't accept me and I don't want to have anything to do with them. In any case I have no intention of staying on here one day longer than I have to. All I can say to my husband's parents and many others around me is "*Kedu*" or "*Odinma*" . . .'

'That's good,' interrupted Ukadike, smiling gleefully.

'No, no! I can't live that kind of life much longer. Imagine me blowing my eyes out so as to cook with firewood, or eating meat smoked over the fire because I can't use a fridge. My son has been unable to understand why the pit latrine hurriedly dug for us does not have a flush handle!'

'The house Doctor is building for you will soon be ready. I am sure he will install everything you want there.'

'With the blockade on? Anyway, I've told him I'm not interested in his house. I don't want any more of this village life in which I do nothing but blow firewood and am pestered by Civil Defenders. I've given him a month to fit us in where he lives at Umuahia. When that month is up, you won't see me back here any more.'

'I will be sorry if you leave us.'

'Save that for somebody else,' Fatima said, rising. 'I'm sure everybody here will be only too glad to see this Hausa woman leave their village to them. I'm afraid it's late and the water for my bath must be getting cold. Thanks for your concern for my welfare.'

'Good night, Madam.'

Chief Ukadike heaved a sigh of relief as Fatima moved to the rear of the compound where a space had been fenced round for her use as a bathroom. Her fearlessness, her dare-devil attitude (to be more exact) stunned him. As she trotted off in the short dancing steps characteristic of white girls or been-to's*, Chief Ukadike shrugged his shoulders. He would not like to be Fatima's husband. She was definitely the type of wife who wore the trousers; he was certain that her chest would be a jungle of masculine hair!

'*Nwata gbujie!*' he shouted Mazi Kanu's salutatory name.

'Are you through with speaking English?' Mazi Kanu answered from another part of the backyard.

'I thought you had retired for the night.'

'Am I a chicken that I should retire before the fall of darkness?'

'You speak like one with food in your mouth,' observed Ukadike.

'Your guess is correct, and your share is awaiting you if you are prepared to eat in the backyard. Wartime food is no longer the type you were served by your front gate. It is much wiser nowadays to stay in the back of your house; if your meal is no more than palm kernels and fried breadfruit, nobody will know except you and your family.'

'I will come over to the backyard, but not to eat. If you had provided for my stomach, you would have invited me to join you without waiting for me to remind you.'

'I didn't invite you because you and Doctor's wife were speaking English, and an illiterate is not expected to foul the air when learned people are speaking English. Now that you are through, join me in swallowing cassava.'

'Is any food greater than cassava now?' Ukadike asked. 'Don't our people liken the cassava to the person who came to settle a dispute between two combatants and suddenly found himself bearing the entire brunt of the fight?'

Mazi Kanu licked each finger of his right hand meticulously and loudly, after which he asked his youngest daughter, Obinna, to serve him water for washing his hands. Having washed his hands, he rinsed his mouth vigorously, swallowed the water, and then picked up his horn for the remaining palm wine.

'The men in Lagos have said we should not snuff tobacco any more,' he said, belching most of the time as he spoke. 'Can they

* African girls who have been to England.

86

also blockade my cassava?'

'Who knows what they and their English masters plan for tomorrow?'

'They can plan their fathers and their mothers,' Mazi Kanu cursed, 'so long as nobody moves me out of my house; if they want to blockade cassava too, let them do so. Who knew Andrew could live one day without snuff? Since the Hausas took Calabar and blockaded tobacco, Andrew has forgotten all about snuff. He even talks about snuff soiling the nostrils!'

'Can I have one more cup of your "Kanu Special" before I trace my way home?'

'Since you did not eat my cassava let me see.' Mazi Kanu shook the calabash. 'I think it will fill a cup for you, leaving the bottom for me.'

Chief Ukadike licked the last drop before dropping the cup on the table. 'Your Special is better than Nigeria's Specials!' was his verdict. 'Mazi,' he switched to a more serious tone. 'My conversation with Doctor's wife was revealing . . .'

Mazi Kanu sat up as if afraid to miss a single word.

'. . . . She is not happy at being left here by Doctor,' Ukadike continued. 'If care is not taken, she may expose the head of a masquerade in the market place. A grown-up man does not stay in the house and let a goat go through the process of delivery in tether. You should tell Doctor to take his wife away to Umuahia or any other place.'

'Welcome, my son who has also become my father! Your words are excellent. You know very well that the wife I have married is the kind with whom I cannot converse without hiring an interpreter. Doctor wants her to stay here until the house he is putting up for her is ready. Is it not a big shame that my son should be the long-mouthed mouse which waits until labour pains set in before building a nest for its use? It is true that Doctor is my son. He is also your own body and both of you are friends. Speak to him about it. Go to Umuahia and discuss it with him. Perhaps he will listen to your words, since you can speak English and I cannot. One thing I must admit is that I have noticed an improvement in my daughter-in-law's attitude to me and my wife. She has ordered new clothes for us, and she no longer calls the little boy away when he comes over to us.'

'Mazi, your words are also excellent,' replied Ukadike, elated at being addressed as Dr Amilo Kanu's friend. 'You see that my visit to your house tonight has accomplished something. I will speak to Doctor, even if it means leaving my tremendous responsibilities here to travel to his house at Umuahia.'

'Thank you. If you can make Doctor change his attitude to me, you would have done a big job for me.'

Chief Ukadike rose to leave. 'Any drop of your Special left?' he asked, knowing what the reply would be.

'Shake the calabash yourself,' Mazi Kanu replied. 'Do you think it is Ofomata's wine which never gets exhausted?'

'I was only joking,' Chief Ukadike said, though he had not removed his eyes from the dregs in Mazi Kanu's horn.

'Unless you think the bottom of the wine belongs to you?' Mazi Kanu asked.

'May our ancestors never hear that! How could I drink the bottom of the wine when my father is present?'

'All right.' Mazi Kanu took a long draught . . . 'take it.'

'No, Mazi,' Ukadike protested weakly.

'Go on; I am giving it to you,' Mazi Kanu urged.

'If you say so . . .' Ukadike took the horn. 'The fire a child receives from an adult will not burn its hand.'

He drained the horn, bade Mazi Kanu goodnight, and left for his house, whistling one of his favourite tunes:

> Save my bullets when I die, O Biafra!
> Save my bullets when I die, Alleluiah!
> If I happen to surrender,
> I'll die for ever.
> Save my bullets when I die.

10

Fatima walked to the back of the house to blow her stuffed nose on the sand, Kleenex and other brands of facial tissue paper having disappeared from the market as a result of the blockade on Biafra. Initially she had switched to toilet rolls but even these were fast disappearing, with the result that you were not always certain that you would find any to buy, even if you were prepared to pay the prohibitive price of ten shillings a roll. She therefore saw no alternative but to blow her perpetually stuffed nose outside. Like everyone else around her did. She restricted the use of the toilet roll to wiping the nose afterwards.

When she dipped her fingers into the pocket of her housecoat for the toilet roll, the fingers touched something tougher than toilet paper. It was an envelope.

'I'd forgotten all about my husband's letter! I'd better read it before I move up to the new house or I may never read it!' She had shoved the letter into her pocket the previous evening when it was handed to her by the orderly sent by her husband to stay with her as her escort and bodyguard. Her husband had also sent her an Igbo-speaking driver, both additions to her household resulting from Chief Ukadike's visit to him. The orderly and the driver had been sent without prior warning, and Fatima had been at her wit's end finding somewhere for them to sleep at night, with only an 8' by 6' room to accommodate her, her son, and their personal effects, including even cooking utensils. She thought it was just like Ami to do a good turn so thoughtlessly that the beneficiary is left to wonder whether the good turn was worth it. Why he could not have waited for the new house to be ready in a week or two, she could not fathom. In her confusion, she had forgotten all about the letter in her pocket.

Her son was asleep in their room. His name had had to be changed from Hassan to Emeka to appease her father-in-law and the family. They would not have their grandson answer to a Hausa name, so nobody would call him Hassan. In order not to rouse the boy, Fatima took the letter to the orange tree at the rear of the compound (where she often sat to have some privacy) and tore the envelope open.

'You can trust Ami to be all syrup and honey – on paper . . .' soliloquized Fatima as she noted that her husband addressed her 'My Sweet Lollipop'.

'. . . Taking every factor into consideration, our best bet is for you and Emeka to stay on at Obodo . . .'

'Stuff and nonsense!' shouted Fatima, flinging the letter on the ground in her rage. 'You stay there at Umuahia, having the best of everything – clean, pipe-borne water, electricity, civilized society, shops, everything desirable – while I am tucked away in this jungle and told to thank God for little mercies? Stuff and nonsense!'

Life at Obodo had been a sharp drop from the standards of living she had known for the past few years. The first morning after her arrival in the village from Enugu, she could hardly believe that she had spent the night in such a decrepit-looking shack. Her father-in-law had magnanimously vacated his own room for her, as the only other room in the two-bedroom house could not take her bed, Emeka's cot, and their personal effects. It was an earth house with a thatched roof hastily mended to stop the rain from pouring through. Separating the two rooms was a space too small to be of any use, and so poorly lit that it was enveloped in darkness most of the day. The 20′ by 8′ space at the front of the building was Mazi Kanu's *obi*, where he received his guests, ground his tobacco, and lazed away the early hours of the night on his cloth chair while waiting for his supper. Mazi Kanu transferred his bamboo bed into the second room in his wife's house, situated at the rear of the compound; his two daughters who previously slept there moved into the second room in his house, the room in which the doctor had grown up. Although the walls and floors were regularly scrubbed, the floors had become uneven over the years, and Emeka stumbled several times before he learnt which parts of the floor to avoid instinctively.

Mazi Kanu could not give up his *obi*, and this meant that Fatima had no place of her own to receive her visitors; moreover, while her father-in-law had his own visitors, she had little peace even inside her room, particularly when the wine from Mazi Kanu's raffia palms flowed freely. Mazi Kanu tried to be as helpful as possible, by shifting his cloth chair to the foot of the cola nut tree several yards from the building – in the morning hours as well as in the cool of the evening. Lack of adequate seating, however, compelled him to return to the *obi* whenever the visitors exceeded three in number; the *obi* had permanent mud beds lining the foot of its walls. Fortunately Fatima was not plagued by many visitors. Initially people flocked to the compound to welcome their wife, each visitor staring at her as you would stare at a Chinese panda at the London Zoo, anxious not to miss any detail of the girl with the carved face who made Doctor forget all the girls he should have married from Obodo and its environs. Fatima's not too inviting attitude and her inability to communicate with her visitors soon thinned the number of callers down to a trickle. Apart from occasional callers such as Chief Ukadike who wanted to demonstrate their ability to speak English or Hausa, most others were content to leave after enquiring about her health and her son, and expressing the hope that she heard frequently from Doctor.

The only kitchen in the compound was at the back of her mother-in-law's house. It was an open verandah, with a roof so low that you could not stand erect if you were taller than five feet.

To the three existing tripods was added a fourth for Fatima. She however, preferred to cook on her three-point kerosene stove which she installed on the narrow back verandah of Mazi Kanu's house, except when she ran out of kerosene and had no alternative but to use firewood in the main kitchen.

The toilet used by Mazi Kanu and his family was outside the compound, and appropriately called the 'spittle bridge'. Mazi Kanu lost no time in commissioning a professional pit latrine digger to dig a twenty-foot toilet for Fatima and her son.

'. . . Stuff and nonsense!' exclaimed Fatima, picking up the letter and shaking off a reddish giant ant which had dropped from the orange tree. She could not imagine what factors her husband had taken into consideration before condemning her to such primitive living in the twentieth century.

'. . . The air raids make life at Umuahia a nuisance. I would never have any peace of mind if you and Emeka were to join me here. Each time an enemy plane is around – and it could be every other day, or every day if you include the days we receive inaccurate information – I would develop stomach ulcers wondering where you and Emeka are. Remember Enugu . . .'

'Stuff and nonsense!' cried Fatima, using the letter to knock off the reddish giant ant which was on its way up her right leg. 'Who does Ami think he's kidding? Certainly not me! Probably thinks the air raid bogey will scare me out of my wits and I'll forget the hell I've been roasting in for two months . . . Two months?' she pondered. 'Amazing how time can drag. I could have said I'd lived two long years in this black hole of Calcutta . . .'

She dismissed the air raid scare. Umuahia could not be a city of men only. There must be hundreds of women and children living there, and if these could escape the air raids, why not she and Emeka?

'. . . Remember Enugu. Was Ami Junior not singled out of the thousands of children by the first shell? . . .'

'Stuff and nonsense!' Fatima exclaimed in an attempt to stifle the inner voice which warned her not to dismiss the air raid danger that easily. 'That was shelling, and we happened to be living just within range of the shelling machine,' she argued with the voice. 'Air raids are a different matter. Did the Nigerians ever get any person at Enugu with their bombs?'

She applied the brakes suddenly. Had she described her own people, her kith and kin, as Nigerians? 'Madness! What am I?'

'Somebody wants to see Madam,' Obinna announced, after striving in vain to catch Fatima's eye.

'What!' Fatima exclaimed as if a man had suddenly caught her masturbating.

Obinna, whose staid countenance hardly ever gave away what she was thinking, said, 'Somebody wants to see Madam.'

'Who is it?' asked Fatima, regaining her composure.

'One woman and a child,' Obinna replied. 'She says she is from Northern Nigeria . . .' Obinna dipped her eyes as she came to "Northern Nigeria". The woman had actually said she was Hausa, but somehow Obinna did not wish to admit that any person could be Hausa and not be a vandal. She had therefore decided never to refer to her sister-in-law as Hausa but as a Northern Nigerian. That way both of them could sleep under the same roof. The thought of any Hausa person, even the wife of a revered brother, sleeping in the same compound with her would have given her nightmares, what with the account she had received of ten Hausa soldiers taking turns to rape her school-friend in Ogoja, the last of them going through it all without even caring that their victim was by then already dead.

'. . . Her husband was killed in Zaria in September 1966,' continued Obinna, 'and she returned to his village in Biafra with their two children. When the husband's village became disturbed she took the children to a refugee camp. One died last month. She is here with the last one.'

Fatima pocketed the unfinished letter and moved to the front of the house to see her guests. Mrs Halima Uche – for that was the visiting woman's name – burst into tears as soon as she saw Fatima. Her son, looking up and seeing his mother in tears, started crying as well, clutching his mother's very much faded wrapper and using it to wipe his tears. Fatima steeled herself, determined not to follow suit. She ruled out using Mazi Kanu's *obi*, for although most people were out collecting one thing or the other for the army, she knew there was no guarantee that a chance caller might not saunter into the compound to find two Hausa women shedding tears and conversing in Hausa. Any interpretation could be given to such an incident. She therefore beckoned to Halima to follow her to the orange tree at the back of the compound. They sat on two *ekwulobia* stools and Fatima invited Halima to tell her why she came.

Mrs Halima Uche dried her eyes and her nose and proceeded to unburden her heart. Fatima was thrilled to hear the Hausa language spoken by a fellow Hausa, something she had missed badly since she left Ibadan for Enugu. She had been deprived of the opportunity of teaching her children their mother's tongue, for fear of causing offence to Biafrans, thereby losing her only opportunity of speaking a language she considered superior to any other language on earth. Three or four young men in the village who claimed to have been traders in Northern Nigeria occasionally sought to please her by speaking to her in Hausa, but it was not the same thing; she had even found herself resenting their gesture. With Halima it was different. She was, like her, a Hausa woman, more or less marooned in a world that had anything but love for the Hausa. Without waiting until Halima had got half-way through her story, and notwithstanding the class barrier between them, Fatima began to feel a bond uniting the two of them, a feeling of warm affection and concern for Halima.

'. . . My husband, Mr Uche, was a tally clerk in the Railway Corporation in Zaria, and we lived in the railway quarters. When a friend came to warn him that he was on the list of *nyamilis* to be killed the following day, he asked me to leave immediately with our two children for the house of my elder sister who was living with her husband in the city. I begged him to come with us, but he refused, saying that our lives would be in greater danger if he came with us. Almost everybody knew him in Zaria, not only as a result of his work but also because he played football very well.

'I begged him to run away from Zaria, but he was afraid he would lose his job and we would have no food to eat. He wanted to stay around and watch things for some days before finally deciding what to do. I begged him not to stay anywhere near our quarters. Before I left with our two boys, we had agreed on the best hideout for him.

'When we left, I feared that it might be the last time we would see him. Events proved me right. My young brother who had been sent by my sister to find out what our plans were and who had missed us on the way, told us what happened. We could not have reached my sister's house in the city before a group of armed soldiers and civilians. carrying a list of Eastern Nigerians they were assigned to kill, rushed into the quarters shouting "Where is Mr Uche?" "Mr Uche, tally clerk, come out at once!" My husband bolted the door on the inside when he heard the sound. He clambered up the wall, but our quarters had no ceiling to hide him. He must have decided to crawl along a beam of the house into our neighbour's room where he would hide until his assailants had given up the hunt and gone.

'Unfortunately our neighbour was hiding in his room, a chicken-hearted Yoruba man who fears even his own shadow. My brother heard him crying later that he did not mean to betray my husband. The mere sound of movement in the roof over his head frightened him and he shouted even before looking up to see what had made the sound. My husband's attempt to hush him up and plead with him was too late. The bloodthirsty murderers heard the sound and rushed into the room. My husband crawled back quickly into our room, squeezed himself into the outer wall and jumped out.

'He ran very fast – he is a fast runner – and before the soldiers could go after him he had gained a good lead. In fact, according to my brother, he could have escaped alive if his pursuers had not begun firing shots in his direction and shouting "Catch am, *nyamili*!" Without knowing it, my husband ran into another group of murderers who were searching for their own marked men. A shot got him on the stomach and he fell. To punish him for resisting capture, the soldiers who had failed to catch him plucked out his two eyes, ripped open his stomach and then left him in the open air to die painfully . . .'

'*Allah so ka!*' shouted a nauseated Fatima. 'Could this really have happened at Zaria?'

'May Allah smite me dead at once if it did not happen,' swore Halima. 'The Yoruba man saw most of it. My brother saw the whole thing. The marks on his face and his features showed clearly that he was Hausa so nobody linked him with my husband and he was free to stay around.'

'I didn't believe any of those stories I heard about the murders in the North, but now that the story comes from you, I have to believe it. Disgusting!'

'My sister,' Halima sobbed, 'that was how I became a widow in my youth. We could not take my husband's body away for burial. Our property was looted, leaving me and the children with only the clothing we had on. I must have flung myself on the ground so violently at the news that I had a miscarriage which nearly killed me. I was six months pregnant then. Yet even so I had to run. My sister's husband got secret information that the murderers wanted my two boys as well; if the boys were allowed to live they would grow up as *nyamilis*. My sister and her husband asked me to hand the boys over and save my life. I was so angry with them for making such a suggestion that I left their house with my boys, still bleeding from my miscarriage and without knowing where I was going. God saved us. A white pastor whom my husband had helped heard of his fate and was driving about seeking news of our whereabouts when we saw him and waved to him without recognizing him. He saw to my cure and brought us safely to Enugu.'

Halima told of the difficulties she had had in locating her husband's home town. She had never been there and could not even remember its name. Her husband's football fame had been very helpful. Everybody was initially hostile to her; nobody in Eastern Nigeria in late 1966 could be blamed for wishing to chop off the head of any Hausa, man, woman or child. But as soon as she told her story, everybody who heard it burst into tears and embraced her warmly. Someone had even conferred on her the salutatory name of *Nwannedinamba* – a close relation can be found among the strange people in a strange land. Although her husband had not built a house of his own in his village, his family rallied round her and her children and helped her to begin a trade. Everyone was delighted with the efforts she made to pick up the Igbo language. The smiles were gradually returning to her face and a new and promising life was unfolding for her when tragedy struck again. Her children had accompanied her to a small market about two miles from their home soon after breakfast, to the man whose machine ground her cow peas for her in preparation for the big eight-day market where she usually sold several pounds' worth of *akara* balls. From the market they heard the sound of gunfire; the Nigerians had infiltrated some armed soldiers to scare away the civilians and seize an important road junction. It had become impossible to return to their home!

Halima and her children had followed the stream of panic-stricken people, heading for an unknown destination. They finally found themselves in a refugee camp, penniless and without food, change of clothing or any cooking utensil or other possession. Worst of all, she could not locate her husband's parents or any of his next-of-kin, and had been unable to see them or hear any news of them ever since.

'That is what has happened to your sister, madam,' she continued.' What pains me most is that it is my own people who have caused me all this suffering. They seem to be determined to follow me wherever I run. When kwashiorkor killed my first son last month, I thought that was the end for me. It is for those two boys, left for me by my husband, that I live. If I lose both of them, what more have I left in this world that I should wish to continue living? It was by chance that I heard about you. I

95

decided I must reach you at all costs, even though I had not met you before and I am no more than a dirty beggar. Please, my sister, save this remaining boy for me and you will save your sister. Make me your housemaid, but save my child for me. If it were at the time I still had tears left in my eyes, I would be weeping now. But I have no tears left so I cannot weep any more. *Allah inana.*'

For several seconds Fatima could not utter a word. Her eyes took in Halima's surviving son who had gone off to sleep in his mother's lap, firmly clutching a small piece of stockfish. The symptoms of kwashiorkor (or *kwashiokpa*, as it had been renamed at Obodo) were clearly evident on him – the distended stomach, the swollen ankles and feet, and those features hitherto found only on the white man: a pale complexion, and the white man's wavy, reddish or golden hair. He was naked, and you could count his ribs as he took each breath. Halima herself was no more robust looking, except that she still retained the complexion and hair of the African. Her blouse was dirty and full of holes, through which could be seen two dangling breasts, as flat as pancakes.

'I will do all I can to help you,' Fatima finally announced in a subdued tone, as if she had still not quite found her voice.

She went into her room and came out with a shirt and a pair of shorts for Halima's son, and one of her own up-and-down wax prints, a blouse, and underclothes for Halima. 'I cannot accommodate you here, at least not until I move into our own house,' she said. 'But you'll eat some food before you go, and I'll do my best for you wherever you are. Meanwhile, I'll send for the Chairman of the War Council to seek his help in finding you accommodation.'

The river which Halima thought had dried up suddenly flooded its banks. Fatima withdrew into her room when she found it impossible to hold back her own tears.

Fatima could not fail to notice what difference it made to move around accompanied by a tall, hefty orderly, armed with a Madsen. He opened the door of the car for her and held it wide open until she was well inside, in the owner's corner at the rear. The orderly shut the door with the minimum noise and maximum professionalism, simultaneously giving the fly-catching Biafran military salute before taking his own seat in front as the OK for the driver to move. He hardly waited for the car to brake to a stop before gliding from his seat and opening the rear door wide open for Madam, his right hand saluting smartly as she stepped out.

During her student days in Britain and their years in Ibadan, Fatima had denounced such ostentation as the bane of the leaders of the developing countries who had a perverted sense of values. This time she felt differently. If secondary school girls could be chauffeur-driven just because they made themselves available to boys who, thanks to the war, had become army officers the day after leaving secondary school, how much more right had she, Fatima, a fully qualified X-Ray technologist, and wife of a lecturer in Medicine, member of the War Services Council and Director for Mobilization for Biafra?

The workmen at the site were more civil to her that afternoon than they had ever been. Idiots! They had probably thought she was just any housewife. They assured her she could move in within a week. 'There's nothing like having *agba*!' she overheard one of the workmen remark. 'All those building items which you and I cannot find anywhere are piled on top of one another here – bags of cement, asbestos roofing sheets, pipes, fittings, tiles. I have never seen any house spring up like a mushroom before. Anybody who tells you that having *agba* is not profitable, don't listen to him . . .'

Fatima did not know what *agba* meant, but she did not care. Whatever it was, she was certain she numbered among the few in Biafra who had it. As the workman said, the building had sprung up like a mushroom. It was a simple, straight-line house, with three bedrooms, the master bedroom having its own bathroom and toilet. A built-in wardrobe was provided in each room. The large kitchen was to be fitted with a gas cooker. Her husband had stated in his letter (which she took along to the house) that the Director for Procurement had commandeered a 3 KVA Lister generator to light the house. If she wanted a deep-freeze in addition to the refrigerator which had already been provided for the house, the Director for Accommodation would look around for one. A separate building would house her domestic staff. A concrete bunker formed part of the outfit.

'. . . I hope you'll find village life as tolerable as one can hope for in wartime when you move into the new house. I too look forward to making the house my hideout, where I can relax once in a while when I want to get away from Wagon's* air raids and the strains of the round-the-clock work schedule we operate here. Nothing like a quiet week-end in reasonable comfort with no one

* Biafran nickname for Gowon, the head of the Nigerian Federal Military Government.

but Fatima and Emeka . . .'

A smile formed on Fatima's lips as she sat on the unfinished bath tub in one of the bathrooms and read through her husband's letter. The smile lingered on like the taste of bitterleaf soup washed down with a glass of water. She forgot her 'stuff and nonsense' exclamation at each point made by her husband; rather she found herself seeing everything with new eyes.

She had previously dismissed the idea of settling down at Obodo, no matter how much her husband lured her by building heaven on earth there for her. She was not the kind of wife a man could tuck away at will in his village; she married her husband with the intention of living with him, and no mansion, however modern, would blind her to the hazards ahead for any foreign wife who leaves her young, handsome, magnetic husband to the mercy of sophisticated girls from his own ethnic group.

She had other reasons for resisting separation from her husband. Because she had no companionship at Obodo, because she had nothing worthwhile or challenging to occupy her, she found herself brooding most of the time. She brooded over the loss of Ami Junior. She wept secretly almost every day when she thought about home in Nigeria, about the fact that she could not communicate with her parents, other relations and friends back home in Nigeria. Were they in good health? She imagined how anxious they must be about her safety. It grieved her that she had no means of informing them that Ami Junior had been killed at Enugu. Two brothers and one half-brother of hers fell within the military age. They were hotheads who had little love for the *nyamilis* and had refused to talk to her after her marriage in London to a *nyamili*. Had they joined the Nigerian Army to fight against Biafra? She had often listened half-heartedly and yet persistently to the Nigerian casualty lists released by Radio Biafra, praying that she would not hear the name of any of them. If only she could send one message home and get a reply, it would make so much difference! At one time she had even contemplated using the medium of the BBC African Service programme CONTACT, but the problem became how to reach the BBC in London and what the repercussions might be for her husband if the BBC carried her message to her relations in Nigeria.

She had argued that life with her husband in Umuahia could provide her with companionship. The cosmopolitan community there was bound to include wives with problems similar to hers, and people who shared her interests. She could put her professional training to good use by working in a hospital. If her husband, out of fear of falling from grace, continued to discourage her from trying to communicate with her family, she stood a better chance of smuggling a letter out of the country if she lived in a city frequented by foreign journalists than if she lived in a jungle hideout.

She had another reason for wishing to join her husband at Umuahia, a reason she could not disclose to him. In her moments of depression, she had wondered whether he was taking all the trouble to fit her out lavishly at Obodo because he did not like the image of a Hausa woman hanging round his neck as he moved in Government circles in Umuahia. Perhaps the Government had even financed the house to save everybody the embarrassment her presence was bound to cause. Although her husband had been careful not to do or say anything that might give her the impression that she was a liability, all the same he had mentioned to her on more than one occasion the names of some high-ranking officials who had tried to denigrate him at the highest levels for no reason other than his marriage to a Hausa wife. Such persons had spoken of the danger of admitting to state secrets a man married to one of his country's enemies; in the final analysis, they had contended, Delilah's loyalty would be to the Philistines, her people, rather than to her husband, Samson, and his people. Could Ami be bowing to such whitemail? She could not ask him such a question, but she could put his motives to the test by joining him at Umuahia.

Yes, all things considered she had decided to proceed to Umuahia at the earliest opportunity, hence when she began to read Ami's letter she was not prepared to see any validity in his arguments. She had seen in the gift of an orderly and a Peugeot the opportunity to pack practically all she brought with her from Enugu and to travel to Umuahia without molestation. There had been no question of retaining the orderly and the car with her at Obodo.

Now she saw everything differently. Mrs Halima Uche had taken away the blinkers which had narrowed her horizon. Halima's account of her wretched experience highlighted some of the noblest ideals of marital life which Fatima suddenly recognized were woefully deficient in her own. Halima had sacrificed personal comfort and risked her very life in her determination to identify herself with her husband. She had demonstrated that Mrs Uche could remain Mrs Uche even when the outlook was bleak. She had thrown in her lot with her husband's people even when it entailed a total break with her own people, like the Biblical Ruth in her attachment to Naomi. She had broken through a major cultural barrier, for which she had won the love and admiration of her husband's family. Even after her tragic separation from her husband's family, her overriding concern remained the protection of her one remaining visible tie with her husband.

Fatima wondered whether the unseen powers had sent Halima to teach her one or two lessons on marital devotion. When Ami had proposed to her in London years back, she was certain they would spend their married life working in the cosmopolitan cities of Lagos and Ibadan or on some international university campus. A flying visit to his village once every five years or so and another to hers would be enough to placate the old people on both sides. She did not need to learn that terrible Igbo language, neither did he have to speak Hausa. As for the children, they would speak English of course, Hausa (if she could teach them) and any other language they picked up on their own. They had it all taped; they could have their cake and eat it – set an example as a couple practising the ideal of a united Nigeria, without exposing themselves to the serious problems of intertribal marriage. Now that she came face to face with those problems, it became glaringly obvious to her after listening to Halima that no real intertribal marriage had ever in fact taken place between her and Ami.

It was initially humiliating – the thought that a woman in rags, with a kwashiorkor child, had so much to teach her about the rudiments of marriage. When she withdrew into her room to weep, it was not only out of sympathy for Halima. She also wept at the shocking discovery that, faced with similar problems, an illiterate, unsophisticated, inconsequential woman had proved better able to cope with the situation than she had, with all her education, professional training, easy life and world-wide experience. Halima taught her her duties to her husband; above all, she taught her the need to make an effort to succeed.

By the time she set out to inspect her new house, she had made up her mind to stay on at Obodo. Ami had gone to great trouble and the Government had incurred considerable expense to make her comfortable at Obodo. She decided not to seek ulterior motives but to accept Ami's proposal at face value. The house had all she could desire, even in peace time. Obodo was as safe as anywhere in Biafra. The enemy at Enugu were several miles away and had shown no interest in moving towards Obodo. The village had no establishment of military significance, and Ami had undertaken to ensure that no publicity-attracting establishments moved there. The thick jungle provided natural cover from war planes; although even one-year-old children in the village knew how to dive for cover, nobody seriously feared an air raid. All the same, Ami had provided the concrete bunker; the asbestos roof of the house was to be camouflaged completely with roofing mats, and palm fronds were already being stuck into every inch of ground on the compound as further camouflage. Fatima had a car at her disposal. Petrol was free and generously provided. What further inducement could any reasonable woman expect before consenting to stay in her husband's village? If Halima could stick to her husband's people with no inducement whatsoever and with all the odds against her, what excuse could she, Fatima, have for grumbling?

She began to see several possibilities in her stay at Obodo. This was an excellent opportunity to overcome the cultural barrier which stood between her and her husband's people. Prior to Halima's visit, she had felt proud and emancipated each time she had proclaimed publicly that her communication with her parents-in-law was limited to an exchange of the elementary greetings 'Kedu' and 'Odinma'. She had felt envious of Halima when she demonstrated a mastery of Igbo language; if Halima could pick up the language, why not she? The months at Obodo would provide the opportunity for her to learn at least some words of Igbo, and to break down at least some of the barrier she had erected between herself and Ami's people.

She admitted that she need not be lonely and jobless at Obodo. Halima's kwashiorkor-stricken son needed somebody to take care of him, to give him the proteins which he lacked. There were bound to be several other such children transformed into white urchins (or 'Harold Wilson's children' as they were nicknamed) by protein deficiency. Her professional training placed her in a position to help such children, and she was certain Ami's medical background would move him to solicit the necessary protein supplements from the appropriate quarters. It occurred to her that she could establish a clinic for kwashiorkor children. She decided to put her ideas on paper and to send the driver off to Umuahia the next day to Ami to solicit his support.

Halima's story had yet another moral for Fatima. Most of Halima's misfortunes were the handiwork of the Nigerians. The same was true of Fatima. She had lost her first son to the Nigerian soldiers. The Nigerian blockade of Biafra had prevented her from reaching her people. Had not the time come for her to forget

Nigeria and think of herself as a Biafran?

How safe was it to leave Ami to husband-snatching single girls at Umuahia who had banded themselves into the 'Cradlers' Association'? She could not be bothered. If he decided to dig his own grave, he had attained the age of discretion. Their separation would keep her a safe distance away, especially as she was not emotionally prepared for another baby while the war lasted. The idea of a pregnant woman diving for cover was not particularly attractive.

11

The explanations advanced had been many. One originated from the Biafran Army, it was claimed. The Nigerian invaders found themselves in a vantage position, the kind that would gladden the hearts and quicken the pace of any invader. Their enemy was on the run, completely disorganized, and completely demoralized. Any good commander would press home such an advantage, allowing the enemy no time to regroup and mount a counter-offensive. The Nigerian Army pressed home their advantage. In October alone, they captured Enugu and Calabar, and compelled Biafra to evacuate Onitsha. A first-rate army could have overrun the whole state of Biafra in that month.

The second, and the most widely accepted explanation, was that the discovery of the abortive coup and the public execution of the four principal characters had come too late. The saboteurs had all along been in close touch with the enemy, passing on Biafra's military secrets, and turning the weapons manufactured by Biafra's Science Group against Biafra. They had also, through outright sabotage on the war fronts, systematically eliminated Biafra's best combatant officers, to ensure easy victory for Nigeria.

Duke Bassey, alias Indigenous, was clutching a glass of wine when a timid tap on the door interrupted his thoughts. He had bolted the door – the safest policy in times of crisis such as this. He deposited the glass on the drink stool beside the half-empty wine jar, pulled together the shirt he had unbuttoned to mitigate the effect of the heat in the room.

'Who's that?' His tone was not very inviting.

'Effiong, sir,' replied one of his shop assistants.

'My, oh my!' Bassey cried when he opened the door and saw Ikem Onukaegbe and Barrister Chike Ifeji behind the boy. 'What brings you here?' he asked as he warmly embraced each of them.

He had not seen them since they parted at the fall of Enugu. He had moved to Onitsha where he had a supermarket, and they had moved to Aba to continue with their war work. He had seen only Professor Ezenwa once or twice when he came to Onitsha to see his family.

'We heard of the fall of Onitsha, and decided we must track you down,' Onukaegbe replied. 'You remember you had told the Prof. that you would move to Port Harcourt if Onitsha fell. It wasn't difficult locating your supermarket where we saw this young man.'

'Well, this is where the fortunes of war have landed Indigenous. Welcome to my mansion!' Bassey opened the door of his bedsitter. 'I was lucky to get this room. The property is mine, including the main house. But I couldn't eject my tenant without notice. Moreover I need the rent, having lost all I had in Onitsha, including everything I evacuated there from Enugu, not to mention my real estate in Enugu. And you must have seen how empty my supermarket is because of the blockade . . .'

'What actually happened?' asked Barrister Ifeji.

Bassey had left Onitsha with nothing but the Biafra suit he had on him, fifty pounds, and his car.

'I wonder which of us is losing weight faster,' remarked Bassey, turning to Mr Onukaegbe. 'Your Biafra suit seems to sit somewhat more loosely on you now than it did when we were at Enugu. As for my beer belly, Nma thought its disappearance was the one silver lining in this war!'

'Where did you see her?' enquired Ifeji.

'At Ikot Ekpene. I thought I should go there first, to let my people know I was alive and well, even though I had lost my possessions. Nma would have had no sleep if I had allowed one day to pass after the fall of Onitsha without letting her know my whereabouts.'

Bassey recapitulated the story of his escape from Enugu. His first attempt to evacuate his personal effects and supermarket from Enugu to Onitsha had been frustrated at Awkunanaw, on the outskirts of Enugu. Unable to persuade the Civil Defenders to let him through, Bassey had returned to Enugu certain that he had no alternative but to escape via the more direct Enugu-Ninth Mile Corner route to Onitsha. It sounded like swimming into the open jaws of a crocodile; the only alternative was to be eliminated by the enemy as they marched into Enugu. Some Biafrans were still using the Ninth Mile Corner road, which meant that the Nigerians had not yet taken it. With luck he might yet get through safely.

At 2 a.m. the following morning, four hours before the time he planned to try the risky route, a couple living at Hilltop drove to his house for refuge. The enemy, they reported, had shelled the Ninth Mile Corner, and the small settlement there had begun to disperse. It took the couple over an hour to recover. They had driven away from their house with nothing but the pyjamas they had on.

'If I hadn't gone to the D.H.Q. that morning, I couldn't have taken anything out of Enugu. The Principal Staff Officer knew that I had contributed £500 to the Government in foreign exchange, towards the purchase of a war plane. Also the two station wagons I donated to the war effort were retained by the D.H.Q. I was given permission to evacuate my supermarket, on the grounds that to abandon such supplies in Enugu would be aiding the enemy. An army Landrover led the way . . .'

The Onitsha story was different. Bassey began: 'It was as if everybody had been at the starting blocks for a cross-country race, waiting for the starter's gun to go off! The explosions were terrifying, I must say . . .'

'Was it enemy mortar?' Barrister Ifeji asked.

'I very much doubt it,' Onukaegbe said. 'I told you that there's strong suspicion in Government circles that the whole incident was the work of saboteurs. Their aim is to cause panic, thereby facilitating the infiltration of the enemy.'

'I didn't stop to ask who fired the shots, and nobody in Onitsha at that time would have thought of doing so,' continued Bassey. 'Even if you had stopped to ask, there would have been no one to answer. The sound was horrifying, and so was the thick black smoke pouring in from the Niger bridgehead. Nobody had time to think. The natural reaction was to run for dear life, and to do so immediately . . .'

No one had time to look for anybody. The traders in the all-engulfing Onitsha Market fled, abandoning thousands of pounds' worth of wares. It was more chaotic than the stampede which followed the unannounced total eclipse of the sun in Eastern Nigeria in 1947. There was no question of running to the house to look for your family or to collect your personal effects. Every child in Biafra had of course been drilled in what action to take in such a situation – to move with the crowd rather than to roam about looking for the parents or next-of-kin. Mr Bassey had taken his car to Leventis Motors for routine maintenance. Fortunately the job had been completed before the commotion began. The cashier could not wait to collect the cheque.

'My driver was so nervous that I had to take over the steering from him,' Bassey went on. 'Luckily since leaving Enugu I had instructed the driver always to keep the fuel tank full. Several people abandoned their cars for lack of fuel. Some pushed theirs to a safe distance, leaving them there to go to Nnewi or Awka in quest of petrol. And you know how our people jump at the first opportunity of making money. The price of petrol at once rose to two pounds a gallon along the Onitsha-Awka and Onitsha-Nnewi roads.'

'I hear some policemen threw away their uniforms and guns to escape as civilians,' Ifeji said, laughing.

'I didn't see any,' Bassey replied. 'I must say I was pleasantly surprised to find some of our soldiers at roundabouts and other major road junctions, directing traffic. Without them the situation would have been impossible, what with the masses of confused pedestrians, cyclists, motor-cyclists and cars vying for the roads. They also compelled motorists to take some helpless pedestrians, especially women with children. Many pedestrians gave up and just dropped by the roadside. I shall never forget the pathetic scene – thousands of people surging forward, with practically no personal effects, to unknown destinations . . .'

'So what became of your property?' Onukaegbe asked.

'It's all gone, my brother! Gone *patapata*, as the Yorubas say. What makes it most painful is that I took all that trouble to evacuate even my brooms from Enugu to Onitsha. It's like washing your hands to crack a palm kernel only to see it snatched away by a chicken!'

'You mean all those fantastic chairs and so on in your house at Enugu are gone?' Onukaegbe asked in a hushed voice, leaning forward.

'Well.' Bassey swallowed hard. He tried to pour himself another glass of palm wine, only to discover that the jar was empty. He raised the glass to his mouth and sucked the brownish dregs which had settled at the bottom.

'We've come to express our sympathy for the loss,' Barrister Ifeji said softly, breaking an uncomfortable silence. '*Ashia*. And may we have your kind of heart when our own turn comes, as I fear it will sooner or later.'

'Life is what matters,' Onukaegbe remarked. 'Everything else is secondary.'

'Didn't I hear that one wealthy trader who had come out alive when everyone left Onitsha decided to go back to retrieve some bags of money he left in one of his stores?' Barrister Ifeji said. 'He got caught in the crossfire, and that was that! He lost his bags of money, plus his life!'

'It is painful losing not only your property but also your means of recuperating from the loss,' commented Bassey. 'But God forbid that I should ever consider my losses so unbearable as to want to take my life. By the way, how is Prof.?'

'The Professor is shattered,' replied Onukaegbe. 'That's the only way I can put it. According to him, the loss of his research papers and personal effects at Nsukka is nothing compared with his current problems. He could not contemplate asking his family to live in open school buildings with no privacy. He could not bring them to join him at Aba where he has only one room in a flat he is sharing with two other members of his Directorate. And it has been impossible finding accommodation in the rural areas, particularly in those villages the enemy are not likely to reach soon. Once the villagers find out that he comes from Onitsha they refuse to co-operate. The characteristic snobbishness of Onitsha people has not endeared them to many others.'

'You know what I heard?' Barrister Ifeji burst out laughing. 'I hear every Onitsha man has suddenly discovered his roots – among the people he had hitherto ridiculed and referred to disparagingly as "ndi Igbo". You know all those insulting stories they told of Igbo people, claiming as they did that their ancestral links were with Benin, not with Igboland.'

'D'you mean that Onitsha people look down on their fellow Igbo?' asked Bassey.

'Didn't you know that?' replied Ifeji. 'But now that the war has hit them hard, they are attempting an about-turn. It's so funny hearing an Onitsha man admitting in public that his father's mother's uncle or some such distant relation came from one Igbo village or another, something they would have previously considered abominable if any non-Onitsha man had dared suggest it.'

'That hasn't solved all their problems, though,' interjected Onukaegbe. 'Many villagers hold the view that Onitsha would not have fallen so easily to the enemy but for the fact that the inhabitants collaborated with the enemy. They fear that any Onitsha man admitted to the village is a potential enemy collaborator, hence a danger to the village.'

'But there is no room for that kind of sentiment in a country in which we constantly proclaim that every Biafran is his brother's keeper,' Bassey protested. 'The Directorate of Propaganda must do something about it.'

'That's the Professor's Directorate,' observed Onukaegbe jokingly.

'You still haven't told me about Prof. though,' Bassey persisted.

'He should be all right,' replied Onukaegbe. 'The mere fact of being on the run again – for the third time – was a bit too much for him. And this was running with a difference. It meant abandoning his family house, with many family treasures to which, as a historian, he had strong emotional attachments. For the first time, he knew of no place of refuge and yet he had had to pick up his wife and children, his mother, his blind uncle, his uncle's family, and so on.

'We couldn't help him; I mean my Directorate. But I took him to my village which is ten miles off the Orlu-Ndizuogu road. If the enemy ever gets there the war will be over.'

'You can't be sure,' said Ifeji.

'If it's that safe, you should probably find me one good house there too,' Bassey remarked smiling. 'I don't think I want to remain in these boys' quarters in Port Harcourt very long.'

'I can't see you living there, man, war or no war! We don't have any good houses there at all. We were able to find an uncompleted house for Prof. Happily it already had corrugated iron sheets on top. Prof. is using mud blocks to raise the unfinished cement walls. He is also arranging for bamboo shutters for the doors. His children were looking for electric switches and what have you. There isn't even a toilet; my people put him in touch with a man who specializes in digging pit latrines. Until he completes the job, they have to improvise. It was a traumatic change for the family, I tell you.'

'War is evil,' observed Bassey.

'It's terrible,' echoed Ifeji and Onukaegbe, rising to leave. They had to return to Aba, forty miles away. It was unsafe and unwise to stay away from your station overnight. Anything could happen any time.

'You know one strange thing . . .' Bassey spoke slowly. It was evident that the idea was only just forming in his mind as he spoke.

'I've lost a fortune at Onitsha . . . It's almost like what the Bible calls a baptism of fire. I'd never bothered to ask what a baptism of fire meant . . . but I now feel that I've been through it. And, having experienced it, I'm a different man . . . a more fanatical Biafran . . . I don't know whether you get me?'

The two men nodded assent, and took their leave.

12

Biafra rejoiced at the dawn of the new year. Christmas 1967 had come and gone. The Christmas Special said to have been planned by the Nigerian Army had failed. Contrary to the plan – to crush the Biafran secession completely before Christmas Day, as a present from Father Christmas to all Nigerians – Biafra was slowly consolidating its identity as a sovereign and independent state.

On 29 January 1968, Biafra launched its own currency and postage stamps. The Nigerian Government had suddenly decided to recall all Nigerian currency notes and replace them with new notes. The decision was seen in Biafra as another method of crushing Biafra, by preventing her from purchasing arms abroad with Nigerian currency. What the Nigerians intended to do with the old notes was not publicized, but many Biafrans sensed the danger ahead for their country unless Biafra introduced her own currency to coincide with the introduction of the new Nigerian notes. To allow the old Nigerian notes to remain legal tender in Biafra would encourage Nigeria to flood Biafra with the useless notes, causing unprecedented inflation. Worse still, the notes could be used to finance further sabotage in Biafra.

It had been an uphill task for Biafra, especially as its independence had not been formally recognized by any country. Intelligence agents, believed to be operating under orders from Nigeria's powerful friends, monitored and tried to thwart every move by Biafran emissaries to commission the printing of the notes and stamps. Biafra did produce the currency notes and postage stamps; the coins were to follow later. The launching of the new currency and postage stamps was celebrated throughout Biafra as the final act of severance from Nigeria and as a triumph of Biafran ingenuity.

The dawn of the new year saw Biafra in its eighth month of existence as a separate entity from Nigeria. Each day, each week, and each month it continued in existence increased its chances of perpetuating its sovereignty. Already its fate had become a subject of international concern. The Organization of African Unity (O.A.U.) had sent its Consultative Mission (later Committee) to Nigeria on 22-23 November 1967. The Vatican stepped in the following month when the Pope sent two emissaries to Lagos and later to Biafra to urge a negotiated settlement. On 9-10 February 1968, the Commonwealth Secretary-General visited Lagos to offer his services in the resolution of the crisis. A month later the Protestant Churches waded in with their own peace overtures. First it was a visit to Lagos as well as to Biafra by delegates from Churches in Great Britain. Then a joint appeal by the World Council of Churches and the Roman Catholic Church, calling for an immediate cessation of hostilities and the establishment of lasting peace by honourable negotiations in the highest African tradition.

The different advocates of peace from abroad had been very tactful in their choice of phraseology, so as to avoid offending Nigeria by acknowledging Biafra's sovereignty. The O.A.U. group had ended their mission by affirming their belief in Nigeria's territorial integrity, and had been roundly denounced by Biafra for their one-sided action. But both the Vatican and the World Council of Churches had directed their appeals to both sides, and their delegates were among a growing number of international visitors coming to Biafra for discussions with Biafran authorities and to see the situation in Biafra for themselves. The world may not have recognized Biafra as a sovereign state, with a seat at the United Nations, but it had indirectly recognized the existence of a territory known as Biafra, and had gone a step further in holding talks with its accredited representatives. The Biafrans saw it as de facto recognition.

Intercepts credited to the Biafran Directorate of Military Intelligence as well as comments by the BBC removed any doubt from the minds of Biafrans as to what Nigeria's real intentions were. The peace overtures were a ruse. Nigeria had announced to the whole world, a month after the war began, that it had advanced from police action to full-scale military operations. Her aim was to crush Biafra militarily, and to do so before Biafra gained de jure recognition as a sovereign state. The Biafrans tensed their muscles, determined to hold out against further Nigerian gains.

The Biafran evacuation of Onitsha in October 1967 marked the beginning of a major military confrontation between the two sides. The capture of Onitsha would be of much greater military significance than the capture of Enugu, and both sides knew it. Only the River Niger separated Onitsha from Asaba in the Mid-West, which was more firmly than ever in Federal hands. If only the Nigerian troops could occupy Onitsha, it would be easy to pour men and ammunition from Asaba to Onitsha, and from there they could fan out into practically every corner of Biafra, using the excellent network of roads linking all major Biafran towns to Onitsha.

A Biafran song described Onitsha as '*odi nso elu aka*' to the Nigerians. On a clear day the Nigerians could see Onitsha from Asaba. It was within mortar range, and they lobbed mortars at will into the ghost town, receiving occasional replies from the Biafrans. Their war planes bombed and strafed the town, destroying abandoned buildings. One thing, however, the Nigerian Army could not do: they could not occupy the town. The author of the song made the point aptly: Onitsha was near, barely a stone's throw away, yet it was beyond reach.

Nigeria's failure to capture and occupy Onitsha was not for want of trying. They did more than 'try, try, try again.' Even when it was certain that the commanding officer was sending the soldiers to their death, he despatched them in ship-loads. And they were never seen again. The Biafran shore batteries took care of them. In their thousands. Including, as the story went, wives who had been told that their husbands were already well-established in Onitsha and were itching to join them.

The Biafran Army had blown the Onitsha end of the magnificent, recently completed Niger Bridge. The only route open to the Nigerian invaders was across the River Niger. The crossing was child's play; you could do it easily in a dug-out canoe. In no time.

October, November, December 1967, January 1968 . . . the months rolled by. The Nigerians kept shelling Onitsha and trying to pour in troops. Every evening Biafrans tuned their radios to find out from the 'War Report' how many vandal boats had been sunk by Biafran shore batteries. Soon Biafra faced serious danger of an epidemic, unless the thousands of bodies of Nigerian soldiers scattered along the bank of the Niger were buried. It seemed that the legendary Mammy Water which had ruled the River Niger from the beginning of history and which had enjoyed the best of relationships with generations of wealthy merchants in Onitsha would not accept the bodies of the vandals as atonement for the unwarranted destruction of the ancient market town. She had therefore ordered the river to wash their bodies ashore. The Biafran Army offered a fee for each corpse buried.

Few Biafrans had any idea what a shore battery was or resembled. What mattered was not its looks but its invincibility, and the fact that it was produced by Biafran scientists. Everyone wished the River Niger had encircled the whole of Biafra: the legendary shore batteries would have taken care of every Nigerian incursion into Biafra. The only event which stole the limelight from the Biafran shore batteries was the Abagana miracle, but that is another story.

The Nigerians had to accept that Onitsha was near and yet beyond their reach by the most direct route. Yet they needed the town for its strategic position. The only course open to them was to get to it by land the long, tedious way – by establishing a supply line hundreds of miles long, up into Northern Nigeria, down through the towns they already controlled in Northern Biafra, and then west to Onitsha on the Enugu-Onitsha Road. The Biafrans would have mined the Enugu-Onitsha road and blown the bridges, but a well-equipped convoy could bulldoze its way through all that.

The motorized column of the Second Division of the Nigerian Army, to which had been assigned the task of taking Onitsha at all costs, had the men and the materials for the cross-country invasion, and it did bulldoze its way through. The deadline for the capture of Onitsha was set for 31 March 1968. The advancing column, more than a hundred vehicles strong, carried more military hardware than Nigeria required to capture every inch of Biafran soil, and estimated at more than three times the armament stocked by the entire Nigerian Army before the blackout. A BBC commentator who appeared to have waited a lifetime for this final act in the Nigeria-Biafra drama, was unequivocal in his prediction that the end of Biafra was in sight. Africa's largest army, Africa's deadliest weapons, were on the march to Onitsha and Biafra lacked the capability and the ingenuity to delay the advance. The stage was at long last set for the capture of Onitsha, and the establishment of the much shorter and more direct link with Lagos across the Niger. With the capture of Onitsha, more men and materials could be poured into Biafra at will. By every enlightened calculation, Biafran resistance was short-lived. Radio Nigeria and Radio/TV Kaduna echoed the good news.

The column advanced steadily. Caterpillars cleared new routes wherever necessary. Army engineers quickly threw Bailey bridges across the narrow streams where Biafran engineers had blown the bridges. Biafran soldiers fought brave battles at Oji River, Ugwuoba, Awka and Enugu-Ukwu. The sum total of it all, however, was to delay the advance temporarily, not to stop it. The BBC prediction was correct. The column was now at Abagana, some twenty miles, or less than an hour, from Onitsha.

Then came the Abagana miracle. A Biafran bullet hit one of the fuel tankers in the column and set it ablaze. That was the end of the invincible Nigerian armada. Hardly any person who had the courage to get near enough to the scene had the mouth to tell the story. It was miles of tankers, trailers, armoured vehicles, military hardware and human beings burnt, burning, charred, exploding, and smoking. A Biafran 'leader of thought' fainted at the sight of the trail of destruction. He was among the Biafrans listed by the Nigerians for extermination at the end of the war, and the thought of what could have become of Biafra and of him had that column reached Onitsha intact was too much for him.

'I told you it would happen! I told you it would happen!' Prophet James shouted and jingled his bell ecstatically as he scurried from one quarter of Obodo to another, stopping wherever he found an audience, to elaborate on the miracle of Abagana. His robe of office reflected the impact of the war on the prophet. It no longer swept the floor as he breezed along; three inches of the length had been snipped off by one of the prophet's female devotees, and used to mend the holes which had developed in the upper half of the robe, exposing the tattered, once white, sleeveless vest (with meshes larger than those on a fisherman's net) which the prophet wore inside. Moreover the robe no longer dazzled the eye with its bluish whiteness. Soap had become a luxury in Biafra, and packets of 'blue', used to keep whites white, had disappeared from the market. The prophet's hair was shaggy, and so was his beard, but these could not be blamed on the war. It was his attempt to approximate to Jesus Christ's appearance as He wandered through the wilderness.

'I told you it would happen! When I called for seven days' dry fast the enemies of the Lord said Prophet James had come again with his false prophecy. The enemies of the Holy One of Israel said Prophet James does not see anything. Thank God some people hearkened to my call, not only at Obodo but throughout Biafra. We fasted and prayed for seven whole days. I knew that one plus God is a majority. I knew that with God on our side, we shall vanquish. Has God not heard my prayers? Has the Holy One of Nazareth not performed a miracle before our very eyes? Go to Abagana and see it! I say go to Abagana and see! Allelu – '

'Alleluiah!' echoed his audience.

'Allelu – '

'Alleluiah!'

Prophet James burst into one of his popular songs, without bothering whether any one else joined him:

Hosanna to the Lord!

Hosanna to the Lord!

Hosanna! Hosanna! Hosanna in the highest!

He danced away, singing Hosanna to the Lord, jingling his bell and sweating profusely, his ubiquitous cross preceding him, held chest-high in his left hand.

The news of Abagana was received with jubilation all over Obodo. 'When I saw what happened,' Chief Ukadike had narrated, 'I did not know when I shouted "*Tonu Ja*".' He had always crossed swords with churchgoers for giving credit to God for every welcome event. 'This time I was convinced that only God could have been responsible for what happened at Abagana. I fell on my knees unconsciously and was surprised that I still knew how to say a prayer!'

The Obodo Youth Front immediately organized a victory march round the town, chanting songs of the revolution as the procession gathered momentum:

> *Biafra binie, nuso Nigeria agha,*
> *Agha! Agha!*
> *Maka gini?*
> *Nihi na ha bu ndi namagh Chineke,*
> *Ndi namagh Chineke kere uwa.*

The Nigerians, the song went, were people who did not know God, the Creator of the world. Biafrans must therefore arise and do battle against them. The 1966 pogrom had already established the Nigerians as a godless people. No god-fearing nation could have perpetrated such carnage on the peace-loving people of Biafra. The trail left behind the Nigerian motorized column as it bulldozed its way to its Waterloo had given further proof of their godlessness. It must have given the vandal soldiers heathenish satisfaction to defecate within the sacrosanct altar of a magnificent Roman Catholic church on their route, in preference to the empty bush all around the church. They had gone further and inscribed boldly above the main archway leading into the church: WE

HAVE COME TO DESTROY NOT TO SAVE. Their humiliation and utter destruction at Abagana was seen by the Biafrans as the hand of God smiting them through the lone Biafran bullet which set the first tanker ablaze.

God had at long last smitten them as, in Biblical times, He smote the persecutors of His chosen people, Israel. He had left His seal at the scene of desolation, so that His people would know that He is God. One building had stood untouched, a tower of strength, as it were, amidst the miles of desolation. It was the home of a Biafran clergyman who had abandoned it and fled at the approach of the vandals.

The victory march gathered strength as it progressed through the town. Women, children, young men abandoned whatever they were doing to demonstrate their happiness. What with the stresses and strains of the preceding months, everybody at Obodo jumped at the opportunity to celebrate something.

The change of currency had been a particularly painful experience. The fall of Enugu and Justus Chikwendu's treachery had jolted the people out of an unrealistic sense of security. The weekly food donations for the armed forces had reduced the quantity of food for consumption as well as the farmers' profits, but nobody at Obodo, not even the refugees, had been reduced to starvation level as a result. The different Civil Defence duties, including the digging of trenches and the combing exercises, meant less time for individual farming, but these were taken in one's stride as a contribution to the national effort. The change of currency was an experience for which there was no suitable expression at Obodo.

'When an old woman like me has to take her money to a bank,' a woman of eighty had declared, 'then the end of the world has come!'

A wine tapper had hanged himself in the wake of the currency change. Nobody knew until after his death why he had chosen the salutatory name 'Echi di ime': tomorrow is pregnant. The remains of a cellophane bag found in his house had provided the clue to his death. The cellophane bag contained at least £300 which Echidime had buried in his compound; it was impossible to tell exactly how much. Termites had discovered his treasure and enjoyed it before him! Nobody at Obodo could believe that Echidime had been worth so much money and yet unable even to cover his buttocks or to take a wife. Unfortunately whatever secret plans he had for the future died with him. The people who had sealed their money in empty beer bottles and buried the bottles were more fortunate.

Amazu, the first man from Obodo to take his money to the bank had returned with a lump on his forehead. A soldier on duty at the bank had struck him with the butt of his rifle because Amazu insisted on returning to his place in the ever lengthening queue, after taking time off to water the grass behind the bank. He had moved up to number fifty-two in the queue early in the afternoon of his second day of waiting. He finally paid in his money on the third day.

Agodi came home with the report of a more pathetic experience. He had chosen a bank temporarily located in a small out-of-the-way village rather than a major town, reckoning that such a bank would attract fewer clients. Many others must have reasoned like him, including car owners from the major towns who were scared by a recent air raid at a bank in Umuahia. The queue was so long that those at the tail end of it could not see the bank premises. By 4 p.m. on the third day of waiting, what with the sleepless nights and hardly any food, the biting rays of the sun sucked up whatever energy remained in him. He suddenly went limp.

Some good Samaritans carried him away to revive him. Hours later when he returned to life, he asked to be shown the way to the bank so that he could return to his place in the queue. But where was his money? He could not feel the heap in the special underwear in which he had hidden it. He tore off his shorts for a thorough search. Only £5 remained of the £180 he had tucked there! He fainted a second time.

Everybody at Obodo had a story to tell. The Biafran Government had had to recall the Nigerian currency notes without being in a position to replace them with Biafran currency. You were required to open a bank account, deposit your money, and go home empty-handed. All you could retain were the coins which remained legal tender in Nigeria and Biafra. Before long another war disease, 'moneyokor', joined forces with kwashiorkor; the new disease afflicted several Biafrans who paid all the money they had into a bank and had nothing except a few coins with which to buy food. It required all the ingenuity of the Public Enlightenment Officer for Obodo to get the people to accept the currency change as yet another challenge. It was no more than part of Nigeria's effort to exterminate the peace-loving, god-fearing people of Biafra for no cause. What they had failed to achieve on the battle front or by the blockade they had decided to try to accomplish through the sudden currency change. But they were sure to fail. Biafra was destined to triumph over even that obstacle.

The miracle of Abagana came as a tremendous tonic for every-body, including Prophet James, the Public Enlightenment Officer, and the Chairman of Obodo War Council. Each person claimed the miracle as a vindication of his faith or his forecast that Biafra was bound to survive. It was cited to substantiate two rumours which had been going round Obodo for some weeks.

'It must have been our new B-26 jet bombers that blasted those vandals,' a warden had told the Catechist of St Charles' Church, Obodo. 'When I told you that we had bought twenty brand-new B-26 jet-bombers you laughed at me.'

'Do you blame me?' the Catechist had replied. 'I thought our Government would have announced such an acquisition either in the 'War Report' or in the news.'

'You don't expect gov'ment to strip all its actions stark naked before the Hausas, do you? Did we announce when we got the first B-26?'

'I admit you have won this time. I hope the twenty jet-bombers will finish those vandals *kpamkpam*!'

'I said long ago that all this claim about Abagana miracle is part of false Prophet James' rubbish.' The speaker, a man who hated even Prophet James' footprints after the prophet had lured his wife away from him, spoke with his lips turned upwards in derision, like a he-goat's. His audience was a school teacher who also served on the Strategic Sub-Committee of Obodo War Council. 'It is now that the true story about Abagana has reached me. There was no miracle at all. When our people saw that the python was twisting too tight for our liking, they sent emissaries to France and China for help. Those people immediately sent us one hundred "Christian Brothers" armed with a kind of gun which they say can reduce Milliken Hill to ashes. The men laid an ambush for the Hausas at Abagana and the python was forced to uncurl itself. That's what that male prostitute who calls himself a prophet says is a miracle!'

The teacher did not sound convinced. 'When our people say that it's the *chi* of a tailless cow that kills the flies which attack the cow, nobody takes it to mean that the cow's *chi* actually comes down to kill flies.'

'It is not the same thing.'

'It is,' argued the teacher, 'and you know it. I think you are allowing what Prophet James did to you to cover your eyes.'

'Was that man from Ugani not called Ezeobuluya? Put yourself in my position and tell me how you would have reacted.'

Whether God acted through agents or by direct intervention,

everybody saw His hand in the disaster which befell the Nigerians at Abagana. It was as if God had declared His stand in the conflict, and every man, woman and child at Obodo rejoiced at the reassurance that God was on their side.

The Youth Front victory march switched from one war song to another as it progressed through the town. When it arrived in the grounds of the small earth building which served as Prophet James' church, the leader switched to the Prophet's popular song. The words were echoed down the long procession:

> Sing Praises to the Lord,
> Sing Praises to the Lord,
> Hosanna! Hosanna! Hosanna in the highest!
> Hosanna to the Lord,
> Hosanna to the Lord,
> Hosanna, Hosanna! Hosanna to the Lord!

Prophet James had never had a happier moment. He failed to notice that his robe of office, soaked in sweat, had parted in two behind him. He threw the tireless bell to one of his assistants to jingle while he clapped his hands with his whole body as he joined in raising Hosanna to the Holy One of Israel. The procession need not have passed by his little church. The building was tucked away in a corner of the town removed from any major road. But for the joyful noise which issued forth from it practically all hours of the day or night, noise far out of proportion to the size and membership of the church, few people at Obodo would have taken any notice of its existence. The Anglican pastor had done all in his power to discredit the church as a hideout for false prophets and threatened to excommunicate any member of his congregation found worshipping there. The threat did not, however, deter his flock for long. Prophet James' methods held a strong appeal for people seeking something to buttress their faith. It was not enough to preach on Sundays that God would not fail his people, especially when the preacher looked more helpless and despondent than his flock on the six days between Sundays. Prophet James had something to offer which the people needed: he claimed prophetic vision and periodic communication with God. He was better placed to ascertain God's plan for Biafra in the war than a pastor who laid no claim to prophetic vision.

The number of Christians who had called at the church had grown since the prophet's call for a seven-day fast. The prophet had rejoiced at the inroad he had made into the Anglican Church, but there was nothing to compare with the happiness he felt as the victory procession sang and danced at his church before moving off to another part of the town.

In between singing and clapping, the prophet shouted at the top of his never-failing voice:

'The miracle of Abagana is of the Lord's doing! If you are happy about it, drop your thank-offering to the Lord in that tray! Allelu – Alleluiah!'

The coins fell one by one, into the tray. By the time the last man in the procession had moved off, an excited Prophet James could not believe his eyes as he counted the coins three different times and on each occasion arrived at the total of five pounds and one penny. Five pounds in coins! This was a princely sum at a time when the new Biafran currency had been launched but had still not gone into circulation and a shilling coin had the purchasing power of one pound. Five pounds in coins was equivalent to a hundred pounds!

A spontaneous offering of a hundred shillings and one penny at a time when most people groaned under the currency yoke was an indication of the mass jubilation at the miracle of Abagana. Prophet James saw in it also an indication of his rising popularity among his people, including some of his arch detractors. He thanked God that he had issued that call for a dry fast.

'Prophet!' shouted the assistant to whom he had thrown the bell earlier on. 'Your robe is torn behind.'

As the prophet turned round anxiously to see how much damage had been done, he heard a sound which meant that the robe was tearing even further. He gave up the effort. 'Never mind,' he replied, smiling like *abacha nmili*. 'I have more than one robe here!' He held up the once-white handkerchief in which he had wrapped the hundred shillings and one penny offered to the Lord.

'I need a robe too, sir,' pleaded his assistant.

'All right. Send me a sister to put out the bath water for me.'

The assistant smiled. Every adult at Obodo knew about the prophet's weakness for women. It was a standing joke that any trap set around a woman's waist would catch him hand, foot and all: he could not survive twenty-four hours without having a woman, and he had scattered his seed like the explosive pods of the oil bean tree. But the people were philosophical about it, especially those men whose wives or daughters had not produced children for him. A wise man does not look too critically at the sides of the stream when he goes there for a drink, or he will never drink from the stream. If you go to Prophet James, shut your eyes to what he does with women and take what he tells you about God.

A dark-skinned woman whose youth, good looks and deliciousness defied the amorphous white robe she wore, walked shyly towards Prophet James.

'Sister, the Lord requires you to meet the needs of the flesh,' instructed the prophet.

'If it is the will of God,' she replied, her eyes lowered, 'may the Holy Spirit enter me through you.'

The prophet led her away to the Inner Room.

13

'When will this thing come to an end?' Chief Ofo asked.

Mazi Kanu Onwubiko used his tubular walking stick to draw short lines on the floor similar to the lines drawn by Ibekwe the bone-setter. The Chief introduced a pinch of snuff into each nostril, just enough to give him the sensation of snuff in his body, and smacked his empty palms noisily in case there was any snuff that needed to be rubbed off. He tucked the snuff-box away in the folds of his heavy loin cloth, like a market woman concealing her precious money in the privacy of her waist.

'Kanu. Uduji. It is you I ask. When will this thing come to an end?' This time his eyes moved from one person to the other. The lines of age which were hardly visible before the war had in recent months deepened into drainage gutters fanning out from the nose and separating the cheek bones from the mouth.

'You probably forgot that you have not passed the snuff-box round, hence you are tucking it away,' observed Mazi Kanu Onwubiko, stretching out his right hand for the Chief's snuff-box. 'Are you Chief in name only?'

'I don't think the news of the entry of the Hausas into Calabar has reached you, eh?' Chief Ofo asked, tucking the folds of his heavy loin cloth more securely as if to ensure the safety of his precious snuff.

'If you ask me to speak my mind, I would say that the entry of the Hausas into Calabar has dealt us the severest of blows since this thing began,' remarked Uduji, a trader.

'Because that was your route for importing those items you always hawked inside your big black bag?' Kanu asked.

'Do you blame him?' asked Chief Ofo. 'After all, our wise men say that it is the roof over a man's head that he worries about keeping in good repair.'

'Leave Kanu alone,' Uduji retorted. 'He can talk the way he does because he has not lost anything since this trouble began.'

'What did he say?' Kanu asked, as if he could not believe his ears.

'I say you have lost nothing of yours as a result of this war. That's why you can talk that way. If you had run with only your head – as we did in Northern Nigeria two years ago – leaving all the property you had taken so many years to acquire, or it you had run from Calabar without taking even a broomstick from your house, you would not be talking that way.'

Mazi Kanu gnashed his teeth for a while; it helped him to bridle his temper, and to collect his thoughts. When he spoke, it was with a note of seriousness: 'Uduji, let the winds obliterate my words . . . I failed to remember that it is only persons wealthy enough to build "plots" in townships who have been hit by this war . . .' His teeth resounded as he ground them masterfully, one against the other.

Uduji got the message, and promptly went on his knees in supplication.

'Mazi,' he began, 'here are my knees. I did not mean what I said. How can any sensible person forget the tragedy that befell you – I should say all of us – at Enugu when our enemies began shelling?'

Chief Ofo was quick to intervene.

'Arise Uduji,' he said, using his hand to strengthen his words. 'Kanu carries no anger in his mind against you. It's only that each one of us you touch now will snap like the dry *tie-tie* on a harmattan afternoon. Nobody stands firmly on his two legs now. Something stronger than the cricket has found its way into the cricket's hole!'

'Odo, I salute you all – ' Chief Ukadike removed his cap as he paid obeisance to the Odo of Obodo ' – but I do not agree with you, O!'

The three men were startled by Chief Ukadike's entry. They heard the voice before they saw the speaker. He wore his usual breezy, pompous air.

'Ezeahurukwe,' Uduji gave him his salutation before realizing from Chief Ofo's countenance that he had committed his second crime of grave indiscretion. Chief Ofo hated the sight of Chief Ukadike, more so when he posed as Ezeahurukwe, the chief who was easily recognized at sight, as if Chief Ofo's regal status was ever in doubt. Mazi Kanu Onwubiko stepped in promptly, to steer the canoe away from the hazardous current.

'With what do you disagree?' Mazi Kanu asked Ukadike.

'I don't agree that something stronger than the cricket has found its way into the cricket's hole,' Ukadike replied. 'It suggests that the Hausas and the Yorubas are stronger than we, the Igbo, which I consider complete rubbish.'

'You think you are stronger than they?' Kanu asked cynically.

'Not that I think, but that I know!' Ukadike shouted as if he was playing to the gallery. 'I fought side by side with their men in Arakan Yoma during World War II, and they are more cowardly than girls in a secondary school. Post a Yoruba soldier as sentry on night duty and as soon as he hears the slightest noise he will throw away his ack-ack gun and run away shouting "*O pa mi O*, he has killed me O!" Don't you know how the Yoruba people behave when you lift a matchet? They'll abandon whatever they have, including their wives as they run for dear life. As for the Hausa man, all he knows is how to shoot an arrow. Where has he handled a gun before? . . .'

'When I don't accept what you say, I'll tell you. O,' protested Uduji. 'If you were in the North in 1966 you would not come here to say that the Hausa people do not know how to kill.'

'That's a different thing. Our people were not prepared then . . .'

'Are we prepared now?' asked Mazi Kanu.

'Jesus wept!' Chief Ukadike shouted. 'Have you not heard our Head of State say that no power in Black Africa can conquer us? You think he can talk like that without knowing what we have in stock? Shore batteries, B-26 jet bombers, she-berets, Madsens, ferrets, not to talk of our home-made *ogbunigwe* and rockets. Have you forgotten what we did to them in the Mid-West? Have you forgotten what we did to them at Abagana? Have you . . .'

The words froze on his lips as the sound of a shot pierced through the cool evening air. Chief Ukadike promptly went flat on the floor in the 'take cover' position. Uduji did the same when a second shot followed. Chief Ofo and Mazi Kanu rose uneasily to their feet, uncertain what to do. The two men looked at each other without uttering a word.

A third shot followed, this time from another direction.

'That sounds as if it was fired from my house,' muttered Mazi Kanu. 'I'm going.'

'Are you mad?' said Chief Ukadike.

'Yes.' Mazi Kanu was already moving as he replied.

'You'll be making yourself a target if you move out into the open. And you will attract the enemy to our location!'

'The madman keeps his sense with him,' was all Mazi Kanu was prepared to reply as he quickened his pace, impelled by a fearless determination to face whatever odds lay between him and his responsibilities as head of a household.

'When a dog heads to his death he loses the sense of smell,' observed Chief Ukadike ominously.

'Man, won't you keep quiet?' Uduji chided, nervously. 'You will soon attract the Hausas here!'

Chief Ukadike jumped smartly to his feet, smacking off as much of the red dust as he could, as footsteps were heard approaching Chief Ofo's *ogbaburuburu*. He felt for his medals, and the sound of their existence restored his self-confidence.

'It can't be the enemy,' he muttered, in an attempt to reassure himself more than his companions. 'They would open fire before moving in . . .'

Some of Chief Ofo's wives and their children ran into the hut, trembling visibly with terror. Chief Ukadike's presence heightened their fears; he must have come to apprise their master of the entry of the enemy into the town. One of the women was carrying a pot of half-cooked bitterleaf soup in a basket.

The next shot was so close that it sounded as if it was fired from Chief Ofo's backyard. One woman could no longer hold back her sobs. Others followed suit as they closed in round their master, clinging to their children. The woman with the soup pot abandoned it in a corner of the room. Chief Ofo sat on his chair and reached for his empty snuff-box.

'I can't understand this,' Chief Ukadike said as he stepped out of the house cautiously. He left the impression that he was off to see what was brewing; his aim was to extricate himself from the crowd. His experience of the war had taught him that it was best during air raids and other moments of danger to keep away from the crowd. He kept close to the wall, like a prisoner in an escape bid. Or like the wicked Odo masquerade stealthily edging his way towards an unsuspecting victim.

'What's that?' He paused to strain his ears. Laughter . . . A war song . . . Yes, one of the songs of the revolution . . . The words became clearer as the singers drew nearer.

> *Nuru olu ayi, Nna, nuru olu ayi,*
> *Nuru olu ayi, Nna, nuru olu ayi.*
> *Odigh mgbe ike Gowon gakari ike Ojukwu.*

Odigh mgbe ike Gowon gakari ike Ojukwu,
Nna nuru. Chuku kere uwa nuru olu ayi.

Chief Ukadike changed direction. baffled but with some sense of relief. He made for the gate, stepping somewhat more confidently at the sound of the familiar song.

'Biafra win – war! Biafra win – war!' shouted the jubilant group as they advanced towards Chief Ofo's compound. A double-barrelled gun discharged a cartridge amid all-round acclamation.

Ukadike took cover behind a tree until he had identified Okeke Eni, Udoakpuenyi, Mazi Kanu . . . Satisfied that it was not one of the techniques adopted by the Nigerian soldiers to infiltrate into a Biafran stronghold, he strutted towards the jubilant group.

Chief Ukadike nearly collapsed at the news that the Republic of Tanzania had recognized Biafra as a sovereign state. The sudden change from fear to unbounded joy was more than he had bargained for.

'How did you hear about it?' he enquired.

'I heard it both from the BBC and from Voice of America,' asserted John Nwosu, Secretary of Obodo War Council.

'If it is only the BBC I will not believe it. You can't trust those – what does our radio call them again? . . .'

'Perfidious Albions!!' echoed his audience.

'O.R.T.F. carried it too,' Andrew the lorry driver put in.

'If the French radio said so, then it must be true' replied Ukadike. 'But we should send somebody to Okpeze just to make sure that their own radio also carried the news.'

'I have already done that.' reported John. 'The whole town is dancing with joy.'

Mazi Kanu expressed surprise that Chief Ukadike did not know about the recognition when he had always claimed prior knowledge of every Government move.

'Of course I knew about it,' Chief Ukadike lied. 'I knew when our men went to Tanzania to sign the agreement and I had put aside one he-goat to celebrate the good news one of these days. I wanted to make sure that the recognition had now been made public. that's all.'

'So we shall eat *ngwo ngwo* in your house today?'

'I invite all of you to my compound this evening to celebrate!'

Chief Ukadike's offer was greeted with 'Ezeahurukwe'! He promptly took over the leadership of the group, buying the floor (as it were) by shouting 'Biafra win – '

'War!' echoed the audience.

'Biafra win – '

'War!'

As the jubilant group advanced towards Chief Ofo's compound, picking up more dancers along the route, Chief Ukadike led them in a popular war song:

> *Enyi Biafra le le*
> *Enyi Biafra ala – la.*
> *Enyi Biafra le le*
> *Enyi Biafra ala – la.*
> *Chetakwanu thirty thousand,*
> *Thirty thousand bu umu Biafra.*
> *Chetakwanu Aguiyi-Ironsi,*
> *Aguiyi-Ironsi bu nwa Biafra.*
> *Chetakwanu Major Nzeogwu,*
> *Major Nzeogwu bu nwa Biafra.*
> *Chetakwanu Chris Okigbo,*
> *Chris Okigbo bu nwa Biafra.*
> *Chetakwanu . . .*

14

'It looks certain now that he will make it,' concluded Professor Ezenwa, shaking hands warmly and appreciatively with Dr Azinna Obinani, Consultant Physician at Queen Elizabeth Hospital, Umuahia and a former class mate at school.

'I told you from the start that there was no cause for alarm,' Dr Obinani replied, parting his thick beard with a smile. 'But you Arts men are always Doubting Thomases!'

'With more and more evidence coming to light that medicine is not an exact science, can you blame me?' laughed Professor Ezenwa.

'Come off it, man!' Dr Obinani, impeccably dressed as usual, his maroon bow tie contrasting with his white shirt and well-laundered white overall, gave the Professor a friendly smack on the back. 'I've handled several such cases before. Nothing more than a combination of shock and depression . . .'

'I was only teasing,' said Professor Ezenwa. 'Ikem and I moved Mr Bassey from Aba to this hospital because of the confidence we've always had in you . . .'

'It should be no problem getting him back on his feet. What you might consider is finding him something to do soon after he is discharged which I reckon will be a week from now or two at the most. He could suffer from a relapse if he has nothing positive to occupy his time. I don't know how you can organize something worthwhile for him, but you can be sure Ikem will know how to break through the cordon our bureaucrats, otherwise known as civil servants, have erected around themselves . . .'

'Won't you ever let up in your onslaughts on civil servants, Azinna?' Ikem Onukaegbe protested.

'This is the day of the civil servant, and that's the truth pure and simple,' Dr Obinan went on. 'They strut about like peacocks, calling themselves Director of one thing or the other and enjoying more amenities in wartime than ministers did in the political days, while professionals like us slave away without any recognition. I have to continue my ward round but we must find time one of these days to discuss the despicable role which you civil servants are playing in the prosecution of this war. See you.'

The month of April and May 1968 had been depressing months for Biafrans. The entire Ibibio-speaking area and the greater part of the Annang Province had capitulated to the enemy or, as Radio Nigeria proudly proclaimed, had been 'liberated' by Federal troops. The Provincial Administrator for Uyo and Annang Provinces had consequently joined the ever-growing group of Provincial Administrators without Provinces to administer – namely Nsukka, Abakalik, Enugu and Calabar.

The recognition of Biafra by Tanzania on 13 April had cheered the hearts of every Biafran. Gabon followed suit on 8 May, and nearly a week later Ivory Coast also recognized Biafra as a sovereign nation. It seemed the recognitions, coming in such rapid succession, had compelled the enemy to greater ferocity. Their target was Port Harcourt, Biafra's remaining seaport and airport, and home of the million-pound petroleum refinery which supplied Biafra (and previously Nigeria) with petroleum products. The capture of Port Harcourt would seal off Biafra completely from the outside world. Biafrans would be unable to fly arms in, meaning of course their inevitable capitulation. The sands were running out for Biafra. Even the rains appeared to have conspired with the enemy. The rainy season was late in coming. Heavy rains would have helped to slow down the enemy.

Professor Ezenwa felt light-hearted as he and Mr Onukaegbe walked to the car. This was their third visit to Umuahia (from

Aba) to see how their friend Duke Bassey was responding to treatment, and the first occasion on which he and Mr Onukaegbe were prepared to share Dr Obinani's optimism that Bassey would make it. Bassey had given them the greatest fright of their lives.

After the crippling losses he had suffered in the fall of Enugu and the evacuation of Onitsha, Bassey's immediate reaction had been to return to his home town outside Ikot Ekpene and stay put with the only precious possessions left to him – his family. What if the enemy broke through from the Calabar front? He had seen the chaos at Enugu and Onitsha when the two towns capitulated, and knew how imperative it was for a head of family to stay on the spot to take the split-second decision when the moment came. If it became necessary to take to the bush, his presence would reassure his family in the way the wings of the mother hen make her chicks feel warm and safe no matter what the external threat to their lives.

Mr Bassey had been dissuaded from going home by Mr Uko, Director-General (War Services), who came from his Province. As a man from a minority area of Biafra, his action could be misconstrued and he could be branded a saboteur. Once this happened, everyone would forget all his contributions to the war effort, and he could well become a victim of mass justice – or injustice. So Mr Uko had reasoned.

As he moaned over the fate of his family, he wished he had acted on his hunch rather than on the advice of a civil servant who had no problems and if the worst came to the worst could fly his family out of Biafra anyway.

Everything had happened with the speed of lightning. A letter had been hand-delivered to his supermarket staff in Port Harcourt, where he had taken refuge since the fall of Onitsha. The letter was written on behalf of an illiterate uncle who played the role of father to the extended family after the death of Bassey's father. His home town was seriously threatened, and it was imperative that he should attend a crucial meeting that night to discuss the defence of the town. Failure to respond to the invitation, the letter said, would endanger the lives of his wife and children.

Mr Bassey was not in the supermarket when the letter was delivered, and the bearer did not leave any information about his whereabouts. He gave his name as Okon which was of no help as Okon was such a common name. However, for some time there had been conflicting accounts of the fighting in the Calabar sector. There had been a persistent rumour that Biafra had injected some 'Christian Brothers' into the area, in a desperate effort to clear Uyo Province and recapture the port of Calabar. Bassey had, in fact, kept his ears very close to the ground, to pick up all available information on the fighting. His car was always standing by with a full tank, to take him to Ikot Ekpene whenever it became necessary to evacuate his family, although he kept hoping that such an evacuation would never become necessary. The possibility that his family was in danger was all that he required to make a dash for home. The identity or whereabouts of the messenger was immaterial.

Mr Bassey had been in such a hurry that he could not stop at Aba to notify his friends that he had passed through to his village. To be on the safe side, he decided to take the Port Harcourt-Aba-Umuahia-Ikot Ekpene road rather than the Port Harcourt-Aba-Ikot Ekpene road. It was a much longer road but it was the safest. Moreover he could call at Mr Uko's at Umuahia to obtain the latest information on the situation at home. Mr Uko was not available, but what Mr Bassey saw was sufficient to quicken his heart-beat and his urge to get home. Mr Uko's two-storeyed house as well as his boys' quarters were crammed with members of his extended family who had been evacuated. Their account of the situation at home was neither encouraging nor helpful, more like the stories of people on their guard. The situation was confused as far as he could make out; some Nigerian soldiers wearing the Biafra Sun had infiltrated the town in unknown numbers. No one could tell Bassey the whereabouts of his wife and children. As far as they knew, nobody had been killed so his family ought to be safe somewhere.

Bassey waited in vain for Mr Uko to come home, to see what additional information he could obtain from him. He did not know that the man he sought was in the house. Mr Uko had recognized the car as he drove in and instructed the steward to say that he had gone out. He was reluctant to face Bassey, remembering that it was his advice which had stopped I -y from going home. Somehow he had hoped th   ..ssey had got wind of developments and evacuated his family. If Bassey had lived in Umuahia he could have whispered a warning to him at the appropriate time, but it was a different thing sending a message to him all the way to Port Harcourt. Suppose the message were intercepted, or Bassey inadvertently disclosed his source? His detractors would promptly capitalize on it and accuse him of spreading wild rumours in order to discredit the Government, and in no time H.E. would be under pressure to strip him of his key responsibilities . . .

It was already dusk when the white Mercedes negotiated the

roundabout by Queen Elizabeth Hospital and sped along the well-surfaced Umuahia-Umudike-Ikot Ekpene road.

'Ette,' Bassey called his driver. 'Drive fast, but carefully. Be on your guard, especially after Ikwuano County when we cross into our province. If you see any checkpoint, slow down and switch your headlights full on so that I can see what's happening and decide whether we go ahead or turn back. There's no cause for alarm, so don't panic. Is that clear?'

'Yessir!'

The unsteadiness in his master's voice, together with the sight of the refugees in Mr Uko's house were enough to convince the driver that there *was* cause for alarm. He made up his mind that he too must satisfy himself that no danger lay ahead before driving on to any road block. If he sensed danger he would swing the car round and speed back to Umuahia, and if his master disagreed with his judgement he would leave the ignition key to him and jump out into the bush.

Mr Bassey sat on the edge of the rear seat, struggling to collect his thoughts and at the same time to keep his two eyes on the road to take in everything as the car zoomed past. He succeeded in keeping the road under constant surveillance but failed woefully in the effort to collect his thoughts. Conflicting visions of the fate of his family made it impossible for him to decide on any line of action.

Surprisingly, they did not run into any road blocks from the time they crossed from Umuahia Province to Annang Province. The road was deserted, even though it was only 8 o'clock. The only person they saw fled into the bush as soon as the car slowed down and swerved towards him. Bassey could feel the sweat collecting on his forehead.

'Drop me here and drive to the house,' he instructed the driver. 'If Madam is in, tell her I've gone to see Ndiyo. I won't be long.'

'Yessir!'

The thought had flashed through his mind and he seized on it. Before going to his house it would be a good idea to drop in on his childhood friend, Ndiyo. If there was one man he could trust in his village it was Ndiyo. They had grown up together, fished together, played masquerades together, even shared the cotyledons of a groundnut. Their childhood bond had been so tight that it was generally agreed that the creator had intended them to be twins but changed his mind at the last moment and sent them to two different mothers! Education parted them. Ndiyo's father would not send Ndiyo to school as he wanted the boy to take after his own profession – fishing. But the parting was only superficial: the bond of friendship continued, notwithstanding the wide material gap which had developed between the owner of a chain of supermarkets and real estate and an ordinary village fisherman. Ndiyo remained Bassey's closest friend and confidant in the village. Bassey gave him every financial support; it was he who replaced Ndiyo's mud hut with a more permanent structure.

'Sh . . . sh! Come this way . . .'

Bassey felt his skin crawl. He was still several yards from Ndiyo's house, but near enough to be heard when he whistled their childhood call signal. It was as if a Nigerian soldier had pounced on him from nowhere; he was so taken unawares that he momentarily failed to recognize Ndiyo's voice.

'Where's your car?' Ndiyo asked, shaking hands with Bassey and at the same time drawing him off the footpath.

'I asked the driver to proceed to my house,' Bassey replied, trying to regain his breath.

'Did you tell him where you were going?'

'Yes. I asked him to tell Nma that I had dropped in to see you.'

Ndiyo asked Bassey to wait for him while he nipped into the house. In a trice he was back. 'We mustn't hang around here,' began Ndiyo. 'Whether or not your driver tells them your whereabouts, they'll start looking for you at Ndiyo's house so let's move away quickly before they come.' Ndiyo led the way, cutting through the bush as if he was a seasoned hunter rather than a fisherman.

'What is happening? Who are the "they" you are talking about? Did you know I was coming? . . .' Bassey shut up when he saw that Ndiyo pressed on much faster than he did, and without uttering a word.

Suddenly there was an outburst of small arms fire. Ndiyo at once fell flat, followed by Bassey.

'The shooting must be from your house,' whispered Ndiyo. 'I'm sure they will soon rush down here, which is why I left word that I had not come home since dusk, to put them off . . .'

'But who are they?' Bassey was panting loudly.

'The Nigerians.'

'What!' gasped Bassey. 'In my house! What about Nma and the children?'

'Sh . . . The night has ears. Let's move away from here first. Nma and the children were alive today . . .'

'Hm!' Bassey calmed down.

'I don't know how it happened,' began Ndiyo, still in a hushed voice even though they must have covered at least two miles along a rarely-used bush path, hardly wide enough to take the width of a bicycle tyre. Bassey could not tell where they were.

'. . . People say it was Chief Inyang. They say the Hausas established contact with him through one Ibibio boy fighting with the Hausas who had been his house-boy before the war broke out. The Hausas sent Inyang tobacco and hot drinks. They promised to make him a Commissioner in the government they intend to set up if he helps them to come in. I don't know how they did it, but people say the town is now full of Hausa soldiers.'

'Where is Nma?'

'She is in hiding with the children. It was only last night that I heard of the plot to lure you in today. I immediately sent word to Nma and she and the children escaped in the dead of the night. Fortunately no Hausa soldiers had been sent to the house by that time.'

'I still can't understand.' Bassey was utterly confused. 'Thank God Nma and the children are safe. But I still can't understand what is happening. Why do they want to bring me here? Was it "they" who sent the message to me from my uncle that I should come home for a meeting?'

'You know Chief Inyang has never been happy since you put up your mansion. I think there was something also between him and your father.'

'So he used my uncle's name to summon me home? For what purpose?' asked Bassey.

'You ask like a child.' Ndiyo replied. 'What do the Hausas do to the people who support Biafra? Don't you know those shots we heard must have been fired at your car, probably in the belief that you were inside it?'

'O God!' gasped Bassey.

Ndiyo moved on briskly, followed by a silent Bassey. Neither man uttered a word from then on. Bassey forgot that he had had no dinner. The threat to his life had driven off all hunger and weariness. Shortly before midnight, they reached a small fishing village. You could see the few stars in the sky by looking at the huge lake in front. Ndiyo led the way to one of the huts. The householder was a professional friend, and he admitted the travellers as soon as he recognized Ndiyo.

Before retiring for the night, the three men agreed on their strategy. Ndiyo would not listen to Bassey's plea to lead him to Nma. It was foolhardy action which could endanger the lives of all concerned, including the people Bassey was trying to save Ndiyo was sure that Chief Inyang would comb every bush in their village to smoke Bassey out. When a man thirsts for blood there is no limit to what he can do. Ndiyo knew his own life was also in danger, and that his house would be under constant surveillance: nobody would believe him even if he swore on oath that he had not set eyes on Bassey. He would have to snatch some sleep and set off on his own before cock crow, hoping to reach Nma at the earliest opportunity and brief her on developments. If his own life was spared, he would do his best to shelter Nma and the children until conditions improved sufficiently to allow Bassey to arrange their evacuation.

Bassey would remain in hiding at the fisherman's hut until the following night, when the fisherman would give him a trusted guide to take him several miles across the boundary to Umuahia Province. From there he was to take care of himself, and find his way to Umuahia.

Bassey stripped down to his vest and underpants and curled up on a mat for the night. The house was hot and stuffy. It had been built without windows to keep off mosquitoes, but they came in all the same. One arm served as a pillow. Soon he fell into deep sleep, in spite of the heat, the mosquitoes and the hard floor. He did not know when Ndiyo stepped out into the lonely night, at 3 a.m.

The Chief of the Ndoro clan in Umuahia Province was having his morning ablution when six Civil Defenders marched in a worn-out captive, whose hands were securely strapped behind him. The shortest of the Civil Defenders (he was under five foot) for the hundredth time that brief morning pulled out his razor-sharp two-edged dagger from the scabbard he had belted round his waist. For the hundredth time he bared and clenched his teeth as he demonstrated with the hungry dagger what would happen to the captive's throat if the story he told them turned out to be a lie. The way he handled that dagger, he must have been a butcher by profession. Having run out of Hausa cows to slaughter, he seemed more than eager to try out his dagger on human throats. Had he been the one who found Bassey squatting in the market stall where his guide had left him, he would have slashed his throat without any qualms. He had no mercy on saboteurs, he repeated several times. Luckily for Bassey, the little butcher stumbled on him and his captors as they were already on their way to the Chief's house, and they would not yield to his pressure to deal with the case summarily without causing the Chief unnecessary bother.

'Come on!' shouted the short man with the hungry dagger as soon as Bassey and his captors stepped into the hall where the Chief received his guests. 'You told us it was the Chief who sent for you. Now that we have brought you to the Chief you are tongue-tied!' He pulled out the dagger, but was restrained by the leader of the group.

Bassey stepped out towards the Chief, but was immediately grabbed by his captors and dragged back. The short man with the dagger reminded the leader that he had warned them that the man was dangerous and they should have disposed of him summarily.

'J.M.J.' Bassey addressed the Chief, using the Chief's popular nickname at Enugu where, before the war, he owned a motor vehicle spare parts shop. 'Believe it or not, this is Duke Bassey, alias Indigenous, standing captive before you!'

'What!' cried the Chief rising from his throne and moving slowly and regally towards the captive as he recognized the voice. 'Indigenous?'

'Yes.'

'Jesus Christ of Nazareth!' shouted the Chief, rushing at Bassey and giving him a warm hug.

'Cut those ropes at once!' he ordered.

The short man for once forgot that he had a dagger, until the Chief gave him a smack and ordered him to use it to sever the rope.

'Indigenous, is this you?' The Chief ran his eyes over a man who counted among the wealthy men of Enugu, nay, of Biafra, and could not believe what he saw.

'This is what your friend has been reduced to,' Bassey replied. 'But I thank God and men like you that I am alive.'

It was his fluent Igbo which had saved Bassey. Had his captors known that he came from Annang Province they would have killed him straight away. Protracted boundary disputes had created so much bitterness between the border towns that each side jumped at the opportunity of claiming a head from the other side whenever one presented itself. Moreover the events around Ikot Ekpene had led to the belief on the Umuahia side of the border that the Annangs were enemy collaborators. If you gave them shelter you might be digging your own grave.

Bassey had insisted on being taken to the Chief without knowing who the chief was. He knew J.M.J. was a chief, but his mind had been too disorganized to think of J.M.J. and his chiefdom. He insisted on being taken to the Chief as his only hope of survival. The atmosphere around the Chief would be more relaxed, and the prospects of someone being able to identify him greater. Also a Chief would be less likely to authorize the kind of summary action advocated by the short man with the dagger.

Chief Iroanya regretted his car was not in good shape to take Mr Bassey to Aba where he wanted to stop over with his friends. However, he got in touch with the P.S.O.1* at the Tactical Headquarters a few miles off and a commandeered Peugeot was placed at his disposal.

Bassey woke up feeling as if every part of his body had been beaten to pulp with a mallet. The cumulative effect of the long trek, longer than he had ever undertaken even as a child, and the two nights on the hard floor in the fishing village and in the market stall, made it impossible for him to raise himself from the bed. It appeared nature had deliberately played down the pain and discomfort, waiting for him to arrive at his destination safely. His host, Ikem Onukaegbe, offered to give him hot water fomentation, but he needed to get up from the bed and this was absolutely impossible. It required pain-relieving tablets to get him out of the bed to tell his story.

'When misfortunes pile up like this,' continued Professor Ezenwa slamming the door of the car, 'you ask yourself what special crime you have committed.'

'That was precisely what Bassey was shouting hysterically when I unwittingly gave him the news I had picked up on the situation on the Ikot Ekpene front,' Onukaegbe said. He slammed his own door, inserted the key into the ignition, folded his hands over the steering wheel, and went on talking without starting the engine. ' "Oh my God!" he kept shouting. "My entire family wiped out! My business gone! My houses gone! What have I done? Was I the one who started the war?" '

'It was heart-rending.'

'Of course, you were there,' Onukaegbe recollected. 'I almost forgot that we all helped to hold him down to enable Dr Nwene to give him the injection. You know, I've wondered whether I should have told him about the car and so on at that time.'

'Why not?' Professor Ezenwa asked. 'He was bound to know about them in the end.'

'I know. But maybe I should have allowed him to recover from

* Principal Staff Officer 1.

his horrible experience first – the ordeal of escaping death by the skin of his teeth two times in two nights. He was picking up gradually, but it seemed my news came as the last straw . . .'

Two days after Bassey's arrival at Aba, Onukaegbe had travelled to Umuahia to see what information he could pick up on the situation at Ikot Ekpene. The authoritative Radio/TV Kaduna had already announced with fanfares the 'liberation by gallant Federal Forces' of the entire Efik, Ibibio and Annang areas, including Ikot Ekpene, reporting that the villagers had turned out in large numbers to welcome their liberators. Radio Biafra had emphatically denied the report, which gave Onukaegbe the hope that things might still improve. Radio Biafra did not tell outright lies. Rather it maintained dignified silence when a Nigerian claim was incontrovertible. Onukaegbe had gone to Umuahia in the hope that he could pick up bits and pieces from Mr Uko and the army boys. He hoped the news would be good, to expedite Bassey's recovery.

Unfortunately the news had been terrible. Bassey's car was reported to have been burnt and abandoned by the road. The driver had made a courageous attempt to turn the car round and escape when he found that he had driven into a trap, but a bullet got him just as he was speeding off. Bassey's mansion had been blown to smithereens. The Nigerians had intended to turn it into an Officers' Mess, but their inability to capture Bassey dead or alive had so infuriated them that they ordered the mansion and its compound walls to be mortared down to foundation level.

Neither Mr Uko nor any one else could give him any information on Nma and the children, except that many people had gone into hiding in the bush. The Biafran Government had conceded Ikot Ekpene to the enemy, and mines had already been laid across the road on the borders with Ikwuano County in Umuahia Province. Massive 'combing' exercises had been mounted all along the border to stop any infiltration.

Bassey had gone berserk at the news. He had failed in his duty as husband and father, he kept shouting. He was a deserter, deserting his family when they needed him most, all because he listened to advice from Mr Uko who had promptly evacuated even his most distant relations at the appropriate time. What was he alive for? He would take his life so as to join Nma and the children . . .

'I'd better keep my mouth shut over the fall of Port Harcourt.' Onukaegbe placed a finger on his lips as he spoke. 'To hear that he has also lost his supermarket and real estate in Port Harcourt would finish him off completely!'

'I'm sure we aren't the only people who see him,' remarked Professor Ezenwa. 'What guarantee is there that others won't go to sympathize with him about Port Harcourt?'

'We'd better go back to the ward and leave word that every visitor must be warned not to mention Port Harcourt to him,' suggested Onukaegbe, opening his door.

'Yes, let's go back . . .' Professor Ezenwa got out of the car. '. . . I wonder, though, whether it would not be best to mention the problem to Azinna and see what he thinks about it. Maybe he will consider it advisable to give Bassey the full works while he is still here under intensive care . . . I just hope this whole thing blows over soon, one way or the other. I'm sick of it.'

'It's terrible,' Onukaegbe replied. He knew Professor Ezenwa's feelings about the war and did not want to fan the embers. 'I'm hoping that something positive will come out of the current peace moves.'

'Peace moves my yash!' exploded Professor Ezenwa. 'How many so called "peace moves" have we had since this thing began? September last year – Organization of African Unity met in Kinshasa only to assure Nigeria of its support. An O.A.U. delegation went to Lagos in November. What did they achieve? They assured Nigeria of O.A.U. backing. The poor Pope tried to intervene in December, but with what luck? We've had delegates from the churches in the U.K. – that was two months ago. If I had had the opportunity to meet those delegates I would have advised them to go home and ask their home government to stop backing genocide. If Britain withdrew military and diplomatic support from Nigeria this war would be over in no time. What other peace moves have there been?'

'You forget the attempt by the Commonwealth Secretary-General in February . . .'

'There you are! He didn't even bother to come to Biafra.'

Onukaegbe went on: 'Actually what I was leading up to is that that was one channel which held out high hopes, especially after the preliminary talks between both sides early this month. For once the Nigerians were serious, largely because Tanzania had recognized us last month. And as you know, within days of that meeting Gabon recognized us. Then Ivory Coast. I had never been so optimistic! . . .'

'Then what happened?' interrupted the Professor. 'Nigeria pumped all they had into the war, to crush us before any more recognitions or peace talks. They made sure they took Port Harcourt before the so-called peace talks under the aegis of the Commonwealth Secretariat were to start in Kampala. And you think they are going there to talk peace with you?'

'The latest report that came in today says the peace talks ended in deadlock. The Nigerians became arrogant because they had captured our last air and sea link with the outside world, as well as the oil refinery. As far as they are concerned, the war is over!'

'I wish it were!'

15

'Somebody must have been responsible for it!' exclaimed Chief Ukadike. 'Somebody here in our midst. That person must have used his transmitter to tell the vandals where to drop the bomb. If I do not smoke that person out today and tomorrow, then I am not the Chairman of Obodo War Council!' The medals rattled as he smacked his chest.

Everyone at Obodo saw it as a callous, unprovoked and unprecedented slaughter of human beings. The Obodo War Council had joined Civil Defence Committees in other parts of Biafra in disseminating information on what to do in the event of an air raid. The few houses at Obodo roofed with corrugated iron or aluminium sheets had been camouflaged with palm fronds. Girls at Obodo had learnt to plait their hair in the 'take cover' style, yet nobody had seriously expected an air raid at Obodo. The nearest military camp was ten miles away, and that constituted the only thing that could be described as a military target in the vicinity. Obodo did not number among the towns and villages privileged to offer accommodation to State House, neither did it play host to any War Directorate or Ministry. The Nigerians were not, therefore, in a position to gain any military advantage by bombing or strafing it. Dr Kanu's major justification in requesting his wife, Fatima, and their surviving son to 'take cover' at Obodo was the safety of the town from enemy air raids. 'The Nigerians don't have the bombs or rockets to waste at Obodo,' he had written in one of his letters to Fatima.

It was about noon on a bright and peaceful June day. The Russian-built Ilyushin jet-bomber swooped down noiselessly,

Those who saw it as it descended at first thought it was one of the B-26 jets alleged to have been acquired by the Biafran Government, probably on a test flight. A white man was seen piloting it; some said they also saw an African sitting beside the pilot, pointing at the locations to be destroyed. One woman was prepared to swear by Amadioha that the African was the discredited Justus Chikwendu. If Justus had been killed by a firing squad as had been rumoured, then he must have been reincarnated in Lagos, the woman had asserted. The plane could not have been over them for more than a minute or two; when it sped away, it left behind a gruesome spectacle. It also left behind the sad reality that there was no escape from the Nigerian war planes, not even in the most remote and inconsequential village.

The bomb craters which generally characterized other Nigerian air raids and formed part of the topography of Enugu, Port Harcourt, Aba, Owerri, and Onitsha did not feature in the Obodo raid. Instead the harbinger of death left behind a circle of death, with a radius of no less than a hundred yards. No one could explain it. Some pointed at an iroko tree, the once majestic branches of which had been untidily split asunder as evidence that the demolition bomb exploded in mid-air after striking the tree, and thereafter opened its dragon's mouth towards the earth, spewing forth destruction as far afield as its fiery breath could reach. Some said it was a napalm bomb which burns everything with which it establishes contact.

The ingredients of the bomb were hardly relevant to the people of Obodo. What concerned them was the death and destruction the bomb inflicted. The top branches of the battered yet defiant-looking iroko tree retained their foliage, but that was because they stood just off the circumference of the circle of death. Every plant within the circle instantaneously went brown as life was burnt out of it; even a cluster of banana trees within the circle lost their boat-like leaves, and their juicy stems drooped like the discarded skins of moulting snakes. The earth on which the plants stood resembled a piece of land burnt for yam cultivation. And the mystery of it all was the absence of any flame. Or smoke!

Prophet James' thriving church was at one side of the circle and all that remained of it was the red laterite which previously constituted its walls. The thatched roof simply disappeared; nobody could say whether it had ascended into heaven with the prophet or had been burnt without leaving behind any ashes. It was impossible to identify the prophet's remains, or to tell from the ruins how many worshippers perished in the disaster. Bits of human flesh and fleshless bones were strewn over the entire area. Someone suggested throwing earth over the disaster area and turning it into one mass grave.

About sixty yards from the church, disaster struck a recently completed bungalow, wiping out an entire family – father, mother, and all the children except the eldest daughter who had gone to the parsonage to assist in making dry packs for soldiers. On the battered gate leading into the compound hung two photographs of the owner of the compound who had perished with his family. He was of medium height, in his thirties. In one photograph, he wore a Western suit, evidence of his debt to Western civilization; he was for many years a teacher. The second photograph must have been taken after he had given up the chalk and gone into business and local politics. In it he wore a voluminous damask *agbada*, black in the black-and-white photograph, but probably much more colourful in reality. He also wore a beaded, expensive chief's cap. He held high a double-barrelled shotgun which he had recently acquired at the time the photograph was taken, with the belt of cartridges hanging down from one hand instead of being fastened round the waist. He aimed the gun at the sky, as though he had a premonition that his death would come from that direction and was trying to offer some resistance. Most of the aluminium sheets used in roofing his house looked like crumpled tinfoil.

An old man dressed like a sunbather on the Riviera, with just enough towel-like material to cover the essentials, told the pathetic story of the unprecedented disaster. He lived in a mud-walled house located safely beyond the circumference of the circle of death, and had hidden beside some banana trees in front of his compound, straining his eyes to see the plane through the dense jungle. The man in the photograph would have escaped with his life. He was clearly outside the circle of death when he recognized the war plane and rushed back to his compound to ensure the safety of his family. The devastating bomb took care of them all, father, mother, and five children, smearing what was left of the battered gate with their blood and fragments of their flesh. A few yards off, the first son of the dead man's elder brother ran from his father's house into the death circle, to play the role of mother hen to his younger brother and sisters who had gone to play with their cousins. The bomb turned all four of them into minced meat.

The old man scratched his dry, ashy skin as he told the story of a man said to repair knives who was rolling his bicycle past, on his way to – who can now say? A refugee woman lodging with her son in a nearby house hailed him, saying she had a knife with a broken handle she wanted him to repair. The man parked his bicycle at the ill-fated gate and went to see the knife. The bomb shattered knife repairer, woman, child, bicycle and knife. The scrap which survived it all resembled a rare archaeological find rather than the bicycle that was parked only a few minutes prior to the disaster. The owner of the house was away at the time; he had gone to give his raffia palms the midday tap. His wife and two children were, however, caught by the deadly bomb, his wife chopping firewood at the back of the house. All three perished. All that remained to testify that life once existed there were the dilapidated mud walls, the burnt-out yam barn and the brownish, drooping, banana trees.

Two other houses were razed to the ground, all life inside them obliterated. A third house was partially destroyed. It stood on the periphery of the death circle. Three children who ran out of the house were smashed to death. Their mother who was breast-feeding her last child in the kitchen did not receive a scratch, neither did her baby; the circle of death just missed them. The half of the bungalow within the circle was completely smashed. Most of what remained of the cement-block walls gave the impression that a mischievous child had tried to turn the walls into a cassava grater by punching holes into them with sharp nails, except for the bits of reddish human flesh stuck here and there.

Such disaster had never befallen Obodo within living memory. It had not befallen any of its neighbours either. It was the kind of disaster that would have evoked a call for the highest degree of mass fasting by Prophet James, but the disaster had, as it were, deliberately silenced Prophet James. Even the Anglican parson who had the habit of attributing any inexplicable misfortune to man's sinful nature, found his theory inadequate for such an unprecedented degree of suffering. It was inconceivable that the sins of one generation alone could have evoked so much indignation from God.

'Somebody in our midst joined the evil spirits to kill our brethren and is now joining us humans to mourn our loss,' asserted Chief Ukadike. 'The Hausas could not have known about Prophet James and located his church merely by sniffing their palms. Somebody must have told them about the prophet and the efficacy of his prayers. Somebody must have told them that Prophet James was responsible for the miracle of Abagana, and used his transmitter to direct their Egyptian-piloted Russian jet-bomber to the spot.'

'Don't say that kind of thing,' chided an old woman who was passing by. 'How can a human being do such a thing? Of what profit is it to him?'

'Keep moving, woman!' Chief Ukadike retorted, his eyeballs bulging as they usually did when the Chief wanted to intimidate someone. 'What do you know that you should feel qualified to dismiss my words?'

'I go on my knees, my master,' apologized the woman without going on her knees. 'I was not dismissing your words. It's only that I cannot imagine what profit any sane person can derive from such an abominable act.'

'If you cannot imagine it, I will tell you. It is money. Money!' Chief Ukadike spoke disgustedly about money as if he would not touch it for anything.

'Money?' the woman asked, as if to her the idea was repulsive, 'this thing that termites lick as easily as a child would lick a plate?'

'That's right!'

'*Tufia!*' The woman exclaimed. 'We know that money is what the whole world is after, but would mere love of meat drive somebody to eat deer stricken with hernia? *Tufia!*'

'You talk as if you don't know our people. Some of our people will sell their mothers, fathers, and children if only that will fetch them money.'

'Let such people continue to make money that way . . .'

Chief Ukadike did not let the woman complete the sentence before he broke in: 'We shall not let whoever this person is make any more money in this way, at least not while I remain Chairman of Obodo War Council.' He smacked his medals, sticking his chest out like an uncapped Biafran soldier walking past a superior officer. 'It is all right to pick a few fruits from another man's palm tree without his permission; to do so with a basket is outright theft!'

The net gradually closed in on Mr Sandy, a refugee living at the Ugwu Centre refugee camp. The security Sub-Committee of the Obodo War Council had built up quite a dossier on him prior to the disastrous air raid. The Security Guard posted to the camp had filed several reports on him, indicating that he was a man to be watched closely. He spoke Igbo, Efik, Ibibio, Hausa and Yoruba, each of them fluently. He was extremely evasive if you tried to establish his home town or the origin of his un-Biafran name. No one could understand why he chose to live in the refugee camp; he drove a car and was evidently sufficiently well-off to rent accommodation for himself in a private home. He was hardly ever seen cooking in the camp. He took his rations of stockfish, formula 2,* *garri*, etcetera, raw; because he used sleeping mats to screen off the end of the school building in which his Vono bed and lounge chair were installed, no fellow refugee knew what he did with his rations. He generally drove off from the refugee camp early in the mornings and returned at night. The stringent rationing of petrol following the fall of Port Harcourt did not seem to have hit him in any way.

Every refugee in the camp believed Mr Sandy had a transmitter, even though nobody had any idea what a transmitter looked like. They alleged hearing sounds that were not the sounds o. a radio emanating from his room at night. The Security Guard claimed to have eavesdropped one night, at the invitation of the refugees. That night he thought he heard Mr Sandy playing back a highly suspicious recorded message. The War Council had promptly followed up the report of the Security Guard by rushing in the police to investigate. Nobody in the camp believed the police when they said they found nothing incriminating on him. The consensus was that the police had, as usual, succumbed to their lust for money.

This time the War Council went for the army rather than the police. Mr Sandy was whisked off minutes after he had alighted from his car, two nights after the air raid disaster. Chief Ukadike was transparently displeased with the Staff Sergeant who made the arrest for not subjecting Sandy to the firing squad in the grounds of the refugee camp. The Sergeant had instructions to shoot only if the suspect resisted arrest. Mr Sandy offered no resistance whatsoever. Moreover the Sergeant knew that instructions had been received from the D.H.Q. that no Biafran accused of being a saboteur or an enemy collaborator must be shot without trial.

'That murderer should thank his stars that he was living in a refugee camp with other foreigners,' grumbled Chief Ukadike loudly after Sandy had been stripped of his shirt and trousers, bound hand and foot and dumped into the waiting vehicle. 'If so many foreigners were not in our midst, we would have shown him how we took care of criminals in these parts!'

Two days after Sandy's arrest, the Directorate of Propaganda sent a high-ranking official to address a mass rally at the scene of the air raid disaster.

'The Government and entire people of Biafra grieve with you at

* Enriched cornflour distributed to refugees and other needy Biafrans.

the untimely loss of so many loved ones,' he had begun. It was on that account that the Head of State had sent him to Obodo, to mourn with the people. He urged the people to view the act of genocide in its wider context.

'. . . This is not the first time the vandals and their Anglo-Soviet-Arab collaborators have committed an act of genocide on the peace-loving people of Biafra. Some of you may have thought that our radio exaggerated the number and extent of such barbarous and genocidal acts. Today every man, woman and child in Obodo has seen the vandals in their true colours. What crime did the children killed in that raid commit?' he asked.

'None!' shouted his audience.

'What crime did the old women, old men, and other innocent people wiped out, commit?'

'None!'

'As for Prophet James, that holy man of God, that . . .' He was interrupted by the piercing cry of a woman in the audience who could no longer hold back her tears.

'What's that I hear?' asked the official disapprovingly. The woman instantly stopped.

'That's better!' he shouted. 'We don't cry in wartime! Those men, women, and children mercilessly massacred by the vandals are not asking you to cry for them. They don't want your tears. You know what they want? They want you to avenge their deaths, and you can only do so by pressing on with the war more vigorously than ever before. The jaw cannot go to rest when there are palm kernels yet uneaten. The vandals think they can conquer us by bombing our old men, women and children. Will they?'

'No!'

'They cannot. We will not allow them! History tells us that no war of survival has ever been lost. Will ours be different?'

'No!'

As he sat down, the Secretary of the War Council set the crowd singing:

> Armour'd-u car,
> Shelling machine,
> Fighter and bomber – Kpom!
> Ha enwegh ike imeri Biafra.
> Biafra win the war!
> Armour'd-u car,
> Shelling machine,
> Fighter and bomber – Kpom!
> Ha enwegh ike imeri Biafra . . .

The mass rally adopted four resolutions before it rose. It expressed unflinching loyalty to the Head of State and absolute confidence in his ability to pilot the ship of state through the present tempestuous seas. It denounced Britain, Russia, Algeria and 'all other visible and invisible partners in Nigeria's genocidal act' for the untimely death of over a hundred innocent civilians in the recent Obodo air raid, and called upon all men of conscience throughout the world to join in the denunciation. The third resolution urged the Queen of England, in her capacity as a mother, to bring pressure to bear on her arrogant Prime Minister so as to call a halt to the massacre of the innocents in Biafra. Finally, the rally pledged the determination of every Obodo man, woman and child to see the war through to a successful end, and their preparedness to continue to contribute to the war effort in men and materials.

16

'Luke,' Fatima called faintly, her housecoat wrapped round her as she emerged from a hot bath. A splitting headache warned her not to shout too loudly. Emeka, her son, abandoned his bowl of Quaker Oats to look for Luke, the army chauffeur.

'Luke! Mummy!' the little boy shouted, pointing towards the bedroom, before Edna, his baby nurse, grabbed him and whisked him back to the breakfast table.

Luke combined tucking in his shirt with rushing to answer Madam. By the time he arrived at the door of the master bedroom, his green army shirt was already tucked into the green trousers. He hoped Madam would not notice that the belt was missing.

'Luke here, Madam,' he announced, his arms stiffening by his sides and his chest nearly hitting the door.

'You and the orderly should get ready.' Fatima spoke with some effort; the headache made her uncomfortable. 'We're leaving for Umuahia in an hour's time.'

'Yes, Madam.' Luke stood to attention.

'Tell Edna to dress Emeka as soon as he's through with his breakfast, and to get ready herself to go with us.'

'Yes, Madam.'

'Tell Jude to prepare scrambled egg and Ovaltine for me.'

'Yes, Madam.'

When Luke suspected that Madam was through, he pulled himself up and enquired: 'Is that all, Madam?'

'Yes,' Fatima replied.

'Yes, Madam.' Luke stiffened, did an about-turn in military fashion, and walked away. As soon as Fatima heard the retreating steps, she flung her dressing gown on the bed and began to dress for breakfast and her first ever journey to Umuahia.

She had developed the idea while in the bath. She needed a change of environment if she was not to go mad; she needed the companionship which no one in Biafra except her husband could give her. The Obodo air raid disaster the day before had shattered her completely – nearly, if not as much, as she had been shattered by Ami Junior's death at Enugu several months back. Halima and her son had called at her feeding centre not quite two hours before the arrival of the harbinger of death. She had given Halima enough salt, formula 2, stockfish, beans, rice, milk and other relief materials to last her and her child one week. She had expressed great pleasure at the amazing progress Halima's child had made since she began to supply him with special high-protein foods. Although she had not mentioned it to Halima, she had hoped that at that rate the boy would be fit enough in a week or two to play the role of elder brother to Emeka. Halima had been unable to restrain her joy at Fatima's invitation to join her in running the feeding centre. It had made her feel so light at heart, the thought that she would be able to repay at least part of the tremendous help she had received from Fatima. Moreover a full-time job would sweep away the evils of idleness. But for the social barrier which she knew existed between the two of them, Halima would have hugged Fatima.

That was barely two hours before the vampire swooped down. Fatima simply could not believe that Halima and her son were no more. She could see them so clearly in her mind's eye, very much flesh and blood, yet the evidence had been unmistakeable. The tribal marks identified one of the few skulls not completely smashed as Halima's. Nobody knew what took her and her child towards the scene of death. She had often referred derogatorily to Prophet James for making passes at her, so she could not have gone to worship at his church. It was Fate, pure and simple.

Fatima had been too dazed to shed tears when Chief Ukadike broke the news of the death of Halima and her son. It was like the feeling you have when you sustain a serious injury; it takes time for the pain to register, but when it does it is unbearable. Halima's death meant more than the loss of a kinswoman, a sister she had discovered in a foreign land. It rammed home to Fatima an ugly reality which the death of Ami Junior at Enugu had underlined – the utter stupidity of the Nigeria-Biafra war. A war said to be waged against rebels, it was in fact no more than the cold-blooded slaughter of innocents. Ami Junior was no rebel. Halima, her son and all others massacred at the Obodo air raid were no more than statistical data on a population census chart; none of them contributed to the decision to separate Biafra from Nigeria, and none was in a position to influence the course of the war. Their massacre made no sense.

The irony of it was that Halima, and her son Ami Junior, symbolized the united Nigeria which the Nigerians claimed as their motive for waging the war. Yet they were among the innocents massacred by these same Nigerians. Halima had also symbolized the best in a wife and mother. What a shocking end to such an exemplary character!

Fatima's nightmare that night showed how insecure she felt as a result of the raid. What if the dragon had directed its fiery breath towards her house? She and her son would have been dead before they could reach the entrance to their bunker. It had been blood-curdling, that nightmare. A jet fighter had been sent specifically to kill her. She could see the white mercenary who piloted it. By his side sat Aliyu, her erstwhile suitor. Aliyu had felt hurt by Fatima's decision to marry Dr Amilo Kanu. So did Fatima's parents. Aliyu came from a good family, had a fair chance of passing the conjoint examinations at the second shot and qualifying as a doctor. Aliyu and Fatima belonged not only to the same ethnic group but also to the same Emirate. Aliyu felt hurt that another man, a *nyamili* at that, could snatch his girl from him. He had threatened to shave off his hair, to fail his conjoint examinations, and finally, to gas himself if Fatima went ahead and married Dr Kanu. Fatima had done just that. Aliyu shaved off his hair, failed his examinations, and –

'I decided it was stupid to kill myself because of you,' Aliyu shouted to her from the jet bomber. He bared his teeth at intervals, and this made him look horrible, like the head of a goat after it has been roasted in the fire. 'Instead of eliminating myself and giving you and that bastard full rein to enjoy your ill-fated marriage, I decided on something much more sensible – to eliminate you, your so-called husband, and your children. So I joined the army. I lobbed the shell that took care of your first son . . .'

'O God!' Fatima shouted at that point, ran out from under her bed and into her concrete bunker, tightly clutching her little son, Emeka, as if to resist any malicious attempt to eliminate him too.

'You're wasting your time running into that bunker,' Aliyu shouted through the loudspeaker, sweat dripping down his face into his Air Force uniform. Fatima could hear him gnash his teeth, something he never did in their years of association. 'We have a special bunker demolition bomb here, so you're no safer there than you were under the bed.' Aliyu gave a dry, ghost-like laugh as Fatima rushed out of the bunker, hugging Emeka to her more tightly than ever.

As she ran across the lawn, sweating profusely and with no particular destination in mind, the loudspeaker shouted her to an abrupt halt. 'We don't have all day to waste here. We still have to get to Umuahia to eliminate that *nyamili* who says he's your husband. We've covered him for some weeks and know where to get him any minute of the day or night. My mission is to wipe . . . all . . . of . . . you . . . out!' Aliyu dragged out that bit for greater effect.

'Unless! . . .'

Fatima jumped at the first ray of hope.

'Unless you drop that bastard in your arms, renounce everything *nyamili* and return with me to Nigeria right away.'

'No! I won't!' shouted Fatima.

'Then here we go!' Before Aliyu reached the end of his sentence the jet bomber dived and opened fire, spewing forth bullets and rockets in the way a sprayer spews forth insecticide.

'Save me! Jesus Christ save me! Save me! . . .' Fatima sprawled in a pool of blood, clutching Emeka and shouting.

'Madam! Madam!' called Luke and the orderly, pounding on the door to the master bedroom where Fatima slept. 'Madam! Madam!'

Fatima had suddenly stopped shouting. She gradually regained control of her senses, realized that she had come through a nightmare, and dismissed her frightened staff before rising from the carpet onto which she had fallen from her bed.

The nightmare and Halima's death were too much for Fatima. The dose of tranquillizer which she took after rising from the floor had been of little help. The trip to Umuahia would be the most effective tranquillizer. From the very moment she issued the orders to Luke to get ready, life began to return to her.

'Mummy, look!' Emeka shouted, pointing at each approaching

vehicle. 'Zoom!' he cried as the vehicle shot past. He would then spin round on the middle seat where he stood beside his mother, to follow the vehicle until it disappeared behind one of the innumerable bends on the road, or until Edna, his nurse, (who sat on the collapsible third row seat of the station wagon) drew his attention to an approaching vehicle in front.

'Mummy, look! . . . Zoom!'

The drive buoyed up Fatima's spirits. The cool, refreshing midday breeze seemed to go right inside her and to resuscitate her. On the advice of the orderly, they had decided to take the earth road to Umuahia rather than the tarmac. Experience had shown that the Nigerian war planes used the tarmac to get their bearings, thereby making those roads much more vulnerable than the innumerable earth roads with which the enemy pilots were not familiar. The road they chose was well wooded on both sides, providing natural cover for the car as it sped through. The potholes were many, but the station wagon appeared to have been built to withstand them.

'I didn't know there was still so much of Biafra left . . .' The fall of Enugu had seemed the end for Fatima, coupled as it was with the loss of her first son. Since then she had been confined to Obodo, never travelling beyond Ndikelionwu – less than ten miles away – to collect drugs and relief materials from the provincial representatives of Caritas Internationalis and the World Council of Churches for her feeding centre. Radio accounts of the war, particularly the BBC and Radio Nigeria accounts of final pushes and 'final final' pushes, had made her feel that virtually the whole of Biafra had been overrun. Her husband had painted such a terrifying picture of the situation that she had expected Nigerian ambushes dotting the entire road to Umuahia. It was a pleasant surprise not to find any signs of military activity on the way. Men, women and children moved about unconcerned, as if the war were being fought in a foreign land. The numerous checkpoints along the road, each preceded by giant road bumps which ruined many silencers, were the only visible reminders that the country was at war.

Fatima began to see how bottled up she had been at Obodo, cut off from civilization and from her equals. Thank goodness Emeka was still too young to go to school; she could not have allowed him to mix with those urchins in the village. Her husband had surprisingly done nothing about her request to install a telephone in the house, so she could not even telephone any of her friends. It had been a total blockade! The death of Halima plugged any loopholes. She and her parents-in-law were now getting on quite well, but language was still a serious barrier. Chief Ukadike breezed in from time to time, but she soon came to the conclusion that the man's concern was only with what he could get out of her. In any case there was little in common between them except that the misfortunes of war brought them together in a small village.

The clouds did, however, have a silver lining. Her months at Obodo had proved rewarding, thanks to her first meeting with Halima which had transformed her so much. Her feeding centre had, within a relatively short time, turned out to be an indispensable humanitarian venture. It appeared to have been established in the nick of time, when the protein deficiency disease, kwashiorkor, exhibited its first signs at Obodo. Her centre had saved many children. The mere fact that she was the wife of the Director of Mobilization had been a tremendous help with the relief agencies: they stocked her centre more than adequately with high-protein foods and all other requirements. The World Council of Churches also sent a medical officer to the centre once every week to see the more serious cases.

As the car steadily reduced the distance between Obodo and Umuahia, it struck Fatima that she had made no arrangements for the running of the centre while she was away, nor had she notified the medical officer. 'Just too bad . . . Things are bound to sort themselves out. In any case I won't be away for long. The children won't die before I return, not with the goat scheme in progress . . .'

Fatima smiled with satisfaction as her thoughts flashed back to the goat scheme. At the time the idea occurred to her, she doubted whether the people of Obodo would buy it. Surprisingly they did, and before she knew what was happening, two neighbouring villages had launched similar schemes. The scheme aimed at making animal protein available to children in the village in spite of the prohibitive prices that kept meat outside the diet of most villagers. The idea was that the village should contribute money to buy one or more goats. Once the goat had been slaughtered, the meat would be sold, and the entrails used to prepare a protein-rich soup for the children to drink. The money realized from the sale of the goat meat would become the capital for the purchase of another goat, and so the scheme continued.

The car slowly climbed over a bump, consisting of the trunk of a palm tree. A few yards later, a police corporal with a rifle slung behind him signalled the car to a stop.

"tate house,' said Emeka rather timidly, as the policeman bent down to check the vehicle.

'State House,' announced the orderly, almost condescendingly as if to warn the police corporal not to waste any further time. The policeman immediately withdrew his head, gave Madam the salute, and ordered his civilian assistant to remove the barrier. The car scaled two more trunks and gradually picked up speed again.

'Idiotic Civil Defenders! If I have any more of their foolish questions . . . !' Fatima pulled off her cardigan, as if to bask more fully in the sunshine of greatness whose rays fanned out towards her.

'How many more miles to Umuahia?' she enquired.

'About ten, Madam,' Geoffrey, the orderly, replied. 'Then we do five miles to Agricultural Research, Umudike, where Doctor lives.'

'We're almost there, then,' Fatima said, straightening herself and feeling the back of her blouse to see if it was wet.

The car had not done another mile before a man riding towards them on a bicycle suddenly jumped off his machine, abandoned it on the road and made for the bush. A pedestrian pointed to the sky as he made for a nearby farm.

'Stop, Luke!' cried the orderly. 'Enemy plane!'

'What?' exclaimed Fatima, panic-stricken.

'Enemy plane, Madam!' replied the orderly, though a reply was unnecessary. Even the vagrant chickens by the roadside knew something dangerous was overhead.

Fatima threw Emeka out of the door held open by the brave orderly and followed him at once. The nerve-racking sound of the jet planes was now unmistakeable.

'Look at them,' shouted the driver who just managed to turn the ignition off before darting into the bush, leaving his door wide open. 'There are two!' Fatima glanced in the direction from which the sound came, saw two jet fighters making for her, held tight to Emeka with both hands and made for the cocoa jungle without caring what lay on her path. Her high-heeled shoes slowed her down as she ran and she discarded them. By now the planes were overhead. She shut her eyes tight and prayed to God for her son and her life. The planes flew past without incident.

'Thank God!' she muttered rising.

'They are turning, Madam!' cautioned the orderly. 'They will come back!'

Fatima promptly went down again. Then she decided she and

her son were not safe where they were. She saw a big gutter several yards ahead of them and decided to make a dash for it. Her ankle-length, wrap-round skirt proved a nuisance. She forgot the price tag on it, held it by the slit on the right side and tore it as far as the knees. Thus liberated, she ran as fast as she could in the closely planted cocoa jungle. By the time she reached the wide gutter, she was too exhausted to think.

'They're coming again!' shouted the orderly from his hideout.

Although Fatima could not see the planes from where she was the crescendo in the sound above meant that the rams were ready to charge. She went down on her knees and elbows, shielding Emeka who clung to her chest. Her heart pounded as the planes approached.

'O God!' she groaned as the rockets, cannon balls, bullets or whatever they were began to fly. For a moment her heart was too frightened to beat. A palm tree which towered above the cocoa trees crashed down, cut in two. Soon the sounds disappeared in the distance. The planes had completed their death mission for the day. The chickens began to emerge from their shelters.

Fatima slumped in the gutter, dejected and confused, with Emeka clinging to her chest. A hole in the ground a few yards away showed that one of the shots must have missed her narrowly. Undoubtedly if she had been standing at the time it would have passed through her. Who knows whether that might not have been the best thing for her, she wondered. How much longer could she put up with this kind of life, living in holes and crawling in forests like a rabbit!

'Ready to go, Madam!' The orderly used his shoulder to hold back a cocoa branch while he gave the salute.

As Fatima rose she became aware of the mess in which she had knelt and sat. No offer, however high, could have made her set foot there under normal circumstances. Her skirt was wet and brown at the seat and knees. Her blouse was also wet and brown. Her feet resembled those of a farmer making yam mounds in the swamps. She had never looked so dirty and dishevelled in all her life – and only minutes before she had been going to spring a pleasant surprise on her husband!

'See what went through our car?'

The orderly handed over to Fatima a heavy lump of lead, as big as the palm of a hand but several times its weight. The edges were ragged and sharp enough to cut through human flesh, metal or rock. The giant piece of shrapnel was still warm, even though minutes had elapsed since it broke away from its rocket casing.

Fatima momentarily forgot her pig-sty appearance and her ripped skirt when she saw the car from which she had fled minutes before. The front windscreen had disintegrated and shed pieces of glass all over the front seat and car floor. The shrapnel had gone through it to pierce the seat, which was normally occupied by the orderly. It had cut neatly through the upper part of the seat, penetrated the middle of Fatima's seat and the bottom of the rear seat, finally bursting out from the rear of the car on the left side of the number plate. Fatima felt as though a plane in which she was flying had suddenly found itself in an air pocket. Her heart jumped out of her mouth as the thought came to her that she, the orderly and possibly Edna would have been dead if only they had remained one minute longer in the car.

'Can it move?' she enquired, after her heart had returned to her.

'Yes, Madam,' Luke replied, shutting the bonnet which he had opened to check on the engine.

'We're lucky it did not hit the fuel tank,' added the orderly.

'Move, Luke, before all these urchins begin to gather here,' Fatima instructed.

She covered her face with her special camouflage sun glasses as soon as the car moved, anxious to avoid running into any friend in her present state. Fortunately Umuahia township was a ghost town following the air raid. The market and the streets were deserted; the banks, War Directorates and government offices had shut for the day as was usual immediately after an air raid. Most people had left either before or immediately after the air raid for their hideouts on the wooded outskirts of the township. They normally went home from there; only a handful of workers returned to their offices after a major raid.

'I hope you're not taking me to master's office?' Fatima enquired as she saw the trafficator blink repeatedly.

'No, Madam,' Luke replied without disclosing much.

'Is that the way to the house?'

'No, Madam.'

'Then why are you going there?'

'I want the P.W.D. engineer to check some trouble in the car . . .'

'Take me straight to the house first!'

Luke did not think it was fair to take Madam to the house without alerting Master. The idea had, therefore, occurred to him to swing into the Ministry of Works garage, get a mechanic to fidget with the engine while he telephoned the house to announce

Madam's arrival. Just in case . . . However he did not need a psychologist to tell him that Madam was not in the mood for trifles. He switched off the trafficator, negotiated the Queen Elizabeth Hospital roundabout and made for Umudike.

17

'Oh, this car!' Luke sounded completely disgusted. 'Why must it give trouble again when we have almost reached the house?'

He swung the car a little recklessly through Gate Zero, brought it under one of the few trees on the laterite road linking Gate Zero with Gate Two, and then allowed it to stall to a stop With uncharacteristic agility he swung the bonnet open and was seen studying the heated engine as if he had graduated from a Peugeot factory.

'Let me go and see if Moses is in so that he will bring Doctor's car to pick up Madam,' announced Geoffrey as he trotted away from the car.

Luke had hit on the idea after Madam had thwarted the plan to phone the house from the Ministry of Works, and he had taken Geoffrey into his confidence without rousing Madam's suspicion. It was natural for a man to take advantage of his wife's absence, and Doctor would be abnormal if he did not do so. Moreover he was the kind of married man for whose love girls were prepared to trade blows. It was therefore unfair to land his wife on him without notice. Luke was to declare the car dead a Gate Zero. Before Madam could put two and two together, Geoffrey was to take the shortest cut to the house and give notice of Madam's arrival. Luke would decide how best to handle the situation from then on.

Geoffrey was panting when he arrived at Dr Kanu's bungalow. Doctor's official maroon-coloured Mercedes stood majestically in the garage. Geoffrey went first to the boys' quarters to find his own level.

'Hannibal the Ogbunigwe!' shouted the long-whiskered Sergeant who served as Dr Kanu's bodyguard, surprised that Geoffrey should materialize from nowhere. Geoffrey gave a stiff salute. Having paid that obligatory military respect to a superior in rank, he decided to get on with his mission post-haste.

'How you come like this without warning?' continued the

Sergeant. 'Any better for that place?'

Geoffrey drew closer to the Sergeant and asked in a hushed voice whether Doctor was in.

'Yes,' replied the Sergeant.

'With a woman?'

'Why do you ask that kind of question?' The Sergeant was visibly puzzled and on the point of getting irritated. 'Did that Hausa woman send you to spy on Doctor?'

'Madam is at Gate Zero now.'

'*Nmagwu Okoro!*' exclaimed the Sergeant. 'And Doctor has just gone in with one first class baby he picked up recently! Darkness has descended in broad daylight!'

A quick conference. Agreement reached on the procedure to be followed. No time to draw Doctor's driver and cook into the full picture. Neither was it necessary. Something had to be done at once. Every second was precious.

'Who the hell is that?' Dr Kanu shouted angrily as the knock on his bedroom door, which he had initially ignored, went on persistently and impatiently.

'Sergeant, sep!' The Doctor could hear the thud of the Sergeant's foot as he came to attention barefoot and stiffened on the other side of the door.

'Are you mad to knock on my door like that?'

'Madam at Gate Zero, sep!'

'What?' bellowed Dr Kanu, jumping away from the bed.

'Luke pretend car spoil for Gate Zero, sep! Send Geoffrey with signal, sep!'

'Oh no!' shouted Dr Kanu, making for the giant towel rack on which he had flung his clothing.

'Is it a plane?' enquired Love anxiously, sitting up on the bed, a nude model any artist would pay a fortune for.

'My wife, and she's at Gate Zero!'

'I'm dead O! They've killed me O! *Ewo!*' Love behaved like a lunatic. The thought of a woman's talons cutting her face and flesh to pieces chilled her bones. And then the scandal to follow. How could she appear in public after that? Why must ill luck dog her steps always? In no time she was crying loudly, the tears blinding her as she wandered from dressing table to wardrobe to towel rack to bed, without accomplishing much.

'Where's my pantie?'

'It's here,' Dr Kanu replied, sounding more relaxed than he actually was. This was a totally new experience for him, and he was struggling to keep his head above water. He needed all his wits if he was to emerge unscathed from this imbroglio.

'Where's my bra?'

'Everything is here. And, please, Love, take it easy. I'm sorry about the mess . . .'

'Oh! It's not fair! To bring me here to be disgraced by your wife! Oh, I'm dead! . . .'

'Come on, Love. Dress up immediately. I'll get you out of it without difficulty, but you must stop shouting.'

Dr Kanu's firm tone, his assurance that he would save her from the approaching avalanche, brought Love a ray of hope. She was in her third year in the secondary school when the war broke out. She had celebrated her seventeenth birthday only the week before, and Dr Kanu was the first man she had ever known in her life. The only man. Their attachment was barely a month old. She had come to see her brother who worked in his Directorate. The brother had introduced her to him, in the hope that he would help her to get some employment. She had all he longed for in a girl. Beauty – if only for the psychological satisfaction it gives. Sophistication – enough to assure him that he was not descending below his social status. Youth. He had remembered the famous words of the greatest living authority on sex in Biafra: 'Take a teenager to bed, and you wake up feeling brisk!' To crown it all, the girl went by the name Love. The most intriguing and tantalizing name he had ever associated with a girl.

Dr Kanu had cast his bread upon the waters by inviting Love to his house. She accepted, to the Doctor's surprise. She had been fed up with a life of *garri*-grating in her village, and was prepared to visit any Director who could get her a job in Umuahia.

Dr Kanu had not only secured her employment as a clerk in a Directorate headed by a friend, but had also turned out to be a wonderful man. And his house offered such comfort at a time of mass deprivation. The difference between the Director's house and Love's brother's room on Agulu Street was as pronounced as the difference between life at an oasis and life on a dry and dusty desert. Love did not therefore require excessive persuasion to accept another invitation.

The birthday party had been organized at Dr Kanu's suggestion and insistence. He paid all costs as well, including the purchase of a £16 jar of Mompo wine and a goat. Love found such acts of kindness incomprehensible. She readily agreed to spend the night with him. The rate at which men were making passes at her, her virginity was unlikely to last many months more unless she returned to her village. If it must be broken some day she could not imagine anyone better qualified than Dr Kanu – so hand-some, so pleasant, so rich, so generous, and, above all, a medical doctor who could take care of any complications.

The idea to take her home that fateful day had come to Dr Kanu when he saw her at the Ikot Ekpene Road roundabout on his way to Umudike shortly after the air raid earlier on. At the time he made the proposal to her, it had sounded an excellent idea for brightening up a day that had been clouded by the visit of the dreaded enemy planes. Little did either of them imagine that a more ominous cloud was looming up, waiting to descend upon them just when they were about to forget that they were still part of a war-torn Biafra.

'Sergeant!' called Dr Kanu.

'Yessup!'

'Tell the driver to get the car out of the garage at once. He will drive this Madam to town. He should go through Gate Eight and take the Olokoro road. No waste of time.'

'Yessup.'

The Sergeant stopped dead between the house and the boys' quarters as if he had been struck by lightning. But he was quick in regaining control of his reflexes. He returned to the house without giving the impression that he was running. This time he did not wait for Doctor to ask who knocked.

'The other Madam is here, sep!' he whispered loudly.

The long-whiskered Sergeant panted and perspired as if he were in Dr Kanu's shoes.

'O my God!' shouted Love. 'I'm dead O! I'm . . .'

Dr Kanu gave her a smack. 'Shut up!' He sealed his mouth with a finger, as if he were addressing his little child. Love obeyed spontaneously, still struggling to hook her bra. She presented the picture of an actress miming the age-old maxim 'More haste less speed'.

'Take all your things into the next room. Dress quickly and stay quietly in there until I tell you what to do next. Right?'

'Yes, sir.'

Dr Kanu made a hurried survey of the room to ensure that no clues remained. A glance at the mirror, which revealed only a guilty countenance. He wiped it, wrapped the key to the guest room in his handerchief and put on the bold face which he needed to receive his wife. The sound of footsteps in the living room warned him that he had little time to spare. As he emerged from the master bedroom Fatima was already in the corridor into which all three bedroom doors opened. An excited Emeka ran towards him. By the time his father had thrown him into the air and caught him three times, happiness was written all over him.

'You're getting too big for Daddy, now, aren't you? Mummy must be looking after you very well. My! What happened to you? Did you have to take cover on the way?'

Fatima seemed more concerned with trying every door on her way than with extending any courtesies to her husband. The first bedroom had a bed, a writing desk and three chairs.

'I use that as my study,' said Dr Kanu cautiously.

Fatima did not show any sign of realizing that the information was intended for her. She peered into the two giant-size wardrobes and under the bed before banging the door behind her as if she had forgotten that Amilo and Emeka were in the room.

'That doesn't sound a warm homecoming,' Dr Kanu protested, opening the door and carrying Emeka into the corridor. Fatima was already inspecting the guest bathroom.

'I'm not concerned yet about warm homecomings,' Fatima replied curtly. 'Please open this room.'

'What's all this in aid of?' Dr Kanu asked, sounding irritated. 'Won't you sit down first and relax before . . .'

'I'll sit down when I want, and please be informed that I haven't come here to be ordered around.' Fatima could not have sounded more aggressive. Dr Kanu knew why she was angry, but it was in his best interest to feign ignorance and righteous indignation.

She continued, walking into the master bedroom: 'I want that door opened before the stuff comes out of that lousy car.'

She paused briefly by the bed as if the creases on the sheets and pillow slip could admit her into their secrets. She flipped the pillow round. Dr Kanu's heart skipped a beat, though he pretended not to be watching her. She pulled out a few drawers here and there, looked into the built-in wardrobes, and inspected the bathroom before shouting to the steward to make up the second bed in the master bedroom. Dr Kanu felt as much relief as if word had just reached him that Love had taken a magic carpet home. He thanked his stars that it had occurred to him to bundle Love into the guest room.

'The water heater is on,' he ventured to pilot Fatima away.

'So I see. Thank you.'

Dr Kanu was pleased to note some welcome thawing in her attitude, and decided to press his advantage.

'But why don't we first mark your arrival with a Dubonnet on the rocks? Then you can tell me why your clothes look so filthy.'

That was as sure a way of catching Fatima as any you could name. She hesitated as a fish hesitates before going for its bait.

'Not after the shabby treatment you've just given me.' Her voice sounded coquettish.

'What shabby treatment?' Dr Kanu spoke as if he had just heard a most outrageously false allegation.

'I didn't believe you could leave me stranded less than a mile from your house. If you felt too grand to collect your wife and son, at least you could have sent the driver. You did neither.'

'I don't know what you're talking about, darling.' He sounded convincing.

Fatima sat on the unused bed and faced him for the first time since she arrived: 'Didn't Geoffrey tell you anything?'

'Geoffrey?'

'Yes. I sent him to tell you that we had a breakdown at . . .'

'Geoffrey!' shouted Amilo without waiting for Fatima to end her sentence. He could not contain his anger.

'Yessup!'

'Come here at once.'

'Yessup!'

'Had you any message for me from Madam?'

Geoffrey stood at attention, his uniform soiled at the cocoa plantation but starchy and stiff all the same. 'I knocked on the door, sep, but Doctor was sleeping, sep. So I waited for Doctor to wake, sep. Then I saw Madam approaching.' He gave the salute, to announce that he was done.

'All of you are numbskulls,' Fatima said with disgust. 'If Doctor was asleep, it did not occur to you that you should ask the driver to come for us?'

'The key was in Doctor's bedroom, Madam.'

'OK, Geoffrey. That will do. Go with Moses now and make sure that both cars and all Madam's belongings reach here in five minutes.'

'Yessup!'

Geoffrey gave the fly-catching salute and withdrew, wondering what tip to expect from his master for covering him up so effectively.

'Now that you see you've condemned me before giving me a hearing, may we go to the living room for the Dubonnet on the rocks?'

'Don't I look too filthy for your living room?'

'It's just you and me, darling.'

Fatima yielded. 'I'm glad your failure wasn't deliberate,' she said, approaching him.

'How could it have been deliberate?'

She offered her lips. He planted a noisy kiss on them. Emeka covered his face shyly and shouted: 'Mummy!'

Fatima kissed the lips he offered. He then swung round to Daddy who also kissed them.

'It's a pleasure to be with my darling husband after I've been through so much.' Fatima leaned on Dr Kanu as they retired to the living room.

'So you treat yourself to Dubonnet here while you condemn me to that flat Mompo wine at Obodo?' asked Fatima while Amilo poured the drinks in his spacious kitchen.

'Wait first till you drink it.'

'Sure this is Dubonnet?' asked Fatima after they had knocked glasses and she had taken her first sip.

'Mompo in a Dubonnet bottle,' announced Dr Kanu. 'That's the nearest I can get to Dubonnet.'

'Tastes more delicious than my Mompo. Almost like real Dubonnet on the rocks.'

'Because it comes from me, you mustn't forget.'

'Of course. I nearly forgot.'

'Mummy, look. Balloon!' Emeka rushed towards Fatima, trying without much luck to inflate his 'balloon'. Amilo suspected nothing until Emeka broke into the living room, holding up a Durex condom. Amilo snatched it away so ferociously that the frightened child burst into tears. Fatima had seen it, and the sight resuscitated the tigress in her.

'Amilo!'

Husband and wife stood looking at each other, Emeka clinging to his mother and crying.

'I want the key to that room!'

Fatima's tone warned Dr Kanu that the game was up. But he would not give up. No, not voluntarily. It was not fair to Love. She had come at his invitation and he had to protect her. Neither was it fair to Fatima. Nor to him. His mind worked fast, in quest of words which could still avert the impending catastrophe. If only he could explain away that condom, and keep that door under lock and key until Fatima went in for her bath, he might yet save everyone embarrassment and preserve his family.

Fatima was quicker than he was. She stormed to the contro-versial door and shook it as if she would tear it open.

'Whoever is in there, you had better open this door yourself before I break it open!' She sounded as though she meant every word of that threat.

'Don't make a fool of yourself, darling. I'm sure this isn't . . .'

Fatima was more concerned with the lady she believed was inside the room than with her husband's jabbering. 'This is my last warning to you to open that door,' she shouted threateningly. 'If you don't want to be handed over to the army . . .'

Smash went the glass louvre windows on the opposite side of the room, facing the well-kept lawn and flower garden. Smash again! Then a sound like that of a medium-sized breadfruit falling on wet ground.

'Are you running away, coward? Eh? Are you running away?'

Fatima nearly tripped over Emeka as she rushed out like a mad woman, determined to catch the girl who had come to snatch her husband from her before her very eyes. Dr Kanu opened the door just in time to see Love leap over a hedge and into an experimental farm. The young girl's courage, her presence of mind, endeared her to him. The bloodstain on some pieces of broken glass meant that she must have shattered the louvres with her bare fists. She held her shoes in one hand as she ran, yet she ran as if it made no difference to her where her bare feet landed. She held a small bundle to her body with the other arm – undoubtedly her wig, wrapped in a scarf, and her handbag. She could not have run faster, even if she had been pursued by a doped Nigerian soldier intent on a rape. Yet she retained her graceful appearance.

'Maybe she should have been a little more patient and waited . . .' Dr Kanu soliloquized. 'Maybe I could have manoeuvred Fatima into the bath and all might have ended well . . . but can I really blame the poor lamb? How could she anticipate what I could do to save her? She had been patient all along . . . until Emeka unwittingly laid hands on that thing and Fatima decided to behave so primitively. No . . . she probably did the best thing . . . At least Fatima will never know who she was . . . nobody need ever know. Saved the poor lamb tremendous humiliation. That thing . . . Why on earth did I forget to dispose of it? Throw it into the toilet, or something . . .'

'Geoffrey!' Fatima shouted midway down the garden. 'Bring a rifle and shoot down that bitch! Geoffrey!'

She had stopped running, acknowledging that the bird had flown. From where she stood she poured all the invective she could muster at the retreating figure, as though invective would scorch the bitch to instant death. Then the idea of mowing her down with a rifle seized her. When she received no reply from

Geoffrey, she rushed back into the house to find the rifle herself before the figure disappeared completely.

'Enough of that!' Dr Kanu grabbed her firmly by both hands.

'Leave me alone, you male prostitute.'

When he did not, and she could not wriggle free, she bent low to bite her way through. Dr Kanu took advantage of his training in karate and led her without any effective resistance to the master-bedroom.

'Ouch! Not on that polluted bed!' Amilo led her to the unused bed.

'You stay quiet there,' he instructed her. 'I am not going to have you damage my reputation for nothing, just because you frightened an innocent girl into nearly committing suicide. If you have no respect for yourself, you must bear in mind that I have an image to protect. Thank goodness the recent air raid has sent most householders around here and their families into their hideouts. I don't know how I could have stood by to watch you make such a public fool of yourself – without checking your facts.'

He paused, ostensibly to cool down, but more to watch Fatima's reaction. She probably saw that she was powerless before Amilo – physically at least. Probably she was wondering whether she should go crazy over Amilo's sexual relationships with a bitch who lacked the guts to confront her.

A car pulled in. Amilo, convinced that he had stilled the tempest – at least temporarily – moved to the living room.

'Mummy, our car!' Emeka shouted, running in. He had forgotten all about the trouble he had unwittingly precipitated.

'Call Edna,' Fatima told him.

The little boy ran off, returning soon with Edna, his nurse.

'Edna.'

'Madam.'

'Clean up the bedroom next to the sitting room – that is, the last bedroom from here. That's where Emeka and I will sleep tonight. Tell Luke and Geoffrey to move this bed into that room as soon as I have my bath. You make some *okro* soup quickly so that Emeka and I can eat some *eba*. You understand?'

'Yes, Madam.'

Fatima could not believe her eyes when, on stirring and opening her eyes she found her room bright as day. Her watch registered 8 o'clock. Was it 8 in the night or 8 in the morning? It could not be so bright everywhere at night, not even with the brightest fluorescent lights. Edna gave her a 'Good morning, Madam.' So it was morning. She could not remember when she fell asleep, but it could not have been later than 6 p.m. She had decided to lie down so as to avoid all callers. She had put off taking her tranquillizer until later to ensure that she was not kept awake in the small hours of the night when it was hell to stay awake. She had slept without the tranquillizer, and slept more soundly than Emeka. She had slept for at least fourteen hours in spite of everything!

18

'Man! I've had it!' Dr Amilo Kanu shook his head as he took Mr Ndubuisi Akwaelumo's outstretched hand. 'I'm in the soup!'

'What's the matter?' asked Akwaelumo, waving Dr Kanu to one of the three lounge chairs in his office.

'Let's get out of here or we'll be constantly interrupted by contractors.'

'You make me extra curious! Give me a minute.' Mr Akwaelumo nipped over to his deputy to tell him that he was going out with Dr Kanu but would be back in time for the meeting at 10.30 a.m. with the heads of divisions in the Directorate.

The two friends drove to Dr Chidi's house at Queen Elizabeth Hospital. Dr Chidi was busy at the hospital, with an unusually large number of serious casualties from the Port Harcourt front.

'Fatima arrived yesterday,' began Dr Kanu hardly waiting to be seated.

'What!' cried Akwa. 'You didn't say she was coming, and yet we saw each other after the air raid.'

'I had no idea that she was arriving.'

'I hope nothing terrible happened in the village.'

'We haven't had time to talk about the village,' Dr Kanu replied. 'My headache is here at Umudike. Love was in the house when she arrived.'

'Mary Magdalene!' exclaimed Mr Akwaelumo, rising from the lounge chair and perching on its edge as if to come as close to Dr Kanu as possible to pick up every bit of the hot news.

Dr Kanu unfolded the story. Mr Akwaelumo knew all about his first meeting with Love and the friendship that subsequently developed, so there was no point repeating that part of the story. He ran into Love as he was leaving Umuahia for Umudike after the air raid. She said she was on her way to his office, to satisfy herself that nothing had happened to him during the raid, which was thoughtful of her. She looked prettier than ever, the air raid notwithstanding. The bashful smile had acquired greater confidence. Her rather large eyes were moist, more moist than usual, and he saw in them a sex appeal which challenged everything masculine in him. Her V-neck blouse revealed a sprinkling of jet black hair springing from the foundations of the most inviting bosom he had ever had the privilege of caressing. For Love's breasts were the nearest approximations to the text-book illustrations of craterless volcanic mountains he had ever come across. He did not even notice that she wore the set of brown wig and matching brown shoes he had given her on her birthday. Her wet eyes and her hairy 'headlights' had completely overpowered him, and his overriding desire had been to whisk her off to his Umudike residence. He had done so without meeting much resistance. All she had wanted was an assurance that she would be driven back home before 4 o'clock, as she had not told her brother that she was going out of town.

As soon as they got to the house he lost no time in peeling his ripe pawpaw. The only thing left was to arm himself with a 'troop carrier' – it was one thing that gave Love the usual assurance that no 'troops' had been left inside her to cause trouble later. It was at that point that his orderly banged on the door. The boys had done their best in the circumstances, and so had he. It was that blasted condom that spoilt everything. Well! When your *chi* says you will be caught, you will be caught. Otherwise why should he have forgotten that he had kept the condom inside the bedside locker for easy access?

'It's tragic!' Dr Kanu summarized, hissing loudly and shaking his head from side to side.

'Oti serious, as the Yorubas say,' echoed Mr Akwaelumo.

'Whichever way you look at it, it's tragic,' Dr Kanu went on. 'Love is an angel. She does not deserve what she's got. You know me . . .'

'You certainly wouldn't call yourself an angel?' cut in Akwa.

'All through my married life I have made every effort to ensure that I never give Fatima any cause to doubt my fidelity.'

'By strict adherence to the eleventh commandment: "Thou shalt not be found out"?'

'No, no!' objected Dr Kanu. 'By keeping to the straight path!'

'Have you ever been into any one that was crooked?' teased Akwa.

'You know what I mean. I don't do it indiscriminately. I was quite active as a bachelor, and I'm glad I was because it taught me one lesson. White or black, red or yellow, post-graduate or illiterate, beauty queen or owl, I have tried them all, and I know that these distinctions have no effect per se on the satisfaction a woman gives you in bed, when you settle down to the real thing. So once you have taken a wife, and you are also lucky that she can give you what you want, what's the point in running after girls? It's the war. If Fatima had been here with me all the time, last night would never have happened.'

'Certainly not!' It was clear from Akwa's tone that he took Kanu's last sentence literally.

'You don't agree?' asked Kanu.

'How could you have invited a girl to your house if your wife had been in? Don't let last night worry you unduly, my friend. Neither you nor I is a knave, and I'm sure our wives know it. If unusual circumstances compel us once in a while to be human, they should understand and bear with us. Rose once found me in an awkward situation at Enugu – I believe it was in 1965. She has never talked about it since then, and I have been anxious not to give her cause to doubt me again. I told you that's why I had to find a reason for not leaving a car for her in the village. With so so girls milling around you from morning till night here, with all the frustrations of wartime, and without a wife to ease the tension, I don't think anybody can blame us for "shelling" once in a while. You can't even work at night. With the fall of Port Harcourt and Afam, electricity supplies are cut drastically so no lights after 8 o'clock. Am I a chicken to retire so early?'

'I hope Fatima will understand,' Dr Kanu said, considerably relieved at the reassurance that he was not a bad husband.

'What about Love?' Akwa asked.

'I haven't seen her yet. But I must see her. She is such an unspoilt – yes, surprisingly unspoilt – jewel and I must help her to get over the shock, even though with Fatima around there can't be any more of that kind of relationship.'

'Is Fatima here permanently?'

'I don't see her moving anywhere else,' replied Dr Kanu, 'especially now that the vandals have decided to send their war planes even to the villages.'

'That's terrible.' Akwa shook his head sadly. 'It makes one wonder if anywhere in Biafra can now be considered safe!'

'If only our boys could have held out in Port Harcourt . . .' said Dr Kanu.

Yes. If only . . . Both men recalled the recent disasters.

The boys had made a valiant effort to defend Port Harcourt. It had not been like Nsukka or Enugu. The shore batteries had maintained their legendary reputation, claiming the lives of thousands of Nigerian soldiers as they had done at Onitsha. Biafran scientists, now known as RaP (Research and Production), had gone one step further. They had produced a Biafran gunboat, which in a combined action with Biafra's lone, famous but over-worked B-26 bomber, had seriously damaged the Nigerian flag-ship 'NNS Nigeria'. One unconfirmed account claimed that the Biafran Navy captured two enemy submarines which they promptly turned against the enemy.

But, as usual, the odds had been heavily against Biafra. Unlike Onitsha, Port Harcourt was a major seaport. The Nigerian Navy could not send its warships up the River Niger to Onitsha. The best the Nigerians could do there was to give the launches convey-ing the troops across the Niger as much covering fire as possible, or to ferry them over when the Biafrans were off their guard. The Onitsha shore batteries could and did foil all their efforts. Port Harcourt was a different story. The Nigerian Navy came with all it had, the way the motorized column of the Nigerian Second Division had been equipped to bulldoze its way into Onitsha. Biafra had no warship, no submarines . . . It was an unequal combat. The Nigerians had the 'right of weight', and once again God sided with the bigger battalions. The Nigerians successfully landed troops in Port Harcourt.

Biafran efforts had been concentrated solely on preventing the enemy from landing there. Little thought appeared to have been given to what would happen if these efforts failed. As a result, when the hour came, everyone in Port Harcourt appeared to have been caught unawares. They saw the mass exodus and instinctively became part of it. There was no time to think of alternative lines of action. You merged into the panic-stricken mass of human beings first, and then remembered your family and your precious material possessions later – and there was nothing you could do about them if you valued your life.

Port Harcourt, the Garden City, was suddenly snatched from Biafra. With it went Biafra's only remaining seaport and all the hopes of importing tons of ammunition and essential requirements by sea. With it went the only petroleum refinery in the country. With it went important oil installations which had strengthened Biafra's bargaining power with potential foreign backers. And with it went Biafra's last international airport. Lagos had thrown all it had into the siege, knowing how crucial Port Harcourt was to Biafra's continued existence. The 'Liberation' of Port Harcourt, as they termed it, would deprive Biafra of its source of petroleum products as well as its major source of electricity at Afam. Biafra would be completely surrounded and cut off from the outside world, and if she still persisted with the war the Federal troops would simply converge from all sides into what remained of the Igbo heartland. Any foreign country which chose to back Biafra from then on would make itself a laughing stock. So certain were the Nigerians that Biafra had been crushed that they went to Kampala for peace talks arranged by the Commonwealth Secretariat without expecting that any Biafrans would be there to negotiate with them. For how could any Biafran leave or enter Biafra, with the capture of their only remaining airport in Port Harcourt?

'I understand that when the Nigerians saw our delegation in Kampala they nearly collapsed, thinking they had seen ghosts,' remarked Akwa, laughing.

'It wouldn't occur to them that we are capable of building our own airports, since they would normally fly in overseas experts to do such jobs for them!' Dr Kanu said. 'I must say I wasn't keen on the idea of sending the peace delegation to Kampala. The Nigerians, I would bet anything on it, would rather defeat us militarily than swallow their pride and negotiate with us. They pretend to be interested in peaceful negotiation only when things are going badly for them at the war fronts.'

'You know how opinions differed at our meeting over the Kampala talks. The point made by the Director-General was that we must not give the impression that we preferred war to peace, and it was incontrovertible.'

'I see the point,' agreed Dr Kanu, 'but we all know that neither Nigeria nor her collaborators – including the British-manipulated Commonwealth Secretariat and the O.A.U., which our radio boys have aptly re-named the Organization of Arab Unity – want to see Biafra survive. So the peace moves are no peace moves at all, but gimmicks to put us off our guard so that the vandals will rout us. Look what they attempted on the Abagana-Anambra sector.'

News had spread in Biafra of the unofficial ceasefire between the two sides on the Abagana-Anambra sector where Biafran soldiers had proved more than a match for the enemy. The miracle of Abagana had been sustained by remarkable feats of bravery by Biafran soldiers. The Awka-Abagana-Anambra axis had proved that, soldier to soldier, the Nigerian was no match for the Biafran, and many Biafrans wished Biafran forces in the other war sectors would do likewise. It seemed that the vandals, having tried all the tactics planned for them by their overseas advisers without gaining an inch of ground, had borrowed a leaf from the tortoise. It is not clear how the initial contact was established, but the following conversation is said to have taken place between the two sides:

Nigerian Soldiers: The Hausas have cleverly withdrawn all their boys from this sector because it is a hot sector, leaving us the Yorubas and Binis to kill you and be killed by you.

Biafran Soldiers: Is that so?

Nigerian Soldiers: Yes. And yet we have no quarrel with you. It is the Hausas who are your enemies. They killed your people in the North.

Biafran Soldiers (after conferring among themselves): That's true. So what?

Nigerian Soldiers: Why then do we continue killing one another? Let us stop fighting.

Biafran Soldiers: All right. We agree.

Nigerian Soldiers: Go and tell Ojukwu that you won't fight us any more.

Biafran Soldiers: Will you go and tell Gowon the same?

Nigerian Soldiers: We agree to do so.

According to the rumour, the two sides returned to their trenches and observed the official ceasefire for two weeks, during which period all guns remained silent: what the war reports describe as a lull in the fighting. Then came a new commanding officer for the Biafran side who knew nothing about the ceasefire. He ordered his boys to open fire, anxious to make his mark at the earliest opportunity. The boys obeyed. No reply came from the Nigerian side. The following morning the Biafran soldiers found bags of rice, beans and *garri* deliberately left for them by their enemy. They also found a note pinned to one of the bags bearing the following message! 'We know our agreement with you still stands. You may have fired at us to test our sincerity. We send you these bags of food as proof that we stand by our agreement.'

The new Biafran commander was intrigued on receiving a full briefing, and he quietly reported the development to the D.H.Q. for instructions. Meanwhile he allowed the unofficial ceasefire to continue. The Nigerian soldiers could be seen listening to transistor radios as they basked on top of their trenches. To remind themselves that the war had not ended, each side periodically fired a few shots into the air!

'I am glad H.E. put his foot down against that ceasefire rubbish,' continued Dr Kanu.

'He had no alternative,' Akwa echoed. 'To have allowed the tête-a-tête to continue one day longer would have rocked the whole basis for the existence of Biafra. It is hypocritical of the Yorubas or the Binis to say they love Biafrans more than the Hausas. Where were they all through 1966 when atrocities upon atrocities . . .'

'Don't mind them,' interrupted Dr Kanu. 'What happened to our people in Lagos and Ibadan? What has been happening to the Igbo-speaking people in the Mid-West, since we lost the Mid-West?'

'The Yorubas said they would join us in breaking away if we seceded. They said they would not live to see Lagos carved out of the West. All empty talk. I often wish I were in a position to teach those vandals a lesson. I would have mowed down all of them who had the cheek to attempt to woo our boys out of their sacred duty!'

'I see you haven't given up your pet wish of joining the army?'

'I'm afraid it comes back from time to time,' Dr Kanu replied. 'It seems the only – or, should I say, the most effective – way in which I could satisfy my conscience that I have given my utmost to Biafra.'

'Now that you are back to your pet wish, I think it's time to change the subject,' said Akwa. 'In any event we'd better be going if I'm to hold my scheduled meeting with my divisional heads.'

Mr Akwaelumo recapitulated his proposed expansion plans. One possibility was to set up a special unit to take charge of the procurement of motor vehicle spare parts. The economic blockade had hit the spare parts trade severely, and unless urgent action was taken most vehicles in Biafra, including vehicles on essential duties, would grind to a halt. The unit, if established, would assume responsibility for procuring spare parts from Biafra and from abroad. It would be empowered to cannibalize abandoned vehicles, to salvage any parts that might still be of use, and to commission the local manufacture of spare parts, where possible.

The second possibility was to establish a unit to encourage food production. It was becoming more and more difficult to find food for the Armed Forces. Biafra was losing more and more farm lands to the enemy, and many farmers were becoming refugees. A deliberate policy to boost food production throughout the country was imperative to stave off a major famine.

'Sounds great,' Dr Kanu commended Akwaelumo. 'My own

headache is how to get more young men to join the army without having to resort to outright conscription. I haven't quite figured out what new techniques to introduce, but I've been wondering whether we couldn't tap the Government offices. How would it sound if we asked each Ministry to "donate" so many young men for military service, to supplement the donations from the various divisions?'

'Makes sense to me,' Akwaelumo replied. 'There must be quite a few young men who are not fully occupied.'

'I'm glad to hear that.' Dr Kanu was visibly pleased. 'I'm also thinking of soliciting volunteers from refugee camps . . .'

Akwaelumo interrupted: 'You see that one can give his utmost to Biafra without necessarily bearing arms?'

'Yes, and no!' Dr Kanu replied.

19

'If this war has taught me one thing,' Mr Bassey said as he placed two bottles on the coffee table, 'it is to thank God for small mercies. If it was before the war, champagne would have flowed today. But I now realize that champagne is nothing. Today is better than yesterday, and I'm sure tomorrow will be better than today.'

'*Ise!*' echoed his friends, Professor Ezenwa, Barrister Chike Ifeji and Mr Ikem Onukaegbe.

'Dr Osita brought me these two bottles this morning, all the way from RaP, Aba. It was such a pleasant surprise. He had only just heard about my illness and wanted to extend his best wishes. He couldn't stay till now because they are off to test a new weapon . . .'

'That must be the flying *ogbunigwe*,' interposed Onukaegbe. 'The vandals called the ordinary *ogbunigwe* "Ojukwu's bucket"; I wonder what they will call this one!'

'But there's nothing like *ogbunigwe*, O!' exclaimed Ifeji, looking strange in his Biafra suit. He had had to give up his three-piece suit with gold chain. It was his own way of rejecting Britain for her role in the war: others had reacted by renouncing their knighthoods and calling on the Queen of England to come and collect her medals. Even the Chief Justice and Clergymen had switched to the Biafra suit, and Ifeji was beginning to look ridiculous in his three-piece striped suit with gold chain and bowler hat. From the practical point of view, his special collars were wearing out fast and he had no means of replacing them.

'When the history of this war comes to be written, the *ogbunigwe* and the shore batteries will receive special mention as Biafra's greatest saviours. We've been able to wipe out more Nigerians with those devices than with any imported weapons.'

'The flying *ogbunigwe* is expected to be an improvement,' reported Onukaegbe. 'You must have heard that the Nigerians are now so mortally afraid of *ogbunigwe* that each advancing battalion is now preceded by a herd of cattle. If our boys have buried any *ogbunigwe* in their line of advance, it will go off on the cows!'

'I didn't hear that,' Professor Ezenwa said.

'Oh yes, it's true,' Onukaegbe continued. 'But the flying *ogbunigwe* will spring a surprise on them. This time we shall not wait for them to activate the *ogbunigwe*, we shall activate it on their heads. When our boys fire it, it will just go *fiam*, and descend on the vandals like fire and brimstone!'

'War is terrible, O!' Barrister Ifeji shook his head. 'See how we sit here talking about thousands of human lives being wiped out as if they were thousands of soldier ants! It's sickening!'

'Do the Nigerians think about that when they drop napalm on innocent civilians in remote villages?' asked Onukaegbe. 'Anyway, our microbiologists are working round the clock to develop special bombs for biological warfare, just in case the vandals think they can drop napalm on defenceless market women and get away with it.'

'What drink I go pour for master?' Mr Bassey's steward enquired from Professor Ezenwa. The two bottles were originally beer bottles. The bottle tops had been replaced with stoppers carved out of the inside of the raffia bamboo. Each bottle carried a special RaP label, giving the brand name and the potency of the spirit it contained. The one thing RaP could do nothing about was the PROPERTY OF NIGERIAN BREWERIES LTD moulded on each bottle at the time it came out of the Port Harcourt glass factory before the outbreak of the war.

'I'll have some of the Nene Sherry,' replied Professor Ezenwa. 'That's the mildest of the RaP drinks.'

'I'll go for the Veroma Gin,' put in Ifeji. 'Although it is 90% proof, I prefer it to the others because it has no colour. I understand the colouring in some of the locally produced spirits could be dangerous.'

'Either of them will do for me,' announced Onukaegbe. 'One must die of one thing or another some day. If it is the spirit distilled by our scientists that will kill me, it's better than being smashed by a Nigerian bomb!'

'May the Lord have mercy on our livers!' intoned Professor Ezenwa as he downed his sherry.

'Amen!' replied the others.

'The gin isn't bad at all,' remarked the lean lawyer as he recharged his glass. He had taken a small quantity first, to sample it. 'I must confess I was becoming sceptical of the growing market in locally made drinks. You can hardly find good palmie nowadays because these mushroom distilleries buy up all the palm wine. And some of the things they produce are horrible.'

'You know even the DMI have gone into distilling?' Professor Ezenwa added with disapproval. 'Why on earth a Directorate of Military Intelligence should get itself involved in distilling spirits beats my imagination.'

'Have you sampled their whisky?' asked Onukaegbe. 'It's two hundred per cent proof! The thing simply burns its way through your mouth, throat, intestines and all!'

'Oh my God!' shouted Ifeji shrugging his shoulders and clasping his head with his hands as if to prevent anyone forcing the burning spirit down his throat.

'Someone ought to tell the DMI to face their assignment and leave distilling spirits to the chemists,' suggested the Professor. 'If they had done so all this time maybe we would have had fewer tactical withdrawals.'

'Gentlemen,' announced Bassey, emerging from the kitchen. 'Here's *ngwo ngwo* to go with the spirits. It should have come at the same time as the drinks, but my steward is new and we are still adjusting to each other.'

Ifeji spontaneously burst into song, and was promptly joined by Ezenwa and Onukaegbe, all three dancing round the table with the drinks and the hot plates of *ngwo ngwo*, and with Bassey standing beside the table:

> *Ihe nile zuru oke n'ala Biafra;*
> *Ihe nile zuru oke n'ala anyi;*
> *Aku na uba zuru oke n'ala Biafra,*
> *Nani onwu, onwu, onwu zuru uwa!*
> *Nani onwu, onwu, onwu!*

'Long life and prosperity to Indigenous!' toasted Ifeji.

'And a happy reunion with his family at the earliest opportunity,' added Onukaegbe.

'We must give you the title of Omenuko,' Ifeji went on, turning to Bassey. 'It is only a man of substance who can produce goat meat at this time in Biafra when a goat costs more than two wives.'

'My brothers,' began Mr Bassey, 'I owe everything I have today, including my life, to God and to the three of you. Yes, God acts through man. If anybody had told me four months ago that I would be alive today, I would not have believed him. But here I am today, living in a furnished house provided by the Government, with an opportunity to earn my own living. I know that since we lost Aba and you came over to Umuahia we have spent a great deal of time together. In fact we lived together here for a week until you were assigned your own quarters. All the same, I thought I should do something special to let you know how indebted I feel to you . . .'

'Come off it,' interposed Professor Ezenwa. 'Formal speeches embarrass me. What's all this for? We have done for you no more than you would have done for any of us in trouble. No more than Ikem did for me when I had my whole family on my hands last October. That's all.'

'And after all,' added Ifeji, 'doesn't our Directorate drum into everyone's head the fact that every Biafran is his brother's keeper?'

'One thing I'll never forget is that it was my own people who betrayed me, who wanted me to die, while you saved me, nursed me back to life, and found me shelter and a job.'

'Don't forget Ndiyo,' Onukaegbe reminded Bassey.

'How can I ever forget him?' Bassey answered. 'But Ndiyo is my kinsman. We grew up together. We were childhood friends. You are different. We knew each other before the war began, but not that well. It is the war that has brought us close. You have been more like brothers to me than my own kith and kin. To think that Uko, my kinsman, would go and evacuate even his distant relations and leave my immediate family to perish, knowing our village politics . . .'

'I thought you had got over all that,' chided Ezenwa.

'I have, but . . .'

'No, no,' Ezenwa interrupted. 'If you have, you have, let's get on with the *ngwo ngwo* before it's cold.'

Ifeji, Ezenwa and Onukaegbe had solicited the help of a top army officer to brief H.E. on Mr Bassey's pathetic condition.

He was to underline the fact that Bassey had given foreign exchange and vehicles to help with the prosecution of the war, and that it was because of his total commitment to Biafranism that he had been unable to evacuate his immediate family from Ikot Ekpene. H.E. had been so concerned that he had gone in person to see Bassey in hospital. He followed up the visit with instructions to the Directorate of Accommodation to assign a furnished house to Bassey in Umuahia, rent-free. He also instructed the Directorate of Procurement to award contracts to him for the supply of foodstuffs to the Directorate. A man who had given so much to Biafra deserved something in return.

With his brilliant record as a businessman, Bassey lost no time in finding his feet. The Director for Procurement, Mr Akwaelumo, started him on plantains and *garri* for the Armed Forces. A couple of weeks later, when arrangements for the importation of stock-fish were concluded, he was among the handpicked reputable businessmen who received the import licences. Stockfish had suddenly risen from 'that wooden thing eaten in Owerri Province and which gets between your teeth' to a status symbol. Two Permanent Secretaries were known to have exchanged blows over the distribution of stockfish. Stockfish had also revealed that men in holy orders shared the same weakness as members of their flock. As an Anglican bishop put it, love of stockfish had swayed clerics away from the true gospel of love they were expected to preach. One consignment of stockfish, and Bassey became solidly established. The only fly in his ointment was the lack of any information on the whereabouts of his wife and children. He had not shaved since the fateful night he escaped from Ikot Ekpene, and said he would not shave until he was reunited with his family.

'My brothers,' resumed Bassey. 'When I call you my brothers, I mean it literally. I feel towards you as though we are of one blood. There's nothing I'll keep a secret from you . . .'

'Except the girl you "shell",' said Ifeji.

'That's a thing of the past,' replied Bassey.

'Meaning what?' Ifeji asked.

'I've given up girls.'

'That's the greatest news of the year!' cried Barrister Ifeji. Professor Ezenwa and Mr Onukaegbe also looked excited.

'You may not believe it, but I mean it,' Bassey went on. 'In fact it's what I was getting at when I began by saying that I could not keep anything secret from the three of you. The thought came to me during those weeks I lay in the hospital. Or rather a nurse in the hospital suggested it to me. I couldn't of course go anywhere then, but I kept returning to the idea and turning it over in my mind. It was not until I moved into this house, while you were still at Aba, that I decided to visit the man whose name the nurse gave me.'

There was tense silence as Bassey narrated his story. 'He is a very ordinary man. Well-shaven, unlike these shaggy so-called prophets one sees around. He does not belong to any of these new, wartime churches; he is an Anglican who goes to church regularly every Sunday. But his small sitting room has become a sought-after prayer house. I did not want to believe the nurse's account of his prophetic vision, but I finally succumbed to the urge to see him because I wanted very badly to know the fate of my wife and children.

'As soon as I walked in and we had exchanged greetings, he said I looked like a hen which had lost its brood. And yet I had never met him before . . .'

The man – he asked to be addressed simply as Brother – had invited Bassey to join the prayer group if he wished.

'. . . He said he was not a soothsayer and so could not just look at a mirror or a bowl of water or some such thing and tell me the fate of my family. But he believed in the power of prayer. "In order for prayer to be powerful, however", he said, "both the person praying and the person for whom the prayer is being said must believe in the power of prayer. Above all, they must rid themselves of sin because that is what is responsible for man's estrangement from God. There's no point bruising your knees praying when your sinful actions erect an impregnable barrier, an iron curtain between you and God".'

'You've become an Evangelist already – or a Brother?' teased Ifeji.

'I'm no Evangelist, and only the leader is addressed as Brother,' continued Bassey. He said he accepted the invitation on the spot and had not regretted it since. Within a week, Brother had seen a vision. Some bones rising to life in the jungle. The vision was not very clear, so he did not wish to raise Bassey's hopes unduly. He had seen the outline of children and women, but the features had been blurred, hence he could not attach too much significance to the vision except that it held out a ray of hope.

Not long after the vision, Biafran troops attempting to recapture Ikot Ekpene stumbled on the hideout of several women and children who had gone into hiding when the enemy captured Ikot Ekpene. Rather than fall into Nigerian hands, these women had taken to the forest, or hidden in the ceiling of their houses, hoping that the enemy would leave soon.

It was Mr Uko who told Bassey about it, and offered to take him to the special camp set up for these women and children whom the Biafran Army had rescued. Mr Uko still had a bad conscience, and the fact that H.E. had taken a personal interest in Bassey made matters even more awkward. He could not predict what would happen if Bassey denounced him to H.E. As soon as he received the report of the evacuation, he got in touch with Bassey and offered to drive him to the Red Cross transit camp opened for the women and children at Oboro.

'It's an experience I'll never forget,' Bassey said, 'the sight of those women and children. You couldn't say they were ghosts: they were all filth, and ghosts are said to be sparkling white. You couldn't call them witches: witches are said to be spritely while these women could hardly stand on their feet. If you can imagine the body of a car abandoned several months anywhere in Northern Nigeria at the peak of the harmattan haze, you would have an idea how filthy these women and children looked. You could not tell the colour of the skin from the colour of the rags they had on – those of them who still had rags. Their bones could be seen under their skin, more clearly than on an X-ray film. Most of the children had no energy left even to cry: they crouched on the floor at a corner of the transit camp, looking like diseased chimps. The only two people who looked normal were the two children who still suckled their mothers. Their mothers, however, were so shrivelled and weak that it was difficult to imagine how anything could have trickled into the mouths of their robust babies from those flabby, lifeless breasts . . .'

Bassey had had to muster all his power of self-control not to burst into tears at the sight of those women and children, who could not even stare back at him. The first attempt at feeding them with powdered milk proved futile. It was like sucking fluid through one end of a siphon and promptly discharging it through the other end. The idea that his wife, Nma, and her kind might have been reduced to such a state did not bear thinking about.

'It was not until they had been bathed and clothed and fed for three days or so,' continued Bassey, 'that I had the heart to interrogate them. At first they couldn't say much. It had all looked to them like a dream. They had been through hell. They had seen other members of their household give up the ghost and had been unable to help them. They had been unable even to scratch shallow graves to bury them, so they had seen their bodies gradually decompose, the stench overpowering the stench of human excrement. It had been a state of utter hopelessness, just waiting for your turn to die!'

'Did any of them have any news about Nma and the kids?' asked Onukaegbe.

'I'm afraid not,' Bassey replied.

'And your friend, Ndiyo?' Ifeji followed up.

'No. The way it all went, you had no courage to enquire about anybody else. They say the vendetta unleashed on the villages around Ikot Ekpene following the infiltration of Nigerian soldiers was unprecedented. It wasn't so much Nigerian soldiers slaughtering at random. I believe our propaganda machinery and mounting world opinion against Nigeria has helped to reduce such genocidal tendencies among the Nigerians. It was rather our own people using the bloodthirsty Nigerian soldiers to eliminate anyone they disliked.

'Mr Uko and I went over to Tactical Headquarters in Ikwuano to make further enquiries, but still no clue as to the fate of my family. It was confirmed that they were not in the house when the vandals blew it up. So I have decided to regard no news as good news. Since no one has reported seeing them killed or hearing of their death, I take it they are alive.'

'I'm sure they are,' Professor Ezenwa said. 'If it were some other wife, I would worry. But Nma is equal to any situation.'

'You know Brother said almost the same thing?' Bassey was excited. 'And yet he has never met Nma before. I used to have doubts before about people who call themselves prophets. Having come to know Brother, I am now convinced that some men are nearer God than others . . .'

'I don't know whether I want to be that near to God, though,' cut in Barrister Ifeji. 'Life would be lifeless!'

'It's not the way I see it,' disagreed Bassey. 'I can't claim yet to be nearer to God than any of you, but from my limited experience of Brother and his small group I'm already beginning to understand what the Bible means by that peace which passeth all understanding.'

No one spoke, so Bassey continued. 'I've told Brother about you, and he says he would be very glad to meet you. Today is one of our prayer days, at half past six, barely half an hour from now. You are welcome to come along, if you wish.'

'Not today,' Ifeji lost no time in replying.

Ezenwa, Ifeji and Onukaegbe drove off in Onukaegbe's car, the car they often used because Onukaegbe received a regular quota of fuel on the special P.Q.A. coupon, which meant it was free of charge.

'I don't know what the two of you think,' began Professor Ezenwa when he was certain Bassey was well out of sight. 'What has just happened strengthens the fears which have been lingering in my mind since we rushed Bassey to hospital, namely that he might be going round the bend.'

'When I see a man like Bassey who at Enugu used to go to Church only for weddings, christenings and so on, when a man like that begins to talk about going regularly to prayer houses and all that jazz, I fear something has snapped,' Ifeji said.

'I don't know if any of you have been inside his bedroom,' said Onukaegbe. 'It's full of candles. He must keep a candle burning all night.'

'I wonder how we can get him to see a psychiatrist?' Ezenwa pondered.

'I'm sure what will cure him is news that Nma and the children are alive and well,' said Mr Onukaegbe.

'Only God can reply to that,' Ifeji observed.

'That's why he's after God, day and night!' Professor Ezenwa found he could not laugh at what he had intended as a joke.

20

'I must get out of here!' shouted Fatima, sobbing without shedding tears. She pressed her left palm against her face as if she needed a double screen to cut off some ghastly sight.

'You'll get over it, darling,' Dr Amilo Kanu gave his wife a soothing and understanding pat on the back.

'I don't want to get over anything else!' she snapped back. 'You must get me out of here immediately.'

Dr Kanu went to the fridge for ice cubes. In an effort to save his marriage, he had been able to obtain a bottle of real Dubonnet from one of Biafra's roving ambassadors.

'Have a drink,' he offered her the glass.

'I don't want a drink. Get me out . . .'

'It's Dubonnet, real Dubonnet on the rocks,' he interrupted her, sounding like a magician articulating the word Abracadabra.

'No. I can't drink anything. Not after what I have just seen.

No!' She shouted hysterically.

It was the most devastating air raid Umuahia had seen. Four Russian Ilyushin jet fighters had descended on the town without warning. The usual warning shots had not been fired because the Provincial Secretary had no idea that any planes were heading for Umuahia and so had not given the necessary orders. Biafra had no radar to detect the approach of a war plane. Whenever an enemy plane was sighted in any major town, the Administration, Civil Defence, or military authorities in that town had been ordered to alert the nearby major towns by telephone (where available), indicating the direction in which the plane appeared to be heading. This was the way that the Umuahia Provincial Office normally received its advance information and ordered the firing of warning shots. Little wonder that most warning shots ended up as false alarms.

This time the four Russian planes had not been spotted at all, hence no advance information and no warning shots. Being supersonic, they descended on an unsuspecting people ahead of the sound they emitted, faster than the reflexes of the boys who manned the anti-aircraft guns and rockets. And they timed their descent very well – around 2.30 p.m. which was lunch time for Red Cross workers, merchants, tradesmen, a time most people were indoors, in their homes or offices.

The air raid was over before you knew it had begun. By the time the anti-aircraft boys opened their barrage of fire the four planes had completed their mission and were nosing their way into the skies. The lightning speed of the raid resulted in conflicting accounts of what actually happened. Some eyewitnesses said the planes fired rockets as well as spraying innumerable bullets. Some others said they dropped bombs and sprayed bullets. An army officer claimed that they dropped special bombs mounted on warheads designed for speed and accuracy. What was in no doubt was the disastrous outcome of the raid.

Two young men had been playing the card game 'Whot' inside a house. Whot had become easily the most popular indoor game in Biafra. Ingenious and not so ingenious printers had copied the original version of the game and mass-produced the 'Biafra Whot' which could be purchased everywhere in Biafra. One of the young men was a bank cashier whose plan to study banking in London had been frustrated by the war. The Branch of the African Continental Bank for which he worked had been forced to move. The other young man was an undergraduate. He had transferred to the University of Biafra in October 1966, along with hundreds of other students of Eastern Nigerian origin who considered it unsafe to continue their studies at the University of Ibadan. He had a year to graduate in Physics. Like most other science students, he served in RaP. His group had the special assignment of producing the casing for the 'Dodan Barracks Special' – the demolition bomb which would shatter all the bunkers in Dodan Barracks, Lagos, the place of refuge of the Nigerian Head of State.

'Last card,' announced the undergraduate, with the confidence of a man sure to win. His companion had five cards in his hand. No matter what he played, the undergraduate was certain to win as his only remaining card was a Whot.

'Plane!'

The young men instantly flung down the cards as they heard the shout.

'Let's go under the bed,' whispered the bank cashier, throwing up the curtain which cut off the bed from the rest of the room and diving underneath.

'No. I'm going outside,' the undergraduate replied, dashing into the common passage towards the outer door.

A crash followed, the noise of which could hardly be described. It was a combination of horrible sounds – exploding bombs, machine-gun fire, collapsing buildings. The house in which the young men had played Whot seconds earlier, a house completed in the course of the war and barely twelve months old, was immediately reduced to débris, as if a giant bulldozer had gone over it in the twinkling of an eye.

The bank cashier struggled out from under the bed, pushing aside fallen blocks and smashed furniture, his head and clothes enveloped in cement dust. He shook his head vigorously, not only to get rid of the dust but also to reassure himself that he had emerged from the most terrible nightmare of his life. When he looked around him it did not help his memory; nothing resembled what he had seen only a couple of minutes previously.

Some of the spectators who saw him emerge from the débris had beaten a hasty retreat as if they had seen a ghost. The stunned look on their faces showed that some tragedy had happened. He walked out, following the direction of their eyes and taking care not to step on shattered glass, crumpled corrugated iron sheets and sharp pieces of wood. Suddenly he stopped, bent over to have a close look at the figure sprawled in the débris in front of him and then shut his eyes and screamed. His undergraduate friend lay full length on the wreckage, his head completely smashed by a falling wall, like the head of an unlucky lizard smashed by a lorry.

Fatima had allowed curiosity to override her sense of judgement and accompanied her husband to inspect the disaster area. As the remains of the late undergraduate were being transferred into an ambulance, she and her husband went over to the next block, where the only survivor was in a coma, following severe head injuries. He was a wealthy businessman, one of the many who had transferred their foreign exchange holdings abroad to the account of the Biafran Government to help with the war effort. There he lay in a coma, oblivious of the calamities that had befallen him. His wife and six children were crushed to death where they had taken cover underneath the dining table. His massive thirty-bedroom house, which brought him a regular income every month, was razed to the ground. At least ten tenants were said to have been killed as well. They had come home for lunch. The man's two lorries which were parked in front of the house were smashed beyond recognition; it was as if the pilot had been sent to eliminate the man and his sources of revenue once and for all. Suitcases, a radio and record-player mounted in a mahogany cabinet were smashed to smithereens. Five gramophone records unearthed as volunteers dug through the débris for human bodies appeared to have been baked in an oven. What once went by the name of mattresses appeared to have been deliberately unstuffed and ground to dust.

In another house, a woman was having a bath when the planes struck. A bullet found its way right into her bucket of water, the first sign that an enemy plane was around. She immediately threw her towel over her soapy body and dashed out of the bathroom in quest of her five children. Each of them answered her call from the encircling débris – all of them were alive.

A trader who lived in a house opposite the 'Lumumba Typing School' recounted his story to anyone who cared to listen. He usually had one main meal a day for which he had come home at around two o'clock.

'Good afternoon, sir,' his wife had saluted him before making for the kitchen to dish out his food.

The trader noticed that she was dressed up. 'Are you going somewhere?' he enquired.

'Yes,' she replied from the kitchen. She was already scooping out the yam pottage from the iron pot into a large enamel bowl. 'Mama Ije sent Ije to tell me that if I came out in time she would plait my hair for me before going off to cook for the soldiers. I thought I should go with Ije straight away. That Nnewi woman who used to do it for me has raised her charge to three shillings. She knows who will pay her that much . . .'

The trader had been too hungry and tired to respond. He went into the bathroom to urinate. He had just undone his buttons when he heard his neighbour's wife shout frantically: 'They have come, O! Enemy plane! My *chi* has killed me, O . . .'

The trader took two steps towards the front door before he suddenly decided to go to his wife in the kitchen. Before he could reach the kitchen the crash came. He threw himself flat along the passage and everything momentarily went blank. The kitchen was not seriously hit. Since all its windows were wooden, his wife escaped without a scratch. The wooden ladle was still in her hand. It was at the front of the house that the war planes scored a bull's eye. Five Biafran Red Cross workers were killed; one of them who had been standing beside a pillar was neatly chopped in two. A woman caught running down the external staircase had been disembowelled, and fell with her intestines spread over the staircase. The trader could not brace himself to contemplate what would have happened to his lean frame if he had taken only three more steps towards the front door.

At the typing school across the road, items of clothing turned out to be the only clue for assembling the different portions of the students' dismembered bodies. The sight was too much for Fatima. She went back to the car shivering, refused bluntly to see any more or to visit the mortuary, and asked her husband to drive her straight home. The dismembered bodies brought back the memories of Ami Junior, Halima and her son, and the terrible nightmare which she had had after the ghastly air raid at Obodo – memories which she had striven to suppress since she took up residence with her husband at Umudike.

'You must get me out of here,' Fatima repeated.

'The house I arranged for you at Imeuno was taken over by the wife of the Brigade Commander of the "S" Brigade because you refused to leave Umudike. If you have now come round to accepting that it is not safe for you and Emeka to stay here, I'll ask my men to scout around for another house. I'm sure this will not be the last of such desperate air raids by the vandals. Whenever they find the going hard at one of the fronts, they take advantage of our deficiencies in the air and pour their arsenal . . .'

'I'm not talking about moving to any remote village; I've had enough of that,' said Fatima.

'Where else could you go?' Dr Kanu asked, as if he did not know the answer.

'I want to get out of here. Biafra, I mean. I want to get out. To Europe. Anywhere. Even Libreville. I can't stand it any more.'

Dr Kanu knew it would come some day, but he had hoped the day would be long in coming. That it might never come.

21

'I must do something before I crack up!' Dr Amilo Kanu muttered as he pressed the electric bell and allowed himself a full yawn. The Sergeant, his omnipresent orderly, flung the door open, jumped into the office and gave the salute, all in one breath.

'Ask Moses to bring the car at once. I'm going out.'

'Yessep!' The Sergeant brushed past a young Captain who had heard Dr Kanu's instructions and wanted to catch him before he went out.

'I don't want to see anybody now, Captain,' shouted Dr Kanu. 'I'm on my way out.' And he stepped towards the door.

'That's why I decided to break in sir, something . . .'

'To hell with whatever it is! I'm going out!'

Dr Kanu picked up the carved walking stick with a near carbon copy of the bearded face of the Head of State, which he had bought from a refugee camp, and strode out of the office without looking left or right at the people waiting to see him. Moses had not brought the car and in the brief moment while he paused to decide whether to wait for the car at that point or to walk to the specially camouflaged car park, the Captain decided to take his chance. He was a young man, no more than 18 or 19, in his final year in the secondary school at the time the war broke out. He had fought bravely both in the Mid-West and the Awka sectors. His left lower arm had been smashed by enemy fire at Enugu-Ukwu, and amputated just below the elbow. He had been promoted Captain after that and assigned to the Directorate of Mobilization, to get him off further combat duties.

'My problem won't take much of your time, sir,' he pleaded. 'My boys who were on a mobilization drive came back with a difficult man who insists on seeing you personally, sir.'

'Because he insists on seeing me, therefore I must see him?'

'No, sir.'

'Why then must I . . .'

'We shall win!' greeted the man from the village, in a combination of Igbo and English, the first two words in Igbo and the last in English, with disproportionate emphasis on WIN. 'Please forgive my boldness, but it was I who insisted on seeing the head man. There is something I want to tell you and nobody else. It will not take time, and it is you alone I want.'

The man's tone sounded serious, sincere and responsible. It was difficult to estimate his age. His head had been clean shaven by his captors and so had his chin, further reducing the clues. He was short but strongly built. His profession as a palm wine tapper obviously kept him physically fit.

'Nothing on him, sir. We've searched him.' The Captain had read Dr Kanu's mind from his wink.

'OK, this way.' Dr Kanu beckoned to the palm wine tapper. They moved off the road to the car park and stopped at a quiet corner some distance from the office block but within the area ingeniously camouflaged with palm fronds. The Directorate of Mobilization was among the best camouflaged buildings in Umuahia, as it was considered a likely military target. It was impossible to tell the shape and dimensions of the building from outside. Neither could you tell that it was originally an elementary school. The football field had become a cassava farm in response to the appeal to grow more food. The roads within the compound, the car park, the teachers' quarters and even the open spaces had been so effectively camouflaged that it was difficult if not impossible to detect any human movement from the air.

The palm wine tapper spoke in Igbo, after once again receiving the assurance that he was standing before the head man in the Directorate of Mobilization.

'I was on top of one of my palm trees yesterday, tapping the tree and collecting the wine for the morning, when I saw two soldiers at the foot of the tree. They made signs at me, so I concluded that they wanted my palm wine. On descending from the tree I gave them the wine to sample, as is customary. Not only did they drain all the wine in the calabash, they said they had come to conscript me into the army. I asked them whether they wanted me or somebody else, and they said they came for me. I asked them whether an enemy sent them or they came on their own. To cut it short, they said I was wasting their time as they had to catch twenty men that day. Only a foolish man willingly disobeys armed soldiers. I obeyed, but pleaded with them to take me to their head man as I had something very important to tell him.'

'Say it, then,' Dr Kanu cut in impatiently, looking at his watch.

It was approaching midday, by which time it was considered unsafe to drive around in a car for fear of enemy planes which had learnt to strafe individual vehicles on the highway.

'Yes, what I want to say is simple,' continued the palm wine tapper. 'My first son, the boy who should have succeeded me when I die, joined the army voluntarily and with my full backing. He was a brilliant boy, always first in his class. He was in his last year at school when the war began. He was killed in Port Harcourt. The two children who came after him are girls. The next boy is still in primary school. If he were old enough, I would have asked him to join the army, not minding that my first son's head has already been sacrificed to the same war. For no person who breathes will say that he has no part in this war. Let the wind sweep away what I have said.

'Now, why did I insist on seeing you? My words are few. If this war has reached the stage when a man of my age is given a rifle by force and sent to the war front, then the time has come for you who hold Biafra in your hands to blow the whistle and end the war. That is all I want to say.'

Dr Kanu ordered the Captain to release the old man, to give him some relief supplies and take him home in a vehicle. He got into his Mercedes and asked Moses to drive him to the Directorate of Procurement on the Umudike road. Mr Akwaelumo was not in. He had been summoned by the Director-General.

'Drive to the Ridge Club,' Dr Kanu ordered.

'The Club does not open before five o'clock,' the Sergeant reminded him. He should have remembered. The Cabinet Office had issued the orders restricting the hours of business of the Ridge Club and all drinking bars in Umuahia to two hours a day, five to seven o'clock in the evenings. The notice had drawn attention to the fact that large congregations of people and cars constituted obvious targets for air raids. It also deplored the fact that such drinking houses were diverting the minds of gallant Biafrans from the war effort and the ideals of the Biafran revolution. The immediate cause of the closure was the action of an army officer who, without consultation with the Directorate of Mobilization, sent soldiers one morning during office hours to conscript all young men they found at the Ridge Club; he hoped that the university lecturer who had hi-jacked his "Cradler" would be there, intelligence reports having informed him that the lecturer usually drank at the Club at that time. The soldiers, behaving like soldiers, indiscriminately arrested every male in the Club at the time, drove them to their headquarters and had their heads clean shaven before reporting back to the officer. The Director of a key Directorate and the head of a RaP group were among the conscripts! The Officer lost one pip from his epaulette for his rashness, but he succeeded in drawing attention to the threat the Cradlers were posing to the war effort.

The Cradlers. They had banded themselves into an Association with pragmatic intentions. The hands that rock the cradle rule the nation and must therefore be accorded their proper place in society, they had contended at their launching ceremony. The snag was that none of them had rocked any cradles. They were mostly female undergraduates, and single. Soon their true role became obvious – to fill the vacuum left by absent wives who had fled to the remote villages or even out of Biafra with their children, to escape the air raids, leaving their husbands to attend to affairs of state in the big cities. The men needed the Cradlers to survive the strains and stresses of the war, and many were in a position to provide them with bed and board for their services. The Cradlers needed the men: most Cradlers earned no more than ten Biafran pounds a month, which could not buy a cup of salt or pay the monthly rent on a single unfurnished room. The Cradler who landed a top Army Officer or Director of a Directorate controlling a scarce commodity straight away hit the jackpot: her fringe benefits could include a chauffeur-driven car with limitless supply of free petrol, expensive wigs and party dresses (for showing off at work), fabulous birthday parties, and such wartime rarities as hair thread, bath soap and panties flown in from abroad. She promptly graduated from eating grasshoppers, lizards, and 'armoured cars' (as crabs had been nicknamed), to eating goat meat. Little wonder that all unattached Cradlers deserted their places of work by ten o'clock each morning, ostensibly to take cover from possible air raids, but invariably to hunt for influential men at the Ridge Club.

Dr Kanu should have remembered. The resolution to close the Club stood in his name. His fellow Directors had toned it down a bit. No matter what your views on morality, the Cradlers were making an invaluable contribution to the war effort. 'Man must wack!'

'Drive to the house,' Dr Kanu ordered. He could not keep wandering up and down the road like Satan, not at an hour when the war planes could swoop down any minute. And he could not return to his office. This was an ideal occasion to have been with Love. Her naivity, her child-like but penetrating questions, her optimism, always helped to take his mind away from the realities of the war. The first day he had her he had spontaneously re-christened her 'Enenebe ejegh olu': she was so pretty that you could spend the whole day just admiring her beauty and forget all about work! He had seen her since the unfortunate incident, and they had sorted matters out. She now lived in a room he had rented for her at the other end of Umuahia, on the Bende road. He ruled out sending for her in her office and taking her to her room. A man who lied to his family that he had gone to work, was killed on top o his mistress when enemy planes struck Orlu! Dr Kanu had decided that he would not visit Love at any time enemy planes could possibly strike. He did not want to enrich the stock of war scandals.

As soon as he arrived at his house, he made straight for the bunker, situated behind the main house where it was readily accessible from the main house, the temporary firewood kitchen he had erected since the fall of Port Harcourt and Afam, and the servants' quarters. It was well camouflaged, with a thatched roof above it and a flourishing vegetable garden surrounding it. Initially, Fatima had shared the prejudice then widely prevalent against bunkers. They were nothing short of ready made graves; it was much better to stay outside, watch the plane, and then decide how best to take cover. She had, however, given up such prejudices, and so had many Biafrans. In the days when the vandals sent a lone, inexperienced and chicken-livered bomber, it was safe to stand outside and watch the movement of the plane. You could see the hatch open and the bombs roll out like giant balls of dung from a cow's anus. So long as the plane did not fly above your head and you ay flat on the ground, you were safe – safe from the bomb and from collapsing walls and débris.

But the enemy had grown wiser. They had switched over to the Mig fighters which unleashed fire and brimstone on a limitless expanse as they escaped from the scene of destruction. Many who stood or ran about in the open were disembowelled or sliced in two. The bunker became the answer. With a zig-zag entrance, the chances of a bullet getting inside the bunker were minimal. The only thing that could constitute a serious danger was a demolition bomb, but if a demolition bomb is used on you, you hardly stand any chance of survival, whether you are inside or outside a bunker. Fatima was not only won over to the safety of the bunker, but soon considered life outside it so insecure that she and Emeka literally lived in the bunker from dawn to dusk every day. It was difficult even to get her to go to the market, even though the markets had changed their hours and, in many

185

cases, chosen new locations in order to minimize the risk of air raids.

'Who's that?' Fatima shouted as Dr Kanu descended the steps leading into the bunker.

'What are you doing there?' Dr Kanu was shocked to find Fatima clutching Emeka as they lay on a mat underneath the Vono bed she had installed permanently in the bunker. The Holy Bible lay beside her.

'Isn't that a plane?' she asked, panting.

'What plane?' retorted Dr Kanu in disgust. 'You must have heard the door of my car bang when I got out.'

'You always say it's nothing . . .'

'Come on, darling, I've just driven in from town, and I'm telling you . . .'

'What's *that* sound?' Fatima interrupted, clinging to Emeka.

'But that's Moses coming out of the car,' Dr Kanu replied, doing his utmost to contain his irritation. 'Come out, darling. Come on, Emeka. There's no plane today.'

'What brings you home at this time of day?' Fatima asked as she made for one of the two lounge chairs in the bunker. It was evident that she was at the same time straining to catch any unusual sound just in case the war planes descended without warning. 'Is it time to be on the run again?'

'Where to?' Dr Kanu asked.

'Are you asking me? It seems to be our life now. Run from Port Harcourt, from Aba, from Owerri. So I wondered whether it's time to run from Umuahia.'

'God forbid! On the contrary, our boys are digging in firmly around Imo River in a bid to recapture Port Harcourt. H.E.'s Special Brigade is . . .'

'May we change the subject,' interrupted Fatima, 'before you accuse me of flaring up. It will take me many years to adopt your attitude over this war. We have recently lost Aba and Owerri, and it should be clear to everybody who can think that Umuahia must be their next target. Instead of concentrating our limited resources on stopping the Nigerians from driving us out of Umuahia too, you have the guts to talk glibly about our boys digging in firmly elsewhere. Where were those boys when Port Harcourt fell? Or do you reckon it will be easier to recapture the town after the Nigerians have securely entrenched themselves?'

'Military strategy is much more complicated than radiography.'

'Thank you, Major-General.'

'I mean what I'm saying. Our international stature will soar overnight if we show that we have the ability to recapture some of our lost territory, particularly in the petroleum-producing areas. Anyway, I agree we should talk about something else. You asked me why I'm home at this time?'

'Yes.' Fatima was curious.

'I missed you in the office, and came back to be with you.' Dr Kanu smiled sweetly.

'Keep that for the Cradlers. I didn't marry you yesterday.'

'OK. If you don't accept that, I've also come home to play with Emeka.' He picked up Emeka who had been leaning on his mother and staring at the wall opposite him, as if in a daze. 'How're you? Been sleeping?'

'Yes,' Emeka answered sleepily.

'Come on, let's go outside and play football. Come on, Fatima.'

'Emeka and I are not leaving this bunker until evening. You can go and play outside.'

'Why?' asked Dr Kanu.

'You know why ' Fatima replied.

'Come on, Emeka.' Dr Kanu was about to lead the boy out of the bunker when Fatima grabbed him by the other arm. He burst into tears.

'If you don't value your life, I value mine.' Fatima's voice was louder than necessary. 'This boy is what is keeping me in Biafra, and I will go to any length . . .'

'What's all this nonsense,' shouted Dr Kanu. 'No one knows how much longer this war will last. If you want to go on living the life of a rabbit every day, I do not want my son to grow up that way.'

'If it is a problem for you, I have told you how to solve it,' Fatima replied in a relaxed but firm tone. 'Send us out of Biafra! Other people have sent out their own families, including some people recently awarded the Biafra Silver Medal!'

Dr Kanu went into the main house and tried Mr Akwaelumo's number. He was in.

'If you had phoned one minute later you wouldn't have caught me,' Mr Akwaelumo told him. 'I'm going over to Uzuakoli right now.'

'May I come with you?' Dr Kanu asked.

'Certainly. Where do I pick you up?'

'From my office. In less than half an hour.'

Dr Kanu returned to the bunker to inform his wife that he was going on duty to Uzuakoli.

'I knew you didn't really come to keep us company,' Fatima

remarked teasingly.

'I did. But what a reception you gave me!'

'I'm sorry, darling.' Fatima jumped as she heard a noise outside. It was Moses slamming the door of his room to return to the car. 'Have a tangelo. We received some this morning from the Agricultural Research Station, and Emeka wanted to eat all of them at once. He said they were delicious.'

'You haven't had any?' Dr Kanu asked.

'I told you I am going on a seven-day fast as from today.'

'What?' cried Dr Kanu. 'Were you serious about it?'

'Ami,' Fatima threw an arm over her husband's shoulder. 'Let's try and respect each other's feelings on this war. I got to know about fasting while we were at Obodo, and I now want to try it. Perhaps at the end of it we may find we get less on each other's nerves. OK? Now have a tangelo.'

The road to Uzuakoli was excellent. It was part of the 65-mile road linking the historic town of Arochuku with Umuahia, built by the pre-January 1966 Government of Eastern Nigeria. Except for four checkpoints, there was little evidence of war on the 12-mile journey to Uzuakoli. Dr Kanu found it refreshing to get out of his office, out of his house, and out of Umuahia township. There was so much fresh air outside, and yet he had been suffocating in Umuahia!

'Who knows how much longer this road will remain peaceful and quiet?' Dr Kanu observed as they sped on.

'Who knows?' echoed Mr Akwaelumo. 'It's because of the uncertainty that the Director-General thought I should review the situation with the army unit at Uzuakoli before deciding whether or not to launch a full-scale food production campaign in Uzuakoli, Nkpa and Alayi zones.'

'It seems this year's Christmas Special is the capture of Umuahia,' Dr Kanu remarked.

'So I hear. Today is December what?' Akwaelumo asked.

'December 10.'

'This will end the same way as their previous specials,' Akwaelumo said.

'We shall frustrate their efforts, what with the recent increase in our fire power, and the high morale of the boys. Moreover,' added Akwaelumo, 'BOFF (the Biafra Organization of Freedom Fighters) has already infiltrated people behind enemy lines on intelligence work.'

'What gives me hope is the fact that everyone in Biafra, including the market women, has at last come to recognize that nothing good will come out of the various so-called peace moves. The outcome of Algiers dramatized the whole thing so effectively.'

Although most Biafrans distrusted the Organization of African Unity, cautious optimism had been expressed when the O.A.U. organized preliminary talks in Niamey, Niger Republic on 20-26 July 1968, particularly as the two Heads of State of Nigeria and Biafra attended. The events of the ensuing months had, however, dispelled even the faintest hopes. Only the Biafran Head of State appeared in Addis Ababa in August when the O.A.U. Consultative Committee on Nigeria was scheduled to meet. The Biafrans thought the O.A.U. should have reprimanded the Nigerian Head of State for being a 'no show'. Then came September when the O.A.U. Committee met in Algiers to negotiate between the two sides. Aba and Owerri fell to the Nigerians on the opening days of the meeting. Even though the Biafrans were prepared to travel in quest of peace to a country which was openly hostile to the very existence of Biafra, they were not permitted to attend. Algeria refused to grant them visas. The O.A.U. proceeded to call for a ceasefire and for negotiations within the framework of one Nigeria.

'You know what I feel?' Akwaelumo began after both men had been silent for almost five minutes, each watching the trees as they sped past the car. 'No matter what we do, and our boys are doing marvellously well in spite of the heavy odds against them, unless a major world power backs us openly, we stand little chance of making it. That's why I have tended to favour peaceful negotiations. I know we've been on opposing sides on this . . .'

'It isn't that I am against peaceful negotiations in principle,' broke in Dr Kanu. 'It's just that I don't believe in hypocrisy. I need to be convinced that there is the genuine intention to resolve the issue by peaceful negotiations. So far, there has been no evidence of this. The vandals are more interested in crushing the Igbo man once and for all than in peaceful negotiations. In any case, their record between August 1966 and May 1967, including what they made of the agreements reached at Aburi, shows the futility of negotiating with them. The O.A.U. does not want peaceful settlement. Many of the Heads of State are afraid that our success may encourage their own people to break loose from years of repression. Those of them who have no skeletons in their cupboards have come out openly and recognized Biafra. The others take cover under the cliché about maintaining the territorial integrity of member states, as if those territorial lines were not the same that many of these same Heads of State criticized in the colonial days as arbitrarily drawn by the imperialists round a conference table in Berlin!'

'President Houphuet Boigny's speech announcing Ivory Coast's recognition of Biafra was particularly moving,' Akwaelumo said. 'I thought that the bit in which he stressed that unity is a concept for the living, not for the dead, would have made an impression on the O.A.U.'

'I used to be naive about the effect of rousing world sympathy.' Dr Kanu picked up his walking stick from the car floor where he had placed it. 'I don't think about it any more. The world knows the Biafran case – before and since the outbreak of the war. Markpress* has made sure of that. Numerous visitors to Biafra have carried stories and photographs of suffering in Biafra to all parts of the world. Even the BBC was compelled to carry the first-hand account of the Presbyterian clergyman from Canada who was eyewitness to the senseless bombing of the Mary Slessor Hospital by the vandals. Where has it all landed us? Nowhere. Nowhere! Major world decisions are not based on sympathy. It is only the language of force that the world understands, but when I say it people call me a hawk.'

'No one in Biafra doubts the fact that we had no alternative but to fight,' conceded Akwaelumo. 'And even the Nigerians will admit that if the two sides were left alone, they would be no match for us. The big snag is that the world has not left us alone to slug it out. The British are vying for first place with the Russians as Nigeria's backers. It's the first time I have seen Britain and the Soviet Union backing the same side . . .'

'And the United States,' Dr Kanu added.

'The U.S. has been somewhat more crafty, sending their excess flour to fatten us while their C.I.A. agents assist the U.K. secretly to prevent us from buying the arms with which to defend ourselves. They regard Nigeria as falling within the British sphere of influence, and in order to maintain friendly relations with the U.K. they allow their attitude to us to be guided by the advice they receive from the British Government.'

'American foreign policy has never impressed me, so I wasn't expecting much from the U.S.,' Dr Kanu replied. 'If this war had been going on in a white country, between whites, America would have moved in at once to stop the fighting without delay and initiate peaceful negotiations between the two combatants.

* The public relations agency based in Geneva which handled external publicity for Biafra.

Not so when blacks are eliminating blacks. They would probably regard it as a welcome development. It's the attitude of the American Blacks that has been particularly disappointing to me.'

'Oh yes,' Akwaelumo nodded as he spoke, 'I remember you were a strong advocate of the proposal to woo Black America to our side.'

'Yes, I was,' replied Kanu. 'I had thought that Black Americans would see in Biafra their hope for final emancipation and for the emancipation of the Black Man everywhere. Here we were, in spite of the deprivations of war, making a major scientific and technological breakthrough . . .'

'And ushering in a cultural renaissance as well,' added Mr Akwaelumo.

'Yes. It was an unprecedented breakthrough on all fronts. With no previous experience, we have constructed and are operating an international airport. With no previous experience, we now refine petrol . . .'

'In fact efforts are now being made to control petrol refining,' said Akwaelumo.

'Could anybody in Nigeria have imagined that a black man could refine petrol without a white man to supervise him?' Dr Kanu continued. 'Shell B.P. would tell you that you need no less than one million pounds to establish a single refinery, and white experts to man it for the next century. Biafra has debunked all that. See what our scientists are turning out, and our engineers. Our home economists have come out with dry packs of practically every local foodstuff, and these can be preserved indefinitely. Our architects have produced unique designs for earth houses, within the reach of the ordinary village farmer.'

Mr Akwaelumo did not want to be outdone by his friend: 'I mentioned cultural renaissance because that is another area where so much is happening. Impromptu musical compositions. Drama troupes. The terrific raffia baskets which have now taken over from imported handbags. Even the palm kernel shell has been turned into a work of art.'

'That's why I thought Black Americans and the Black Man everywhere would have felt proud of what was happening in Biafra. I had thought that they would throw in their lot with us to set Biafra firmly on its feet, knowing that with our rich human and material resources, Biafra is poised to become the first truly independent African country, equipped to uplift the downtrodden Black Man everywhere, having known what it is to be downtrodden. But alas, the Black American is too brainwashed to know where his salvation lies.'

Mr Akwaelumo had a different answer. 'I would say the Black American succumbed to Nigerian propaganda. You know Nigeria had been hailed by the imperialists as Africa's potential leader. To run down Nkrumah's efforts to project the African Personality, the imperialists had always painted Nigeria in glowing and unmerited colours. What those same imperialists have now advised Nigeria to propagate is that the neo-colonialists are propping up Biafra to destroy Africa's most promising nation, Nigeria. Ridiculous! And the Black Americans seem to have bought the rubbish!'

'You're probably right,' Dr Kanu conceded. 'The imperialists never come out in their true colours. They crushed Nkrumah in Ghana because he was proving too independent for their liking. They don't want a black country that will stand firmly on its feet and talk to them on equal terms. They want us to cling perpetually to their apron strings, and if Biafra was allowed to survive, it would upset their apple cart.'

'It's the French attitude I can't understand,' remarked Mr Akwaelumo.

'Neither can I,' Dr Kanu echoed. 'They say they are with us, yet you're not always sure whether or not they are.'

'If only France, or some other big power would come out in the open to declare support for us, the course of this war would change. All we need is three or four fighter bombers and the ability to buy modern equipment in the open market, and then nobody would show the vandals the way back to their country!'

'I couldn't agree with you more,' Dr Kanu said. 'France can do it if she wants, but I'm beginning to doubt whether she will, unless she is waiting until we all die before she comes to our rescue! Our supply of young men for the army has now almost completely dried up, and unless something happens pretty fast you and I will have no alternative but to bear arms.'

'Not me!' shouted Akwaelumo. 'I'm perfectly satisfied that I am making my maximum contribution to the war effort as Director for Procurement . . .'

'Stop!' shouted a guard, his finger on the trigger, as the car approached a barrier at the entrance to the Methodist College, Uzuakoli. 'Advance to be recognized!'

As the car drove into the compound, after the driver had identified his boss, Dr Kanu talked about his concern for Fatima. He had always been vehement in his attacks on Biafran leaders who evacuated their families from Biafra, and he hated to find himself asking for the evacuation of his own family. But Fatima had taken more shocks than those other wives, some of whom had been evacuated in the first week of the war. She was fast becoming a nervous wreck, jumping at every sound as if a war plane perpetually hovered above her head. Unless she was removed from Biafra he might have a mental case on his hands, and this would impair his effectiveness as Director for Mobilization.

'I don't know when next you'll have an opportunity of seeing H.E. face to face, but this is the kind of problem I suggest you take up directly with him,' advised Akwa.

'You think so?' Dr Kanu asked.

'Yes. Don't suggest evacuation. Just present the problem to him and see what he suggests.'

'Thank you. I hope neither of us cracks up before the opportunity to meet H.E. presents itself.'

'You don't look like somebody about to crack up,' teased Akwaelumo.

'Don't be too sure,' Dr Kanu replied.

22

December 15, 1968.

Nkwo Obodo market lacked its characteristic noise and vivacity. Though, like other markets in Biafra, it had abandoned its well laid out stalls and moved into a dense bamboo jungle without stalls, it had continued a busy, boisterous market in spite of the war. After the massacre of the innocents, as Radio Biafra described the tragic raid of Okpa market by two Nigerian Mig fighters, when a hundred or more were killed, every market in Biafra abandoned its readily identifiable stalls and sought refuge in the jungles. The market hours were also changed, to avoid midday when the war planes could swoop down any time, any where, without provocation and without warning.

The Obodo War Council had decided on morning hours for Nkwo Obodo market. By seven o'clock it had already attained its peak, and its din could be heard from half a mile. By nine it had reverted to deserted jungle.

This Nkwo day the market was no more than a quarter full.

There were hardly any buyers and sellers from the neighbouring villages; even the incredibly tough *agbenu* women traders were absent, and so were many Obodo women. One of the war fronts in the Okigwi sector had advanced to within ten miles of Obodo. Christmas 1968, only ten days away, held little prospects of peace and goodwill for the people of Obodo. The noise of small arms fire was clearly discernible, especially at night.

A group of women forgot the wares they had come to sell as they discussed the situation.

'Mama Ebele, do you say we shall survive this ordeal?'

'It will end well,' Mama Ebele replied listlessly.

'I don't think Mama Ebele heard what I heard last night. It was as if they were playing the guitar with their rifles.'

'How could I not have heard it?' responded Mama Ebele. 'Who at Obodo would say he slept a wink last night, with those things sounding nonstop?'

'I asked my question simply because I heard you say "it will end well".'

'What else should she have said?' a chubby-looking woman asked. Although she had been helped to put her basket of cassava down long before the discussion began, she had not remembered to remove the pad from her head nor to display her cassava tubers for sale.

'I used to give the same reply myself whenever anybody greeted me *kedu*,' put in the first woman. 'But after last night's *ngedelegwu*, I hardly know what to say.'

'What you heard last night is nothing,' asserted Nkoli, a 'second degree' refugee who had run first from Ogoja and later from Onitsha, her home town. 'I gather it was our own boys firing last night. The time to run is when the Nigerians bring their ferrets. Then the sound changes, and you'll hear the Nigerian guns sound as if they are shouting *kwapu kwapu unu d-u-u-um!* When that sounds, even the lizard runs without further warning.'

'God forbid that that will happen here,' Mama Ebele cried.

'What can the Hausas be looking for in Obodo?' Nkoli asked. She and her family had chosen Obodo for its remoteness, after running first from Ogoja to Onitsha, and then from Onitsha to Obodo.

'I wonder,' echoed the chubby woman. 'We have no Government department here; nothing of importance.'

'That is what I had been asking myself, until I heard Ukadike say that Radio Kaduna announced that the Federal troops had "liberated" Obodo.'

'Did they announce that?' asked Nkoli, concern written all over her face.

'I heard somebody say so,' Mama Ebele confirmed.

'Then that is serious. If it were Radio Nigeria in Lagos, I would not take it seriously, but Radio/Television Kaduna? That is serious. They are the people in control in Nigeria, so they know what they are saying.'

'It can't be true.' The chubby woman was not prepared to brace up to the imminent danger. 'Who in Kaduna knows this place?'

'You speak as if you forget that there are saboteurs everywhere,' observed Mama Ebele. 'Was it not a sabo who brought the Nigerian jet bomber to kill Prophet James and destroy his church?'

'I said right from the beginning that we must not take in these refugees who allowed the Hausas to enter their own towns,' the chubby woman with the pad on her head said regretfully. 'They are never happy to see people like us who are still occupying our homes, so they use transmitters to invite the enemy so that every person in Biafra will become a refugee like them.'

Nkoli protested vehemently.

'I say my own, hoha!' The woman with the pad was adamant. 'Nobody in this town heard of an air raid before the War Council talked about every Biafran being his brother's keeper and compelled us to take those refugees. Since then it has been one trouble after another. Air raid. Now Kaduna talks about "liberating" us! All because we took those Onitsha people . . .'

'Don't begin to say what will annoy me,' Nkoli retorted, rising from her stool.

Mama Ebele pleaded for peace.

'I did not call anybody's name,' persisted the woman with the pad. 'But I do not say my own things behind people's backs . . .'

'Wait!' shouted Mama Ebele.

It was the sound of the *ikoro*, at first hardly discernible, but soon its clear sonorous message filled the air. The spontaneous screams from the women as most of them abandoned their wares to rush home announced the end of the world.

The sound of the *ikoro* had hardly faded away before all Obodo males had assembled in Chief Ofo's palace, armed with matchets, dane guns, spears, cudgels. No one uttered a word, but the message of doom was clearly inscribed on every face.

'Odo, Ogbuisi, Ogbuisi, Mazi, Mazi, . . .' Chief Ukadike quickly disposed of the elementary courtesies. His characteristic exhuberance had deserted him. He had even forgotten to wear his medals.

'Kinsmen,' he went on. 'You have assembled here at the sound of the *ikoro*. The *ikoro* does not sound for nothing. You heard what happened last night. As soon as I saw the first ray of light I was on my way to the Brigade Commander for the latest sitrep, so that I could know what to tell you. I had hardly reached Ngene junction when I saw a despatch rider on his way to my house with a message from the Brigade Commander . . .'

The atmosphere was tense. The light cool morning breeze had stopped at the sound of the *ikoro*.

'The Nigerian Field Commander of the rag-tag Federal troops in Okigwi has already claimed that he has "liberated" Obodo, and Lagos has congratulated him on the important achievement. Radio/Television Kaduna carried the news two days ago. The vandals are therefore throwing in all they have to enter Obodo. Their hope is to drink champagne at Nnewi, H.E.'s home town, with British and Russian journalists on Christmas day. Since they cannot break through Onitsha – thanks to our shore batteries – they are determined to break through Obodo to Ekwulobia and thence to Nnewi.

'But the Brigade Commander assured me that our gallant Biafran forces will not allow their jigger-infested feet to touch Obodo. We are expecting planeloads of ammo from abroad tonight. Through Dr Amilo Kanu's intervention, the Head of State has directed that at least one planeload of ammo should be sent immediately to this sector. Once our boys receive that ammo, they will flush out all the pockets of vandals from this area. Meanwhile, RaP has been asked to send the Commanding Officer plenty of *ogbunigwe*.

'As a precautionary measure, the Brigade Commander directs that we evacuate all women and children immediately.'

'To which place?' shouted Uduji, unable to hold back his anger, frustration and fear.

'But the Government has warned that all able-bodied men must remain behind to defend . . .'

'You have not answered my question about where we are to send our women and children,' retorted Uduji rising to his feet.

'Uduji sit down!' three voices shouted in unison.

'Why should Uduji sit down?' intervened Mazi Kanu Onwubiko. 'Would anybody here tell me that any person who has asked the question he has just asked is vomiting fodder?'

'There are many places to send the women and children,' Chief Ukadike replied. 'Some can go to Ndikelionwu. There is food there, and the people of Ndikelionwu are friendly to our people. Some can go to Ekwulobia. Some can go to Ndiowu. They are all friendly towns which have not been disturbed . . .'

'And what happens when any of those towns is overrun?' cut in Uduji.

Chief Ukadike was furious: 'Uduji, if I hear *fim* from you again, I will show you . . .'

'Yes, it is Uduji, you will show your strength,' muttered Uduji, 'yet the Hausas are about to drive you out of your home and you can't stop them!'

Chief Ukadike stormed towards Uduji, to tear the ne'er-do-well to bits. Two men held him back. When he had cooled down, he continued: 'This is our home town. Don't our people say that what is ours is ours, but what is mine is mine? It is true that Nigeria is fighting Biafra, but as far as I am concerned, once the vandals take Obodo, my home town, they have conquered me and the war is over for me.'

'*Ndewo*, Mazi!' echoed Chief Ofo. 'Ukadike's fault is that he likes to hear his voice, but when he touches on a solid point he should be commended. Our fathers before us lived and died here. Whatever anybody says, here also will I live and die. What will I tell my ancestors if they hear that I have taken their *ofo* to a strange land? I agreed that the *ikoro* should be sounded to summon every Obodo human being who sports a penis, to plan how to save our town. Those are my words.'

Chief Ofo gnashed his teeth as he foraged for his empty snuff-box in the folds of his cloth.

'Mazi, Mazi,' began Ezeani, one of many traders forced to abandon their wares in the north and return home in 1966. 'While we talk about every male remaining behind to defend the town, the War Council should stop the male refugees from leaving. Many of them left last night. The people living in my compound were packing their things when I came out this morning.'

'We must not allow them to leave!' shouted several voices. No uncomplimentary epithet was spared on the refugees: they were ungrateful, greedy, envious, malicious, wicked, treacherous, disloyal to Biafra, weak-kneed. They were in regular contact with the enemy, using secret transmitters, and once they began to evacuate themselves from a town threatened by the enemy that town was bound to capitulate. Before moving they would have shown the enemy unguarded routes for entering the town. Everyone in the gathering agreed that no male refugee should henceforth be allowed to leave the town. They must learn to take the rough with the smooth; the men among them must stay back to defend the town that had given them shelter and food for one whole year. Four men picked from each of the eleven villages of Obodo were despatched promptly to mount road blocks in their respective villages, to stop every taxable male from leaving the town and to apprehend any infiltrator.

Chief Ukadike took the floor for his final charge: 'My brothers. the whole of Biafra is watching us. If we do as the people of Nibo did, the vandals will not step into our town. Let us disperse now and send away our women and children, with money, clothing and whatever food they can carry. They should set off before dark. Those of us who have no bunkers must dig them today. Kill one or two goats, and dry the meat. If you have no goats, kill some chickens and dry the meat, just in case we have to run into the forest for some time, God forbid! Secretary, do you have any announcement?'

Chief Ukadike was visibly worn out, despite his efforts to keep up his public image as a dare-devil. The civil defence instructions he had just handed down to his audience had, before now, meant little to him, forming nothing more than part of the volume of papers churned out by the Directorate of Civil Defence, first on regular duplicating sheets and, later on, as a result of shortage of typing or duplicating paper throughout Biafra, on torn out sheets of primary school exercise books. He had not envisaged the day he would be in a position to carry them out, in his home town.

'Ezeahurukwe has touched on everything,' began Mr John Nwosu, the Secretary. 'There is only one thing left. God forbid that we shall run from here, but if we have to do so, we must put poison into all food we cannot carry away, including pots of drinking water we leave behind. Lock up your houses, and destroy . . .'

'Is that not a lorry?' shouted Ezeani.

The Secretary moved towards the entrance to identify the vehicle. 'It's a lorry,' he shouted from the entrance, 'and it seems to be going towards Mazi Kanu's house.'

'May the shelling machine silence you there,' cursed Mazi Kanu, 'if it is Mazi Kanu's name that you choose to broadcast to the enemy today.'

'I hope the Hausas have not already infiltrated the town while we sit here talking,' remarked Uduji.

'God forbid!' cried Chief Ofo, rising to his feet.

'The lorry has turned round. It is now coming here,' shouted the Secretary from his look-out point, simultaneously searching for an escape route.

The men rose and some were already disappearing behind the women's huts when Chief Ukadike shouted at them to remain where they were. In the absence of his medals, he did not want to be left alone to face the onslaught.

'Those who wish to stay may do so,' Uduji shouted as he disappeared, followed by several others.

The lorry stopped in front of Chief Ofo's reception hall, and a soldier wearing the Biafra Sun jumped down, carrying a Madsen with the magazine detached. Mazi Kanu, who had stood his grounds alongside Chief Ofo, recognized Geoffrey, the orderly who had been assigned to his daughter-in-law while she lived at Obodo. That ruled out fears of enemy infiltration.

'Who knows whether they have killed my son,' Mazi Kanu muttered to Chief Ofo as he moved towards the lorry. The orderly instantly gave him a half salute and led him away beyond the lorry. Mazi Kanu slumped down on the grass before the orderly could conclude his message. By the time he regained control of himself, an anxious crowd had gathered round him.

'I hope Doctor's wife gave you the keys to their house?' Mazi Kanu enquired slowly, with a deliberate effort to contain his emotions.

'Yes sir,' replied Geoffrey, in a tone devoid of his characteristic boisterousness.

'Go and pack their things. Whatever you want to carry away. But make sure you don't touch any of my things . . .'

'Why should they be allowed to carry Doctor's belongings?' cut in Uduji who had suddenly materialized. 'Does Doctor have two heads, I ask? Don't all of us here own property which we value? Or will whoever asks such questions be branded a sabo and shot?'

'Uduji has a point,' the Secretary of the War Council remarked, watching the orderly from the corner of his eye.

The orderly told the driver to start the lorry, ignoring Uduji, the Secretary of the War Council, and any others who shared their views. He had orders to carry out and little time to do so without risking his life; this was not the moment to quibble with idle civilians. He was about to jump into his front seat, beside the driver, when Chief Ukadike who had not uttered a word, drew him aside.

'Geoffrey, my brother,' Chief Ukadike whispered, 'tell me in a nutshell. Can our boys stop the vandals from getting into Obodo?'

'How can I answer that? Am I God?'

'Don't be angry with me, my brother,' pleaded Chief Ukadike when he saw that the orderly was impatient and irritable. 'You people at Umuahia, especially those of you who see H.E. almost every day, you are the God we see with our eyes. You know what will happen before it happens.'

'Country bad. That's all I can say.' The orderly spoke solemnly and in a hushed tone, 'They say the pilot of one plane bringing tons of ammo for us is a C.I.A. man. After taking off from Lisbon, he threw the ammo into the sea and returned to America.'

'Jesus Christ!' exclaimed Chief Ukadike.

The orderly continued: 'I hear one sabo told the enemy that our ammo has finished, so at once they began a big push. That's why Doctor sent me with this commandeered lorry. The Brigade Headquarters is already moving to Obia . . .'

'What!' Chief Ukadike could hardly believe his ears. The Brigade Headquarters moving to Obia, a good nine miles beyond Obodo, and yet the Brigade Commander orders every man in Obodo to remain in his home! Who would defend the town, if the soldiers who stood between it and the enemy were on the run?

'This is impossible!' The crowd surged round Chief Ukadike whose face was a picture of utter hopelessness. The orderly promptly jumped into the lorry and ordered the driver to move.

'Make una push am for me,' the civilian driver appealed for help when he found the battery had not charged up sufficiently from the Umuahia-Obodo trip to start the engine without help. The men were too engrossed in Chief Ukadike's words to hear him. The orderly jumped out of the lorry and, with his rifle in position, ordered the men to give the lorry a push. The engine started after about fifty yards. The orderly who was already getting back into the lorry instantly jumped down when the familiar but ominous sound rent the air.

Kwapu kwapu unu d-uum!
Kwapu kwapu unu d-uum!

'God, almighty!' the orderly shouted. 'Enemy ferret don' reach here! Driver move! . . . Stop! . . .'

The driver jerked forward as ordered, and stopped as ordered. The orderly, all worked up, rushed to Mazi Kanu Onwubiko: 'I beg you, Mazi, make we go before ferret reach here . . .'

'I'm not going anywhere.' Mazi Kanu spoke slowly but with finality.

The orderly bit his right forefinger, apprehensive of what his master would do to him if he returned to Umuahia without his parents and his property. The idea came to him in a split second. He would bundle the old man and his wife into the lorry after collecting Doctor's belongings from the house . . .

Kwapu kwapu unu d-uum!

Kwapu kwapu unu d-uum!

'Take cover!' shouted the orderly, with amazing presence of mind as something whistled past. The mortar landed four hundred yards away, on the dirt road which joins the trunk road to Nnewi. It immediately disintegrated, hurling lethal shrapnel in all directions. An agonized shriek defied the resultant silence as one victory was registered for the advancing enemy: an old widow, hard of hearing, on her way to Chief Ofo's compound to find out why the *ikoro* had been sounded, was cleanly disembowelled. She slumped down over the bloody mess. The war was over for her.

23

'*Chei!*' shouted Geoffrey, sweating profusely. The mortar which had just landed must have been aimed at his lorry, and it would have scored a bull's eye had he not stopped to take Mazi Kanu. A sabo must have been observing his movements and passing on the information to the Nigerian troops through a transmitter. There could be no other explanation. The realization that he could have been a dead man threw him completely off balance. No warning, no farewell; leaving behind two aged parents, his wife and nine children all of whom depended heavily on the stockfish, formula 2, powdered milk, *garri*, black-eyed beans, salt, etcetera he sent them regularly from the relief supplies delivered at his master's house every week by the Caritas Representative.

The thought that he stood within the reach of a live ferret sapped whatever courage still remained in him. The entire Biafran Army did not own one single ferret, nor initially even the bazooka to destroy one. He was among the few Biafrans who had had the privilege of beholding one with their own eyes. 'Corp'l Nwafo' as it was nicknamed, had been captured intact in the Anambra sector, an act of outstanding bravery by a Biafran soldier after whom the ferret was nicknamed. 'Corp'l Nwafo' had been a spectacle sufficiently harrowing to give one a nightmare. Normal bullets were as effective on it as wooden arrows striking the Olumo rock; even the tyres were impregnable. One ferret alone could fight its way through a Biafran battalion armed with No. 4 rifles; all a sensible soldier in such circumstances could do was to escape with his head before the ferret came within range and reduced him to minced meat.

Every Biafran, including the vast majority who did not have the opportunity to see 'Corp'l Nwafo' on display at Umudike, knew that an advancing ferret wiped out every human being in its path. Every Biafran knew that the ferret could gain several miles in one short day, and that this meant that you did not pause for breath as soon as its sound heralded its approach. Its orders – *kwapu kwapu unu dum* – warned all in its path to pack and quit before it arrived.

Geoffrey hurriedly and nervously removed the things that would give him away as a soldier. He dumped his beautiful stiffly starched camouflage uniform as well as his shining boots into the lorry. For a brief while he scrutinized his Madsen rifle and the magazine, curved like an oil bean pod, wondering what to do with them. Then he also dumped them into the lorry as he made for the bush. With luck, he might take advantage of the confusion and escape as a civilian, without being spotted by vigilant Civil Defenders manning the innumerable checkpoints on the way and handed to the army for immediate deployment to the hottest war front as a deserter. Civil Defenders (and civilians generally) did not take kindly to soldiers running away from the war fronts, and they occasionally took summary action with such stragglers, branding them saboteurs. The driver would take care of the lorry, since it belonged to his elder brother from whom it had been commandeered for war duties by the Directorate of Transport.

The race – that is the literal translation of the Igbo word describing the mass exodus from a town about to capitulate – the race away from Obodo began like the uncoordinated and confused movement of soldier ants disturbed by the foot of an unobservant pedestrian. Many villagers headed for the trunk road to Obia, while many others ran away from the same road as if death stalked them there. Ubaha villagers ran towards Mbom village, while Mbom villagers headed for Ubaha village. A woman who was warming her pot of bitterleaf soup when the ominous *ikoro* sounded put the pot in a basket and ran from the house with the basket on her head leaving behind the cassava *foofoo* which was to go with the soup. The soup spilled as she ran, trickling down her head. When she paused for breath, a safe distance on the footpath to Obia, what remained of the soup was not enough to go with more than a few balls of *foofoo*. She restrained herself from throwing it away, pot and basket included, when someone told her that the pot and the basket would come in handy in a refugee camp.

The Reverend Nehemiah Anwuna had just invited the godparents of one of the two war babies he was about to baptize to 'name this child' when the mortar landed. The child's mother had to chase him into the vestry to retrieve her child from him. It seemed the sound of the mortar had shattered his already jaded nerves. He pulled off his cassock only to put it on again when it occurred to him that it was safer to be seen in it, even if he fell into enemy hands (God forbid!). From under the vestry table where he took cover briefly, he cursed his congregation for not digging bunkers around the church, forgetting that it was he who had dissuaded them from doing so, denouncing bunkers as mass graves. He did not stay long in the vestry. What if the vandals met him there? The inscription they left on the walls of the church near Abagana ('We have come to destroy not to save') reminded him of their hostility towards churches in Biafra. He tiptoed out of the vestry, as if he was escaping from an ambush, and made for the footpath to Obia, ignoring his driver who held the car door open for him and forgetting his Holy Bible, Book of Common Prayer and his reading glasses.

'Where are you going?' a woman shouted as she saw her neighbour, a middle-aged woman, striding past her in the opposite direction.

'Nduka!' she shouted, panting heavily.

Nduka, her only brother, had gone mental. He could not get over the loss of his supermarket at Onitsha. When the enemy mortar landed in Onitsha, he had carefully locked up his precious supermarket and asked his staff to report in a week's time, hoping all would be well by then. He was among the last to leave Onitsha, and went no further than Nnewi from where he hoped he could conveniently nip back to Onitsha every morning to keep an eye on his supermarket. He never went back to Onitsha. All that remained of his supermarket was the bunch of keys in his pocket. His relations had no alternative but to send him to Dibiaezue who had a reputation for curing every brand of madness.

'When you fetch him, where will you take him?' enquired a man leading a goat with one hand and a child with the other.

Nduka's sister stopped abruptly. She had not given thought to that problem. After rescuing Nduka, what could she do with him?

Where could she take him? To a refugee camp? Who would take care of him there? It was only a momentary pause. Her first responsibility was to rescue her brother from enemy bullets; what to do with him after that was secondary. She ran on, unmindful of the consequences, towards the remote village where Dibiaezue lived.

Within two hours of the explosion of the first mortar, the disorderly ants had regrouped into one unending flow, avoiding the trunk road for fear not only of the ferret but also of supporting enemy planes. The mass of human beings followed footpaths as they made their way towards Obia. The man who had been leading a goat with one hand and his child with the other had slung the hefty goat across his back leaving his three-year old son to trudge beside him: the goat would fetch him thirty or more Biafran pounds at the end of the trek, thereby providing him with cash to supplement the slim rations at a refugee camp. It was therefore common sense to take special care of the goat, to ensure that it reached the unknown market in good shape.

In the ancient traditions of Obodo the sun bluntly refused to appear in its usual splendour, as if reluctant to preside over such an abomination. Only once in the history of Obodo had the sun hidden its face for so long at a time. That occasion was shortly before the influenza epidemic early in the century, when a middle-aged farmer debased himself and his kinsmen by cohabiting with a she-goat. The sun had hidden its face for the whole day. The ancestors demonstrated their revulsion by unleashing an influenza epidemic on the town which claimed thirty lives. The farmer had been tied to a rope and dragged round the town, after which his bruised and battered body was dumped into the evil bush, to propitiate the ancestors.

To abandon the town was an even greater abomination. It was tantamount to utter betrayal of all the ancestors of the town, to run, leaving their mortal remains behind to be desecrated by the enemy. It was tantamount to leaving the ancestral homes to grow wild, as if the ancestors had died without male issue. Who would pour libations to the dead and offer them *cola* every morning? Who would attend to the gods of Obodo?

The sun knew it was an abomination which would provoke the ire of the ancestors, and so refused to show its face. The wind knew it, and so sought an alibi by migrating to other towns, leaving Obodo without the mildest breeze.

Chief Ofo knew it. He also knew that tradition forebade him from sleeping outside his palace for even one night; no *Odo* of Obodo had ever done so, as far back as the human memory could go. He dared not carry the *ofo* of Obodo to another town, neither could he abandon it at Obodo without renouncing his title to it. He therefore had no choice but to stay with his *ofo* in his palace.

Mazi Kanu Onwubiko knew it, and he was determined to remain at Obodo no matter what the consequences would be. He was too old to begin a new life as a teacher, going on transfer from one town to another. He had all along refused to organize an emergency pack, knowing that he would not go anywhere. He returned to his house after the fall of the mortar, to coax his wife into joining the 'race' to Obia. He was waiting for her to leave before locking the compound gate and joining Chief Ofo in his palace when a car screeched to a halt outside. It was a green family-size Peugeot, effectively camouflaged with palm fronds to minimize the risk of being spotted by enemy planes. Two soldiers jumped down, rushed into the compound, bundled Mazi Kanu and his wife into the car and drove off before either of them could raise any protest. Dr Kanu knew what capital the Nigerian leaders would make of the capture of his parents. He knew that his father, with his characteristic stubbornness, would decide to remain behind. The Biafran Army had already conceded Obodo to the enemy, so time was not in his favour. He had therefore sent the car with two commandos with instructions to fight their way through if necessary and rescue his parents.

24

April 1969, the twenty-first month of the war.

A camouflaged Volkswagen mini-bus, fitted with a public address system, blared out the message as it moved slowly from one street to another:

THERE IS NO CAUSE FOR ALARM. THE ENEMY MADE A SUICIDE ATTEMPT TO CAPTURE UMUAHIA IN ORDER TO FORESTALL PEACE EFFORTS. THEY WERE HOWEVER REPULSED BY GALLANT BIAFRAN FORCES, WHO INFLICTED HEAVY CASUALTIES ON THEM. HIS EXCELLENCY APPEALS TO EVERY BIAFRAN TO REMAIN CALM, AND ASSURES THE NATION THAT THERE CAN BE NO QUESTION OF CONCEDING UMUAHIA TO THE VANDALS.

Checkpoints had suddenly sprung up in different parts of the town, to check all vehicles for possible infiltrators and also to prevent panic-stricken Biafrans from evacuating themselves and/or their property from Umuahia. The emergence of the checkpoints contributed to the anxiety you could read on every face. During the four miles' drive from Umudike to Umuahia, Dr Kanu found groups of children and adults congregating by the roadside, to ascertain from the movements of the road users whether their turn had come (God forbid!) to be on the run as refugees.

Except when the enemy stormed and captured a town all of a sudden, you could always tell by watching the road (if you lived near a besieged town) when to be on the move. Private cars with mattresses, beds and furniture strapped to the roof tops were invariably the first signs of the impending catastrophe.

The air was too tense and ominous for Dr Kanu's liking. The situation had not been that bad when he drove home not quite two hours earlier. Could it be the air raid? Or could the military situation have changed so dramatically? He saw the Provincial Administrator's commandeered Peugeot in the transit refugee camp close to his office and ordered his driver to go to the camp.

'Things seem to be hotting up,' he said as he got out of the car and shook hands with the Provincial Administrator. 'What's the latest?'

'I should be asking you that question,' replied the Provincial Administrator, drawing Dr Kanu away from the refugees who had surged towards them hoping to pick up bits of information on the military situation.

'I have been out of town for an hour or two,' Dr Kanu went on, 'and anything could have happened since then.'

'The sitrep hasn't been good at all, they say. Our losses in men and materials have been unusually high. The enemy's losses are umpteen times higher, but they seem hell-bent on drinking tea from H.E.'s bunker in Umuahia, according to one of their radio messages which our boys intercepted. The army boys are determined to stop them at all costs, but it appears the vandals sneaked through by an unexpected route and suddenly emerged on the outskirts of Bende town before they were spotted. So Bende is now seriously threatened. However, I've been asked to dispel all signs of panic. For that reason, we are diverting the thousands of refugees who would have flooded Umuahia by now. I have posted men at strategic points on the Bende and Uzuakoli roads, to divert the refugees to transit camps outside the township, and from there they will be sent towards Mbano. Let those refugees into Umuahia and the whole township will be on the run in a trice!'

As Dr Kanu shook hands with the Provincial Administrator to return to his car, the Administrator asked with unconcealed concern: 'You know Bende is only twelve miles away. You think we can make it this time?'

'We have to!' The reply came from Dr Kanu involuntarily.

It was difficult to say what single factor precipitated Dr Kanu's momentous decision. It stemmed from a series of events which had built up, one on top of the other, like the bricks of a house.

The loss of Obodo, his home town, had weighed on him more than he had ever imagined. He had never had strong emotional attachments to the village. He did not grow up there, and had discovered that the higher he moved up the academic and social ladder the greater his estrangement from village life. His marriage with a 'strange' girl whose contempt for Igbo village life was printed boldly on her face had not helped matters, nor his irritability on the one or two occasions he went home after qualifying as a doctor and found the whole village flocking to his house for free medical attention. Apart from walking in as if it was their right and without apology to see him any minute of the day or night, the people had expected not only free consultation but also free drugs – all because he was a son of Obodo!

But like most others who had spurned the village, he had had second thoughts during the war. The more remote the village, the safer from the enemy. The wisdom of putting up decent buildings in the village had become transparent. Those buildings had helped to mitigate the adverse effects on Biafra of the loss of the urban cities. In his moment of despair, Dr Kanu had turned to Obodo. The village had provided shelter for his wife and remaining son, and with the house he had built there, he nursed the hope that Fatima would go back to Obodo sooner or later, if the war dragged on. The fall of Obodo put a stop to that. It threw his parents and relations out of their homes and farm lands, and destroyed their means of earning a living and keeping themselves usefully occupied. He could not contemplate leaving his parents and immediate relations to live in a refugee camp, so he had had to rent a whole house for them near Nkwerre. His father had not forgiven him for forcing him to betray his ancestors by evacuating him from Obodo. His people in the refugee camp resented the fact that in spite of his exalted position, he had allowed Obodo to be taken by the enemy.

Then came the threat to Umuahia. He knew the seriousness of the threat. Everyone who had attended the innumerable meetings at State House since Aba and Owerri fell knew it. The Nigerians were desperate. The war had raged for nearly two years. World sympathy for Biafra was mounting. Some countries had already recognized Biafra and many more were believed to be considering doing so. The capture of Port Harcourt had not had the expected effect on the war. Biafra had built another airport at Uli, and set up its own oil refineries. Their heavy bombardment of Uli airport had not stopped Biafrans from importing arms. Their day and night air raids around the Egbema oil field had not stopped Biafra from exploiting crude oil for its hidden petrol refineries which the entire Nigerian intelligence network could not locate. The drivers who evacuated the oil had learnt to drive for miles at night without lights.

The Biafran scientists were turning out more lethal weapons. The Nigerians knew that it was in their best interests to end the war quickly. Their advance towards Umuahia demonstrated their desperateness. The boys who returned from the front lines claimed that the Nigerians had, for the first time, introduced tanks into the war. And that they had acquired special fighter-bombers to give support to their advancing troops.

As Director for Mobilization, Dr Kanu knew Biafra's major weakness. This time it was not only inadequate supplies of ammunition. It was also a dearth of fighting men. Nigeria had millions of young men; they were like soldier ants let loose. Biafra suffered fewer casualties on the battle front, but as with the Israelis fighting against the Arabs, one dead or wounded soldier meant a much greater tragedy for Biafra than for the enemy. Voluntary enlistment had given way to 'donations' of fighting men from each village and each Government department. The donations had had to be supplemented by outright conscription, with conscription teams storming villages, offices, motor parks, dance halls, markets, refugee camps – anywhere young men and not so young men could be found. It was common knowledge that any man caught was whisked away to a recruitment depot where his hair was promptly shaved off and he was immediately despatched to the war front. To send a young man to the war front with no military training and more often than not in the clothes he wore at the time of his conscription was tantamount to sending him to certain death. Those who could, escaped from the front at the slightest opportunity, notwithstanding the admonition given to them by army clergymen that any soldier shot while escaping went straight to hell! Their accounts of their experience at the front did not encourage others to join voluntarily. On the contrary many young men hid in house ceilings for days whenever conscription teams were around, or wore 'choristers'' robes whenever they went out, to make them look like men in holy orders (who were usually exempt from military service). Dr Kanu remembered the incisive comments of the palm wine tapper. He knew that if the war dragged on much longer Biafra would have no fighting men, even if she had all the ammunition in the world. Unlike Nigeria she had no willing neighbours to send their young men to join her fighting forces.

A meeting at State House Two, some twenty miles from Umuahia, to discuss contingency measures in the event of the loss of Umuahia to the enemy became the turning-point in Dr Kanu's life. It was clear from the trend of the discussions that, contrary to what the loudspeaker had blared out along the streets of Umuahia earlier in the afternoon, the Biafran leadership was ready to concede Umuahia to the enemy.

Dr Kanu could not stand it. He had given up a fine job because of the Nigerians. He had broken all links with the outside world, including his in-laws, in order to get away from the Nigerians, to a place of his own where the fact of his ethnic origin would no longer expose him to discrimination and genocide. The Nigerians were not content with imposing a blockade against him, but they had dogged his footsteps ever since. The Nigerians had slaughtered his innocent son at Enugu. The Nigerians had driven him out of Enugu. The Nigerians had driven his family out of Obodo, his village. Now the Nigerians wanted to drive him out of Umuahia. Where to? Wasn't there a point at which one had to say an emphatic NO to the vandals?

At the end of the meeting, Dr Kanu asked H.E. whether he could have a word with him privately. The time was 2.30 a.m. Dr Kanu expressed his grave concern over the progress of the war right from the start. Biafra was steadily losing territory to the enemy, and if this pattern was allowed to continue it was only a matter of time – the enemy was sure to engulf the entire country. The civilians had given every possible support to the war effort, more support than he had read or heard about in any other war – and he had read all the literature on warfare assembled by the Research Division of the Directorate of Propaganda. This unflinching support had come in spite of the severe hardships and deprivations confronting so many civilians. He was sure the civilians would continue to give their full support. There was, however, one thing they could not do – win the war at the war fronts. That was something left for the soldiers; their own contribution to the war effort.

He recounted the enthusiasm with which thousands of civilians volunteered to join the Armed Forces and, if need be, pay the supreme sacrifice for the young republic. His Directorate had had a difficult job turning away volunteers. Some who were turned away at one recruiting depot had promptly reported at another in the hope that they would have better luck there. One of the things which had heightened his concern was the sad realization that this rush for enlistment had subsided – hence the decision to solicit donations from village communities and, later, to conscript. He told H.E. the story of the old man, suggesting that Biafran leaders should end the war if conscription was to be extended to men of his age as evidence that even conscription had already run into difficulties.

'All our achievements on all other fronts are of no avail unless we also achieve victory on the war front,' Dr Kanu went on. 'I have great faith in Biafra. Our scientific and technological achievements in less than two years as a nation, and a nation at war, the unprecedented involvement in and commitment to the national cause, and the high degree of self-reliance and self-confidence which our people have manifested, prove beyond any doubt that we have the makings of a great nation. I have come to the conclusion that many more of us must join the Armed Forces if our dreams for Biafra are to be realized. Accordingly I hereby offer my services to the Biafran Army in whatever capacity I am considered fit.'

H.E. opened a new packet of cigarettes, pulled one out and took his time lighting it. He took several puffs before he spoke. 'Every Biafran does not have to bear arms in order to serve his country. You are doing an excellent job as Director for Mobilization, certainly more important than commanding one battalion.'

'Someone else can be found to take over from me, Your Excellency,' Dr Kanu argued.

'Just as someone else can be found to join the army,' replied H.E. with a gentle smile.

'I'm not so sure, Your Excellency. It's becoming almost impossible to find good material for the army, whereas I can name several people who can take over from me as Director, and probably do it better.'

'What does your wife think about this?' asked H.E.

'I don't want to discuss it with her because I know what her reaction will be. She will not like it one bit.'

'And yet you feel you must go ahead with it?'

'Of course, Your Excellency,' Dr Kanu replied. 'I would only seek your permission to send her out, with my surviving son, to Libreville. She has had quite a few shocks, apart from the tragic death of our first son, and she is now a bundle of nerves. You know she is in the medical profession, and she would make a valuable contribution if she could be employed at the centre for kwashiorkor children in Gabon.'

H.E. knocked off the two-inch-long ash which he had held expertly in place at the end of his cigarette. He then looked straight into Dr Kanu's eyes as if he wanted to see through their owner. 'Amilo,' he began, measuring out his words, 'I want to speak frankly to you. Biafra has wasted several of its intellectuals in this war. Chris Okigbo, Dr Imegwu, Joe Uchendu, Amamchuku Okeke, Nathaniel Okpala, and so on. I do not want to waste any more if I can help it. Biafra needs their talent and their training for the realization of the goals of Biafranism, both now, and perhaps even more after the noise of war has died away. I do not want to add you to their list. One does not become a good soldier just by picking up a gun. Or by being patriotic. It requires serious training, and experience, both of which you do not have . . .'

'And both of which I am prepared to acquire,' interrupted Dr Kanu.

'All right!' H.E. rose sharply, as if he was going to subject Dr Kanu to a physical examination. 'Go and sleep on it. If after that you haven't changed your mind, go and see the General Officer Commanding. I'll mention it to him. Meanwhile, I'll ask the Commissioner for Special Duties to send your wife to Libreville, whether or not you join the army.'

It was the G.O.C. who broke the news to Mr Ndubuisi Akwaelumo. 'Your friend, the doctor, has had his first baptism of fire! He's all wrapped up in bandages – I almost said in swaddling clothes! – in Queen Elizabeth Hospital.'

'Don't tell me anything has happened to him!' exclaimed Mr Akwa, jumping up from his seat as if to arrest the General Officer Commanding, Biafran Army for first degree murder.

'Nothing serious. A shattered bone here, and a bruise there, that's all. That's nothing for a combatant officer. But I must admit one thing before I run away. The Doc. has courage. What he lacks in military finesse he makes up for with his terrific guts!'

'Where do you say he is?'

'Queen Elizabeth Hospital. I don't remember the ward, but any doctor at the hospital will tell you. I ordered that he should be given the best amenity room.'

Mr Akwaelumo was already on his way to Queen Elizabeth Hospital before he remembered that he had a parcel for Dr Kanu, from his wife Fatima. She had sent it on one of the planes that call at Libreville on their way to Biafra. He promptly directed the driver to go to his house at Umudike. It was irritating to have to drive the four miles to Umudike first before going to the hospital to see his friend, but he knew how much Fatima's parcel would mean to him.

The nurse asked him to wait outside while she went to see whether the patient was asleep. Mr Akwaelumo could hardly hold back his anxiety.

'Come in,' whispered the nurse, opening the door. 'The doctor said he should have as much rest as possible . . .'

Mr Akwaelumo walked briskly past the nurse as if he was rushing to embrace Dr Kanu. He stopped abruptly when he saw the state in which his friend was: literally wrapped up in bandages, as the G.O.C. had described him. His head bandage gave him the look of a sheikh. The right arm was bandaged and in a sling. The unbuttoned pyjamas revealed that the chest was also bandaged.

'Well,' greeted Akwa as he took Dr Kanu's left hand which had been extended to him, and held on to it. 'I didn't know until the G.O.C. told me just now that you were back from the front.'

'I didn't know either when I came here or how. I'm told I was unconscious when I was brought in.'

'Terrible!' exclaimed Mr Akwaelumo.

'Draw that chair nearer and have a seat.' Dr Kanu allowed his friend to be seated before he went on. 'You remember the trying days before the outbreak of the war when H.E. told a foreign correspondent that he regarded every day in which he continued alive as a bonus from God? I have greater cause to regard my being alive today as a bonus from God.'

Dr Kanu cleared his throat and lifted his bandaged right arm in an attempt to turn leftwards in Akwaelumo's direction.

'I hope it doesn't hurt too badly,' Akwaelumo enquired, rising instantly to help.

'Not too badly, at least not when one realizes that I would have been lying dead and abandoned at the front.'

'Come off it, man.'

'I'm serious . . .' Dr Kanu proceeded with his story. His short experience at the front had been beyond anything he could have imagined.

The first week, events had more or less followed a set pattern. The vandals opened fire, and the Biafrans replied. Neither side attempted to advance, nor to retreat. You fired from your trenches, directing your rifles at the enemy in general rather than at any specific target. Occasionally the vandals lobbed some mortars, hoping to strike at the Biafran location, but without luck. Only two exploded anywhere near enough to have constituted a threat.

'It was frightful the first night. O, my God! It was as if you were in front of a firing squad. But your system soon adjusted to the macabre guitar strumming, as the boys nickname small arms fire. On some fronts, I am told, such exchanges of small arms fire are a means of reminding the other side that the war is still on. The vandals of course know that we have no ammo. So when they indulge in this game they hope our boys will soon run out of ammo, and then they advance. Until we run out of ammo, or until they decide to advance at all costs with their armoured cars, the war front is not too hot. It can be terribly hot if they fly in their Migs to give them covering fire. That, however, involves a degree of co-ordination between ground and air which is beyond them. I gather they had to give it up after the Migs emptied the destruction intended for our boys on their own men!'

'Serves them right!' cut in Akwa. 'God will wring their necks!'

'It seemed I was to be started off as a Principal Staff Officer at the Tactical Headquarters,' continued Dr Kanu, 'where my duties would be administrative.'

Dr Kanu was to hold the rank of Lieutenant-Colonel, the rank to which all Directors were entitled. This would keep him out of the actual war front. He had, however, resisted this, making it clear to the G.O.C. that his motivation was to fight at the front. He did not want any rank, as this might create problems, knowing that Lt-Colonels are not sent to the war front. His career was at the Faculty of Medicine of the University of Biafra, and any military rank assigned to him would be no more than a memento as soon as the war was over.

The G.O.C. consulted H.E. again, and they agreed reluctantly that he could be attached to a commanding officer temporarily, to get him to a war front. His future post would be decided after that. He was not given any rank. His uniform carried nothing but the Biafra Sun, on both sleeves.

'. . . but all the boys knew what I was before joining them,' he went on. 'My decision to join them in the trench – dressed like a private – inspired them. I saw this, and thought we could capitalize on it.'

Dr Kanu recounted how, during one of the quiet nights at the front he discussed his plan with his Commanding Officer – a boy who was clearly below twenty-one but had already made a reputation as a dogged fighter. Captain Nwora – that was his name – welcomed the idea, but had to obtain clearance first from Tactical Headquarters.

'My idea was simple. Not only did I find it extremely boring engaging in the intermittent exchange of fire, it was also clear that that was no way to drive the enemy out of Biafra, or even to stop them from taking Umuahia. What our boys needed very badly to boost their morale was to gain some ground from the Nigerians, no matter how small.'

A whole week passed. No clearance. 'In retrospect,' Dr Kanu went on, 'I fear the officers at Tactical Headquarters threw out the proposal, but didn't want to say so definitely, knowing from whom it came. If they had accepted, it would have meant giving me twenty tough boys – and we had them right there with us, willing to go anywhere with me. I had also requested a generous supply of the flying *ogbunigwe*. What I intended was to steal across with my boys and our *ogbunigwe* one night to the enemy trenches, give them a surfeit of the *ogbunigwe* and throw them into utter confusion. I also had my eye on knocking out the Saladin which they had been using to harass our boys . . .'

'My!' Akwa claimed, 'wasn't that a suicide bid?'

'Yes and no,' replied Dr Kanu. 'That was how Chris Okigbo and his boys silenced some trenches on the outskirts of the university campus at Nsukka. After all, how did they knock out the first ferret to be destroyed by Biafra at a time we had no bazookas? A boy crawled to the ferret where it was parked for the night, opened the access hatch at the top and threw in a hand grenade. Take another example. How did our BOFF boys secure the release of Biafrans detained by the vandals on the Nsukka campus? They merely lobbed thirty mortars into Nsukka, taking the enemy unawares. Bedlam was let loose. A group specially trained for the purpose promptly rushed into the campus and released the detainees. The enemy regrouped and came back to attack. They found no one to attack! Simple! Anything is possible in war, man; and my point is that we cannot push back the

Nigerians or even prevent their continued advance unless we try what may not be found in the standard texts at Sandhurst, or what may appear suicidal. Anyway, it seems the vandals read my thoughts and so decided not to give me the opportunity. Or maybe they received additional reinforcements.'

'Our information is that they were on orders from Lagos to capture Umuahia at all costs without further delay,' interrupted Akwa. 'The hypocritical O.A.U. had resumed its deceitful manoeuvres, giving the impression that it was sponsoring a peace conference. Lagos as you know is dead against any negotiated settlement when it thinks it can achieve outright victory, so it has ordered the field commanders to accomplish the immediate capitulation of Biafra while the O.A.U. dilly-dallies. The O.A.U. would then have nothing to settle.'

'How they did it, heaven only knows,' Dr Kanu continued his story. 'If anybody had told me that we could be surrounded and captured without firing a shot, I would have asked the person to sharrap. But those vandals did almost precisely that. One story I picked up after regaining consciousness here was that their bosses in Lagos had received intelligence reports that I was fighting at that sector, and that the vandals had been given specific orders to capture me alive and send me down to Lagos where special treatment awaited me as the man directly responsible for mobilizing young people against their so-called fatherland, Nigeria!'

'There's no doubt that Lagos will pay anything to have a Biafran of substance like you there,' observed Akwa. 'Such a person would have a much higher propaganda value to the world press and to Nigerians as a leader of the Igbo than some of the riff-raff – the dregs whose names nobody had ever heard in Igbo-land – but who are now paraded round the world by Lagos as Igbo V.I.P.s on the Nigerian side. That is of course if the person they catch is the type who will sell his conscience and his people for a mess of pottage. If he is like you and me, then torture of the worst kind awaits him. But I am digressing. Do you credit the vandals with such a high level of military intelligence that they know which Biafran is fighting in what sector?'

'I don't. It's our people I blame for not making more effective use of our innate intelligence and the determination and dedica-tion of our nation. There was I, offering to do what precisely the enemy later proceeded to do. Probably because I didn't go to Sandhurst, nobody took the proposal seriously. The result?'

The Biafrans were sleeping outside their trenches, as it was the quiet period of night when neither side normally opened fire on the other. The enemy had estimated the strength of Biafran defence in that sector, and sent enough men, equipment and ammo to wipe them out while a much bigger, motorized unit simultaneously pushed forward towards Umuahia. What saved Dr Kanu and the few others who survived was that one of the Nigerian soldiers fired his rifle prematurely. The prospects of a grim hand-to-hand encounter with Biafran troops had so frightened him that he unconsciously pulled the trigger. Others followed suit involuntarily. Having let the cat out of the bag, there was nothing else their commander could do but to launch the attack prematurely.

If only the enemy had known the state of confusion in the Biafran camp, they would have pressed on to easy victory. The fact that there had been no immediate reply from the Biafran side instilled greater fear into the Nigerians, who believed it must be part of Biafran tactics. Some of the Biafran soldiers had already begun to flee from the scene until the commander shot at one of them as a deterrent to the others.

'I tell you, man, it is difficult to recapture the state I was in,' Dr Kanu said. 'Fright of the highest order. The feeling a man has when he sees death standing right in front of his nose and quickly closing in on him. At the same time I had the feeling that I must resist even death. That resistance was my only hope of survival. My mind immediately went to our limited stock of flying *ogbunigwe*. Without waiting for my commander's orders I made for them. In a trice I was launching them in the direction of the guns. How I got moved from there to this hospital, I don't know!'

'You have become a hero during your first experience of the front,' Akwa congratulated Dr Kanu. 'You'll get the full details from the army boys. But from what the G.O.C. told me, you have already carved a name for yourself as one of Biafra's war heroes. Your courageous and timely action not only saved your company from complete annihilation, but also dealt a severe blow to the vandals. It seemed your wound came from a mercenary who was directing the Nigerian operation. He missed you but struck a hand grenade lying nearby. Happily one of your boys promptly picked him off, but not before he had fired at the boy who tried to save your life. Well done, man.'

'Thank you.'

'I must leave you to have some rest, after what you have been through.'

'Do stay on, Ndu,' Kanu pressed. 'Don't forget that I'm n only a soldier but also a doctor! I know when I need some rest.'

'It's interesting that you regard yourself first as a soldier and secondly as a doctor,' remarked Akwa, smiling.

'But that's what I am and what I will be till we win this war,' affirmed Dr Kanu.

'Are you thinking of going back to the front after this?' Mr Akwaelumo's voice left no doubts that he expected a 'no' answer.

'Why not? If each soldier absconds after his first experience at the front, how can we ever hope to win?'

'But you are not a soldier,' Akwa said. 'You are the Director for Mobilization.'

'D'you mean H.E. has not named any person to succeed me as Director?' asked Dr Kanu. 'I told him to replace me immediately.'

'If you do not wish to continue as Director, you have an important role to play in the medical field.'

'Is that to say that I could not play an important role as a soldier?' Dr Kanu asked. 'Haven't you just told me the outcome of my recent military operation? With the experience I have now acquired, don't you think I could render even greater service as a soldier?'

Mr Akwaelumo decided to drop the point, seeing how committed Dr Kanu was to his new profession.

'Oh, in case I forget, I have a small parcel for you from Fatima.' Mr Akwaelumo opened his briefcase. 'It arrived several days ago, and was handed to me by a courier from State House.'

'Bless her. I hope she and Emeka are well, and that no busybody has told her that I've joined the army.'

'I hope not,' echoed Akwa. 'I must really be going.'

'What do you mean?' Dr Kanu said. 'Wait, let's see what news Fatima sends – it's her first letter since leaving for Libreville. Please cut the parcel open for me. I have only one hand free.'

Dr Kanu went for the letter first. Six pages of Fatima's tiny writing. He decided he would skim through it so as not to delay Akwaelumo indefinitely and go over it in greater detail after he had gone. '. . . Wished she had had such a job to do in Biafra . . . Most challenging and absorbing . . . Shocking state in which the children arrive from Biafra, including children picked up from parts of Annang Province recaptured from the Nigerians . . . Sight of those children, torn away from parents and home by a war said to be fought to save them, has hardened her attitude to Nigeria and turned her pro-Biafra – that's interesting! Emeka is fine.

Asks about Daddy every day, and wants to know when Daddy is coming or when they are returning to Umudike to see Daddy . . . She saw Emeka taking it out on a little boy, the child of a Ghanaian neighbour. Why the fight, she asked? Emeka replied that the boy called him a Nigerian! Isn't that great? . . . Now the presents. A packet of razor blades for you . . .'

'Me?' said Akwa.

'Yes,' affirmed Dr Kanu. 'And a reel of hair thread plus two cakes of Lux soap for Rose . . .'

'Well, well!' exclaimed Akwa, rubbing his hands gleefully. 'May we be blessed with many more Fatimas!'

'A head of tobacco for the old man, a reel of hair thread, two cakes of soap and a blouse for Mama . . .'

'How extremely thoughtful of her,' said Akwa. 'I am sure your father will be the happiest man on earth to receive a head of tobacco. If he wanted to sell it, he could make a hundred pounds on it. I understand ten shillings worth of snuff is not enough for one nostril!'

'The other gifts are for me,' continued Dr Kanu. 'Listen to this. She's enclosed two packets of Durex . . .'

'What?' cried Akwa, rising in excitement.

'Listen.' Dr Kanu was thrilled. '"I would rather you keep yourself for me, as I am keeping myself for you. But remembering what I saw the day I arrived at Umudike without prior notice, I am enclosing two packets of Durex so that if the devil proves too overpowering for you, you do not contract Bonny disease or whatever they call V.D. in Biafra . . ."'

'Terrific. That's a blank cheque for you, man!'

'You are my witness,' Dr Kanu replied, grinning broadly as he folded the letter.

There was a gentle tap on the door. The nurse who had ushered in Mr Akwaelumo opened the door and came in, looking very excited.

'Doctor,' she addressed Dr Kanu. 'Doctor Anene said I should inform you that H.E. will be calling at your room in half an hour's time, and that there should be no other visitor at that time.'

'H.E.?'

'Yes, doctor.' She replied in a tone that left no doubt that she considered the visit the greatest honour that could be bestowed on any patient. She gave Mr Akwaelumo a look that clearly said 'hop it!' The last bit in her message – that no other visitor should be around during H.E.'s visit – was her own invention.

'I'd better be off before overzealous nurses throw me out,' said

Akwa. 'Congratulations once again. It's not every wounded recruit that H.E. visits in hospital! See you later today, or certainly tomorrow.'

'See you!'

25

'I don't know how and where to begin,' said Mr John Nwosu, Secretary of the Obodo War Council, as he sat on a bamboo bed, the type which had replaced spring beds for most refugee Biafrans. It had earned itself the nickname *agbaba aghalu* (that which can be abandoned when it is time to flee) because it was so cheap and obtainable practically everywhere in Biafra and if you had to run you had no regrets leaving yours behind. Mr Nwosu had not only made his own bed himself within a week of their arrival at the St David's School Agu Refugee Camp, but had also taught and encouraged many of his fellow refugees from Obodo to make theirs and thereby conserve their scanty funds. He had gone ahead to make some for sale.

'What about my house?' enquired one refugee. 'Is it still standing?'

'I left many yams in my barn . . .' began another refugee.

'My cows must be very lean now, with no one to take them to green pastures, that is if the Hausas have not already killed them off and eaten them.'

'Is it any use asking about my raffia palms, since I know the Hausas have no idea how to tap palm wine?'

'How true is the story the BBC carried about Chief Ofo?'

Mr Nwosu met a barrage of questions as the anxious refugees flocked round him as though he had just returned from heaven. In the four months they had spent in the refugee camp, their home town Obodo had gradually receded from them to the point where it had become to all intents and purposes part of an entirely different and inaccessible world. Through Dr Kanu's influence, instructions had been given by State House to the Biafran Army to recapture the town at all costs. The G.O.C. was even said to have manned the artillery personally for a brief while, as a morale booster. Two well-known and highly respected leaders had addressed the soldiers at the war fronts, to spur them on to further action. It was absolutely crucial to flush out the vandals, not only to deflate the Nigerian propaganda which had made a mountain out of a molehill (for what was the strategic importance of the capture of Obodo?) but also to demonstrate to the world press and foreign governments in sympathy with Biafra that the Biafrans were capable of recapturing lost territory. During that period, the Obodo refugees in St David's School Agu Refugee Camp lived on hope. They would not adjust to their changed situation. They would not engage in the usual refugee activities. It was unnecessary to develop roots in a refugee camp when they would soon return to their home town.

Their hopes were shattered by external forces fighting for Nigeria which thwarted all Biafra's attempts to import ammunition. Thousands of rounds of ammunition which finally arrived turned out to be useless: they were the wrong size for the rifles. Even RaP ran out of some of the ingredients for manufacturing the home-made weapons. The Nigerian soldiers were thus able to dig in and, having dug in, it was not easy to dislodge them. The Obodo refugees had to accept their lot as refugees.

St David's Camp took its name from St David's C.M.S. Central School Agu, located at least three miles off the Orlu-Urualla tarmac on a dusty untarred road. Something resembling a giant goal post, darkened with solignum to keep the termites away, constituted a landmark at the point where you left the tarmac. Apart from a pot-hole here and an unanticipated corrugation there, the road surface for the three miles to the camp was reasonably good for an untarred road during a rainy season. A blind corner heralded the approach to the camp, a corner made more blind by the fact that several yards of the road passed through the very centre of a small market, with raw cassava, green maize cobs, heads of coconuts, and vegetables displayed on both sides of the road by women whose cheerfulness made you forget that a gruelling war was on. A smaller market was pitched at the entrance to the camp, primarily for those refugees who were too hungry or too weak to walk the quarter-mile to the market.

The camp had a fence round it, the kind of fence that would not keep out an adventurous six-year-old boy. A bamboo barrier at the entrance suggested that no car was allowed into the camp without authority. The checkpoint was manned by a five-foot-tall Civil Defender, a local man who introduced himself as a special constable even though he wore civilian clothing. The Agu War Council posted trusted sons of the soil to man the checkpoint as a means of monitoring the movements of the refugees, to guard against their indulging in subversive activities. Every vehicle entering or leaving the camp was thoroughly searched.

'I went with two BOFF boys,' continued Mr Nwosu. 'The boys are tough, I tell you. As our people say, they have sold all fear in the market . . .'

'I hear they are given an overdose of "push me I push you",' put in Uduji, referring to Biafra gin.

'You talk as if one gallon of it will turn you into a brave man!' another refugee chided Uduji for interrupting. 'Please go on with your story.'

Mr Nwosu went on. 'Those BOFF boys know everything about the location and movement of the vandals. They know what times they shell, what times they play the guitar as it were, with their automatic rifles. I was so shaken one night that if I hadn't known one of the BOFF boys at school I would have thought they were set on handing me over to the vandals! We were so close to them and it was such a clear moonlit night that through a parting in the bush I could see one of their men – must have been a patrol man – washing his clothes . . .'

'Why didn't you wring his neck?' shouted one of the refugees.

'Easier said than done!' shouted another.

'Actually I was tempted to do something, even if it was only throwing a stone at him and missing. It was the first time I had set eyes on one of the vandals who have turned life into hell for us in Biafra. But my guide read my thoughts and warned me in a hushed tone of the consequences of my action by reminding me of the incident at the Inyi sector in which a Biafran soldier – a crack shot a that – could not stand the sight of the Federal troops relaxing in front of their trenches one evening and passing round what must have been tins of sardines and a bottle of genuine White Horse whisky. The Biafran soldier picked up his Madsen and killed three of the vandals before the others disappeared into their trenches. The Federal troops in retaliation shelled the Biafran location practically non-stop for three days, one day for each dead soldier . . .'

'Tell us about Obodo,' interrupted one refugee who had grown impatient over Nwosu's irrelevant digression. 'What is the truth about the Odo?'

Mr Nwosu groaned. 'Darkness has descended on Obodo in broad daylight.'

The refugees closed in, eager to catch what he said, especially as his ow tone indicated sad news.

'As you all know, from time immemorial, the Odo of Obodo has never slept out of Obodo town for even one night. Chief Ofo did not want to be the first to break that tradition. He did not want to abandon our ancestors whose *ofo* he held in trust. That was why he stayed behind. The vandals did not kill him when they came in...'

'Is that so?' one of the men interrupted.

'Yes. They saw him as good propaganda material, and promptly made him the father of Dr Amilo Kanu. That accounts for the BBC story that Chief Ofo led a group of male and female dancers waving white handkerchiefs to welcome the so-called gallant Federal troops into Obodo. You remember the story said that the Odo denounced the Biafran Head of State and even his own son, thanked the peace-loving Federal troops for liberating his town, and called on all sons and daughters of Obodo, young and old, to come out of hiding and return to their homes and farm lands where the Federal troops would receive them with open arms...'

'You mean he didn't say those things the BBC claimed he said?'

'Of course not.'

'I knew it!' affirmed the refugee.

Mr Nwosu went on with the details. It had been a one-time refugee at Obodo named Collins, a tall, handsome young man who was always impeccably dressed even though he had no visible means of livelihood, who led the enemy into Obodo. He had not forgiven the Obodo War Council for expelling him from the town. The War Council had sent him away to rid himself of the Bonny disease which he was alleged to be spreading among young girls as well as married women all over Obodo.

'The first act of the vandals on entering Obodo was to demolish the house of every member of the War Council,' Mr Nwosu reported. 'Chief Ukadike's house...'

'You mean that if I go to Obodo now I'll not find Chief Ukadike's mansion?' asked one of the refugees.

'You will not find even the compound walls. The house was first set on fire, and later they smashed it to dust. Now it is as if it had been hit by a demolition bomb. Even my own half-built house was completely destroyed...'

Mr Nwosu continued. Dr Amilo Kanu's house was left intact. The Nigerian Commanding Officer moved into it, something the vandals considered a psychological victory. Chief Ofo's palace was also left intact at the initial stages. Mr Collins still hoped to regain the love of Chief Ofo's daughter, hence the show of kindness to Chief Ofo. The BBC story was organized by Mr Collins.

He posed as Chief Ofo's interpreter, and gave the BBC a prepared welcome address purported to have been delivered by Chief Ofo. He brought the male and female dancers who 'warmly welcomed' the gallant Federal forces, waving white handkerchiefs as they danced. He brought the dancers from either Makurdi or Oturkpo.

Everything appeared to have gone well for a time. Collins saw to it that the Federal troops provided Chief Ofo with all his needs, including what he valued most – snuff. Unlike the Biafran soldiers who depended on Biafran-made dry packs and food contributed by the local community, the Nigerian soldiers lacked nothing. They even moved along with Hausa cattle for meat. The psychological war had advanced to the stage in which the Nigerians were anxious to demonstrate that most Biafrans were opposed to secession and were only too glad to welcome the 'gallant Federal forces' whenever their home towns became 'liberated'. To get a Biafran of substance to denounce Biafra publicly and call on his 'misguided' kinsmen still in the 'rebel enclave' to cross the lines to freedom was considered a major victory. Chief Ofo was a singularly important catch being (according to Collins) the father of one of the pillars of Biafra. Possibilities of sending him on a world tour, with Collins as interpreter, were already being considered without his knowledge or assent.

Then disaster struck. Biafran guerrillas attacked several locations simultaneously, blowing up a fuel dump, destroying a ferret, and inflicting casualties by throwing grenades into a hut which had been converted into a mess. The Nigerians, caught unawares, were completely disorganized and Obodo was virtually in Biafran hands. The Nigerians quickly recovered from the shock, regrouped outside Obodo and advanced on the town with ferrets and all. They met with no resistance whatsoever. There was no enemy. The BOFF team had disappeared into the ant holes from whence they had emerged, their orders being to harass the vandals, not to recapture Obodo.

Collins could not save Chief Ofo. An angry soldier had blown his brains out without receiving instructions.

'I had always said it,' observed one refugee, hissing loudly. 'Chief Ofo should have come out with us. He should have come out.'

'To do what?' asked another refugee.

'To do what all of us are doing here.'

'I don't agree with you. Chief Ofo is dead, that's true. But sometimes being dead is better than being alive. It is better to die and be buried in your own soil than to live this terrible kind of life, knowing that even at the end of all that suffering your body will be accorded no more respect than would a bundle of firewood.'

Nobody spoke. A refugee lay dead on the verandah only yards away from the cubicle Mr Nwosu had carved out for his family with mats for some privacy. The dead man belonged to the group who had been refugees for over a year. The Government had evacuated them from their home town for security reasons, leaving Biafran troops in complete charge. Intelligence reports had shown that they would facilitate enemy infiltration if they were allowed to remain in their homes. Many of these refugees refused to adjust to their changed situation. They wanted to be allowed to go back, even though their homes had since been lost to the enemy, confirming the view that they were saboteurs all along.

The dead man's corpse was still warm, he could not have been dead for more than an hour or two. He lay on his right side, his face to the wall and his back as it were, to the world, to Nigeria and Biafra, to a war of which he had become completely oblivious. Close by, in the open air about three yards from the end wall of the same building, a man stirred the contents of a small earthen pot boiling on the fire – some vegetation collected from the nearest bush, boiled without salt, without pepper, without palm oil. He needed something to supplement his ration of *garri*. His skin from the waist up looked as if it had received a first coating of white-wash. It was no longer thick enough to hide the outline of his ribs. He carried a mysterious lump on his left side just above the waist-line. Whatever the lump was, it gave him a stoop. As he walked to and from his pot of boiling vegetation, he hardly took any notice of the corpse. His fellow refugees took little notice of the corpse either. It had become routine to bury one or more every day. Two had been buried the previous day. It happened to be that particular man's turn today, nothing more. A grave would be dug for him later – the camp officials would see to that. The next day it would be someone else's turn.

Lying stark naked at the end of another school block was one more refugee who looked ready to follow the yet unburied corpse. But for the upward and downward movement of his ribs as he breathed you would have counted him already dead. He lay face up, his knees sticking up. Every bone of his body could be identified from the outside. Unless he had deliberately rolled his trunk in kitchen ash, he could not have had a wash for a long long time. He opened his eyes – nearer yellow than white – when the sound of footsteps filtered through to him, took in the approaching figure rather weakly and shut off the light again. The *cocoyam* leaf with which he received his ration of three cups of *garri* was abandoned on top of his ribs; he was too weak to throw it into the bush. His own brother – also fast emaciating, but with enough flesh still left on him to be able to wear a pair of khaki shorts – his own brother walked past him unconcerned as if it meant nothing to him if his brother did not see the light of another day. Only the Camp Director, taking a visiting Refugee Medical Officer round the camp, suspected he might be thirsty and ordered water for him. The water disappeared immediately, and so did a second cup. The Medical Officer did not need to touch him to diagnose dehydration due to lack of salt in the food. The dying man surveyed his surroundings, revealing what with a week's balanced diet, would be transformed into a handsome face complete with a fine moustache. The eyes closed again, shutting out the misery and hopelessness around him.

'We shall win!' sneered an old man when the Medical Officer passed by him. All the camp officials knew him for his bitterness towards Biafra. He had been a parliamentarian in the civilian regime, a Junior Minister, and had thrown himself into the Biafran cause even when some of his townsmen expressed reservations about the wisdom of voluntarily opting for a nation in which the Igbo would be able to dominate them. The ideology that every Biafran is his brother's keeper appealed to him. He donated quite freely in support of the new regime, and encouraged his kinsmen to do so.

Then came the unprovoked midnight massacre of his people by a neighbouring Igbo village, on the flimsy and unfounded charge that they were saboteurs. His wife and four teenage sons – his entire family – were slaughtered in one night. He himself escaped the massacre purely by accident – he had travelled to Umuahia to negotiate with Caritas Internationalis and the Red Cross for relief materials.

The shock destroyed his enthusiasm for and loyalty to Biafra. A nation founded as a protest against genocide could not condone genocide within its own borders. From that moment on, he prayed for the collapse of Biafra. Each time Biafra suffered any reverse, he would go round the camp shouting with a sneer: 'We shall win!'

Deprivation had sapped his vivacity. His hair had gone brownish white, with no dye to keep it a youthful black. His loin cloth kept slipping off his waist in the absence of flesh to hold it in place. At one moment it slipped off completely, and slid down his thighs. He took time over the rescue, taking no notice of the village girl behind him. Each ankle was swollen, retarding his movement as he walked. Kwashiorkor had set in.

The Obodo refugees dispersed in groups. They had already received their daily rations from the camp store – three cups of dry *garri* and a slice of raw yam no more than two by three inches. No palm oil, salt, pepper or any other ingredient. Relief supplies from abroad had dried up recently because of Nigerian bombardment of Uli airport, as a result of which no stockfish, formula 2 or dried milk had been distributed for two weeks. It was not too late to seek work for the day in the village. That was one way to avoid turning into a bag of bones: whoever hired the refugee was required to give him two meals in addition to a cash payment.

Mr Nwosu set off the following morning to Nkwerre, to report back to Chief Ukadike, his Chairman, who had organized the trip. The Chief had made a beeline for Umuahia as soon as Obodo fell, ostensibly to get the Government to do everything possible to save Obodo but in fact to fend for himself. It was unthinkable that he – Ezeahurukwe – should live in a refugee camp. Apart from the humiliation of sharing an open, dwarf-wall school with the dregs of society, he could not throw himself completely at the mercy of refugee camp officials, eating only the rations it pleased them to give him.

His technique was to foist himself on one of his influential friends in the way a shrewd dog attaches himself to a man who has had more food than his system can accommodate. He made a start with his kinsman, Dr Kanu. His glistening medals and imperious airs earned him the guest room (rather than a room in the boys' quarters) in Dr Kanu's house at Umudike. As soon as Fatima understood his strategy, she talked her husband into finding the Chief some war work which would get him out of their house. You would not believe that a beggar could be so selective. Chief Ukadike was not in quest of simply any job. What he wanted was an employment that would ensure enough food for his family and hangers-on. The relief agencies – which ranked top of his priority list – could not take him on. The World Council of Churches had a surfeit of clergymen who had lost their parishes, and so did not require extra hands. Chief Ukadike was not a Roman Catholic so that ruled out Caritas Internationalis. The I.C.R.C. (International Committee of the Red Cross) was hostile to anybody associated with any Government functionary. Chief Ukadike spent a whole month as Dr Kanu's guest before Mr Akwaelumo came to Dr Kanu's rescue. Chief Ukadike was appointed store-keeper for the Directorate of Procurement depot at Nkwerre. The Directorate commandeered a bungalow for him on the premises of the secondary school which housed the depot.

Mr Nwosu had pleasant memories of his earlier visit to Chief Ukadike at Nkwerre. It was the first occasion since he became a refugee that he had eaten to his full capacity. As he journeyed again to Nkwerre he looked forward to more than a good meal. He had a proposal up his sleeves. If Chief Ukadike gave the necessary backing he would embark upon what was becoming the most lucrative occupation in Biafra, namely 'afia attack'. His trip to Obodo had shown him that crossing the enemy line need not be as hazardous as he had feared. The line was so long and so inadequately patrolled that many Biafrans crossed it at will without losing their lives. The Nigerians occupying the abandoned Biafran territories had established flourishing markets where you could buy almost everything lacking in Biafra, at incredibly low prices. But you required Nigerian currency. The old Nigerian coins were still legal tender, but you could hardly find them in circulation in Biafra. Mr Nwosu felt Chief Ukadike was in a position to collect these coins, hence the need for the alliance with him. Ten shilling coins were sufficient to transform you into a rich man if you were not caught by Biafran patrols to or from the 'attack' trade.

26

It was one of those nights when most pilots give up trying. The conscientious among them return to the nearest base for fresh instructions. The straight mercenaries or the secret service agents of hostile countries empty their cargo into the sea and return to Europe without bothering to consider how much that one plane-load of ammunition, relief materials, or brand-new Biafran currency notes meant to the country in which so many vital decisions hung on the number of planes which landed safely each night.

The battle for Umuahia had been fought as much at Uli airport as on the actual war fronts. The enemy had encountered much greater resistance there than at Enugu, Port Harcourt, Aba or Owerri, notwithstanding their sophisticated weapons and air cover. Biafra's fire power had increased substantially. Uli airport had to be put out of action permanently if Biafra was not to turn the scales completely against Nigeria. No plane must be allowed to take off or land at the airport. So Lagos had ordered.

Joe had landed and taken off from Uli several times before, in spite of the Nigerian bombardment, and he was by now familiar with Nigerian tactics. Unlike most of the other pilots who risked their lives to fly to Biafra, he was a Biafran. His training had been in small private planes, but he had undertaken the gun-running flights as his own contribution to the war effort. He began as a co-pilot, but soon took full charge. A message had been transmitted to him from State House to pick up Mrs Fatima Kanu from Libreville and bring her to Biafra.

Fatima had not quite got over her fright the day she and her son left Biafra in a Caritas plane. The fact that they would travel in a relief plane had given her a false sense of security, as if the Nigerians distinguished between relief planes and war planes. It was not until she arrived at the air terminal that she realized that she was heading for nothing other than a war front! It was not the usual air terminal. It was an uncompleted two-storeyed private residential building, hurriedly roofed and fitted with shutters to make it usable. The walls were not yet plastered, neither was the floor. There were no conveniences. It was no different from any other uncompleted residential building around, except that a counter had been installed. Passengers were hustled here at night, under the light of hurricane lamps, until the OK was given to proceed to the airport a couple of miles away. You were lucky if you travelled the first night you reported at the terminal; it depended on whether any plane was able to land and take off.

Notwithstanding the unconventional appearance of the air terminal, passengers were subjected to the conventional drill before receiving clearance to board the plane. Health certificates, passports and baggage were checked by customs officials. In lieu of the regular airline tickets, passengers had to present evidence from the appropriate authorities that they had permission to travel. Except for travel to countries which had recognized Biafra, passengers had to travel on Nigerian passports. The Biafran authorities seemed to be in a position to issue new Nigerian passports!

Enemy planes raided the airport twice that night, dropping countless bombs, while Fatima and the other passengers took

228

cover at the terminal. The vibrations shook everything around. Never had so many bombs exploded so close to Fatima. They brought back the gruesome memories of Halima and her son, and of the devastating air raid at Umuahia. Was it sensible to attempt to board a plane in such circumstances, she wondered. Her husband reassured her: the airport staff and the pilots knew when to act and what to do. What buoyed up her spirits more than the assurances was the thought that once she and her son managed to get airborne they would be free of air raids for ever. It was a gamble worth taking.

The bomb explosions soon gave way to the crackling noise of small arms fire. The airport Commander knew what that meant. The enemy often resorted to small arms fire from the planes after exhausting their stock of bombs. As soon as that happened, activity was resumed at the airport. The special runway squad promptly repaired any damage to the runway, knowing that the small arms fire was short-lived, and did little damage. The Commander ordered the passengers to proceed to the airport.

Fatima would never forget the experience. There was no departure lounge, and all the formality ended after the checks at the terminal. You were responsible for conveying yourself and your baggage to the appropriate aeroplane, all in pitch darkness. Dr Kanu had seen a visiting expatriate group off once so he had some idea of what to do. Fatima was to board her plane at Finger 3. They drove in complete darkness. Fortunately there were no vehicles coming in the opposite direction. On arrival at the Flight Line (the name for the main runway), they had little difficulty in locating Finger 3, one of the hideouts for the planes. From then on the success of the entire operation hung on speed and efficiency, and Fatima had never in all her life seen such a combination of speed and sense of purpose. It made her proud of the black man in a way she had never been before. In no time the plane taxied off from the specially constructed hideout and got on to the Flight Line. The runway lights came on briefly and the plane was airborne.

The fear that the war planes might return and catch them on the runway at first prevented Fatima from taking in all the unusual features of the flight. The plane was in complete darkness; neither the interior lights nor even the statutory aviation lights were switched on until the plane had left the danger zone. There were no seats: you sat on the floor, or on your baggage. When the pilot wished to communicate with the passengers, he sent the Flight Engineer to make the announcement. There was no public address system. There were no air hostesses, and no refreshment of any sort was served on board. It had been a memorable ninety-minute flight to Libreville.

Fatima did not know until after her arrival in Libreville how much her stay in Biafra had shattered her nerves. The unexpected bang of a door gave her the jitters as if a mortar was about to pierce her heart. Her most humiliating experience was at one of the wards in the children's home soon after her arrival. The sound of a commercial plane flying overhead sent her diving for cover under one of the beds.

She had spent barely two months in Libreville before setting off on this sudden journey to Biafra, but the effect on her of that short spell outside Biafra had been incredible. She had regained her nerve. The noise of battle was far, far away, and so was the ever-haunting fear of air raids. She no longer had to live in a hole like a rabbit, coming out only at night. Food and clothing were readily available, and at normal prices. Her job with the children presented a challenge which made life worth living. She had also been able to re-establish contact with her parents who were alive and well and thrilled to know that she had not been killed in the war. They had given up all hope after the fall of Enugu. She had flatly rejected their suggestion that she should fly back to Nigeria, and had warned them not to attempt to pay her a visit in Libreville. It would be sufficient to keep in touch by correspondence until after the end of the war, but they had better watch out what they wrote about Biafra.

She was amazed at herself, after despatching that letter to her parents; amazed that she should reject the offer to return to Nigeria at a time when she was at liberty to go back home without hindrance. She had been taken aback the day she saw Emeka, her son, angrily spanking a playmate for abusing him by calling him a Nigerian. Had she too become so sold on Biafranism that she considered herself a Biafran rather than a Nigerian?

She had been bowled over when the first letter she received from her husband carried the news that he had joined the army. Had he gone crazy? Had he been whitemailed? She had written a harangue, to bring him down to earth. Did he want their only remaining child to become an orphan at such a tender age? Even if he survived the war, what if Biafra lost in the end? What would be their fate in Nigeria when it became known that he had actually borne arms voluntarily against his country?

Fear of possible censorship had made her tear the letter to bits – and burn the bits. Then she suddenly remembered. She remembered that Ami had always wanted a military career, ever since he enrolled at his university's cadet corps in his first pre-clinical year . . . She remembered that he had sought a commission in the British Army Medical Corps, after his pre-registration house job, but his nationality had stood in his way . . . She remembered how terribly upset he had been as Director for Mobilization whenever he thought of the death which awaited most of the young men he was responsible for recruiting or conscripting, as they were sent raw, untrained and ill-equipped to the front lines. She remembered how he had gone without food on one occasion, shortly before she left for Libreville, when one woman, weeping uncontrollably over the fate of her only son, challenged him to take a gun and go to the defence of Biafra now that she had no more children whom he could snatch from her and send to die for him.

No. Ami was not crazy. He had demonstrated the noblest quality in man. Her anger melted away. The letter she sent off to her husband was one of encouragement. And admiration. He must, however, match valour with discretion. He was of much greater use to Biafra, and his family, alive than dead.

She would not at first admit it. But she had become a Biafran!

Joe had been circling high in the air for nearly an hour, safe from the reach of the enemy planes and the range of Biafran home-made anti-aircraft rockets. He was waiting for an enemy war plane to empty its load before he landed, and the war plane was waiting for him to land before bombing the airport. The captain of the invading plane at last radioed Joe, warning him that it was too risky to attempt a landing: another plane which had attempted to do so earlier on had crashed. Joe insisted.

'OK. Let me go in first, then you can follow,' the captain of the Nigerian war plane proposed. He was expected to fly three missions that night and so could not spend an eternity on the first mission alone, nor return to base with his bomb load.

Joe consented. The war plane emptied its bombs on the airport and sped away to Lagos to report a successful raid. Joe received the signal to land. The runway lights came on. He landed flawlessly, and steered the plane to Finger 4. The passengers sat on boxes of ammunition which had been strapped to the floor of the aeroplane: an imperfect landing would have been catastrophic.

Curiously enough, Fatima maintained steady nerves. She could have been cruising on the mail boat for all she knew. Her spirit was somewhere else. Why had she been summoned to Biafra? The notice had been extremely short. A message had come through in the early afternoon, from the officer on special duties acting as Liaison Officer for the children's home, that her husband was having a week off after a heroic military operation, and H.E. had agreed to give him a treat by allowing her to fly in at Government expense to join him. The Liaison Officer said he was under instructions to find her a seat on the first plane taking off from Libreville for Biafra.

The story did not sound convincing at all to Fatima. If H.E. was so interested in arranging another honeymoon for Ami, why not do it the other way round – allow Ami to join her in Libreville where he would be more likely to get some rest? Admittedly this line of action would be fraught with problems for H.E. The impression might be created that he was arranging overseas honeymoons for his officers while Biafra burnt. Or the journey might be misconstrued as an escape from Biafra by the Director for Mobilization turned army officer. Admitted. But why not a letter in Ami's hand? The Liaison Officer's explanation was that a letter could have taken longer as it would have waited until the next flight from Biafra to Libreville, and no one could say when that would be. The message had been radioed.

Fatima came to with a start when she found herself standing in front of Brigadier Mbonu at 2 a.m. in a well-furnished house. She could not recollect what had happened since leaving the airport, or how she came to appear before the Brigadier. She had no idea what part of Biafra she was in at that moment.

'We haven't met before, Mrs Kanu,' Brigadier Mbonu began as he led Fatima to a padded chair. The smile on his handsome face was obviously forced. 'I am sorry that our first meeting should be in these circumstances. H.E. instructed me to inform you, with the deepest sense of grief, that your husband was killed in an air raid yesterday. It was . . .'

'What did you say?'

'Yes, Mrs Kanu,' affirmed the Brigadier, trying to avoid Fatima's staring eyes. 'No tragedy has grieved us so much – everyone, including H.E. himself – not even the loss of Umuahia. It was nothing short of murder which is what . . .'

'Ami dead! Oh my God!' exclaimed Fatima, dropping her handbag and clutching at her face with both hands. The Brigadier pressed a bell and his orderly burst in before the sound of the bell had faded away, gave the salute, took a signal from his master, gave the salute again and disappeared as rapidly as he came in. The door opened again, and Mr Ndubuisi Akwaelumo and his wife, Rose, came in to take Fatima away. They led her gently to a waiting car, and drove her to a village near Dikenafai where Mr Akwaelumo had recently moved in, following the loss of Umuahia. No one spoke, for no one knew what to say. Akwaelumo's mind flashed back to the pathetic scene at the Enugu Progress Hotel in 1967, early in the war, when little Amilo lay wrapped up after being smashed to death by a mortar. His consolation to Ami at that time was that it was only the water that had been spilled; the pitcher was still intact. What could he say to Fatima on this occasion, with her husband lying dead, smashed by a demolition bomb? It was best to shut up. Rose bit her lips as she fought hard to hold back her own tears. As for Fatima, the initial shock had left her dry-eyed. Temporarily.

> Dibe! dibe!
> Ndidi ka nma.
> Onye obialu nya dibe n'uwa,
> Biafra nwe nmeli!

That song, rendered by officers and men of Dr Kanu's battalion as the red earth was heaped over his body, made Fatima weep even more hysterically. She had first heard it at Obodo, sung by the youth after the air raid which wiped out Halima and her son, Prophet James, his church and his congregation. It had been rendered with such solemnity and dignity that the very air had stood still. Even she who did not know what the words meant had been so moved by them that she had requested a translation later.

'When your turn comes, take heart: Biafra is sure to win . . .'

That was the message the song carried, a message easier to give than to accept. In her case, moaned Fatima, how many times must it be her turn, how many turns must she have before the tragic war was over? Her first son had gone. That was her first turn. Halima, whom she had come to regard as a sister, had been brutally slaughtered with her son. That was her turn again. She had gone to Libreville convinced that she had made more than her own fair share of sacrifice for Biafra. And now her very reason for being associated with Biafra, her own husband, had been singled out and smashed to death, not at the war front as she had feared during the flight into Biafra, but in a hospital ward in an unknown village. What special wrong had she done? What crime had she committed to take so many bitter turns of grief in so short a time? Was she responsible for the Declaration of Biafra?

Dr Kanu had still been in hospital recovering from his battle wounds, when the Government finally conceded Umuahia township to the enemy. The hospital, which had become the best military hospital in Biafra, had to be evacuated to a new location. A secondary school, some ten miles from Orlu, had been selected. It was in what was considered a safe area, sufficiently far from the town and at least a mile away from the main road. The refugees who had used it as a refugee camp had turned the playing fields into cassava plots and stuck palm fronds into the few remaining patches of open space which they could not farm, as camouflage. The closest any war plane had come to the village was a raid on Orlu, during which a hotel was destroyed, killing a civil servant and his mistress as they sought to achieve perfect union in their nakedness. The refugees living in the school had heard the devastating sounds, but none of the planes came in their direction.

Dr Kanu had spent barely a week in the new location when the plane seemed to have discovered the hospital. What made the raid look even more mysterious and suspicious was that the plane missed or deliberately spared the main blocks and struck only the staff house which had been converted into an amenity ward for V.I.P.s, with Dr Kanu as its lone occupant. The coincidence confirmed the widely held belief that Lagos had a strong network of military intelligence, operated by disloyal, mercenary Biafrans armed with transmitters, who had direct links with the Egyptian pilots of the Soviet war planes, directing them to their victims. Because Biafra had few, if any, secrets these sabos had ready access to the information required by the enemy, hence they knew everything about the new location of the military hospital. The demolition bomb had gone through the roof, turning what was previously a lovely bungalow into a giant crater.

Mr Akwaelumo had taken Fatima to the scene of the disaster before the packed funeral at the local church. She needed little persuasion after that not to insist on opening the coffin to see her husband's remains.

27

We are Biafrans
Fighting for our freedom;
In the name of Jesus
We shall conquer.
'Lep! Ai! Lep! Ai! . . .'

The part of the Second Lieutenant in the play, commanding the matchet parade at Enugu, was acted by a young man who had a long scar down his right arm, stretching from the upper arm to below the elbow. The right arm was shorter than the left. It was more than ordinary drama for him, for it was he who, as an inexperienced, freshly commissioned Second Lieutenant, commanded the dummy-gun carrying volunteers on the grounds of the Enugu Campus of the University of Biafra in September 1967, eighteen months back. He had subsequently distinguished himself in the Ikot Okpora sector, holding out against the Nigerians with his bare fists as he waited for a reinforcement which never came. That was where he lost an inch or so of his right arm. He was promoted Captain while his bones were being pieced together. On discharge from the hospital, he insisted on returning to the war front. H.E. took him into the 'S' Brigade. His promotion to the rank of Major was announced the previous day, for the part he played in the recapture of Owerri. The Armed Forces Drama Troupe had invited him specially to play that part in the play.

'It's hard to believe it,' commented Ikem Onukaegbe as the play went on, 'but it already sounds like history, and yet it happened only yesterday.'

Mr Duke Bassey said nothing. Mr Onukaegbe glanced at him and could see from the darkness that he was watching the play with every part of his body.

The title of the play was appropriately *We Shall Vanquish*. The plot was the story of Biafra, told in words and action intended to fire the fighting spirit of every Biafran who watched it. The play had been put on as part of the celebrations to mark the recapture of Owerri from the Nigerians.

Owerri was much more strategically located than Umuahia, being the hub of the most important roads still in Biafran hands, roads leading to Onitsha, Umuahia, to Aba, to Orlu, to Okigwi and to Port Harcourt. It was the nearest major town to Biafra's main international airport at Uli.

More important, the recapture of Owerri demonstrated that Biafra had the capacity to regain its lost territory, that Biafra could dislodge the Nigerians, even after they had occupied a town for as long as six months. It raised Biafran hopes that, with increased fire power, Biafra could drive the Nigerian forces of occupation back to their country. One more such victory for Biafra, and Nigeria would take the peace talks more seriously.

'Great!' That was Mr Onukaegbe's verdict at the end of the play. 'It's amazing to see such a first-rate performance in our present circumstances.'

'You say the Prof. is now deployed with one of the RaP groups?' Mr Bassey asked, as if oblivious of Mr Onukaegbe's comments about the play.

'Yes,' replied Onukaegbe.

'Which one?'

'The group at Amaekpelima.'

'Where's that?' asked Bassey.

'Who knows? He says it's an out-of-the-way town, not likely ever to fall into the enemy line of advance. The other attraction is that that group refines its own petrol. It has also been assigned the responsibility for producing engine oil and brake fluid. He is to serve as their admin officer.'

'I thought his Research Department was doing very good work,' Mr Bassey remarked, absent-mindedly.

'Certainly,' Onukaegbe said. 'Practically all the feature programmes on Radio Biafra rely on them for data – "Outlook", "Commissioner's Mail Bag", "This we Believe", and so on. Not to mention the data they assemble for H.E.'s speeches. The point is that the Prof. fears too much. He is afraid to move to Orlu where accommodation has been found for the department.'

'But Chike is at Mbano which is worse in terms of air raids, being next to State House Two.'

'Yes,' Onukaegbe replied. 'The difference is that Chike is much more Biafran than Prof. Sometimes, as you must have noticed, it's not easy to say whether Prof. is with us or not. Chike is so deeply involved in his present assignment that he has not had time to think about air raids. H.E. wants the Biafran Charter ready immediately, and they are working round the clock to produce it. Now that Biafra seems to have finally arrived – with the recapture of Owerri, the successful take off of the Biafra Land Army and the possibilities of a major diplomatic breakthrough – H.E. feels the time has come to spell out in black and white the ideals of the

Biafran Revolution. The tentative arrangement is to launch the Charter on 1 June, at Ahiara ...'

Mr Onukaegbe stopped talking when he noticed that Mr Bassey was not listening. They had found their way to the Peugeot and were waiting for Major O.C. who had offered to drive them to Emekuku, seven miles away, where Brother had found Mr Bassey a house.

'You know what?' began Mr Bassey after they had said good-night to the Major and were about to retire for the night. 'The play we have just seen has thrown some light on a vision which appeared to me yesterday.'

Mr Onukaegbe opened one of the wooden windows in the living room which had already been bolted for the night, to let in fresh air, and took a seat. Mr Bassey also sat down as he went on to describe his vision:

'I normally seek guidance each morning, as soon as I wake up. Yesterday, after I had relaxed in the normal posture, I saw a path opening up in front of me. I followed the path with my eyes, on and on. Then suddenly I found I could go no further. A huge coffin had suddenly blocked the path. The remains of a man gradually emerged. The head, arms and legs had been chopped off. The cuts were fresh, and blood was still oozing out. I shut my eyes tight. When I opened them again, everything had disappeared, including the path. I couldn't make head or tail of the vision. You may have noticed that I was irritable yesterday. I feared that Nma and the children had been wiped out by the Nigerians, hence the coffin. Well, part of the play re-enacted that vision.'

Onukaegbe did not know what to say. He avoided mysticism, and was already finding the Sassarobia perfume exuding from Mr Bassey's bedroom rather suffocating, and counting the days when he would move into his own house at Owerri. It was a pity that they should be celebrating Biafra's glorious achievements in that fashion, and he wished Professor Ezenwa had been around. He would have known how to dismiss Bassey's fantasy without hurting his feelings.

'I intend to discuss the whole thing with Brother,' Bassey went on. 'The only meaning I can give to it, especially after watching the play, is that our path seems to be taking us back to the tragic events of 1966 ...'

'But that hardly makes sense,' said Onukaegbe. 'Certainly not now, when the clouds have cleared again. If the trend continues and we recapture more and more towns from the vandals, I can't see our path taking us back to Nigeria. *Tufia!* God forbid!'

237

'I hope it never happens. The precious lives and property lost since 1966 would have been wasted if we were to return to the Nigeria we left behind. I hope we recapture many more towns. That is my one hope of reuniting with my family, if, as I hope, they are still alive. But what I have told you is my vision, not my wish. What matters is not whether or not it makes sense, but what message the Almighty is sending us through it.'

'Don't frighten me, man.' Onukaegbe rose to his feet as he spoke, rubbing his eyes to keep off sleep. 'Let me rejoice for the victory God has given us today. Tomorrow will take care of itself.'

28

A month after her return to Biafra, Fatima reluctantly accepted the plea for her to go back to her work in Libreville. The Biafran recapture of Owerri had made it easier to persuade her. The last impression she wanted to create was that she was leaving Biafra because the going had become rough. The Biafran victory at Owerri had resulted in a steep rise in public morale. It showed that the offensive mounted by Biafra in the dying months of 1968 had begun to yield rich dividends. The victory at Owerri was also looked on as Biafra's revenge for the cold-blooded murder of Dr Kanu. All told, no time could have been more ideal for Fatima to withdraw quietly from Biafra without being misunderstood.

Mazi Kanu Onwubiko, Fatima's father-in-law, had made an irresistible plea to her to go back to Libreville. He had spoken to her as a loving father to a beloved daughter. And she had accepted the plea in the same spirit. The tribal curtain separating her from her parents-in-law had disappeared. Her presents from Libreville had softened their hearts towards her. A gift of a whole head of tobacco at a time when people had been driven to snuffing sand, went beyond the traditional good gesture of plucking a chicken's tail feathers in the rainy season. The thoughtfulness of it, and the exceptional value of the gifts, had won a special place for Fatima in the hearts of her parents-in-law.

But it was Fatima's attitude to them during the month following Dr Kanu's death which had completely won over Mazi Kanu and his wife. She spent more time with them at Nkwerre than in the more comfortable house assigned to her at Orlu. She shared whatever relief supplies she received with them, and ensured that they had adequate supplies of local foodstuffs. She cooked for them whenever she was around, and showed surprising enthusiasm for Igbo dishes. Her attempts to speak Igbo made everyone roar with laughter. Mazi Kanu and his wife suddenly began to enjoy the advantages of having a devoted, grown-up child, something even their own son, the doctor, had been unable to give them.

Mr Ndubuisi Akwaelumo had made several unsuccessful attempts to persuade Fatima to return to Libreville, arguing that Biafra was unsafe for her. He had also tried to use his wife, Rose, but without success either. Rose had given up when Fatima asked her point-blank why Biafra should be safe for Rose but not for Fatima.

Mr Akwaelumo was amazed at Fatima's transformation from the Northern Nigerian woman bundled out of Biafra to give her husband peace of mind, to a fully-fledged Biafran woman, as Biafran as H.E. himself. If any country deserved her loyalty, she had declared, it was Biafra. The Biafran Government had flown her home to attend her husband's funeral. Her husband had been awarded the Distinguished Service Cross, Biafra's highest military honour, posthumously. The Government had assigned a furnished house to her at Orlu free of charge, and provided her with a chauffeur-driven car with regular supply of free petrol, a bonanza in wartime Biafra when petrol had soared to the astronomical price of £30 a gallon. She was placed on her husband's salary, effective from the date of his death. The Government had also accepted responsibility for the education of her son, Emeka, from kindergarten to First Degree level. To cap it all, H.E. had called on her personally, to console her and assure her of his personal interest in her welfare. He had given her the choice of remaining in Biafra or returning to Libreville, where, from reports he had received, she had been doing an excellent job.

Such kindness and concern for her welfare, in spite of her antecedents, exceeded Fatima's wildest expectations. It made her see her fate as inextricably interwoven with the future of Biafra, and she would not listen to any suggestion that it was in her best interest to return to Libreville. The fear of death had vanished. If anything, death would expedite her reunion with her loved ones. She would notify H.E. of her decision to remain in Biafra, and ask if Emeka could be flown back to her. If H.E. was willing she would be glad to step into her husband's shoes as Director for Mobilization . . .

Mr Akwaelumo had seen no alternative but to ask Mazi Kanu

239

to intervene. Mazi Kanu chose the occasion of one of Akwaelumo's visits to raise the issue, beginning with Fatima's memorable gift of a head of tobacco which, he claimed, had clipped ten years off his age.

'Without snuff, one will run mad in these troubled times,' he asserted. 'If you remain here with us, who will send me another head of tobacco when this finishes?'

Mazi Kanu had moved on to the main issue. Since running from Obodo and becoming a jobless refugee, he said, he had had ample time to chew over the events around him. Each time he had done so, he had come to one conclusion. Nigerians committed abominations against Biafra and Biafrans had fought back like men, notwithstanding the fact that circumstances had compelled the Biafrans to fight with their hands tied behind them, more or less. The recent recapture of Owerri had further demonstrated that Biafrans were not women.

'But will Biafra's salvation come from the battlefield?' he asked, turning his wrinkled stare from Fatima to Akwaelumo. Without waiting for an answer he went on: 'Before you answer me, count the number of lives lost, of young and old: nobody can count them. Think of the betrayal of our ancestors, our traditions, as we are driven from one town to another; think of the broken-hearted old people who died only to be buried in strange lands, away from their ancestors and without the customary funeral rites. Think of the starvation and hardship, with old and young burrowing into the ground like rabbits to escape death from the enemy . . . And what makes it even more serious is that there is no end in sight.'

'The recapture of Owerri is the beginning of the end,' Fatima had put in.

'The recapture of Owerri is good news,' the old man agreed. 'But think of what remains to be recaptured – Onitsha, Calabar, Umuahia, Port Harcourt, Enugu, Okigwi . . . I cannot count them all. And as you are recapturing one town, the enemy will be trying to capture a new town from you!'

Mazi Kanu had gone on and on. His conclusion was that the dispute between Nigeria and Biafra could not be settled by war.

'We are too old now,' he summed up, 'to produce an answer which will be acceptable to young people. I am not sure that even you,' he turned to Akwaelumo, 'can find the answer. You are all too involved in the dispute to be able to see the answer. As for the soldiers, they cannot find the answer: the only answer they know is the gun. We never had any war of this magnitude until they seized power. You will ask me who then can find the answer? For the answer must be found or there will be no human being left to bury the dead, or farm the land. This is my answer. It is children like Emeka who will find the answer, after we are dead and gone. As they grow up and count the cost of this war, they will have to find the answer . . .'

The substance of Mazi Kanu's plea was that the lives of children such as Emeka must be preserved at all costs, as the only hope for the future. Luckily Emeka was still in Libreville, where he was more likely to survive the war than in Biafra. It would be criminal to bring him back to Biafra, to suffer the fate of his elder brother and his father. Fatima must return to Libreville where she had a duty to look after the little boy and the other Biafran children there, to bring them up for the challenge ahead. She must also remember that Emeka was the only male issue left to Mazi Kanu and her late husband. If anything happened to him, that would be the end of Kanu Onwubiko's lineage.

'Amazing woman!' soliloquized Akwaelumo as his car inched away from the terminal building. He had heard the sound of the plane taking off, but he decided to await confirmation from the Airport Commander before leaving the terminal building where he had retired after driving Fatima to the Flight Line. Everything had gone remarkably smoothly, reported the Commander, a lecturer by profession although you would have sworn he had been a commanding officer all his life the way he carried himself. Fatima had got on the plane and the pilot had taken off without the usual downpour from the enemy.

'Amazing woman . . . What an irony that Amilo is not alive to receive his transformed wife . . .'

Mr Akwaelumo decided to spend what remained of the night with a medical doctor at the Roman Catholic Hospital compound at Ihiala. It was an unnecessary risk attempting to drive all the way back to Dikenafai in darkness. As the car sensed its way to the hospital, his thoughts switched from Fatima to Dr Kanu, her late husband.

Dr Kanu's death had created a vacuum in his life. His wife, Rose, could not fill it. She gave him the companionship of a wife, but not Amilo's companionship. In any case he could not count on Rose's company much longer. The enemy had hardly been cleared from Owerri before a decision was taken that as many Directorates as possible, including his, should move to Owerri. Rose did not want to live anywhere near Owerri. While Fatima was around, she filled some of the vacuum. He somehow felt the presence of Amilo as he scuttled around to minister to Fatima's needs. But he was cautious not to let the handshake go beyond the elbow. In fact it was to reduce the possibility of becoming too closely involved with Fatima that he had been so keen to talk her into returning to Libreville, although he never disclosed this. The moment she said goodbye to him and boarded the plane, the emptiness returned in full force.

It was not only a sense of loneliness. It was also a feeling of inadequacy. Mr Akwaelumo found himself measuring his life against Dr Kanu's. He had done something similar with Fatima and Rose, measuring Rose against Fatima. How would Rose have reacted in similar circumstances? His verdict had been in favour of Fatima. There was something about Fatima to which he did not think Rose could measure up: her courage, her independence, her masculinity – a masculinity which did not in any way detract from her feminine charm and grace. He thought of the calm composure with which she had stepped into the aeroplane when a Biafran ambassador who went in after her was visibly shaking, afraid that an enemy plane might descend on them when escape was impossible.

He had on previous occasions measured himself against Dr Kanu. On each occasion he had found himself trailing behind. Dr Kanu was versatile, full of ideas. He was the live wire of meetings of the War Services Council, and Akwaelumo had always considered it a pity that people like him did not have direct access to H.E. instead of sycophants who fed H.E. with what they thought he would like to hear rather than with honest advice.

Where Mr Akwaelumo could not see eye to eye with Dr Kanu was in his decision to join the army as a combatant officer. That was to allow idealism to run riot. One does not have to commit suicide to demonstrate one's love for Biafra. As a Director in charge of an essential war service, Dr Kanu was already giving maximum service to his country. Or had Amilo been trying to advertise himself? To please H.E.? No. It could not be. Amilo had a charismatic personality, but he was not ostentatious. Nor was he a boot-licker. Could it be that it was Akwaelumo himself who was at fault? Lacking in courage? Lacking in conviction? Placing the fear of death above everything else?

Dr Kanu had become a national hero. A chapter had been earmarked for him in the book already commissioned by H.E. on Biafra's War Heroes. He had received the D.S.C. as compared with the B.B.M. (Biafra Bronze Medal) recently conferred on Mr

Akwaelumo and a handful of others engaged in essential services. Dr Kanu's name would be engraved in a memorial plaque to be erected at the end of the war. What more could a man aspire to, even if he lived a hundred years?

'Maybe we should all emulate Amilo and take up arms,' he said to himself.

'What if we lose?' an inner voice cautioned. Yes. What if Biafra lost?

It was the growing prospect that Biafra might lose which had driven Dr Kanu to join the army. True, Owerri had been recaptured, demonstrating Biafra's capability to regain lost ground, but as Mazi Kanu had said, how much remained to be recaptured?

Akwaelumo knew that Biafra had practically exhausted itself. The Nigerians were comparable in a way to the Americans fighting the Vietnamese in Vietnam. Life went on fairly normally for the average Nigerian in his country. Schools and universities continued to function normally. The economy suffered little disruption. The noise of war was too distant to give him sleepless nights. Even football matches continued to be played! It was only if he had a close relation fighting at the war front that he had anxious moments.

The situation was very different for Biafrans. The war raged on Biafran soil. Every inch of Biafra had become a war front and every child in Biafra felt the full impact of the war. It was Biafra that absorbed all the material losses. It was Biafra that had the problem of millions of people becoming refugees in their own country, and the number grew with every military reverse. The hardship was reaching a point where something was bound to snap. It was not just a question of lack of bread, sugar, eggs, bottled drinks and the other luxuries of the westernized middle class. Most Biafrans had long forgotten these things and did not regret them. It was more serious than that. The price of *garri* had risen by at least 6,000% since the outbreak of the war, and so had most of the basic, indispensable foods. If the war dragged on much longer, only a privileged few in Biafra would be in a position to eat one meal a day. Every one of the estimated fourteen million people in Biafra would have to depend on relief supplies flown in from abroad. The International Committee of the Red Cross seemed to spend much of its time in never-ending debates as to whether relief supplies should be flown into Biafra direct or routed through Nigeria to be examined first by the Nigerian Government; whether relief supplies should be landed at night or in daylight; whether the I.C.R.C. should purchase yams, *garri*, palm oil and other essential local foodstuffs for refugees locally with cash as it did in Nigeria or whether it should revert to trade by barter in Biafra and so on. Judging from this, the situation was as bleak as it would be if Biafra's millions depended on nothing but biblical manna dropping from heaven!

Yes, what if Biafra lost?

Akwaelumo gave his driver instructions for the morning and dismissed him. His host had given him the key to the guest room which was accessible from the outside. He shut and locked the door gently, so as not to wake anyone up. Between removing his Biafra suit and tying his wrapper for bed his thoughts returned again and again to that haunting question: what if Biafra lost?

The aftermath of the war would be blood-curdling. The Nigerians would make sure that the Igbo man would never again constitute a threat to the rest of the country. The Nigerian Army would go on a rampage – with instructions to kill every Igbo man of substance at sight. No foreign observers would be allowed into Biafra until this crucial exercise had been completed and all traces of it whitewashed. Radio Biafra and Markpress in Geneva would already have been silenced, to ensure a complete blackout on the atrocities.

Even if you survived the rampage, Mr Akwaelumo wondered, what future awaited you in Nigeria? The person who described Nigeria as a geographical expression was not a numbskull. The man whose slogan in the war against Biafra was 'To keep Nigeria One' had himself admitted previously that there was no basis for Nigerian unity. Aguiyi Ironsi had been brutally murdered in July 1966 because, as Supreme Commander and Head of the Federal Military Government, he had set himself the goal of turning Nigeria into one united and strong country. If Nigerians now appeared united, it was because they had Biafra as a common enemy. When the war ended, the unifying factor would disappear. To be forced back into Nigeria would be a return to the tribal politics and ethnic bitterness of the post-independence era, where it would be impossible to conduct a reliable national census or to hold a fair and free election; where the primary preoccupation would be the sharing of the national cake, not the making of a nation.

Worse still, the Biafran would be returning to Nigeria from a position of weakness. Unless something positive came out of the peace talks. If only those countries which professed to be Biafra's friends could help to obtain favourable terms for Biafra. If only

Britain and the other countries which fought the war for Nigeria would make Nigeria take the peace talks more seriously. If only the hawks in Biafra could face realities, and see in the recapture of Owerri not the signal to prepare for another protracted war, but the opportune moment for Biafra to press home her peace proposals . . .

'Mazi Kanu is right,' Akwaelumo muttered to himself. 'War cannot be the answer.' Every Biafran had seen from bitter experience that issues of morality do not necessarily affect the fortunes of war. God tends to fight not on the side of the oppressed but on the side of the oppressor because the latter has the bigger battalions. If Biafra was unable to retain its sovereignty by force of arms, the next best line would be to press for a confederation which would allow each component full powers over its defence and such crucial areas as education and economic development. Such a confederal arrangement would guarantee security of life and property to Biafrans. It would also allow for a cooling off period to enable the children, as Mazi Kanu proposed, to grow up and find more enduring answers.

Mr Akwaelumo suddenly realized that he had been standing stark naked between two window blinds and staring into the darkness through the glass louvres, his wrapper in one hand. He shook his torch and directed its dim light at his watch. He was staggered to find that it was already 3 a.m. He quickly tied his wrapper, went outside to water the lawn, and folded his Biafra suit which he had spread on the bed. He had told the driver to call him at 6 a.m. if he was not already up, so that they could drive back to Dikenafai before the Nigerian war planes resumed their pastime of menacing the roads. He had already climbed into his bed when he remembered . . .

He went down on his knees, his elbows on the bed and his head bowed: 'Oh God of Abraham, God of Isaac, God of Jacob, who breaketh the bow and knappeth the spear in sunder, who maketh wars to cease in all the lands,' he began. It was his fourth prayer in twenty-four hours. God must not be allowed a moment of sleep until He got His priorities right. Biafra must survive.

DJI-m-m-m . . . Akwaelumo jumped to his feet as the entire house convulsed. The Nigerian planes had resumed their nocturnal assignment at Uli airport. *DJI-m-m-m*. Akwaelumo dived for cover under the bed. The ceiling sagged. A lampshade crashed to the floor . . .

POSTCRIPT

January 14 1970.

Total eclipse over Biafra.

The soul of Biafra had ascended into the heavens. In full military regalia. Complete with human and material resources, like a great soul journeying to another world.

No sign of the Biafra Sun. Not even at noon. Hibernating, like a migratory bird? Gone with the soul of Biafra? Or just disappeared, to avoid presiding over the traumatic experience ahead of every Biafran as he turns the hands of his clock back by thirty whole months? No one could tell.

Radio Biafra broke the ominous silence. The voice was unmistake-able. It was the voice which would have obliterated the entire Nigerian Army at one blow if invectives could kill. It was the voice that had infused hope into Biafrans on the many occasions when all hope had appeared lost. It was the same familiar voice, but everything else had suddenly changed as if by magic. No Biafran fanfare. No invectives. Instead the voice carried an obituary. The Republic of Biafra had been erased from the map. Overnight.

The Biafran Field Commander at Eziokwe picked up the obituary on his transistor and discarded it as a gimmick by the enemy. He had effectively blocked every attempt by the vandals to advance to Uga airport. The latest suicidal attempt – barely three months back – had cost the enemy at least five thousand men. He would not concede one inch of Biafran soil to them, gimmick or no gimmick. He placed his boys on the alert, and sent for more *ogbunigwe*.

Instant moulting. For everyone: Akwaelumo, Duke Bassey, Barrister Ifeji, Onukaegbe, etcetera. From Biafranism back to Nigerianism. Each person sought his own hideout, to bury his discarded Biafran skin.

NOTES

CHAPTER 1

Aburi: a town near Accra in Ghana where Nigeria's military leaders met on 4-5 January 1967, under the auspices of the head of the then military regime in Ghana, in a bid to resolve the differences between them and avert the disintegration of Nigeria. Agreements reached at the meeting included the renunciation of force as a means of solving Nigeria's problems. The Military Governor of Eastern Nigeria, who attended the meeting, later accused the Federal Military Government of failure to honour the Aburi agreements. In a letter dated 16 February 1967 to the Head of the Federal Military Government, he listed the various Aburi agreements which had been set aside by Lagos to the detriment of Eastern Nigeria, and warned that unless the agreements were honoured he would be compelled to take appropriate action to protect the interests of Eastern Nigeria. 'On Aburi We Stand' became a popular slogan in Biafra.

Pogrom: on 29 May 1966, and again on 29 September 1966, thousands of Eastern Nigerians, particularly Igbos, were brutally murdered in parts of Northern Nigeria. The massacres were a deliberate attempt to eliminate the Igbos living in Northern Nigeria, in retaliation for the murder of the Prime Minister of Nigeria (a Northerner) and the Premier of Northern Nigeria (also a Northerner) during the January 1966 coup which brought the military into power, a coup regarded by people in Northern Nigeria as an Igbo coup because no prominent Igbo was murdered at the time. The Biafrans referred to the May and September 1966 massacres as 'the pogrom'.

Kwenu, kwezuenu: Igbo expressions which a speaker uses to call the audience to order before addressing them. Here the speaker requests the different contingents to answer him as he recognizes them. Their response implies that he has their authority to address them.

Ewo: an exclamation, similar to 'Oh!'

Ojukwu bu eze Biafra . . .

> Ojukwu is Biafra's king,
> So it was ordained at Aburi;
> Awolowo, Yakubu Gowon,
> They can't overrun Biafra!
> Biafra win the war;
> Armoured cars,
> Shelling machines,
> Heavy artillery,
> They can't overrun Biafra!
> Biafra win the war;
> Armoured cars,
> Shelling machines,
> Fighters and bombers,
> They can't overrun Biafra!

Sho-sho: derogatory name for one Northern Nigerian ethnic group to which some Nigerian military leaders belong.

Abam: the Abam people from the south-eastern part of Igboland established a reputation as warriors in an age when a warrior's prowess was determined by the number of human heads (especially males) he brought home from an operation.

Akaekpe Akanli ka oyibo n'akpo . . . an invention to break the monotony of Left! Right! Literally: 'It is the left hand and the right hand that the white man calls Left! Right!'

CHAPTER 2

Gowon, itiwe, tiwe . . .

> Gowon, if you rouse the sleeping lion,
> Gowon, if you rouse the sleeping lion,
> Gowon, if you rouse the sleeping lion,
> When the lion wakes, the consequences will be disastrous!

Agbada: a voluminous gown worn by men.

Yoruba: one of the major ethnic groups in Nigeria.

Suya: beef kebab.

Na we-we: pidgin, meaning 'We know one another very well', or 'We are birds of the same feather'.

248

CHAPTER 3

Republic of Oduduwa: some prominent Nigerians from Western Nigeria had announced publicly that they would proclaim Western Nigeria a sovereign state under the name 'Republic of Oduduwa' should any other part of Nigeria secede. The Yorubas are said to have descended from Oduduwa.

Anini: a coin formerly in use in Nigeria, of practically no value.

Buying: literal translation of an Igbo idiom meaning 'monopolizing'.

CHAPTER 4

Wetin: pidgin, here meaning 'What do . . .'

Hausa: the dominant ethnic group in Northern Nigeria. Often synonymous with 'Northern Nigerian'.

Ole ebe unu no . . .
> Where is your country, Biafra!
> Where is your country, Biafra!
> I just can't leave Biafra to settle in Nigeria.
> I just can't leave Biafra to settle in Nigeria.
> Biafra must make it!
> Fellow Biafrans!
> Gird up your loins for the challenge!

N.C.N.C.: National Council of Nigerian Citizens, a major political party in Nigeria which controlled the Government of Eastern Nigeria prior to the 1966 coup.

N.P.C.: Northern Peoples' Congress, a major political party, based in Northern Nigeria. It controlled the Federal Government as well as the Northern Nigeria Government prior to the 1966 coup.

Action Group: the third major political party in pre-1966 Nigeria. It previously controlled the Government of Western Nigeria until a split within the party in 1962 led to the emergence of a new party formed by the splinter group which took over the control of the Government.

Onyenwem: Igbo for 'my lord'. Literally: my owner.

249

CHAPTER 5

Foofoo: boiled and pounded cassava, usually a heavy meal.

Omu: the yellow leaf from a tender palm frond used in securing roofing mats.

Kpulum: Igbo slang, meaning 'I swallow my words'.

Iyiya: an insect said to be very timid.

Kwapu kwapu unu d-uum: Igbo onomatopoeia for the sound of mortar. Literally: 'Pack and quit, pack and quit, all of you'.

Ise: Igbo equivalent of 'Amen, so let it be'.

Combing: Biafran civilians were required to 'comb' regularly through all the forests around their villages to ensure that they did not harbour enemy infiltrators.

Kwom: the sound made by a hen as it searches for food for its chicks.

Ogene: a metal gong used as a musical instrument, but also used by the town crier when he proclaims an important announcement.

Ikoro: a huge musical instrument, made from a hollowed-out tree trunk with a slit on one side. Its sound is heard from all corners of the village. The ikoro is sounded only in times of grave emergency.

Ndo: Igbo for 'Sorry'; 'What a pity'; 'How sad'.

CHAPTER 6

Kpamkpam: completely.

Harmattan: a cold, dry, dusty wind blowing southwards from the Sahara, usually in December and January.

Garri: grated and fried cassava, which is eaten in a variety of ways.

Kpilikom: Igbo onomatopoeia describing the shutting of the mouth.

Igba ndu: Igbo for 'covenant'.

Nkwo: the Igbo week includes four market days. Nkwo is one of them.

Ofo : symbol of authority, generally held in trust for the gods or ancestors by priests, chiefs or medicine men. It is not expected to be carried to another town.

CHAPTER 7

Dane gun : shotgun manufactured by the village blacksmith, fired with gun powder.

Nack you tory : pidgin meaning 'spin a yarn'.

CHAPTER 9

Itibolibo : Igbo slang for an ignoramus.

Istafablushbulfa : mimicry of the English language by an ignoramus.

Bo : exclamation (pidgin).

Chi : personal God as distinct from the God of the community.

Kedu, odinma : Igbo salutation, 'How are you', 'All is well'.

Nwata gbujie : short for 'If a child attempts to fell it (a thorny plant with a tender stem) it will fall on the child, thorns and all'.

Masquerade : an ancestral spirit, believed to dwell in the bowels of the earth, from where it emerges through ant holes when the occasion arises. Anyone who discloses publicly the human being inside the masquerade is regarded as having committed a grievous offence, the punishment for which is very severe.

Ofomata : a man from Nanka in Eastern Nigeria who was so well-to-do that palm wine always flowed freely in his house, available to anyone who cared to look in.

CHAPTER 10

Obi : house for the head of the family, or that part of his house in which he usually receives his guests.

Ekwulobia stool : low kitchen stool.

251

Nyamili: derogatory word used by the Hausa to refer to the Igbo. Believed to be a corruption of the Igbo expression 'nyem nmili', meaning 'give me water'.

Alla so ka: Hausa for 'God forbid'.

Akara: a meal prepared from ground cow peas and sold in small balls.

Allah inana: Hausa, meaning 'God will provide'.

Patapata: Yoruba for 'Completely', 'Nothing left'.

Ashia: expression of sympathy or sorrow, similar to 'Sorry', 'How sad'.

Ndi Igbo: Igbo for 'the Igbo people' or literally 'the people of Igboland'.

CHAPTER 12

Odi nso elu aka: Igbo expression, meaning 'That which is near yet is inaccessible'.

Tonu Ja: Igbo for 'Praise Jehovah'.

Biafra binie, nuso Nigeria agha . . .
> Biafrans arise, wage a battle against Nigeria.
> Battle! Battle! Battle!
> For what reason?
> Because they are people who know not God,
> People who know not God the Creator.

Christian Brothers: Biafran nickname for white mercenaries.

Abacha nmili: slices of boiled cassava soaked overnight in water before being eaten.

CHAPTER 13

Tie-tie: strands extracted from the trunk of the raffia palm.

O pa mi O: Yoruba expression meaning 'He has killed me O!'

Ogbunigwe: Igbo, meaning 'That which kills in large numbers'. A bucket-shaped, devastating land mine invented by Biafran scientists and put to good use by the Biafran Army.

Nuru olu ayi, Nna, nuru olu ayi . . .
>Hearken to us, Father hearken to us,
>Hearken to us, Father hearken to us,
>Gowon's might can never match Ojukwu's,
>Gowon's might can never match Ojukwu's,
>Hearken to us, God the Creator, hearken to us.

Ngwo ngwo: a delicacy, prepared from the entrails of a goat.

Enyi Biafra le le . . . An Igbo song calling on Biafra's friends to remember the atrocities perpetrated on Biafrans. It refers to the thirty thousand 'children of Biafra' murdered in Northern Nigeria; to Aguiyi Ironsi, a son of Biafra who was assassinated by Nigerian soldiers on 29 July 1966 to bring Gowon to power, and to Major Nzeogwu and the poet Christopher Okigbo, sons of Biafra, killed on the battlefield.

CHAPTER 15

Amadioha: the god of thunder.

Tufia: it was believed that the powers of evil could be held at bay if you spat in their direction and shouted 'God forbid!' The exclamation 'Tufia!' has come to represent the act of spitting.

CHAPTER 17

Nmagwu Okoro: a girl's name, but used here purely as an exclamation.

Okro soup: slippery gravy for foofoo, made from the okra vegetable chopped into small pieces.

Eba: foofoo prepared from garri (grated and fried cassava).

CHAPTER 18

Oti: Yoruba, meaning 'It is . . .'

Binis: the people of Benin in Mid-Western Nigeria.

CHAPTER 19

Fiam: onomatopoeia, here describing the speed with which the missile would make for the enemy.

Ihe nile zuru oke n'ala Biafra . . .
>Biafra is self-sufficient in every respect;
>Our country is self-sufficient in every respect;
>Biafra is self-sufficient in material resources;
>Death is universal,
>It is the only thing Biafra cannot brag about.

Omenuko: Igbo name, meaning one who dispenses largesse in times of scarcity.

CHAPTER 21

Man must wack: pidgin, meaning 'A man must eat to keep alive'.

Enenebe ejegh olu: Igbo description of a beautiful girl: 'If you were to admire her beauty to the full you would forget to go to work!'

CHAPTER 22

Agbenu: men and women from a part of Igboland which is too dry for intensive cultivation, who either become professional traders or hire out their services to farmers from the more arable parts.

Ngedelegwu: the Igbo xylophone. Used here to describe the sound of small arms fire by Nigerian soldiers.

Odo: Chief Ofo's title.

Ogbuisi: literally 'head cutter'. A generic title for men who have distinguished themselves in one way or another. (It was a mark of achievement to return from a battle laden with many human heads, especially male heads.)

Mazi: title for adult males who have not chosen their own individual titles.

Fim: onomatopoeia for utterance.

Ndewo: Igbo for 'welcome'. It is used here to stand for 'well-spoken'.

CHAPTER 23

Chei: exclamation.

Cola: a fruit traditionally offered to guests.

CHAPTER 25

Cocoyam: a tuber, smaller than the yam or the cassava.

Afia attack: the nickname for the unauthorized but extremely lucrative trade going on behind the enemy lines. Enterprising Biafrans went behind enemy lines to buy commodities which had become non-existent in Biafra, to sell them at inflated prices in Biafra.

CHAPTER 26

Dibe! dibe! . . .

> Take heart! Take heart!
> Fortitude pays dividends.
> When it's your turn, take heart,
> Biafra shall vanquish!

Fontana Books

Fontana is a leading paperback publisher of fiction and non-fiction, with authors ranging from Alistair MacLean, Agatha Christie and Desmond Bagley to Solzhenitsyn and Pasternak, from Gerald Durrell and Joy Adamson to the famous Modern Masters series.

In addition to a wide-ranging collection of internationally popular writers of fiction, Fontana also has an outstanding reputation for history, natural history, military history, psychology, psychiatry, politics, economics, religion and the social sciences.

All Fontana books are available at your bookshop or newsagent; or can be ordered direct. Just fill in the form and list the titles you want.

_____

FONTANA BOOKS, Cash Sales Department, G.P.O. Box 29, Douglas, Isle of Man, British Isles. Please send purchase price, plus 8p per book. Customers outside the U.K. send purchase price, plus 10p per book. Cheque, postal or money order. No currency.

NAME (Block letters) _____

ADDRESS _____

_____

_____

While every effort is made to keep prices low, it is sometimes necessary to increase prices on short notice. Fontana Books reserve the right to show new retail prices on covers which may differ from those previously advertised in the text or elsewhere.